DON'T CRY FOR ME

This Large Print Book carries the Seal of Approval of N.A.V.H.

DON'T CRY FOR ME

SHARON SALA

THORNDIKE PRESS
A part of Gale, Cengage Learning

GALE
CENGAGE Learning·

Detroit • New York • San Francisco • New Haven, Conn • Waterville, Maine • London

GALE
CENGAGE Learning®

Thorndike Press® Large Print Basic.
The text of this Large Print edition is unabridged.
Other aspects of the book may vary from the original edition.
Set in 16 pt. Plantin.

LIBRARY OF CONGRESS CATALOGING-IN-PUBLICATION DATA

Sala, Sharon.
    Don't cry for me / by Sharon Sala. — Large print ed.
      p. cm. — (Thorndike Press large print basic)
    "A Rebel Ridge novel"—T.p. verso.
    ISBN-13: 978-1-4104-5406-5 (hardcover)
    ISBN-10: 1-4104-5406-1 (hardcover)
    1. Large type books. I. Title. II. Title: Do not cry for me.
PS3569.A4565D66 2013
813'.54—dc23   2012036961

Published in 2013 by arrangement with Harlequin Books S.A.

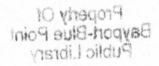
Printed in the United States of America
1 2 3 4 5 6 7 17 16 15 14 13

Soldiers are trained for battle —
trained to fight to the death for
country and their fellow soldiers.
They are trained to be tough —
and to follow orders without question.
They accept that when they go to war
they may not come back and they are
willing to pay the sacrifice to keep
their country free from tyranny.

They are trained to die —
but no one has told them what
to do when they come home
in pieces, shattered in body,
mind and spirit. They come home
forever changed by what they've
seen and what they've done in
the name of war, and the only
other people back home who
truly understand how they function
have either been cremated

and scattered to the winds
or lie buried six feet under.

I dedicate this book to the
wounded warriors of our great
nation, who have come home
from one fight to fight again
every night in their dreams.

I do not know your names,
but I do cry for you.

You are my heroes.

ONE

Rebel Ridge, Kentucky
April
"Sniper at three o'clock. Get down! Get down!"

Bullets ripped through walls. Someone screamed. Someone was praying to God to let him die.

Quinn was on his belly, crawling toward an opening to get a bead on the sniper, when the world exploded.

One minute Quinn Walker was back in Afghanistan watching PFC Wooten's head explode all over again and the next moment he woke up. He sat straight up in bed, his heart pounding, his body covered in sweat.

He threw back the covers and staggered to the window overlooking the high mountain meadow. Less than an hour until sunrise. The sky was already showcasing the imminent arrival of a new day.

Why did this keep happening? Why

couldn't he let it go? He leaned his head against the window and closed his eyes, willing the nightmare back to hell, and wondered if there would ever come a time when that horror faded — when he was able to accept that he was back home in Kentucky?

The little something called PTSD he'd brought home from the war had an ugly habit of recurring just when it was most inconvenient. It wasn't like sand fleas, which fell by the wayside after a good dose of tea tree oil. There were no meds, no vaccines, no magic wand to wave and make it go away. It was the gift that kept on giving, night after night in his sleep, and in the bright light of day when he least expected it. A word, a sound, even a scent, was all it took to yank him back. It was the son of a bitch on his back that wouldn't go away.

Too early to get ready for work and too late to go back to bed, he made a quick trip into the bathroom, and then grabbed a pair of sweatpants and headed downstairs from the loft.

The hardwood floors in the cabin echoed his steps as he turned on the lights and moved into the kitchen area to make coffee. As soon as it was done, he took his first hot, steamy cup outside to the wraparound deck to wait for sunrise.

Disturbed by Quinn's appearance, an owl suddenly took flight from the A-frame roof and flew into the trees.

Fog hovered waist-high above the ground all the way to the trees. He caught a glimpse of something moving off to his left and waited until a large buck with a massive rack slowly emerged from the fog. It was the prince of the forest, and the antlers were its crown. The buck suddenly stopped, as if sensing he was no longer alone.

Although Quinn didn't move, he knew the buck smelled him — or at least smelled the coffee — but it wasn't enough to spook him. After a few moments the buck moved on through the clearing in stately fashion and disappeared into the forest. It was a far better greeting to Quinn's day than his nightmare had been.

He sat on the top step with his elbows on his knees, waiting for the coffee to cool, remembering when this had been his grandparents' place, and he and his family were still living at home. Only this cabin wasn't the house that had been there then. This one was new. Quinn had built it with the help of the family after the old home place was blown up during a gunfight with some hired killers from L.A.

They'd come to silence a witness who was

hiding here in the mountains, intent on keeping her from testifying against their boss. That witness was not only a distant relative but his brother Ryal's long-lost love.

The bad guys lost the fight.

Ryal and Beth and their baby daughter, Sarah, were living happily ever after.

Quinn was still trying to outrun a war.

A few moments later a coyote came out of the tree line near where he was sitting, lifted its head then tucked tail and disappeared.

"Yeah, I know, I'm screwing up the status quo this morning, but mine got screwed up, too," Quinn said, and took a quick sip of coffee before he was satisfied that it cool enough to drink.

He sat with one eye on the meadow, watching the night creatures going to ground and the day creatures coming out, all the while waiting for sunrise.

As a backcountry ranger for the Daniel Boone National Forest Service, the area he kept track of was off-road and unpopulated except for the wildlife. The fewer people he had to deal with, the better he liked it.

Finally the sun did him the honor of rising to the occasion, and Quinn went about the business of getting to work.

By midmorning he was on the opposite side of Rebel Ridge, hiking up Greenlee

Pass to look for Robert Lane and Wayne Hall, two hikers who were over a day late checking out of the park. He wasn't expecting problems, but in country this rough, having an accident and no way to get medical attention could mean the difference between life and death. He carried food and first aid, and was in contact with ranger headquarters by two-way radio. The last reported contact with the hikers was at a location just above Greenlee Pass. Since he hadn't met them on the trail on his way up, it stood to reason they were still ahead of him. Unless they'd done something stupid like diverting off the hiking trail and getting themselves lost, in which case the search would turn to air, horseback and rescue dogs. In the eighteen months since he'd been on the job, they'd only had one such search, which had ended on a happy note. He was hoping that would be the case again.

He'd been walking for almost three hours when he paused at an outcrop to use his binoculars. A careful sweep of the area revealed nothing that alerted him. No smoke. No distress flag. Nothing. He pocketed the binoculars, got a drink of water and continued upward.

Less than a hundred yards later he found the first sign of blood. He would have missed it but for the unusual number of ants swarming on it. After the first sign, he found another and then another. He couldn't tell if it was human or animal, but either way it wasn't good. He didn't want to walk up on an injured animal, but he had no option but to keep following the blood trail upward, in case it was his hikers.

It didn't take long to find the source. Another hundred yards up and he caught the scent of something dead. A few yards farther he found one of the hikers — or at least part of one. An arm and a foot were missing, along with most of the internal organs.

The sight spun Quinn's head back to Afghanistan so fast that for a moment he nearly lost it. He grabbed for the dog tags he still wore and held on as if his life depended on it. The metal dug into his palm, and it was that pain that helped him focus.

He turned away from the sight and began looking at the scene, trying to figure out what had happened. There was one backpack about twenty feet up from the body, hanging from a limb. It appeared to have been ripped apart by teeth and claws. There were black bear in the park. This wasn't good.

When he found claw marks on a tree trunk where the bear had marked its territory, he stopped and stared. The claw marks were nearly ten feet high. That was one damn big bear.

He grabbed his radio and quickly called in to dispatch.

"This is Walker, come in."

"Go ahead, Walker," the dispatcher said.

"Found one of the hikers. Dead. Looks like a bear attack. I've got claw marks on a tree a good ten feet high." He gave the GPS coordinates of the body. "I have a blood trail that leads down the mountain, and I'm going back to follow it. We're still one hiker short. Stands to reason it might be him."

"Copy that, Walker. Stay safe. Over and out."

Quinn slipped the rifle strap off his shoulder, took the gun off safety, jacked a shell into the chamber and headed back down the trail.

Now that he knew what he was hunting, all his instincts kicked in. The forest had gone silent — like everything was holding its breath. He stopped, listening. Not even the air was stirring. After a moment he kept moving, following the blood into the trees, keeping his eyes on the ground and his ears tuned to the sounds around him.

About ten yards in, a twig suddenly snapped. He crouched instantly as he swung his rifle toward the sound. A few moments later a raccoon ambled out from under one bush and disappeared just as quickly beneath another one.

Shit. He let out a slow breath and kept moving.

The earth beneath the trees was spongy — covered in dead leaves and pine needles — but it wasn't the type of ground cover that held prints. It wasn't until he came upon a place void of leaves that he found his first footprint. It was human. Now that he knew he was trailing a man and not a bear, he started calling out loud. He didn't know which man was dead and which one had walked away from the bear attack, so he shouted both names.

"Hello! Hello! Robert? Wayne? Where are you?"

He kept shouting as he walked, following blood drops, broken limbs and the occasional footprint. He'd been on the trail for a good twenty minutes before he heard a faint sound. He stopped to listen, then called out again.

"Hello! Robert? Wayne?"

He heard the sound again. It was a faint call for help. His heart skipped a beat.

"Keep yelling! I'm coming," he shouted, and ran toward the noise.

One moment he was pushing through a thicket of brush, and the next he had to jump to keep from stepping on the body.

The man was lying on his side, covered in dirt and leaves and an abundance of dried blood. One leg had claw marks all the way from thigh to calf, with ants swarming the wounds. When he rolled over onto his back and saw Quinn, he started to cry.

"Thank God, thank God."

"Are you Robert or Wayne?" Quinn asked.

"I'm Robert Lane. Wayne is . . . Wayne is . . ."

Quinn put a hand on his shoulder. "I found him. Just rest easy, man. I'm Quinn Walker with the ranger service. Help is already on the way. Give me a second. I need to let them know I found you." He took out his two-way.

"Dispatch, this is Walker, over."

"Go ahead, Walker."

"I've got one alive. I'm sending GPS coordinates. Send me some help, ASAP."

"Copy that, Walker. Help is on the way."

Quinn eyed the area carefully, then dropped his backpack and knelt by Robert. He took out his canteen and lifted the man's head, slowly pouring water into his dry,

15

cracked lips.

Robert grabbed frantically at the water, wanting all of it at once.

"Easy," Quinn said. "A little bit at a time so you don't choke, okay?"

Then he poured a little on a rag and wiped some crusted blood from one eye.

Robert groaned.

"Sorry, man," Quinn said softly, and doused the leg liberally with water, washing off the ants. "Did the bear follow you?"

"I don't know."

"What happened? Why did it attack?"

Robert moaned and then started to cry. "I don't know. It was coming up the trail toward us. The minute it saw us it charged. We never had a chance. It swiped at me first. I went down, and Wayne grabbed a branch and started screaming and yelling, trying to get the bear's attention."

Robert paused, choked on a sob and then broke down and wept.

Quinn let him cry. He knew how it felt to watch a friend die. He gave Robert another drink of water, and finally he was able to finish the story.

"Wayne saved my life. The bear ripped his belly open with one swipe. I heard him scream." Robert shuddered. "He was screaming and screaming, and then all of a sudden it was over. Wayne was . . . you know, and the bear was tearing into him like he was starving. I got up and ran. I ran. I ran away and left him like a coward."

"No. He was already dead," Quinn said. "Would you have had his sacrifice go for nothing? He did what he did to save your life. It would have been a stupid move not to try and get away, okay?"

Robert nodded, but he was crying again.

"How old are you, Robert?"

"Twenty. Wayne was twenty-two. We've been best friends since I was in the sixth grade. Oh, my God, this is going to kill his mom and dad."

Quinn touched the other man's forearm. "Death is always a hard thing to face, but it comes to all of us eventually. Just hang in there."

Robert moaned. "I think I'm gonna pass out. Don't lea—"

"I won't leave you, man. I promise."

Robert Lane's eyes rolled back in his head.

Quinn felt for a pulse. It was too rapid. The wounds were showing signs of infection. The guy would be lucky if he didn't lose the leg.

He stood up with his rifle steady in his grip. It wasn't the first time he'd stood guard over a man who was down.

He contacted the ranger station again.

"This is Walker. Do you copy?"

"Go ahead, Walker."

"From what the hiker said, I think we've got a rogue bear. It's either sick or been injured. Might need to send some trackers up here to find it before it attacks someone else."

"Copy that, Walker. I'll pass the message on."

"Walker out," Quinn said, and pocketed his radio, then resumed guard.

It was close to an hour before he heard a chopper, and somewhat later before he heard people coming up the trail. He was deep into the trees, but they had his coordinates. They would find him. When he began to hear voices, he called out until the rescue crew came into view.

Within minutes they had the hiker's condition assessed, started an IV in his arm, sluiced the rest of the ants out of his wounds with disinfectant, loaded him onto a stretcher and strapped him down. The eight-man crew would take turns, two at a time, carrying him down the mountain to the clearing where the evac chopper was waiting.

Another crew was recovering the other hiker's remains. It would be dark before

Quinn got home.

Quinn drove up to the cabin, turned off the headlights of his Jeep and got out. With the sun down, the air was already getting cool. He took his boots off on the deck, unlocked the door and then carried them through to the utility room. He would clean them up later, but not now. He needed to wash the blood off himself first.

He stripped where he stood, tossed his clothes into the washing machine and started it up before heading through the house to his loft. Within minutes he was standing beneath a spray of hot water with his eyes closed, willing away the gore of what he'd seen.

His life was solitary for a reason. Until he could figure out how to cope with his flashbacks and nightmares, he wasn't in any frame of mind to build a personal relationship. He knew this and accepted it, but it didn't make the lonely nights any easier to get past.

A couple of hours later he'd finished cleaning up in the kitchen and grabbed a beer as he headed for the sofa. Even though living in the mountains was usually a recipe for poor-to-no phone or TV signals, the satellite dish he'd had mounted on the roof served him well. There were a couple of shows he liked to watch, and later he hoped to catch the local news to see if they reported on the injured hiker's condition.

He'd just kicked back and reached for the remote when his cell began to ring. The Caller ID showed an Out Of Area message. He frowned as he answered.

"Walker."

"Quinn, it's me, B. J. Pettyjohn."

The hair crawled on the back of Quinn's neck. It had been over three years since he'd heard from anyone in his old unit.

"Hey, B.J. How the hell did you ever get this number? And tell me this isn't bad news."

"No, oh, hell no, sorry. I didn't mean to give you a start or nothin'. And I called a good number of Walkers before I found one who would claim kin to you. He gave me your number."

Quinn grinned. "Then it's good to hear from you."

B.J. laughed. It was a silly kind of nervous laugh, but a three-year gap made chitchat difficult to pick back up.

"Look, the reason I called . . . I remember you saying you were from Kentucky, right?"

"Right. Why?"

"You remember Conrad from our unit?"

The smile slid off Quinn's face. "Yeah, why?"

"So I heard through the grapevine that Conrad — who by the way is a corporal now — was in a Humvee when it hit a land mine and has been stateside at the army hospital in Fort Campbell, Kentucky, for the past two months. The doctor's about ready to sign off on a release, and I remembered hearing Conrad grew up in foster care, without any family or anywhere to go. I just hated to think about one of us turning into some homeless vet and sleeping on the streets, you know? Thought you might know of a place that could help."

Quinn didn't have to think twice. "Yeah, I know a place. Don't worry. I'll take care of it."

"That's great! It's a worry off my mind."

"Yeah, sure. Are you home on leave or what?" Quinn asked.

"No. I'm out for good as of six months ago. Can't wrap my head around normal living yet, but hey . . . it's bound to come back one of these days."

Quinn knew exactly what he meant. "One of these days for sure," he echoed.

"So, talk to you soon, and tell Conrad I said hey."

"Will do, and thanks for the heads-up."

"Right."

Quinn ended the call, and then set the phone aside and reached for the remote. He found the show he wanted to watch and then kicked back and took a drink of his cold, yeasty beer.

But the show was the furthest thing from his mind. He kept remembering the last time he'd been with his unit. They had been doing a sweep of some empty buildings when the world had blown up in his face. He'd been burned and bleeding and half out of his head when someone grabbed his arm. It had been Conrad, shouting, "We got you, Hillbilly, hang on! Hang on! Don't you dare die."

Now Conrad was the one hurting. The least he could do was provide a place for R & R until his fellow soldier was one hundred percent. Tomorrow he would make a few calls. Make sure the doctor didn't sign the release papers before Quinn could get there, and see if he could borrow Ryal and Beth's SUV. The backseat lay down flat, making the rear of the vehicle into a fairly decent bed. It was a long way to Fort Campbell, which meant it would be a long way back here. A hard drive for anyone who was healthy — and the ride from hell if everything hurt. They had a history of getting on each other's last nerve but also had a great respect for each other as soldiers.

Just after daybreak, Quinn began making phone calls. He found out Conrad's doctor was a man named Dr. Franks, then called around the hospital until he located him. After he explained the situation to Franks, the doctor assured Quinn that he wouldn't sign the release papers until he arrived.

Then he called Ryal.

"Hey, brother, are you up?" Quinn said.

"I am now," Ryal said, and then chuckled.

"Yeah, sorry about that. Look, I need a favor. A soldier from my unit is in Blanchfield. That's the army hospital on base at Fort Campbell, remember?"

"Yes, I remember. That's where *you* were, right?"

"Right. So this friend is about to be released and needs a place to stay. I'd like to borrow your SUV so I can make a bed in the back for the drive home."

"Yeah, sure! When do you need it?"

"Day after tomorrow."

"Come get it. Anything else I can do for you?"

"I have to go back up on the south side of Rebel Ridge and help look for a rogue bear

23

or I would do this myself. But since you asked, there are some things I'm going to need. Are you up for a trip into Mount Sterling?"

"Wow, this must be some good friend."

"It was Conrad who pulled me out of the fire after the explosion."

Ryal frowned. "Enough said. Bring your list and your money, brother. I'll do anything you need me to do."

"Thanks. I'll owe you."

"No, I'll never be able to repay you for saving Beth's life. Just consider it a favor from one brother to another."

"Thanks."

"Yeah . . . but what's the deal with the bear?" Ryal asked.

"Killed a hiker and tore another one up pretty bad. We're thinking it's either sick or wounded, and it's still out there. Even though the attack happened on the far side of the mountain up on Greenlee Pass, I would nix any personal hunting trips until further notice, okay?"

"Definitely, and I'll spread the word in the family."

"Thanks. Kiss Sarah for me and tell Beth I said hi. See you soon," Quinn said, and disconnected.

After that he began gathering his hunting

gear. By the time he reached the ranger station and checked in, he learned that the trackers and their bloodhounds were already on the mountain.

The backcountry of Daniel Boone National Forest was huge, and there were places he had yet to see. Given that they'd had a pretty dry winter, he needed to check out the amount of deadfall on the mountain, which could impact firefighting should a blaze break out. Deadfall was also a place where a sick bear might shelter. After picking up a handheld radio and a map of the area, he headed out in one of the forest service trucks.

The day passed without incident, as did the following day. The bear was still in the wind but had not been seen again. They'd passed the message on to all the people living in the area and hoped they could find the bear before it killed again.

For Quinn, it was all he could do to focus on work. It was going to be weird having someone else in the cabin, and he had no idea how messed up Conrad was. The possibility existed that he was making trouble for himself, but he couldn't turn his back on the situation, either. He slept fitfully, knowing that tomorrow his life was going to take a drastic turn.

Quinn was on his way to Ryal's house by sunrise to trade vehicles. Upon arrival, he wasted no time transferring the pillows and blankets that he'd brought or pulling down the backseats to make the rear of the SUV into a bed.

"Need any help?" Ryal asked.

"I got it," Quinn said, and folded a quilt until it fit the space, then threw in the pillows and a blanket. "That should work."

"You said you had a list?" Ryal asked.

Quinn took a paper and a hundred dollar bill out of his pocket. "I think this should cover it, but if it's more, we'll settle up when I get back."

"Was Conrad hurt bad?" Ryal asked.

Quinn stopped.

Ryal didn't know what was going on, but all expression had just disappeared from his brother's face.

"I don't know, but it won't matter."

Ryal sighed. "I didn't mean it like —"

"Let it go, brother. It's just me being me," Quinn said softly. "I'd better hit the road."

"Yeah. So . . . drive safe and we'll see you soon."

"You, too, and thanks for helping me out,"

Quinn said.

As Ryal watched Quinn driving away, he had a sense that Conrad, whoever he was, was going to make a positive difference in his brother's life.

As Quinn drove in one direction toward Fort Campbell, Ryal, Beth and the baby went the other way into Mount Sterling to fill Quinn's list. Once they finished, they headed back to Rebel Ridge and took everything up to the cabin.

Beth washed and dried new sheets while Sarah played on a blanket nearby. Ryal pulled out the sofa that made into a bed and pushed some furniture around to accommodate it. As soon as the linens were ready, Beth made up the bed, adding an extra quilt at the foot in case of cool nights, then went to tell Ryal she had finished. She found him standing on the back deck with Sarah in his arms, looking out across the meadow.

"Hey, I'm ready if you two are," Beth said, and kissed her baby girl, who was almost asleep.

Ryal slipped an arm around his wife, holding her a little longer and tighter than usual.

She sensed something was bothering him.

"Honey, what's up?"

He shifted Sarah to a more secure spot on his shoulder, then looked back across the meadow. "I was remembering what happened here and how close I came to losing you."

Beth leaned against his shoulder, the one without the baby. "It's you we nearly lost, and all because you threw yourself over me when the house blew up."

He shuddered. "If you had died, living without you wouldn't have been possible."

Beth cupped the side of his cheek. "But I didn't. All that's in the past, and look at what a beautiful place Quinn has made here."

"Yeah, it suits him."

"Because of the solitude?" she asked.

He nodded. "And the memories. This was Granddaddy Foster's old homestead, remember? We loved coming here as kids. I think this is a good place for him to heal."

Beth frowned. "Do you think he will? Heal, I mean."

He shrugged. "He's already healing, but who knows to what extent? War changes people. He'll never be the same."

"But he'll be the best Quinn that this Quinn can be."

Ryal smiled. "That's for sure. He'll never settle for less."

Two

It had taken just under four hours for Quinn to reach Fort Campbell. Since it was the same hospital where he'd been sent after he was wounded and where he'd mustered out, he knew the base setup. He drove straight to the visitors' center at Gate 4 to get a pass. Although he hadn't been here in over three years, he had the weird feeling he'd never left.

The feeling persisted as he drove through the base, and the closer he got to Blanchfield Hospital, the more his anxiety grew. By the time he pulled into the parking lot the skin on his body felt tight and hot. He resented the anxiety. It made him feel weak, and weak was not an option. This was about Conrad, not him.

He got out of the car, checked the bed in the back one more time, making sure nothing had shifted out of place, and then made a call to Conrad's doctor to let him know he was there. The doctor answered on the third ring.

"Dr. Franks."

"Hello, Dr. Franks, this is Quinn Walker. I spoke to you a couple of days ago about having one of your patients, a Corporal Conrad, released to my care?"

"Yes, yes, I remember."

"I'm here on base and in the parking lot at Blanchfield. How do I go about getting Conrad signed out?"

"Hang on a sec, let me check," Franks said, and put him on hold.

As Quinn was waiting, a van drove up and pulled into a handicap parking space across from where he was standing. A woman got out, then circled the van and opened the side door. He glanced up just as a platform slid out, lowering a man in his wheelchair. Quinn's gut knotted, and then he looked away, feeling guilty for being thankful that wasn't him.

When Franks came back on the line, Quinn's focus shifted.

"Mr. Walker, are you still there?"

"Yes, sir."

"I remember you telling me you'd been a patient here before. Do you remember where Physical Therapy is located?"

"Yes, sir."

"Conrad is there now. I'll meet me you in PT in about fifteen minutes."

"Thank you, sir. I'll be there."

Quinn dropped his phone in his pocket and headed into the hospital. Now that he was here, he was anxious to find out what he'd let himself in for.

He headed for the bank of elevators, refusing to make eye contact with the people in the lobby. When he got on the elevator, he quickly turned his back on the other occupants and stared at the door, waiting for it to open. It was as if the past three years had never happened and he was still on crutches, with healing burns and scars that screamed *Look at me!* He was startled not only by the anxiety that he felt but also the insecurity. This hospital was not a good place to be.

When he entered the physical therapy area, he was even more hesitant, eyeing the patients in various stages of rehabilitation. As he began scanning the room, looking for Conrad, he heard someone cursing.

Quinn smiled. He'd just found his comrade.

"Damn, damn, damn, that effing hurts!"

The physical therapist eyed the frown on his patient's face. They had been working at this one exercise for nearly fifteen minutes and he knew Conrad was tired, but it took pain to get progress, and so he kept pushing, urging the wounded vet up and down a set of steps to stretch and strengthen the injured leg muscles.

"You know and I know that's how you get better, so try again, okay?" the therapist said.

"Hell no, I'm not going to try. I'm going to *do* it!"

"Hey, Conrad, how's it going?"

Mariah Conrad froze. That was a voice straight out of her past, a voice she'd never thought she would hear again. She looked over her shoulder, and then her heart skipped a beat.

"Oh, my God."

Quinn grinned. "It *has* been a while, but I thought you would at least remember my name. It's not God, it's Quinn."

Mariah blinked. "What are you doing here?"

"I came to get you."

The physical therapist smiled at Mariah and patted her on the back.

"Since you have a visitor, we'll call this session over. Just let me know when you're ready and I'll take you back to your room."

Mariah nodded but couldn't quit staring.

A muscle in her leg was beginning to knot. She needed to sit down or move, but she couldn't think past looking at Quinn's face. The last time she'd seen him, he'd been so bloody and burned she'd been scared he wouldn't make it, and when she'd never heard from him again, she had finally allowed herself to accept that he was out of her life. Then she remembered what he'd just said.

"You came to get me? What are you talking about?"

Quinn saw panic in her eyes and realized he hadn't considered the possibility she would refuse him.

"I heard they were going to release you and thought you might like to spend a little R & R in the mountains with me."

Mariah grabbed on to the step rails with both hands and then sat down to keep from falling.

"In the mountains — with a hillbilly?"

Quinn grinned. "Yeah, with a hillbilly."

A surge of emotions ran through her. Without family to turn to, she'd been in something of a panic, wondering what was going to happen to her when they kicked her out of Blanchfield. Quinn was a godsend, but she was a long way from the woman she'd been and felt obligated to

33

warn him.

"Are you sure? I don't think you know what you're getting yourself into. I'm a wreck. My honorable discharge just went through. I'm so screwed up the army doesn't want me anymore."

"That's okay. *I* want you."

She looked anxious, which was an emotion he never would have associated with her. The Conrad he'd fallen for had been a first-class grunt with a daredevil gene. Over the two years he'd known her, they'd made love in every isolated place they could find between Iran and Afghanistan. War had definitely kicked her butt, but he had to believe she was still in there. All she needed was peace and time to find her way back.

"Are you sure?" she asked again.

"I know exactly what I'm asking for. I've already cleared it with your doctor. Now it's up to you. Are you going to come?"

She blinked back tears. "Yes."

"Aces."

She looked up. "Here comes my doctor."

"Hey, Mariah. How's it going?" Dr. Franks asked, and then eyed Quinn. "Mr. Walker?"

"Quinn, and yes, sir."

Franks put a hand on Mariah's shoulder. "Are you in agreement with being released to this man's care?"

Mariah frowned. "In his care? What does that mean? I'm ready to be released on my own. I'm just going with him, right?"

Franks smiled. "Sorry. Poor choice of words."

"Just so we understand each other," Mariah muttered.

The doctor eyed Quinn. "Are you sure you're ready for all that attitude?"

The red flags on Mariah's cheeks were something Quinn had seen before. "All that and then some," he said.

"Then I suppose we need to get some paperwork signed so you can get on the road. I believe you have a ways to go to get home, isn't that right?" Franks asked.

Mariah looked up at Quinn. "How far?"

"Does it matter?" he asked.

She started to argue, then caught herself. She had nowhere else to go. Her shoulders slumped.

"No."

Quinn held out his hand. "Trust me?"

She turned loose of the railing and grabbed his hand.

"Yes."

The doctor waved at an orderly. "Let's get Conrad back to her room so she can pack."

■ ■ ■ ■

Two hours and a ream of paperwork later, Quinn was in the parking lot, tucking a pillow beneath Mariah's injured leg and then another under her foot to keep it elevated during the ride.

She was wearing sweatpants and a loose, army-issue T-shirt that had seen better days. In bright daylight the healing scar from the head wound she'd suffered was easier to see through the short dark curls of hair.

"You okay in there?" he asked, as he pulled the covers up to her waist so she could reach them.

Mariah nodded. The quilt on which she was lying was thick and soft, and the pillows and blanket smelled like lavender. She reached for his hand, briefly clasping his fingers.

"Thank you."

He nodded. "It's good to see you," he said, and then shut the hatch and pretended he didn't know she was crying.

Mariah couldn't believe this was happening. She had awakened again this morning with the same feeling of dread that had been with her for the past two weeks. The closer she got to a release date, the more panicked she'd become. She'd never had a family, and had grown up in foster homes in and around Lexington.

By the time she'd aged out of the system she was a street-smart eighteen-year-old with a chip on her shoulder. She'd wanted something more out of life than what she'd been dealt, but with no way to attain it, she'd joined the army. Even though the country was already at war, it had seemed like a good idea. She'd been fighting just to exist all her life. Surely she could fight a few more years for something bigger, and learn a trade at the same time. The decision was a combination of ignorance, näiveté and the best-laid plans.

Within six weeks of leaving basic training she was on her way to Afghanistan, and it didn't take long for her to realize that enlisting wasn't the best idea she'd ever had. Besides the ongoing war, she'd never been as hot in the summer or as cold in the winter as she was over there.

And then she'd met Quinn — a kindred soul with a daredevil heart — and fallen hard. The chemistry between them had been instantaneous, and they took advantage of every moment of downtime they could to be together, which usually meant having sex. She'd told herself it was just part of what was happening. No promises. No ties. She'd never meant to fall in love with him, but she had. After he'd been wounded, his absence left a huge hole in her life. She hadn't expected to ever see him again, but his arrival today had been the answer to a prayer.

She was most worried about what he expected from her. At this point, it was all she could do to walk six feet without stumbling, and her head was a mess. Between the flashbacks and the memory loss, she wasn't anywhere close to a functioning human, but dear God, she was grateful to him — as grateful as she'd ever been to anyone in her life. The only problem was that she was in no state of mind to resume their prior relationship, but she had been too big a coward to tell him that for fear he would change his mind.

Lying in the back of the SUV was far better than having to sit up for hours, and the pillows Quinn had shoved under her healing leg were lifesavers. The last thing she remembered was looking at the back of his head. Lulled by the motion of the car and the soft music from the radio playing in the front seat, she cried herself to sleep. Only when she felt the car slowing down did she begin to stir.

Mariah woke up and rolled over, but it wasn't until she bumped against the back of the seat that she remembered where she was. She sat up gingerly, wincing when a muscle knotted in the back of her healing leg.

"You okay?" Quinn asked.

"I slept."

He hid a grin. "I know. I'm stopping for gas. You'll want to take a bathroom break here, because we have another two hours to go."

"Okay." She hesitated, then knew the sooner she got it said, the better. "You'll have to help me into the store."

"I know that, honey, and it's no big deal to me, okay? If I hadn't had my family to help me when I came home, I would have been in a world of hurt."

The word *family* suddenly sank in. She began to wonder if she'd signed herself up to be staying in a house full of strangers.

"Do you still live with them?"

"Lord no," Quinn said. "I have my own place up on Rebel Ridge."

"What's Rebel Ridge?"

"The name of the mountain where I grew up, remember?"

39

Her expression went blank. "No. I don't. There's a lot of things I don't remember."

Quinn glanced up in the rearview mirror. "But you remembered me, right?"

All she could see were his eyes looking back at her. "Yes, I remembered you."

Their gazes briefly locked, and then his attention shifted as he turned off the highway into a large quick stop. He gassed up, then pulled up to the convenience mart and parked.

"Hang on and I'll help you out," he said.

Mariah ran her fingers through her hair and then rubbed the sleep from her eyes. It would feel good to stand up.

The hatch opened. Before she could think what to do, Quinn scooted her slippers onto her feet and then held out a hand.

"You move at your own speed. I'm just here to steady you, okay?"

"Yes." She rolled over to the edge and then sat up.

Quinn grabbed on to her arm as she slid out, then locked the car.

"Ready when you are," he said.

She took a deep breath and then a first step. Her body was stiff, but as soon as she began to move, it became easier.

"What time is it?" she asked.

"Almost two in the afternoon. Are you

hungry?"

She nodded.

"We'll get something to eat before we leave here," he said.

"I have some money," Mariah said.

"That makes two of us, and we'll be using mine," he said, as he opened the door for her.

She gave him a look, which he ignored.

Quinn paused at the counter and asked the clerk, "Which way to the bathrooms?"

The clerk pointed.

Quinn slid his hand under Mariah's elbow as they moved in that direction and then into the small hallway at the back of the store. Two doors faced each other. When Mariah tried to go into the women's bathroom, she discovered that the door was locked.

"Somebody's in there," she said. "I'll wait."

Quinn reluctantly left her standing there as he went into the men's room.

She leaned against the wall to take the weight off her bad leg and waited for the door to open. It didn't take long for her to realize there was more than one person in there, and they seemed to be having a good time, which was weird. She could hear laughing and talking, and an occasional

41

thud, like one of them had bumped against a wall. She'd had fun in a lot of places, but a Quick Mart bathroom wasn't one of them.

A couple of minutes later Quinn came out, and when he saw that she was still leaning against the wall, he frowned.

"Are you still waiting?" he asked.

She nodded and rolled her eyes. "Sounds like a party going on in there."

He moved toward the door, then stopped as if he'd just been punched.

"I smell smoke," he muttered.

She nodded.

He leaned closer. "No. I smell pot."

Her eyes widened. "Seriously?"

Suddenly he doubled up his fist and began pounding on the door.

"Police! Open up!"

The clerk up at the front jumped off his stool and ran to the end of the counter to see what was going on, while inside the bathroom the sounds of squeals and shrieks grew louder, followed by a sudden flushing and a lot of running water.

"Open up!" Quinn yelled again, pounding harder.

The door swung inward. Two teenage girls came stumbling out of the bathroom. They took one look at Quinn and then stopped.

"Hey. You don't look like the police."

"I lied, and smoking weed will rot your brains," he muttered, and pulled them out of the doorway so Mariah could go inside.

She was struggling not to laugh as she shut and locked the door. The bathroom smelled like the back room of a bar she knew down in Lexington, but at least it was finally vacant. By the time she came out, the girls were long gone and Quinn was leaning against the wall with his arms folded across his chest.

She grinned.

Quinn looked her up and down, then slowly smiled, like he was trying her on for size and had decided she was a fit.

"Corn dogs, burritos or overdone chicken strips are in the deli case," he said.

She wrinkled her nose. "Do they have any cans of Vienna sausages in the grocery section?"

His smile widened. "Why yes, I believe they do. What would you like to go with them?"

"A dill pickle, crackers and a Pepsi."

"I am so remembering why we clicked," Quinn drawled.

Mariah rolled her eyes. "And all this time I thought it was about my boobs."

He laughed out loud. "For that, you also get dessert."

"A Butterfinger? I haven't eaten a Butterfinger candy bar in forever."

"You can have anything you want. Do you want to go back to the car to wait, or are you still okay?"

"I'm okay, but I'll wait up at the counter and let you do the shopping."

Quinn hesitated, then touched her cheek. "I am so sorry this has happened to you, but I can't tell you how glad I am to see you again."

Mariah shrugged. "Just wait until I come unglued on you, then see if you still feel the same."

He frowned. "We're all fucked, woman. It's how we came back. Doesn't mean I'm ready to quit living."

Her eyes widened. "You mean you still have —"

He interrupted. "Let's get our stuff and get back on the road. We can talk later."

It was obvious he didn't want to talk about himself any more than she wanted to admit what was going on inside her head.

Instead of making her worry, it was oddly reassuring.

"Don't forget my pickle," she said.

"I won't," he said, and then held out his hand. "I didn't forget anything about you."

Mariah took it gratefully to steady herself.

44

"Everything I remember is in a jumble in my head."

"It will get better," Quinn said. "I promise. However, all you have to remember today is who you're going home with, and that's me. Let's go get the grub so we can get back on the road."

The remnants of their meal were in a sack between Mariah's feet. She'd fallen asleep in the front seat with a half-eaten Butterfinger in her hand, pickle juice on the front of her shirt and tears on her face. A muscle jerked in his jaw as he shifted his gaze back to the road. He could imagine what was going through her head, but he couldn't fix it. At this point all he could do was keep driving, because he wasn't going to wake her.

The next time she woke up, Quinn was slowing down again. When he took a turn off the highway onto a two-lane blacktop road, she sat up, wincing as stiff muscles complained.

"Where are we?" she asked.

"Pretty close to home. Welcome to Rebel Ridge," he said.

Her eyes widened. "This is where you grew up?"

"Yeah. Are you okay? Do you want to lie down in the back again? This has been a hell of a ride for you today."

"I'm okay."

"We'll be at my brother's house in about fifteen minutes. You can stretch your legs and go to the bathroom there before we head up to my place."

"How far is it to your place from there?"

"About an hour."

Mariah looked up through the windshield, but all she could see was a winding road disappearing into the thickly growing trees. She was used to cities and people. Even when she'd been deployed, there were always lots of people around. This was definitely out of her comfort zone.

"This is a really big mountain, isn't it?"

Quinn nodded. "It's very quiet where I live. No sirens. No neighbors to hear me freak out in my sleep . . . just the critters and me."

"Critters?"

"Raccoon, owls, deer and the occasional coyote, but nothing scary, honey."

"I'm not afraid of anything on four legs," she muttered, then sat for a moment, absorbing the concept of that much peace and quiet. The longer she thought about it, the calmer she became. Then she looked up at Quinn.

"It sounds like heaven."

46

"We're high enough up that I'd say we're pretty darn close."

THREE

Ryal was in his woodworking shop staining a special order dining table when he heard Beth calling his name. He dropped the brush into a container of paint thinner and stepped outside. She was standing on the porch with their puppy, Rufus, at her side and Sarah on her hip, pointing toward their driveway.

He saw Beth's SUV coming up the road and waved to let her know that he'd seen it, then headed toward the house at a jog. They would finally get to meet the guy who'd saved Quinn's life.

When he reached the porch, Beth was grinning.

"What?" he asked.

"Look in the front seat," she said. "And whatever you do, don't make a fuss."

Ryal turned. "Why would I . . . ? I'll be damned! He's a *she*!"

Well aware of how the Walker brothers

teased each other, Beth felt obligated to repeat herself. "Ryal! Do not make an issue out of this, especially in front of her. You don't know what she's been through or what condition she's in. Understand?"

He tweaked her nose and then winked. "I'm not completely dense. Of course I understand," he said, then jumped off the porch and went to meet them with Rufus at his heels.

Quinn was trying to see Ryal's house from the perspective of a stranger, rather than a kid who'd grown up inside those walls, wondering what Mariah would think. Granted, Ryal had done some remodeling with the wrap-around porch and a fresh coat of white paint after their parents moved out, but it was still a mountain house, simple in style and size. The fact that his brother was a master carpenter didn't hurt, though, and since Beth had come to live there, the landscaping had taken on a softer, more feminine look. Flowers local to the area had been planted along both sides of the rock walk leading up to the house, and the bushes were trimmed, rather than al-lowed to grow wild.

He sneaked a glance at Mariah, trying to judge what she thought, and was surprised to see a slight smile on her face.

"What do you think?" he asked.

She pointed toward the house, and the man and puppy coming down the walk.

"Your brother looks like you."

"Yeah, I guess he does. You can pretty much always find the Walkers in a crowd. We're all pretty tall."

Mariah's eyes widened. "There are more of you?"

"Ryal and Beth have a daughter, Sarah, who's a little over a year and a half. I have another brother, James, and his wife, Julie, and their two kids. And there's my sister, Margaret — but we call her Meg — our mom, Dolly, and a whole lot of cousins."

She couldn't imagine. "It must be a good feeling to know who your people are and where you come from."

"I'm ashamed to say I never thought about it, just took it and them for granted. But it *is* exceedingly good to know there are people who have your back," Quinn said.

All expression was gone from her face, and he hated that he'd caused her one moment of pain. He reached for her hand.

"I have your back, Conrad. We all do. If you don't believe it now, you will in the days to come."

Mariah was saved from having to answer

as Quinn pulled to a stop.

"Sit tight. I'll help you," he said, and quickly circled the car.

A cool breeze flowed past her as he opened the door. Mariah took his hand as he helped her out, then stood for a moment to get her bearings.

"Hey, brother, you made good time," Ryal said, as Beth came down the walk behind him, carrying Sarah.

Quinn didn't bother with chitchat. He knew they were surprised and curious, but he wasn't going there, and the sooner they figured that out, the better.

"Ryal, Beth, this is Mariah Conrad. Mariah, my brother Ryal and his wife, Beth. The cutie Beth is holding is Sarah, and this very shy pup is Rufus."

Mariah pushed a shaky hand through her hair and grinned at the puppy, who was licking everybody's shoes.

"Nice to meet you. Thanks for loaning Quinn your car. It made the trip a lot easier for me."

"We're the ones who should be thanking you for saving Quinn's life," Ryal said. "He can be a pain in the ass, but we were grateful to get him home in one piece."

Mariah was surprised that Quinn had credited her with his rescue.

"I wasn't the only one there," she said.

"You're the only one I remember," Quinn said.

Beth handed Sarah to Ryal and slipped an arm through the crook of Mariah's elbow. "Why don't you come into the house with me while they switch stuff from one vehicle to the other? It'll give you time to freshen up and stretch your legs for a bit."

Mariah glanced at Quinn. "Do we have time?"

"We have all the time you need," Quinn said.

Beth led Mariah into the house at a leisurely pace, while Ryal and Quinn transferred things from the SUV to Quinn's Jeep.

"You neglected to mention that Conrad was a girl," Ryal said.

"And now you know," Quinn said, as he transferred the quilt and pillows into the backseat of the Jeep.

"She really saved your life?" Ryal said.

"Pulled my ass out of a burning building."

Ryal glanced toward the house. "She must be one tough lady."

"As tough as she needs to be," Quinn said, and tossed her duffel bag between the seats. "Did you get the stuff on my list?"

"Yes. Beth and I have already been to your

52

place, made up the bed and left the rest on your kitchen table."

"Thanks. I appreciate it. Did you have enough money?"

"Yes. Your change is on the table, too. So do you have any feelings toward her besides gratitude?"

Quinn turned, his face suddenly expressionless. "That's none of your damned business. Are we clear on that?"

Ryal held up his hands. "Clear as day."

"Good. Be sure to pass that along to the rest of the family, because I'm not going to satisfy anyone's curiosity at the cost of her privacy."

"Absolutely," Ryal said.

Quinn glared. "You're grinning."

"Am I not supposed to?"

"Not unless something is funny," Quinn snapped.

"But you're so damned entertaining," Ryal said, and punched Quinn on the arm.

Quinn sighed. "Damn it, Ryal . . ."

"Chill out, bro. It's all good. If you have everything transferred, come up to the house. Beth made an apple pie this afternoon. I'll bet they're already digging in. Here, kiss your niece hello. It'll put you in a better mood."

Quinn picked up the baby, kissed her soft

cheek and grinned when she poked a finger up his nose, then followed Ryal into the house. The interrogation had ended, but he knew his brothers too well, and this wasn't over. They wouldn't stop until they were completely satisfied they knew all his business, or at least thought that they did. He just hoped they didn't spook Mariah into thinking he had an ulterior motive, because he didn't know why he'd done this, either. It wasn't going to be easy living with anyone, especially someone who might have the same kind of issues he had. The fact that she didn't remember a lot of her past was a little sad. They'd shared a lot besides sex.

"See . . . I told you they would be hogging all the pie," Ryal said as they entered the kitchen.

Beth shook her head as she dished the pie onto plates. "Such a baby. There's plenty for everyone."

Quinn glanced at Mariah. She was quiet but seemed at ease. Then Beth took the baby and put her down for a nap, and the moment passed.

Mariah was taking everything in and had learned more in the past five minutes about Quinn Walker than she'd known the entire two years of their mutual deployment.

Watching him so at ease with his niece was unsettling. She was trying to picture herself that way and failing miserably. Then she made herself focus on them and not herself.

His brother's house wasn't elaborate, but it felt homey. The furniture was simple but beautiful. Family pictures on the walls rooted the house and its occupants in a past she would never know, and the pie Beth was cutting was like something out of a magazine. If it tasted half as good as it looked it would be amazing. She couldn't cook worth a darn, and didn't have a marketable skill beyond her sharpshooter medal and a better-than-average eye when it came to pinpointing liars.

Then she reminded herself that it didn't matter, because she wouldn't be here long enough for anyone to judge. As soon as she was able to stand on her own two feet again she would be gone. She and Quinn had a history, but nothing that had ever warranted a forever kind of bond. They'd shared a war and a bed, and that was all.

"How about that pie?" Ryal said.

"As you can see, I'm cutting it," Beth said. "Why don't you get the iced tea out of the refrigerator and make yourself useful?"

Ryal grinned. "Yes, ma'am."

Beth rolled her eyes. "He's not usually this

malleable. I think he's just showing off for company."

Mariah's leg was throbbing. She needed some of her pain meds but was embarrassed to ask. When Beth put the pie on the table, Quinn scooted a piece toward her and handed her a fork. She took a bite and rolled her eyes.

"Oh, my gosh, this is good," Mariah said.

Beth grinned. "It's a recipe my Granny Lou gave me. She's the best cook in the family."

"Lou Venable is the best cook in both families," Quinn said, then added for Mariah's sake, "We're actually distant cousins to the Venables, who happen to be Beth's family, too."

Mariah didn't bother to hide her surprise. "You two are related?"

Ryal nodded. "We're very distant cousins, which is not all that unusual on Rebel Ridge, although we all grew up knowing each other. Not a lot of people ever move off the mountain, and those who do usually wind up coming back. What about your family? Where are they from?"

"I have no idea," Mariah said. "I was an abandoned baby who grew up in a series of foster families. Aging out of the system at eighteen means a kid like me winds up on the streets. I needed to belong somewhere, so I joined the army in the hopes of learning a trade and ignored the fact that we were already in a war."

"I'm so sorry," Ryal said. "I didn't mean to —"

"No, don't apologize. I don't want anyone to cry for me. It is what it is, and Quinn already knew all this, which I assume is why he offered to babysit me through the rest of my healing." She wouldn't look at Quinn, couldn't look for fear she would see pity, and that was something she couldn't bear — not from him. "I am unbelievably grateful, but I can't promise to be the ideal houseguest. My memory's shot, and my leg is a mess."

"But you're alive," Beth said. "And trust me, I know how to appreciate that more than most. But that's enough serious stuff for now. Who wants ice cream on their pie?"

"I do," Ryal said.

"Well, we all knew that," Quinn drawled. "The only person in the family who eats more than Ryal is James."

Mariah smiled and held out her plate. "I've been eating hospital food for two months. I won't turn down ice cream."

Beth doled out the ice cream, and for a few minutes conversation was sparse. As soon as they finished eating, Quinn carried their dirty plates to the sink.

"Thanks for the loan of the car and for helping out, but we need to get moving."

Then he glanced at Mariah. Her hands were curled into fists and the knuckles were white. *Damn it. How had he let her get that bad without noticing?* He walked over to where she was sitting and leaned down.

"How bad are you hurting?"

"Enough."

"The doctor gave you pain pills. Where did you pack them?"

"They're in the outside pocket of my bag, the one with the zipper, not the snap."

"I'll be right back."

Beth turned just as Quinn walked out. She started to ask where he was going, then saw the pain on Mariah's face and guessed what was happening. She got a glass of water, then took it to the table and sat down beside her.

"I'm so sorry. Here we were acting like this was a party, and you just got out of the hospital. Why didn't you say something?" she asked as she set the glass in front of Mariah.

"It just started getting bad a few minutes ago," Mariah said.

Beth touched the top of Mariah's head,

then the side of her face. "You don't have to hide how you feel from us. We don't judge, okay?"

"Yeah, okay," Mariah said, then breathed a sigh of relief when Quinn came back.

"Here," he said, and dropped two pills into her outstretched palm.

Mariah downed them quickly. "Thanks."

"You're welcome. Do you need to go to the bathroom before we leave? Like I said, it's about an hour to the cabin."

"I guess," she said, but when she tried to stand, her leg went out from under her. Quinn grabbed her before she fell. "Damn it!" she muttered.

"I got you," he said, and slipped an arm around her waist to walk her down the hall to the bathroom door.

"Can you make it from here?"

There were tears in her eyes. "Yes. Just wait for me."

"Don't worry, kid. I'm not going anywhere without you."

By the time they said their goodbyes and he got her to the Jeep, the pain pills were having enough of an effect that she was feeling some relief. He put a pillow on the passenger seat before helping her inside.

"The Jeep's shocks aren't as good as the

SUV's, but if you sit on this pillow I think it'll help."

"You don't need to worry about me," she said, as Quinn reached across and buckled her in.

He was so close she could feel the warmth of his breath against her skin. What she was thinking was disconcerting in the midst of so much pain. Then he turned, and she found herself caught in his gaze.

"What happens if I want to worry about you?" he asked.

Longing washed through her. "I don't know. I guess I can't stop you, can I?"

Quinn's pulse was racing. He was so close he could almost taste the kiss, but he wouldn't go there. Not until she was standing on her own two feet and no longer dependent on him for her care. It wouldn't be fair, and if he had a chance in hell of rebuilding this relationship they had to start on equal ground.

He winked to lighten the moment, then backed out of the Jeep and closed the door. By the time he got inside, she had her emotions in check.

"I know you must be exhausted, but this is the last leg of the trip. Once we get to the cabin you can sleep, relax and watch some TV, whatever you want."

"I'm okay. The pain pills are kicking in."

"Good. Next time, don't wait so long, okay?"

"I won't."

She waved at Ryal and Beth, who were standing on the porch, then leaned back against the seat as he drove away.

"Your family is really nice."

"Yeah, they're pretty special, but they're also nosy. You'll probably meet more of them than you're ready for over the next few weeks."

She shrugged. "I'll take my chances."

"Just don't say I didn't warn you," he muttered.

Mariah grinned. "Take a breath, Quinn. I've been fighting insurgents for almost five years. I'm not afraid of your family."

The smile on her face was like a breath of fresh air. It was the first time since they'd left the hospital that he'd gotten even a glimpse of the Mariah he'd known before. It gave him hope that the rest of her was in there somewhere, waiting until it was safe to come out.

When they got back to the main road he turned left and headed up the mountain. Just a little bit farther and they would be home.

It didn't take long for Mariah to notice

the houses they were passing. Some were bunched together in twos and threes, and others were set so far back off the road all she saw was the driveway and the roof. A lot of them were in varying stages of disrepair. She knew what it meant to choose food over shelter.

Most of the vehicles she saw were up on blocks or were being stripped for parts. Children playing in their yards paused and waved as they drove past. A couple even gave chase until called back by a family member keeping watch from a nearby porch. It was obvious that the job market around here was weak.

Quinn caught the changing expressions on her face as they drove and couldn't help but wonder what she was thinking.

"I'm guessing this lifestyle is pretty foreign to you," he said.

Mariah frowned. "The rural part, yes, but the obvious poverty, not so much. Some of my foster homes weren't much better, and after I aged out of the system I was homeless. I would have gladly chosen any of these houses rather than sleeping in an abandoned building or a sewer pipe with a half dozen others just like me. In fact, these people are all better off than me. If not for you, I would be homeless again."

"You never said anything about being homeless before," he said.

She shrugged. "Why would I? We were too busy trying to stay alive to dwell on what I'd left behind me. I never thought I'd come back all messed up, or that I'd be right back where I started before I signed up. No, that's not the truth. I have a ways to go to get back where I started."

"And you have all the time you need to do it," Quinn said.

She frowned then shook her head. "I can't stay with you forever."

"You're not looking at this from the right angle. All you need to do is take one day at a time, honey. One day at a time."

She leaned back and then sighed. "You're right. As usual, I want everything put back together yesterday so I can get on with tomorrow."

Quinn frowned. "If you think like that, then you forget to live for today."

She'd never thought of life that way before. It was something to consider.

A short while later he began pointing out places of interest, and her focus shifted.

"My brother James and his wife live down that road," he said. "They have two of the cutest kids."

"Beth told me she's an illustrator and Ryal

makes furniture. What does James do?" Mariah asked.

"He farms a little tobacco, but his main job is with the postal service. He's the mail carrier for all of Rebel Ridge and parts south."

"I don't mean this to sound prejudiced, but how come your family seems to have a higher standard of living than a lot of your neighbors?"

"I don't know. There are plenty of others like us. We find ways to support ourselves knowing we won't ever be rich, but we know how to be happy with what we have. The people on Rebel Ridge aren't any different from people down in the city. Some are willing to settle for less, some aren't. It's just a fact of life."

"Do you have a job you go to every day?"

He nodded. "I work for the Daniel Boone National Forest Service as a backcountry ranger. I'm not in constant contact with the public like some rangers, which suits me."

"Then what *do* you do?"

He shrugged. "It varies. Just before I went to get you we had two hikers go missing."

"Did you find them?" Mariah asked, and then knew from the set of his jaw that something had gone wrong. "I know that look," she said. "What happened? Couldn't you find them?"

"No, I found them, but one was dead and the other severely injured."

"Oh, no. What happened?"

"They were attacked by a rogue bear, but that was on the other side of the mountain. He killed one. The other managed to get away. He was in bad shape when I found him."

She shuddered, her eyes widening as she peered into the trees lining the road. "Did you kill the bear?"

"Last I heard they were still tracking him. But don't worry, they'll find him and do what they have to."

She shuddered and wrapped her arms around her waist. "What else is up here that I need to be concerned about?"

"If I had to guess, I'd say that would be me. I snore. I have some serious flashbacks that turn into living nightmares, and I've been known to shout in my sleep."

She rolled her eyes. "At least now I know I won't have to worry about making a fool of myself in front of you."

"There are no fools where I live, girl — only members of the same survivors' club. Now stop worrying. It's all good. You'll see. I only have one bedroom, but my sofa makes into a bed, and we've got it all fixed up for you. I would have let you have the bedroom and taken the sofa myself, but the bedroom is up in the loft and the stairs are steep."

"Loft?"

"Yes, my place is an A-frame. Two stories, with one bedroom and bathroom upstairs, and one big open room downstairs, with a kitchen at one end and the living area at the other. There's another bathroom downstairs, next to the utility room. It makes more sense for you to be on the main floor. And there's a wraparound deck that will be great for you to get your exercise without having to walk on uneven ground. It's not luxurious, but it's pretty new, and I'm not a slob."

Mariah was silent, picturing the home and him in it, when he added, "We'll be okay. No pressure to do anything but relax and get well. Understand?"

Relieved that he'd finally brought up the issue of nothing personal expected between them, she could finally relax. Whatever happened, she was grateful to be with someone she trusted.

Up in the high country on the other side of Rebel Ridge, Jake Doolen, his sons and their bloodhounds were still trying to pick up the bear's tracks, desperate to find it before it attacked and killed someone else, but the signs were scarce to nonexistent. It was as if the bear had just vanished.

As far from the hunters as it could get, the bear was carrying an arrow in its rump, and the wound was infected, making it impossible for it to hunt as it once had. It was sick and in pain — two issues that drastically increased the danger quotient. Within hours of first sensing the dogs and the hunters it had made an about-face and begun moving in the opposite direction. If the Doolens didn't find it in time, it would emerge from the reserve and right into populated territory.

FOUR

The sun was already sliding toward the western tip of the mountaintop by the time Quinn and Mariah reached the cabin. Her first glimpse of the site he'd chosen for the simple A-frame made her think Quinn was still in soldier mode. He'd set the cabin in the middle of an open meadow that was surrounded on all four sides by trees, with only one road in and out.

In fact, the original homestead had been built in this same place nearly a hundred years before for essentially the same reason: distrust of the federal government in general. The first Walkers to live here had believed that if you couldn't be found, you couldn't be counted, and if you couldn't be counted, then you were off their radar. That mind-set still lingered in some of the more remote areas of Rebel Ridge and the rest of the South.

"Home sweet home," Quinn said, as he

pulled up to the cabin and parked.

Mariah couldn't quit staring. All it needed was some gingerbread on the eaves and snow on the roof, and it could pass for a fairy-tale cottage from a picture book. The deck was deep and wrapped around the cabin on three sides. The railings were strong and sturdy, built for sitting or leaning. And just like that, all the tension she'd been feeling was gone.

"It's absolutely beautiful," she said.

Pleased that she hadn't freaked about the isolation, Quinn relaxed, too. The first hurdle was over.

Mariah opened her door, carefully swung her legs toward the side, then slowly slid out of the seat.

"It feels good to stand up."

Quinn quickly circled the Jeep and slid an arm around her waist to steady her.

"The ground can be a little rough. Hang on to me until we get up the steps."

Mariah didn't argue. The last thing she wanted was to bust her nose before she got in the house, although it wouldn't be the first time she'd taken a tumble since she'd been wounded.

Once they got up on the deck, Quinn stopped to unlock the door. It swung inward on silent hinges, revealing a large open room

with a two-story ceiling and a shiny hardwood floor. The walls were cedar paneled,
and the massive stone fireplace at the far
end of the room was a statement in itself.
She could imagine being snowed in up on
this mountain with a fire blazing and Quinn
at her side, then shook off the fantasy. No
need dwelling on things that weren't going
to happen.

"You must love living here."

"It's okay for a hillbilly, I guess."

She frowned. "I wasn't making fun of you.
I only called you that because I . . . liked
you, and because you always called me
twerp."

"Well, you were a twerp. Now you're a
corporal," Quinn said, and started to tousle
her hair when he felt the scar on her head
and stopped short.

"Ooh, sorry. Did I hurt you?"

Mariah traced the crooked ridge of scar
tissue with absent fingers.

"No."

"How bad were you hurt?"

"Bad enough. It makes me nuts that my
memory's scrambled," she admitted.

"But that means if I tell you that you
always used to rub my feet and scratch my
back, you'd have to believe me."

She laughed out loud, startling herself

70

with the sound. It had been a long time since she'd felt like laughing.

"Sorry, mister, but I'm not that bad off. I'm not the foot-rubbing, back-scratching kind."

"Oh, I don't know about that," Quinn said. "You were damn good at scratching certain itches."

"And so were you, but that doesn't mean we're picking up where we left off, right?"

"Right."

"So stop making me nervous and show me around, okay?"

"You get the fifty-cent tour, which means all of the downstairs. If you get strong enough to walk up the stairs on your own, you'll get the other half."

He proceeded to show her the bathroom, the little utility room next to the kitchen, then the kitchen itself. He stopped by the kitchen table to sort through the things Ryal and Beth had left for him, then moved to the sideboard and took a cell phone out of a drawer.

"As soon as I charge this up, it's yours. It'll keep me in touch with you, and you with the outside world, when I'm at work, okay?"

Another niggle of worry had just been laid to rest. "Very okay," she said.

"I assume you know how to use a gas stove?"

"I can turn one on and off and I can use a can opener, but cooking like Beth cooks . . . no way."

He frowned. "I didn't haul your cranky ass all the way up here to cook for me. I just need to make sure you know how to heat a can of soup when I'm not here. Understood?"

She stifled a grin. "My cranky ass?"

He ignored her and led her out onto the back deck.

"This is a good place to critter watch or, if the weather's nice, read a book."

Now she was the one frowning. "Critter watch as in cute critters, right? Not killer bears?"

"Definitely not killer bears," Quinn said, but he wasn't entirely truthful. He didn't want to scare her, but until the bear was found and put down, he couldn't really guarantee anything. "However, you would be smart if you stayed inside the cabin or, if you're out, don't go farther than the deck when I'm not here."

She shuddered. "Consider it done."

He eyed the setting sun. "I need to unload the Jeep before it gets dark. If you want to walk around a bit before you go inside, you can hold on to the deck railing for stability. You saw your bed in the living room. The TV remote is on the table beside it if you'd rather stretch out. I'll make us some supper later."

"Do what you have to do and don't worry about me."

He'd started to go inside when, despite her words, she stopped him with a touch.

"Quinn?"

"Yeah?"

"I would never have believed when I got up this morning that I would be here with you before nightfall. The fact that I am is beyond amazing, and I want you to know how grateful I feel."

He ran a finger down the side of her cheek. "I didn't do it for your gratitude," he said, then went back inside, leaving her alone.

She would have pursued the conversation just to ask him why he *had* done it, then, but she was afraid she wouldn't be able to handle the answer.

Using the railing as he suggested, she walked the length of the deck and back again a couple of times, but as the sun finally dropped behind the mountain, she went inside.

Quinn was at the kitchen stove. A bowl of

salad was on the counter, a pitcher of what looked like iced tea beside it.

"Something smells good," she said.

"Hamburger steaks and fried potatoes."

"Oh, my Lord, that sounds good," she said. "I'm going to wash up."

"Don't dawdle. I'm dishing it up now."

"Yes, sir, right away, sir," she said, and headed to the bathroom.

She was halfway across the room when something hit her in the middle of the back. She turned, looked down and saw a wadded-up dish towel on the floor.

"Hey!"

"You're dawdling," Quinn said.

She rolled her eyes, picked up the towel and tossed it on the table as she passed.

Quinn could see the stiff set of her shoulders as she walked away, but he smiled as he filled their plates. If he kept her guessing, she would have less time to dwell on her situation. As for the nights, there was no way to prevent the inevitable as they slept. Hell was a hard thing to climb out of when your defenses were down.

One thing between them had not changed. Quinn knew he'd always had the ability to get on Mariah's last nerve, and it was still happening. Before, they'd always ended their squabbles by making love, but that release was no longer available, and he found himself pushing and teasing to keep from taking her back to bed. By the time the meal was over and the dishes were done, Mariah wanted to hit him and Quinn knew it. He needed to disarm the situation and decided the best thing he could do was leave her alone.

"I'm gonna go upstairs and shower. Do you need anything before I go up?"

"Where's my bag?" she asked.

"I put it on top of the washing machine so it would be close to the bathroom."

"If I take a shower, will it use up your hot water?"

Quinn began to smile. "I don't know. Wanna race to find out?"

Her eyes widened. "Are you serious?"

He shrugged. "I want a shower. You want a shower. I'm going up to my bathroom. You've got the one down here. I guess we'll find out if the water heater holds up, won't we?"

She didn't know whether to laugh or light into him. "You have got to be kidding," she muttered, as she swung her aching leg around and headed for the bathroom.

Quinn waited until he heard the door swing shut and then he headed upstairs, grinning as he went. Bringing her here to stay with him just might turn out to be the best idea he'd ever had.

Mariah stripped without digging into her bag and was a little anxious as she turned on the shower, afraid the water would get cold before she was through. She couldn't believe Quinn was actually planning to take his shower now, too. Chances were they would both wind up finishing in cold water.

A fresh towel, a new bar of soap and a small bottle of shampoo were on the little counter, and she guessed he'd put them there for her. His thoughtfulness was touching, but a cold shower was not. By the time she stepped in, she was caught up in the idea of racing to get clean.

The water pressure was good. The water was nice and hot. She squirted a small dab of shampoo into her hand and lathered up, racing through the suds and rinsing faster than she'd ever rinsed before. By the time she got to washing herself, the water had gone from hot to comfortably warm.

"Oh, crap," she said, and began rinsing the soap off her body as fast as she could. Her bad leg was hampering her, because she had to hold on to the railing with one hand as she scrubbed at her skin.

Then the water went from warm to luke-warm.

"No, no, no," she squealed, as she turned around to rinse off her back.

At that point lukewarm shifted to straight-from-the-well cold, and Mariah screamed and turned off the taps.

There she stood, dripping wet, shivering and listening to the booming laugh right above her.

Quinn! The jerk. She still couldn't believe he'd done that.

She rolled her eyes, grabbed a towel and wrapped it around her body, then got another one and began to dry her hair. The dryer she got, the warmer she became — and, grudgingly, she began to grin. That was, without doubt, the funniest shower she'd ever taken. In fact, she couldn't remember the last time she'd done something just for fun.

Once she was dry, she realized the bag with her clothes was still on the washing machine on the other side of the door. She peeked out, saw the coast was clear and started to go get it just as she heard footsteps coming down the stairs.

"Oh, no, no, no!" Moving as fast as she dared on her gimpy leg, she grabbed the bag and darted back inside the bathroom, and none too soon.

"Hey, are you okay in there?" Quinn asked.

"I'm just fine," she said.

"Do you need any help?"

"I've got this."

"Are you sure? In case you don't remember, I'm good in the shower."

She grinned. Clearly he was gonna play that "lost her memory" card as long as she let him.

"Hey, Quinn?"

"Yeah?"

"Shut the hell up."

He grinned. "Yeah. Okay. I'll just be in your bed watching TV."

"Oh, for the love of —"

She heard footsteps. He was walking away. She didn't know whether to be glad the pressure was off or worry about what she would find waiting for her in her bed.

Quinn figured he'd pushed enough of Mariah's buttons for one night and left her on her own in the bed watching television while he finished some work.

He was busy on his laptop at the kitchen table, finishing a report on his last trip up to the area around Green-lee Pass where the rogue bear had last been seen. As soon as he was done, he hit Save, then emailed it to the office.

According to the latest info they'd sent him, the trail had gone cold. After forty-eight hours without a solid hit, the powers that be had made a decision, and pulled the Doolens and their dogs off the mountain. Until there was a new sighting, they were at a loss as to where to look. But this decision had led to another one.

Come Monday, all the rangers were to begin notifying people in their areas about the possibility of a bear attack and advise them to stay out of the woods until the bear had been found.

Quinn read that directive without any confidence that it would be heeded. Telling mountain people to stay out of the woods was like telling them to stop breathing. They hunted the mountain and fished the creeks to feed their families. He would follow orders and spread the word, but he had no faith in anyone listening. Discouraged and more than a little bit worried, he finally turned off the laptop and went to check on Mariah.

The television was still playing softly in the background, but she had fallen asleep with her leg propped up on a pillow and the covers in a wad at the foot of the bed.

He picked up the remote and turned off the TV, then straightened out her covers and eased them over her, taking the time to assess her more carefully when she wasn't aware.

She was pale, and much thinner than he remembered, but all of that figured. Two months in a hospital would do that to anybody. Her dark hair was much shorter, as well, but he assumed that was because they'd probably shaved most, if not all, of it off because of her head injuries. As he watched, her eyelids began to flutter, and he knew she was dreaming. When she suddenly moaned, it was like someone had just shoved a knife into his gut. It was startling to realize he was that connected to her distress.

He started to wake her, but he knew how hard it was to get back to sleep once the nightmare took over and changed his mind, hoping she would just sleep through it. Instead he began turning off the lights until the house was completely dark except for a night-light up in the loft by his bed.

She moaned again, this time mumbling beneath her breath before the moment passed. Then she flinched, and he kicked off his shoes, pulled back the covers and slid into bed beside her. As many times as they'd made love, they had never had the luxury of sleeping together. But this wasn't a night for passion, and she wasn't sleeping in the true sense of the word. She was still fighting a war, and he couldn't let her do it alone.

He eased as close to her as he could get without bumping her injured leg, then rolled over onto his side and tucked her close against his body. There was a moment when he felt her tense.

"Easy, soldier, easy," he whispered. "I've got your back."

He heard a sob and rose up on his elbow. She was crying in her sleep, but her body had begun to relax. For now, it was enough.

He eased down and let go of his own tension. Within minutes he, too, had fallen asleep.

Ten miles over and another mile higher, the bear had taken shelter beneath an overhang of trees and rock. The festering wound in its hip was a constant pain that kept it in a pain-filled daze. It was sick and starving — a recipe for disaster. The cougar that usually bedded down in this lair smelled the bear and the festering wound. And sensed the danger. It was enough for the big cat to give the bear a wide berth and slip quietly away.

About two miles from where the bear had holed up, a couple of hunters had taken to the woods to run their dogs. They were sitting around their makeshift camp with their lanterns lit, laying bets as to whose dog would strike a trail first, when they heard one of the pack began to bay.

"Woowee, Warren, you hear that bugle? That's my big red, Samson. You owe me five dollars. I told you he'd be the first to pick up a good scent."

Warren rolled his eyes. "Son of a bitch," he muttered, and handed over the five, which his buddy promptly pocketed.

They picked up their lanterns and shouldered their guns as they listened to the rest of the pack begin to sound. The dogs would bay in a different tone once they treed their prey, and the hunters wanted in on the kill.

"Sounds like they're running something a little east but coming this way," Millard said. "What say we head out?"

"I'm with you," Warren said, and they disappeared into the woods.

The bear was in a sleepy daze when it heard the hounds. If circumstances had been normal, the sound of the dogs would have sent the bear in the opposite direction, but not this time. In its pain-addled brain, that was food on the move.

As it began to move, it recognized its own weakness, which in turn fueled its desperation to kill.

Warren and Millard were following the pack by the sounds of the yips and bays when all of a sudden they heard everything change. The barking went from trailing to full-on attack. Even though the men were more than a half mile away, they could hear the howls and growls, the shrieks and the yelps, in what they could only assume was an all-out fight.

"What the hell?" Millard said, and started to run, holding his lantern with one hand and a finger near the trigger of the gun he carried in the other.

Warren was right behind him.

Even as they ran, they could tell something bad was happening. The dogs were no longer in fight mode. They could hear constant cries of pain, until, one by one, the pack went silent.

The hunters kept running, but by the time they reached the kill site the bear was gone and seven dogs were dead or dying — bones crushed, bodies eviscerated.

"Oh, sweet Jesus," Millard said, going from body to body in disbelief.

Warren held up his lantern as he made a 360-degree turn, his gaze fixed on the inky darkness of the woods.

"What in hell did this?" he asked.

Millard was crying. "Samson's not here. I can't find him anywhere. Maybe he ran off. Maybe he got away."

"Look. Here's drag marks," Warren said, as he swung the lantern to their left. "What in hell could do all this without the dogs bringing it down? I don't understand. It damn sure wasn't a cougar. It would have just took to the trees, not fought a pack of dogs like this."

"Maybe a bear?" Millard said.

"I guess, but not even a full-grown black bear would take on a pack of eight dogs."

"Well, something did, and whipped 'em bad," Millard said.

"Here, the drag marks lead —"

He stopped in his tracks, staring down at the ground.

"What?" Millard asked.

Warren swung his lantern again. "Come here, Millard. Look at this."

Millard moved closer to the light, saw the paw print and squatted down, using his hand to measure the size.

"Son of a bitch," he whispered, then stood abruptly and swung his rifle into position against his shoulder.

"I never saw a black bear big enough to make a track like that," Warren said.

Millard shuddered. "We need to get back to the truck."

"But what about the dogs?" Warren asked.

"They're dead. You wanna be next?"

Warren shook his head. "It's not right to just leave them out here to rot. They're like family, damn it."

"We'll come back in daylight," Millard said.

"I don't know about you, but right now I'm not too sure about where we are. How the fuck do you suppose we'll find 'em again?"

"Buzzards," Millard answered grimly. "Now let's get the hell out of here while we're still in one piece."

The men eyed the sky, found the North Star and started running.

Mariah woke up the next morning to the sounds of birds singing and the scent of freshly brewing coffee, and wondered where the hell she was. Then she heard Quinn talking to someone on his phone and remembered that her life had taken a one-eighty for the better.

Without registering the indentation on the other pillow, she threw back the covers. Her muscles were stiff and, as usual these days, aching in too many places. But she silently gave herself the "at least you're alive" pep talk as she swung her legs off the mattress and stood up.

Almost immediately, her injured leg gave way. She grabbed the back of the sofa to steady herself, and waited until the feeling came back and she was confident it would hold her weight before trying to walk.

She waved self-consciously at Quinn as she headed for the bathroom. He winked and waved back, but she could tell by the tension in his face that something was wrong. Whatever it was, she would prefer to hear it fully dressed. After she used the bathroom and washed up, she dug a pair of clean sweats from her bag and then finger-combed her unruly curls. The fact that her heart-shaped face was devoid of makeup was standard for a female soldier in combat. Her eyebrows and eyelashes were as dark as her hair, and her eyes were what Quinn called cat-green. In her opinion, there was nothing remarkable about any of it. Anxious to find out what had put the frown on Quinn's face, she headed back into the kitchen.

"Do you want eggs and bacon or something lighter, like cereal?" Quinn asked.

"Forget feeding me. I can do that myself. What's wrong?"

"We may have a new lead on that rogue bear."

"Oh, Lord, please tell me it did not attack another person."

"Two hunters were running their dogs about fifteen miles from here last night. They heard them strike a trail, then what sounded like a massacre. By the time they found them, seven dogs were dead and one had been dragged off. They found tracks from a very large bear. My boss down at the ranger station said they've called back the trackers and their dogs. I hope to hell they find it this time. If it's no longer in the national forest area, then it's way too close to civilization."

Mariah shuddered. "What do you have to do?"

"The local authorities will tell the residents to stay out of the woods, and keep kids and animals close by. I wasn't supposed to work today, but this has changed everything."

"I don't need anyone to babysit me, Quinn. This sounds like a dangerous situation. Go do what you have to do. I'll be fine. I'm grateful to be here."

Quinn didn't have a choice. But he wasn't willing to leave her unprotected.

"Pour yourself some coffee. I'll be right back," he said, and bolted up the stairs to the loft.

Mariah poured a cup of coffee and was stirring in sugar when he came down carrying a rifle and a box of shells.

"I don't believe the bear will ever make it this far down before it's found, but I saw what it did to those two hikers, so I'm playing it safe. Under no circumstances should you be outside today, okay? Bears can move really fast, and you can't."

She reached for the rifle. "Can I see it?"

He handed it to her. He knew she could use it, but he didn't know how this would affect her mentally.

"I need to ask you something," he said.

"Okay, ask away."

"Can you be here by yourself, under this kind of tension, and not suffer some kind of setback?"

"You mean, is this gonna make me freak?"

He grimaced. "Yeah, something like that."

"Then the answer is no. I have that phone you gave me. I have a house full of food, a bed and a TV, and if I need to protect

88

myself, I obviously can. Go do your job and quit worrying about me."

"I'll call to check on you, and if you get spooked about anything — and I mean *anything* — then by God, you better call me."

"I promise."

He started toward the door, then stopped. "Damn, I hate this. This isn't the way I planned to get you settled in."

"Yeah . . . the best laid-plans and all that," Mariah said.

Quinn patted his pockets, making sure he had everything he needed, then started for the door.

"Hey, *f* Quinn?" He turned to face her.

"Don't be a hero."

He grinned. "And don't *you* eat all my cookies."

She was still smiling as she watched him drive away. Then, the moment the Jeep was out of sight, she locked both doors, and made sure all the windows were shut and locked before pouring a bowl of cereal. There were plenty of things she could do today. Without the physical therapist dragging her through an exercise regimen she might actually get in a little extra sleep. And when the mood hit her, she could do her exercises on those stairs that led up to the loft. Being able to scale those steps might

come in handy some night when she
couldn't sleep — and *Quinn* couldn't sleep
— and the world was a kinder place.

FIVE

Lonnie Farrell had been born and raised on Rebel Ridge, but his journey away from home sweet home began when he was fourteen. He got himself arrested for making and selling meth, which resulted in a four-year stint in a youth offender facility. He came out a wiser criminal than the kid he'd been going in and headed straight for Chicago, where he hooked up with the uncle of a kid he'd met in jail.

Among other things, Uncle Sol was a bookie with a somewhat tenuous hand in the business of prostitution. It soon became Lonnie's job to make debtors pay up, which included dunning the "girls" who worked for Sol, making sure they didn't shortchange him. Within twelve years Lonnie had revamped the whole prostitution angle from streetwalkers to high-class hookers, more than tripling Sol's income.

But for Lonnie, the world of hookers and

pimps was growing stale. He wanted more — more money, more challenges, more risks — which took him straight back to the reason he'd first gone to jail: making and selling drugs. No more cooking meth for Lonnie Farrell, though. He wanted in where the big money was: cocaine. He had everything in place except where he was going to set up shop, and for that he wanted a location that would be extremely secure. He'd thought about it long and hard before it came to him in a dream, and once it took hold, he'd considered it genius. Not only would it take him off the radar, but it would be unbelievably easy to protect. And the best part of it was he had a built-in link to cheap labor in the residents of Rebel Ridge. All he had to do was contact the long-distance owner and he would be in business.

Sylvia Dixon was furious. As of today she was officially divorced, and in her eyes that meant she had been cheated out of a proper settlement. Her ex, Robert Dixon, was worth a fortune — the last heir to one of Louisville's old-money families. It was her opinion that the fact that she'd been married to him for less than four years should not have mattered, and she was still pissed at herself for signing that prenup.

Here she was, at the waning age of thirty-nine, with only a lump sum settlement of a quarter million dollars, her BMW, the uptown condo and no prospects in sight. With her lifestyle, that money would be gone within the year. She needed to make new plans — fast.

The three-inch heels of her Jimmy Choos marked her rapid stride with a *clip, clip, clip* as she stomped back to her car, slamming the door behind her as she got in.

"Smarmy bastard," she muttered, as she pulled the settlement check out of her purse and quickly endorsed it before driving by the bank.

Her cell phone rang as she was about to leave, and the tone of her voice when she answered still mirrored her anger.

"Hello."

Lonnie Farrell heard anger and immediately shifted into a different mode of approach than the one he'd planned.

"Hello. Mrs. Dixon?"

"Yes, who is this? How did you get my number?"

"I'm sorry. I should have identified myself first. My name is Lonnie Farrell, and your family lawyer gave me your number. I represent a company interested in buying some property you own back in Rebel Ridge."

Sylvia smiled as her heart skipped a beat. *In your face, Robert Dixon. I can still land on my feet.*

She immediately shifted mental gears. "I apologize for my abruptness, but a woman in my position can't be too careful."

"Of course, I completely understand. Now, as to the reason I'm calling. Are you interested in selling your property?"

"You are referring to the Foley Brothers Mine and surrounding land?"

"Yes, ma'am. The company I represent is interested in buying it."

Robert Dixon was not Sylvia's first husband, nor had she hooked her well-to-do exes by being stupid.

"The mine is played out."

"Yes, ma'am. We know."

"What are you planning to do with it?"

Lonnie hesitated, choosing his words carefully. "Right now the plans are in a development stage, but that shouldn't concern you if you're interested in selling."

Sylvia had run her own cons, and this sounded suspicious.

"You want to buy an abandoned mine, but you're not interested in mining?"

Lonnie was getting pissed, but there was

too much riding on making this happen to let it show.

"I understand your curiosity, but I assure you, it's not a secret. It's the dark, damp interior and the constant temperature that make it ideal for our needs. We want the space for mushroom farming."

Sylvia blinked. There couldn't be much money in that. "I don't know if this is going to work out. I can't imagine there's all that much profit in selling fungi, and I'm not in the market of giving things away."

"You'd be surprised," Lonnie drawled. "We're willing to offer you half a million dollars."

Sylvia stifled a gasp. "A half million dollars to grow toadstools? Obviously you think I'm an idiot. I do not want to be involved in anything illegal."

"Toadstools are poisonous, and you're overthinking our offer, Mrs. Dixon." He threw in an amused chuckle for effect. "Do you want to do business, or shall I inform them you're not interested, in which case we will just look for another source?"

Sylvia felt trapped. If Robert hadn't divorced her, this conversation would have ended before it began, but a half million dollars? How could she refuse?

"I'm sure you understand my concerns,

but it won't be necessary for you to look any further."

"Perfect! I'll have the papers sent to you. The check will be with the papers. Just sign them both. You send me one copy and keep the other, as well as the check." He waited, guessing that the offer of a lot of easy money would be hard to reject.

"I want a cashier's check," Sylvia said.

Lonnie grinned. "Of course," he said. "What address should I use?"

Sylvia gave him the address of the condo where she would be living.

The call ended a moment later, and she dropped the phone in her lap and grabbed the steering wheel with both hands as she looked out the windshield.

The sun was still shining. The sky was still clear, and if that call had been on the up-and-up, she would soon be another half million dollars to the good. So why did she feel like she'd just sold a piece of her soul to the devil?

Quinn checked in at headquarters, got the location of the kill site and headed up the mountain. He couldn't quit thinking about the condition of the hikers he'd found. Knowing the bear had taken down eight full-grown hunting dogs highlighted the growing danger. He just hoped to God that they found the monster before anyone else crossed its path.

Nearly an hour passed before he reached the location where the dogs had been killed. Although the carcasses had been moved, the ground was still black where the dogs had bled out. He could have found the trackers by following the sounds of their dogs as they moved farther up the mountain, but they didn't need him.

If the bear was sick or wounded, then there would be no rhyme or reason to its movements, and it would likely be in serious pain. Any wound would have become infected, and the bear would be extremely feverish. The fever would keep the bear in a constant state of thirst, and immersion in water would be soothing, as well. He'd been thinking about this scenario ever since the first search had been called off. There was a creek less than a quarter of a mile from where he'd found the dead hiker that snaked downward in this direction.

He first needed to find the water, then search it for sign. If he was right and the bear was walking the creek to cool its feverish body, it would explain why the dogs had lost the trail on the first search, and would also pinpoint the track the bear was taking downward toward civilization.

Concern for Mariah was at the forefront of his mind, and while he hadn't mentioned it to her, he'd already made a call to his mother and his sister, Meg, asking them to "drop by" and check on her. This was supposed to be his day off, so their appearance wouldn't be suspect, and they could play dumb about knowing he'd been called in to work.

Of course they'd agreed far too willingly, which told him they were beyond curious about the woman he'd brought home. He sighed. In the long run he would pay, but he would endure whatever interrogation they gave him as long as he was assured that Mariah was okay.

He glanced around the kill site one last time and then checked his map before moving off into the woods. His rifle was hanging at the ready in the crook of his arm, his ear attuned to the sounds around him.

Within a short time he'd found a creek with swiftly moving water. He checked the coordinates and confirmed his suspicion that it was the same one he'd found up near the hikers. Now he needed to see if he could find bear signs. When he waded into the water, it immediately washed over the tops of his hiking boots, soaking his feet in an ice-cold rush.

"Oh, shit," he said, then ignored the discomfort and began walking up-creek.

The bear's gut was full. It had gone back to the kill site the same night and fed on three other carcasses before returning to the overhang. The meat had given it a burst of much-needed energy, and while the wound on its hip was still festering and running with pus, having a full belly gave it one less pain to address.

Just before sunrise a coyote returning from a night of hunting startled it awake. The bear growled in disagreement and then headed for water to slake its thirst. Once that was accomplished, it lay down in the creek, letting the cold, rushing water wash over its suppurating hip until it was blessedly numb.

By the time the Doolens and their dogs had reached the kill site, the bear was already moving downstream.

It was just before noon when Mariah woke up. The talk show she'd been watching was long since over and a soap opera had taken its place. She wrinkled her nose and switched off the show before making a slow, achy trip to the bathroom, dragging her leg as she went. It occurred to her that she was going to have to maintain a regimen of physical therapy whether she liked it or not, or she would be left with a pronounced limp.

Instead of the high-powered painkillers, she popped a couple of the over-the-counter kind and hoped for the best as she began to poke around the kitchen for something to eat.

She was standing at the cabinet, trying to decide between a can of chicken noodle soup and a can of beef stew, when she heard what sounded like a car engine. Thinking it would be Quinn, she smiled as she headed for the door. But the vehicle she saw through the window wasn't his Jeep, it was a pickup, and two women were getting out.

One was older and gray-haired, wearing a loose-fitting dress. The other was much younger, but Mariah recognized her features. It was like looking at a female version of Ryal, right down to the slim build and height. These had to be some of Quinn's family.

She looked down at herself and sighed. Gray worn-out sweats and a U.S. Army T-shirt with a tear under the arm. Not the outfit she'd hoped to be wearing to meet more members of his family.

What the hell? It was only clothes, and she didn't adhere to the theory that clothes made the man — or the woman, as the case might be. Instead of waiting for them to knock, she opened the door and lifted her chin.

Dolly Walker was both anxious and curious. Quinn was the only one of her children who'd never married. In fact, he'd never had a girlfriend he considered serious enough to bother bringing her home to meet the family. The fact that he'd suddenly brought a woman home with him out of the blue had the whole family curious. Ryal had filled them in on who she was and why she was there, so after Quinn's call this morning, she and Meg had been more than willing to check on her.

She'd baked a dried apricot cobbler, and Meg had made a meatloaf and roasted some potatoes. They knew the drill. Supposedly they were bringing some food to help Quinn out, thinking he would be there to introduce them.

As they drove up the winding driveway and across the open meadow, Dolly couldn't help but think about how different the new cabin was from the old house she'd grown up in, but different in a good way. Her children would never be wealthy, but their occupations and lives were already steps above what hers had been, and for that she was proud.

"Hey, Mom, what are you thinking?" Meg asked, as the cabin came into view.

"That I need to keep an open mind and not judge."

Meg frowned. "Are you thinking you won't like her?"

"Oh, no, no, I didn't mean that. I was thinking about what shape she'll be in. Remember how Quinn was when he first came back? Whatever we said or did for him was wrong. He wouldn't talk about it, and he didn't want any help."

Meg sighed. It had been hard on all of them to watch him suffer and be unable to help, but it had been hardest on their mom. When they were young, she'd always been able to fix their boo-boos. It had to be hell for a parent to see that kind of suffering and not be able to do anything about it.

"It'll be okay, Mom. I think the main thing is to follow her lead."

Dolly nodded as she got out of the car, but she wasn't convinced. And then the door opened. The young woman standing in the doorway had her chin up and her shoulders back. She looked like she was gearing up for a fight, not greeting guests.

"Oh, crap, she doesn't look happy," Meg said.

"She doesn't know us," Dolly said, determined that if Quinn liked this woman, then she would like her, too.

She picked up her cobbler and headed for the cabin.

Meg followed with her own offerings as they walked up the steps.

"You must be Mariah," Dolly said. "Meg and I brought you and Quinn something for supper tonight."

"Quinn's not here," Mariah said, shifting nervously as she stepped aside to let them come in.

Meg frowned. "Oh, we're sorry. This is his day off, so we just assumed . . ."

Mariah shrugged. "There was some trouble about a bear. I think they called everyone in to the ranger station."

"Well, then, we'll just introduce ourselves," Dolly said, and set her cobbler down on the counter. "I'm Quinn's mother, Dolly Walker, but you just call me Dolly. This is my daughter, Margaret Lewis, but we all call her Meg."

"It's nice to meet you, and the food smells wonderful," Mariah said. "I'm sorry the sofa is out of commission, but you're welcome

103

to take a seat on what is now my bed."

"We can sit out on the deck," Meg offered.

Mariah didn't want to argue, but Quinn had given her orders she wasn't inclined to ignore.

"Quinn told me not to spend time outside until the bear was caught."

Dolly glanced at the worry on Mariah's face. Quinn had warned them about the danger, but she hadn't taken it seriously until now.

"Then we can sit at the kitchen table just as easily." She glanced at the clock. It was after twelve o'clock. "Have you had anything to eat yet?"

Mariah shook her head. "I was debating on which can of soup to open when you drove up."

Meg waved toward the table. "You two sit. I'll poke around and get all three of us something."

Mariah sat because she didn't know what else to do. She was already out of place here. Trying to play hostess would be a joke. She wanted these women to like her, but her track record with women friends wasn't the best. She supposed it had to do with a lack of bonding as a child. The few times she'd actually gotten attached to a foster parent, she had been moved. After a while she'd quit trying.

Dolly could tell Mariah was ill at ease, but there was one thing they all had in common that would be safe grounds for conversation, and that was Quinn.

"So, you and Quinn were in the same combat unit in Afghanistan?"

Mariah nodded.

Dolly smiled as she reached for Mariah's hands, holding them firmly in her grasp to punctuate her words.

"I know you saved my son's life, and for that alone you will always hold a special place in my heart. Thank you, my dear. Thank you very, very much."

The woman's warmth was infectious. Mariah's nerves began to settle. She felt embarrassed to be singled out like this when there were others who'd been there, too.

"We were just lucky to find him when we did," she said.

"And how are *you* doing?" Dolly asked.

" 'Slowly but surely' is a good way to put it," Mariah said, and glanced at Meg, who was banging cupboard doors and opening drawers with confidence.

Dolly caught the look. "Don't worry about her. She's been here enough times in the past year that she knows where things are."

Mariah nodded, but she still felt useless.

She was scrambling for something to talk about and then remembered Quinn telling her that his mother had grown up on this property.

"Mrs. Walker, Quinn said —"

"No 'Mrs. Walker' business. Call me Dolly."

"Okay. So, Dolly, Quinn told me you grew up on this property."

Dolly's eyes widened as memories washed over her. "Oh, yes. There were six of us kids, plus Mama and Papa. The old house wasn't much, but it was home. All the girls slept in one bed. All the boys slept in another, and Mama and Papa were in the loft upstairs. Papa worked the mines, and Mama grew a big garden. The boys learned to hunt almost before they went to school, and all of us girls learned how to manage a house and feed a family with little to nothing to start on. We were dirt-poor and wore hand-me-downs until they were thin as tissue paper, but we always had each other and a whole lot of love."

The words painted a picture that warmed Mariah all the way to her bones. What a gift it would have been to grow up like that.

"You were very lucky."

Dolly shrugged. "There are plenty of people who would argue that with you. Living on the mountain can be a hard life."

"Now, Mom, you know good and well money isn't everything," Meg said, and then winked at Mariah.

Meg's wink made Mariah think of Quinn. "You and Quinn look alike," she said.

Meg nodded. "I know. All of us Walkers look enough alike that you can definitely tell we're kin."

"I think I remember Quinn mentioning nieces and nephews. Are any of the kids yours?" Mariah asked. The smile on Meg's face shifted just enough for Mariah to know she'd asked the wrong question. "I'm sorry. I shouldn't have gotten personal. You don't have to answer that," she said quickly.

Meg shrugged. "It's old news, sugar. Besides, if you're here, you're considered part of the family and can ask anything you want. To answer your question, I do not have children. I would like to, but I'm minus a man in my life, so it's not likely to happen."

Dolly frowned. "Finish the story, Meg, or I'll do it for you. It's time you stopped being ashamed of something you didn't do."

Meg's shoulders slumped, but she managed to put a smile on her face.

"What Mom's trying to say is, I had a husband, but he's now in the state penitentiary. I divorced him after he murdered a man down in Louisville over drugs."

Mariah rolled her eyes. "That's probably where a good portion of the kids I was in foster care with wound up. It's also why I joined the army. The first eighteen years of my life pretty much sucked. I was looking for a place to belong, and in a lot of ways the army served me well."

Dolly blinked. "You were in foster care your whole life? You never knew your parents?"

Mariah tensed, bracing herself for that look she got when people realized she was a throwaway.

"I was an abandoned baby, only a few hours old when someone found me. I grew up in the foster care system in Lexington until I aged out. After that I was on my own."

Meg stopped making sandwiches and stared at Mariah, trying to imagine what it would be like to be that alone in the world.

But for Dolly, the story was shocking. "Oh, honey, I'm sorry I brought up a touchy subject."

"No, it's nothing like that, at least not for me. It's a fact of my life and definitely taught me to be independent."

Dolly got up, walked around the table and

wrapped her arms around Mariah's neck.

"Every motherly gene I have is imploding. This just breaks my heart, honey girl," she said, and laid her cheek against the crown of Mariah's head.

Mariah didn't know how to react. She was confused and more than a little embarrassed, and Meg saw it.

"Ease up, Mom. If we scare her off before Quinn gets to work his magic, he'll kill us."

Dolly looked embarrassed, but Mariah laughed. And the moment the sound came out of her mouth, a little bit of the sad child she had been disappeared.

"Sandwiches are ready," Meg said. "Looks like you have cold pop and iced tea to drink. What's your pleasure?" she asked.

"Iced tea for me," Dolly said.

"And for me," Mariah added.

Dolly put the plates on the table, chattering as she worked. Meg was putting ice in the glasses and pouring tea while acting as the straight man for her mother's monologues.

For Mariah, it was a peek into what a relationship between mother and daughter could be. It didn't really make her sad, but she could definitely tell what she'd missed. And it was also an interesting view of how his family had molded Quinn into the man

109

he was today.

They continued talking even after the food was gone, and Mariah was still smiling an hour after they left. When she finally lay down to take a nap, she rolled over and fell asleep without feeling a moment of panic. It was the first time since she'd been wounded that she slept without dreaming.

Every nerve Quinn had was on alert as he kept moving upstream. The squirrels chattering in the trees along the creek was normal, but the sudden silence that followed was not. He was jumping at every rustle in the brush, afraid he was missing clues beneath the water because he was so anxious about walking up on the bear.

Still, he couldn't quit on this. His gut instincts kept telling him this was how the bear was getting away and why the dogs were losing the scent. Except for feeding, the bear was actually using the water as a highway.

He'd gone about a mile upstream from the kill site when he spotted something in the creek bed that gave him pause. There was a large, moss-covered boulder jutting out of the water with four long, distinct scratches cut into the moss. They were equally spaced and went all the way to the rock. It made him think of claws cutting flesh down to the bone, like he'd seen on the leg of the hiker he'd rescued.

He straightened abruptly, scanning the area to make sure he was still on his own, then took another step, slower this time, and began looking closer as he continued to move upstream. The next clue he found was on the actual creek bank, where a large chunk of earth and grass had been broken off, as if something very large and heavy had stepped too close to the edge and it had given under the weight.

He climbed up onto the bank to back-track, eyeing the forest floor for further prints. But the ground was covered in leaves and pine needles in different stages of decay. If anything had passed that way, it wouldn't have left any prints. He moved a few yards farther, still looking for signs of scat or the remnants of a kill. He was so focused on looking down that when something large suddenly darted out of the brush to his right, he fell backward. He was scrambling for his rifle when he realized it was only a deer. The doe leaped across his line of vision before disappearing downhill.

"Shit," Quinn muttered, as he got to his feet and shifted his rifle to a better position.

He paused and looked up, then caught

himself staring at the trunk of a sixty-foot pine. The gashes that had been cut into the tree were at least ten feet off the ground, maybe higher — just like the ones he'd found at the site where the hiker was killed. It was the bear — still marking territory.

He pulled out his two-way.

"Ranger Walker to dispatch, do you copy?"

"Go ahead, Walker."

"What's the status on the team of trackers? Over."

"They lost the trail again about two miles from the canine kill site, over."

"Are they still on the mountain? Over."

"Yes. They're moving down and east from Greenlee Pass."

"I'm going to send you my coordinates. Tell them I'll be waiting. I think I found something. Over."

"Will do. Waiting to receive them. Over," the dispatcher said.

Quinn ran his GPS, sent the location and settled in to wait. At best guess it would take most of an hour for the men to reach him. He glanced at his watch. It was already after 2:00 p.m. Once it got past 4:00, it got dark fast, and he had no intention of leaving Mariah home alone in the dark, nor did he relish a hike off the mountain after the sun had gone down.

He sat down on a rock, shed his backpack and then dug out a bottle of water and an energy bar. It wasn't home cooking, but it served a purpose. As soon as he finished, he put the wrapper in his pocket, put the empty bottle in his backpack and settled down to wait.

Six

Quinn glanced at his watch, then pulled out his phone to check on Mariah. He made the call, and while he waited for her to answer, he wondered if she was on to him for the sneak visit from his mother and sister, then decided it was too late to worry about that now.

The phone rang several times. Just when he was about to become concerned, she answered, and he could tell she'd been sleeping.

"Hello?"

"Hey, it's me," he said. "You sound sleepy. Did I wake you?"

"Yes, but that's okay. I'm glad you called. I've been worrying about you . . . uh, I mean with the bear and everything."

He smiled. "I'm still all in one piece."

"Oh, my God, do not even joke about that," she muttered. "Your mother and sister were here. They brought food for dinner tonight."

The tone of her voice took care of one concern. She didn't sound pissed.

"Oh. I'm sorry I wasn't there to introduce you. Were you okay with that?"

"Of course I was okay. They stayed and ate lunch with me. I liked them, Quinn. They're really nice."

He grinned. "And you were surprised that they were nice . . . as opposed to me, you mean?"

"Oh, shut the hell up," she said.

He laughed.

Mariah grinned and then changed the subject. "What's going on with that bear?"

"Not sure just yet, but I have a theory. I'm waiting for the trackers and their dogs to get to my location."

"You'd think dogs would be able to track it. Why is that not happening?"

"That's part of my theory. There's a creek that winds nearly twenty-five miles on Rebel Ridge before it hits a river. It was close to where the bear first attacked the hikers, and a few miles down the mountain that same creek is also close to where those hunting dogs were killed. I think the bear is using it like a highway, which leads me to think it's either sick or injured. If I'm right, that's one reason why the dogs keep losing the trail. It doesn't just go in and out of water but stays in it, maybe for miles. That's also why it's so important to find it. A weakened animal is a desperate one. It'll take chances it wouldn't normally take in its drive to survive."

She shivered. "I didn't know all that. Now I *am* worried."

"I survived the worst the Taliban threw at me. One sick bear is not going to be how I meet my end."

"And you know this how?"

He had no intention of telling her that he planned on living to a ripe old age with her. Not yet.

"I just do." Then he began to hear barking. "Hey, I hear dogs. I guess the trackers were closer than I thought. I'll try to be home before dark. Take care of yourself, and don't forget to do your exercises."

"In the meantime, is there anything I could do? I mean for you?"

"Just take care of yourself."

He disconnected, shouldered his backpack and his rifle, and waited for the trackers to arrive.

Everyone on Rebel Ridge knew Jake Doolen's bloodhounds were the best trackers on the mountain, maybe even in Kentucky. Jake was on call with the Kentucky State Bureau of Investigation, as well as anyone else in need, on a twenty-four-hour basis, but to the best of Jake's memory, neither he nor his sons, Avery and Cyrus, had ever been called out just to track a bear. It wasn't that the hounds couldn't do it, because he had faith that they ultimately would. But this was like tracking a ghost bear. Every time his hounds picked up a trail, it always ended when the bear went into the water. And they'd never been able to pick up the trail again on the other side.

When he got the message from ranger headquarters about a possible new lead, he was ready to jump on it. He was sick at heart from the loss of life, both human and animal, and scared shitless the bear would kill again before they took him down.

According to the directions they'd been given, they should be near the site where the ranger was waiting, and when the dogs suddenly began to bay, he realized someone or something was coming their way.

Cyrus took his rifle off his shoulder, while Avery flipped the safety off his. Just in case. Then they saw the ranger coming toward them and relaxed, Cyrus lifting a hand in welcome.

When Jake saw it was one of Dolly Foster's

boys he felt a twinge of regret. If he'd been luckier in love he could have called them his sons, but Dolly had fallen for Tom Walker and that had been that. He'd settled for his Amanda without too many regrets, and he'd loved her in the best way he knew how right up until the day she died.

"Zeus! Blue! Red! Sit," Jake said sharply, and all three hounds dropped as Quinn approached.

Avery cradled his rifle as he smiled a hello. The Doolens had gone to school with the Walkers and were old friends.

"Hey, Quinn."

Quinn nodded a hello, eyeing the big raw-boned men. Jake's hair used to be as red as his sons', but it had gone fully gray. They were all outfitted in heavy-duty denim because of the rugged terrain into which they'd been sent, with orange hunting vests for safety.

"Avery, good to see you. Cyrus . . . Jake, you're both looking good."

Jake nodded. "You, too, son. I hear you have some information. I sure hope it's good."

"It's a theory with substance, how's that?" Quinn said.

"Right now we'll take anything that might

118

lead us in a new direction. So what do you have?"

"You know I'm the one who found the two hikers, right?"

"Yeah, we heard."

"As you know, the paw print I found on-site was huge, and the claw marks the bear left on a tree were much farther up the trunk than you would have expected a black bear to leave."

"We saw the markings on the tree, but the paw print was gone by the time we got to the site. We did find a big one near where the dogs were killed, but the floor of the forest is thick with leaves or rocky as hell. Hard to find tracks, and with the dogs losing the trail, it's been frustrating."

"Follow me back toward the creek. There's something I want to show you," Quinn said, then led the way.

As they drew closer, the hounds suddenly bayed. They'd already picked up on the scent.

"You got something!" Jake said, as his dog strained on the leash.

Quinn paused and then pointed up at a pine tree in front of them. "Look at that."

Cyrus cursed beneath his breath. Avery just stared. But Jake grunted in shock.

"Hell's fire, that's got to be ten, maybe

twelve feet up, just like the marks where you found the hiker's body."

"There's more," Quinn said. "This way."

All three dogs were straining on their leashes and baying as Quinn reached the creek bank. He stopped, then squatted, pointing out where the earth had been dislodged.

"See this? Looks like something really heavy dislodged this chunk as it stepped down into the creek."

The men nodded, but in their opinion, it was just more of the same stuff that they'd already seen. The bear had gone into the water. So what?

But then Quinn didn't cross to the other side of the creek. Instead he began to wade downstream.

"Follow me down a few yards," he said.

The men walked along the creek bank, paralleling him.

As soon as Quinn got to the rock where the moss had been scratched, he pointed again.

"Look there."

Jake stepped out into the water with his dog, Zeus. As soon as they reached the middle of the creek where the rock jutted out of the water, Zeus sniffed the moss and bayed.

"Yeah, I'd say that's bear," Jake said. "So, did you find where he went out on the other side yet?"

"Now we get to my theory," Quinn said. "I've said from the start that something's wrong with this animal. It's either sick or injured. So say I'm right, and say it's feverish, that means it will be constantly thirsty. You agree?"

Jake nodded. "Makes sense."

"And it won't be able to hunt, so it takes the easiest prey it finds, and that happens to be whatever crosses its path, which is how I view the killings so far."

Jake was still listening. "I don't disagree. But if it's so sick and crippled, then why haven't we found it laid up somewhere? Why do we lose the trail at the water's edge and not pick it up anywhere on the other side? It doesn't backtrack, because we've already ruled that out. And we've found numerous places where it's spent a day or two, but it never goes back to the same location."

"Because I think it's using the water like a highway. There's that constant thirst, for one thing. And if it's feverish, or it's been injured, lying in this cold mountain water at a moment's notice would soothe the heat and the pain. I think the only time it comes out of the creek is when it hears something that leads it to a kill. That's why your dogs can't find another trail on the other side, because the water *is* the trail. If I'm right, the only chance we have of finding it is to either follow the creek down, or go all the way down to where the creek runs into the river and come up to meet it. And — again, if I'm right — when it kills again, it will be somewhere that's not far from the creek."

Jake's shoulders slumped. What Quinn was saying nullified the chance of the dogs being able to locate the bear.

"This sucks."

"I agree," Quinn said.

"We need more men for sure," Jake said, then eyed the sun through the trees. It was too close to sundown to set this new plan in motion. "And I can get them, but I need to notify your ranger station. What I am saying is we're not doing this in the dark. Not with this one."

"I agree," Quinn said. "So, unless I'm ordered elsewhere, I'll see you tomorrow?"

Jake nodded. "Yes, and for the record, that's one damn good theory."

Quinn shrugged off the compliment. Knowing the animals and the region was just part of the job.

"I'm headed back down to where I left

my truck," he said.

"We'll go with you," Jake said. "I have a lot of phone calls to make and some extra plans to figure out."

"And in the meantime, we pray to God no one else gets hurt before we find that bear," Avery added.

The sun was about to slip behind the peak of Rebel Ridge when Quinn got his first glimpse of home. He could not deny that his anxiety had nothing to do with wet feet and an empty belly. It was all about Mariah. As a grown man, he'd never had anyone to come home to before. It felt good.

Mariah came out onto the deck as he pulled up and parked, then frowned when she saw the expression on his face. She'd seen that look before. It spelled both mental and physical exhaustion.

"You look tired," she said, as he came up the steps.

"You look good," he countered, smiling as a blush of pink swept up her neck and across her cheeks.

"Well, that's a lie, but thank you anyway," she said.

Quinn stopped at the door and pulled off his hiking boots and socks, then started to strip out of his clothes when it hit him that he couldn't do that anymore without an audience.

"Um . . . I usually strip out here and throw my clothes straight in the wash," he said.

Mariah crossed her arms. "Okay with me."

His eyes narrowing, he tried to decide if she was kidding or if this was a test. It wasn't like she'd never seen him naked before.

"It's your call," he said, as he shed his shirt and dropped his pants. His thumbs were in the waistband of his briefs when she sighed and walked away.

"Whatever," he muttered, then picked up the wet, muddy clothes and headed for the utility room.

When he emerged the washer was filling with water and Mariah was outside, walking the deck with a stiff, lopsided stride. He couldn't decide whether she was pissed or just frustrated. Either way, he could identify. He felt a little bit of both himself.

Determined not to make an issue out of this, he went straight upstairs and into the shower. By the time he came out, the scent of heating meatloaf brought him down the stairs double-time. Mariah was at the sink washing her hands. He walked up behind her.

"Something smells good," he said.

"Your sister's cooking. Meatloaf and roasted potatoes. Do you want a salad or a vegetable? I can open a can or chop up some lettuce."

Quinn put his hands on her shoulders. "I'm sorry I was such an ass. I don't know what made me do that."

She hesitated. "I do. This whole thing is awkward. We have a history, right?"

"Yeah, I'd say that's a fact."

"Only it was nothing but sex, right?"

This time Quinn didn't answer.

She turned around. "Quinn?"

"I vote for salad."

She blinked. "What?"

"You asked me if I wanted a vegetable or a salad. I vote for the salad, but if you want, I'll chop it."

Mariah sighed. Maybe he was smart to avoid discussing their past. Not when she was like this anyway — crippled in both body and brain.

"Fine. No onions in mine," she said, and turned away too fast to see the disappointment flash across Quinn's face.

The bear had managed to kill a small doe that morning, which had given it a brief burst of strength that had carried it nearly two miles farther down the creek. But the wound in its hip was like a sore tooth — the pain never went away. And it was hungry again. By the time it was dark, the bear had stopped.

As it sat, the water was just deep enough to wash over the infected wound and work a bit of medicinal magic. The cold, swiftly moving water both numbed the pain and flushed the running pus from the still-open flesh.

An owl hooted from a nearby tree.

The bear uttered a soft woof.

The owl took flight.

The bear sniffed the air, sensing a change in the weather.

Clouds were gathering to the southwest. A storm would blow through before morning. Minutes passed as the forest came alive with the creatures of the night.

Somewhere off in the distance, a dog howled. The bear lifted its head and sniffed the air again — anxiously this time. Nearby, a calf had become separated from its mother and bawled in a long, plaintive cry. Moments later, the cow answered back.

The bear's belly was empty. The calf was near. Without hesitation, it stood up, waded to the creek bank and, grunting in pain as it climbed up and out, disappeared into the dark.

The calf was still bawling for its mother cow.

Then, all of a sudden, a roar ripped through the night, sending small animals scurrying into hiding and the night birds into flight. The calf's crying shifted from plaintive to an indescribable sound of terror and pain.

Nearby, a dog began to bark.

The mama cow was bawling as she ran, but there was no longer an answer from her baby.

The bear was already dragging the calf's carcass into the woods. It would gorge, then find a place to sleep off its meal.

The clouds continued to gather. A couple of hours later the storm moved in. Lightning could be seen in the distance, followed by the distant sound of thunder.

The bear didn't care. It was holed up in a small niche on the side of the mountain just large enough to shelter it from the storm, asleep with a full belly and a rising fever.

Mariah's sleep had been fitful at best, and when the sound of thunder suddenly blasted over the cabin, she woke up screaming. She rolled out of bed, bumped her lip on the floor and tasted blood, which just added to the delusion that they were being bombed.

"Incoming! Incoming! Get down! Get down!" she shouted, crawling on her belly, trying to find her gun.

The shaft of lightning that tore through the darkness was the flash as the shell exploded. The rush of wind as the storm front hit was the blast of impact. Corporal Conrad was under attack without a gun.

Quinn had been awake for nearly half an hour. He'd heard the storm coming long before it hit and had been lying in bed, frustrated by the fact that whatever bear sign might have been left behind was going to be washed away by the oncoming rain. It felt as if the weather and the mountain were conspiring against them.

Even though he'd known the storm was coming, he jumped when the first blast of thunder rattled the windows. The moment he heard Mariah scream, he knew what was happening, but before he could get the light on in the loft and get downstairs, she was already on her belly, crawling across the living room floor.

Quinn turned on the lights, calling her name as he ran.

"Mariah! I'm here, I'm here."

She was halfway under the sofa bed when he reached her. But in her mind the hand on her leg belonged to an insurgent. Despite her injured leg, she kicked and fought with all the strength she had, certain she was about to be captured.

Quinn rolled sideways just before her foot caught him on the chin and then stopped. Fighting with her wasn't going to pull her out of this. Instead he grabbed the remote and turned on the television, frantically searching for something that was the opposite of what was going on inside her head. He landed on the channel carrying classic TV reruns and found *I Love Lucy*.

He upped the volume until the laugh track and Lucy's antics drowned out the sound of thunder and lightning, then settled back against the wall with his heart in his throat, waiting for her sanity to return.

Mariah would have been screaming, but she was shaking so hard she couldn't breathe. In her mind she'd gone from hiding to being trapped under debris, just like she'd been when she was injured. The pain in her head was as real as it had been the day she was wounded, and she could feel the blood running down her leg and soaking into her uniform.

And then she heard laughing.

It didn't fit the scenario. She pushed frantically against the weight on her back, trying to get herself free.

The laughter persisted, along with the sound of a woman's voice. Maybe help was at hand.

"I'm here! Help me!" she cried.

The moment Quinn heard that, he was on his feet. He grabbed the end of the pullout bed and flipped it up, folding it back into the sofa, then lifted Mariah off the floor and into his arms.

"Honey, it's me. It's Quinn. You're okay. Look at me, look at me."

The desert morphed into the interior of Quinn's cabin, the artillery fire into thunder and lightning. She touched her head, then moaned. All she could feel was the scar.

"Oh, my God," she mumbled, and then pulled out of his arms and staggered to the chair where she curled up into a ball and, still shaking, hid her face against her knees.

Quinn sighed. He knew just how she felt. Disoriented. Crazy. Lost. All of the above.

He turned the sofa back into a bed and straightened the covers, then took off one blanket and draped it over her without saying a word.

Mariah felt the weight of the blanket and

pulled it close, but she wouldn't look up — *couldn't* look up. The laughter was still rolling through the room, and it made no sense. None of this was funny.

Quinn turned off the television. The wind was blowing rain against the windows and hammering it onto the deck. Lightning flashed. The sky belched thunder.

"Mariah?"

She shook her head, denying him an answer.

It didn't stop Quinn from saying what he needed to say. "This happened to me at least twice a day for the first year after I came back. I still have my moments. I think I always will, although it's getting easier to rein it in."

She shuddered. He'd been out over three years and this was still going on? She wanted to die.

"Talk to me, honey," he said softly.

Mariah pulled the blanket all the way over her head.

Quinn sighed. He wasn't a shrink. He didn't know what else to say or do.

Lightning struck, lighting up the meadow in a flash of white so bright it was momentarily blinding. The thunder was so loud he could feel it in his bones. He'd grown up on the mountain. He knew what storms were like here. But Mariah was a city girl. Granted, she was tough and street-smart, but it took more than guts to face what sounded like the wrath of God.

He turned the television back on but lowered the sound so that it was playing in the background, then stretched out on the bed near her chair — just in case.

The faint scent of her shampoo was on the pillow beneath his head. He bunched it up so that he would have a better view of the chair where she'd taken refuge and remembered being in the same frame of mind. Nothing any of his family could do had helped, even though they'd been desperate to make things better. He had to remember that. She had withdrawn to recover, not to reject him. And if she was anything like he'd been, she would not want to be reminded of this later.

Time passed, as did the storm. Within an hour the cabin was quiet except for the gentle sound of rain still falling.

Quinn had fallen asleep on the bed with the lights in his eyes and the television playing.

Mariah had made herself as small a target as she could and was still curled up in the chair. She'd pulled the blanket from her head but had been unable to sleep. Instead she'd watched Quinn lie there with one arm flung out on the bed beside him and the other over his head, and wished she'd never come. The humiliation of coming undone like this was hard to get past. It had happened in the hospital, but there she hadn't been the only one having flashbacks.

Here, there were no nurses running interference with sedation, or shrinks trying to help you get through it by "sharing your feelings." Still, she knew that if they'd released her from Fort Campbell with nowhere to go and she'd freaked like this on a city street somewhere, the authorities would have arrested her, the courts would have sent her to a loony bin and she would never have seen the light of day again.

What she couldn't get past was thinking this was hell at its finest. Just because she hadn't died in Afghanistan it didn't mean she'd escaped the war. It had simply followed her home.

As she sat there feeling sorry for herself, Quinn suddenly jerked and then moaned. Her attention immediately shifted from feeling sorry for herself to what was happening to him. She sat without moving, watching the play of emotions across his face.

He moaned again, and then kicked before rolling over onto his side.

That was all she could take. She threw the blanket off her shoulders and tried to stand, but her leg was numb from having been in one position for so long, and she nearly took a header.

"Damn it," she muttered, then made her way across the floor to where Quinn lay sleeping, dragging her blanket and stumbling as she went.

Without knowing what he was reliving, she knew better than to curl up behind him. Instead she got in bed, then scooted as close to him as she could get without invading his space, pulled the blanket over both of them and took his hand.

His fingers twitched, then curled within her grasp. She held her breath, waiting to see what happened. When he twitched again, then moaned, she tightened her grip and spoke his name.

"Quinn."

He sat up with a jerk. "What's happening?"

"You were dreaming."

That was when he realized she was in bed with him. Her eyes were red-rimmed and swollen. She'd been crying beneath that damned blanket. It hurt his heart.

"Thanks," he said.

The empathy in his eyes was her undoing.

He saw her chin quiver. "Damn it," he said softly, and pulled her close, tucking her beneath his arm so that they were lying face-to-face with his chin resting at the top of her head. Every muscle in her body was tense, and he felt it. "We're just sleeping here," he said.

"Okay."

He took a deep breath and then closed his eyes. Despite the fact that every light in the house was on, they slept.

SEVEN

Lonnie Farrell was a man on a mission, and everything was coming together. Right after Sylvia Dixon had agreed to sell him the mine, he'd sent the money and papers by overnight express with a request for her to sign, fax him a copy then mail the originals back. When the fax came through with her signature on it, he knew it was the time to pick up the phone. It had been a good while since he'd called home, but he hadn't lost touch with his roots or with his mama.

They'd had a special relationship when he was growing up as the man of the family, and, right or wrong, those memories were part of who he was. Right after he'd begun making the big money, he'd bought her a fancy double-wide trailer, and had a new water well drilled at the old home place and the septic tank replaced. Compared to a lot of her neighbors, Gertie Farrell was living high on the hog, and she never missed an opportunity to brag about her son, the successful Chicago businessman.

There weren't many on Rebel Ridge who swallowed the story that whatever Lonnie Farrell was doing was legal, but money was money, and he funneled it to her on a regular basis.

What he needed now was local labor, and he knew exactly who to call to spread the word. His sister, Portia, and her lazy-ass husband, Buell, along with all three of their kids, lived with his mama now. He knew Buell was inclined to drink too much, but he wasn't stupid, and Lonnie was about to give him the first steady job he'd held in over five years.

It was after dinner when he made the call, and Portia was the one who answered.

"It's your nickel. Start talkin'," she drawled, her version of hello.

"Hello, Portia. It's me, Lonnie."

"Well, hey, Lonnie. How's the big city treatin' you?"

"Fine. Just fine. Is Mama around?"

"Yeah, but hang on. I think she's on the pot."

Lonnie frowned. It had been a long time since he'd been around people who spoke as crudely as his family. This was a blunt reminder of the world he was about to rein-habit.

He heard Portia shouting, and then heard Buell in the background telling her to shut the hell up because he couldn't hear the TV. A few moments later he heard his mother's voice. She sounded a little breath-less, as if she'd been hurrying, but there was also joy in her greeting.

"Hey, son!"

"Hello, Mama. How have you been?"

"Why, I've been just fine, thanks to you. I hadn't heard from you in a while and was beginning to worry."

"You don't ever have to worry about me, Mama. I know how to take care of myself."

Gertie couldn't quit smiling. "Yes, yes, that you do."

"I have some good news," he said. "I'm coming home for a visit."

At that point she squealed. She actually sounded like a little girl, and there was a moment when Lonnie felt real regret for not going home sooner. He could hear her relating the news to Portia and Buell, and then heard a door slam and the sound of kids screaming and talking all at once. Portia's kids didn't even know him, but they obviously knew *of* him as the man who sheltered and fed them, so that was enough.

"You got a special reason for coming?" Gertie asked, still giggling as she talked.

"I do. I'm coming to Rebel Ridge because I'm starting up a new business not far from the house, and I'm going to need some local labor to clear brush and trees, and fix some roads."

"Oh, my word! That's wonderful, Lonnie! You don't know what that will mean to the folks around here."

"Yes, I do know, Mama. I used to be one of them, remember?"

"You were barely a man when you left here."

Lonnie's voice hardened. "I was the *only* man of our family, and you know exactly what I mean. I took care of you then, and I'm still taking care of you. That's what a man does."

A fleeting memory of the time from before he left — something she'd long since put behind her — hit without warning. She heard his anger and quickly made her amends.

"You're right. I didn't mean no disrespect. So what kind of business are you planning to start up?"

"I'll tell you about it when I get there. In the meantime, put Buell on the phone. I'm about to put your lazy-ass son-in-law to work."

Gertie gasped. "Are you sure? I mean —"

"Don't worry, Mama. I know what I'm doing."

"I know you do. Hang on just a minute while I hand him the phone. Buell, Lonnie wants to talk to you."

The look on Buell Smith's face said it all. Lonnie didn't like him, and he knew it. Whatever this was about, it couldn't be good. His voice was a little shaky as he took the phone.

"Yeah, I'm here. How you been, brother?"

Lonnie swallowed the retort on the tip of his tongue. He didn't have any brothers, and if he had the urge to claim one, Buell Smith would not be in the running.

"I have a job that needs to be done up the road a bit from Mama's, and I need you to find at least two dozen men who are willing to work." His disgust came through in his voice as he added, "I'm not talking about any of your drinking buddies. I need people who will work their asses off. The money will be fair. Depending on what I think of their work ethic, they could be hired on permanent. I'm going to put you in charge, but if you fuck up, not only will you not get paid, but I will personally beat the living shit out of you. Are we clear?"

Buell thought about his own little side business and how this might impact it, but he didn't have the guts to tell Lonnie no.

"Yes, yes, we're clear as glass. What's the job about? What are we gonna be doing?"

"Initially, clearing trees and brush, and repairing a road. I'll tell you more after I get there. Can you do what I'm asking?"

"Yes, hell yes, I can do that. So these men you want are going to ask me questions, like when will the job start, you know, and assurance that this is for sure gonna happen, so if they turn down another job offer they aren't gonna lose out."

Lonnie's voice softened threateningly. "Here's the deal, Buell. That's the last time you get to question my word or my authority. Do you understand me?"

Buell had sense enough to be scared and was nodding anxiously until he realized Lonnie couldn't see him.

"Yes, I understand," he said quickly.

"You tell the men to be at the entrance to the old Foley Brothers Mine day after tomorrow at 1:00 p.m."

"I'll do that. You can count on me," Buell said, but he was already frantic.

He was expected to find two dozen men in less than forty-eight hours for that kind of work. He didn't have a good personal relationship with any men who were inclined to break a sweat. But he was more afraid of Lonnie than he was of approaching men he knew did not hold him in high regard.

"Now let me talk to Mama again," Lonnie said.

Buell handed the phone back to Gertie. "He wants to talk to you again."

Gertie was still smiling. "I'm here, son."

"I'm going to need a place to stay while I'm there. Do you have a spare bed I can use for one night?"

"Absolutely," Gertie said. "I had a pig butchered a month ago, so I got pork in the freezer. I'll fry you up a pork chop and make a dried apple pie. Does that sound good to you?"

Lonnie thought of the Cordon Bleu dining to which he'd become accustomed and sighed. He was so far removed from fried pork chops it wasn't funny, but he could endure whatever it took for at least one night.

"That sounds real good, Mama. I'll be there day after tomorrow."

"I can't wait. I love you, son."

"I love you, too, Mama," Lonnie said, and hung up.

All things considered, he felt like his work

for the day was done. Within six hours of receiving the bill of sale, he was already assembling a local crew who would be clearing the main road to the mine. It was going to be a trick to pull this off, but he'd faced bigger challenges for less reward. Growing the mushrooms was going to be a front for the drug business he intended to start.

His chemists were on notice, and he had already ordered the material needed to restructure the abandoned mine into an operation for growing mushrooms. That would be set up first so that the drug operation could hide beneath the cover of the legal operation.

Damn but he did love it when a plan came together.

The cold rain was a boon to the bear. Its belly was full, and the creek was swollen with the runoff from the storm. The chill of the night and the rain that continued to fall worked as well at cooling its fever as the creek. Instead of holing up somewhere to sleep, the bear took to solid ground and continued to move downstream. Once it would have had a den it returned to at night, and a territory in which it lived and fed. But its injury had changed every instinct it had but the one to survive.

Tomorrow the scent of its passing would have washed away in the storm and it would already have taken a stream less traveled. By the time the Doolens and the search teams gathered and began moving upstream, the bear would already have reached the juncture where three creeks met and moved on.

As the residents of Rebel Ridge slept, the bear was heading east along a lesser creek. As fate would have it, by the time the sun rose, it was sleeping in a cave less than a half mile above Quinn Walker's cabin.

Quinn woke up before daybreak, surprised to find Mariah asleep in his arms with her head pillowed on his chest. It would have been difficult for him to express the emotions that hit him, but it was fair to say that she was insinuating herself ever deeper into his heart.

After the episode she'd had last night it was obvious they had a long way to go, but he would consider himself blessed if they took that road together. How to approach the issue with her would be the trick. He sensed her reluctance to ask for help and even understood it. PTSD was as emotionally wounding as any IED could ever be. Flesh would heal, but the mind . . . that was an entirely different story.

He glanced at the clock. It was just after five o'clock. He needed to get up, but dear God, he hated to move.

As if sensing his quandary, Mariah opened her eyes, realized where she was and abruptly rolled off him. When she realized he was watching her, she felt her face flush.

"Sorry about that," she said.

"I'm not," he said. "I hate to get up and leave you in the bed alone, but we have a big hunt scheduled this morning, and we're meeting early."

"Don't worry about me," she said. "You know I'll be fine." The moment she said it, she thought of the flashback she'd suffered last night and knew how silly her words must have sounded. When Quinn didn't call her on it, she wanted to hug him.

"I know you will," he said. Instead of kissing her, he ruffled her hair and rolled out of bed.

Mariah sighed. She would have preferred a kiss instead of a pat on the head, but she wasn't ready to go where the kissing would lead. She got up, as well, and, after standing for a few moments to get her balance, went to the downstairs bathroom as Quinn ran upstairs to the loft to shower and get ready for work.

As soon as she came out, she began to make coffee, then got a box of cereal, some bowls and spoons, and sat down to wait for the coffee to be ready. It wasn't on a level with real cooking, but it was the best she had in her this morning.

When the coffee was done, she poured a cup and then took it out the back door to the deck overlooking the meadow. The air was chilly, the fog just beginning to lift. It was the half-light between night and sunrise that always made her believe there could be such a thing as magic.

In the woods, dark shadows morphed into one thing until she blinked, which turned them into another. A large bird took flight from the roof above her head and headed toward the trees. It looked like an owl, but she couldn't be sure.

She took a sip of the coffee, savoring the flavor and the warmth as it slid down her throat, then moved a few steps for a better view to the east, waiting for that moment when a new day was born. A hinge on the back door squeaked. Quinn emerged from the house with his own cup of coffee.

"I'm here," she said, waving from her end of the deck.

Out of habit, he gave the tree line a slow searching gaze, looking for anything out of place, but he saw nothing to cause him alarm.

"What do you think?" he asked, as he walked up beside her.

"About this place? It's beautiful."

A slow smile spread across his face. He was pleased that she felt the same way he did, but his smile quickly faded.

"It *is* beautiful, but you have to remember, like everything else, there are always hidden dangers. I know you're more capable of taking care of yourself than most women, but you're at a disadvantage here just by not knowing the territory."

"You're right. I know cities and, thanks to the army, I know the desert and the Taliban, but I do not know this world."

"When you get a little more mobile, I'll be glad to teach you."

She nodded. "If you don't get sick of babysitting a nut job, I'll take you up on that."

Quinn frowned as he cupped her cheek. "Don't ever call yourself a nut job again."

She sighed. "It's how I think of myself."

"Then change your way of thinking. Are you gonna come eat cereal with me?"

She glanced to the east. The sky was awash in shades of pink and orange.

"Yes, I'm coming," she said, and followed

him into the house.

They poured cereal, added sugar and milk, and took their bowls to the table and began to eat with the ease of a couple who'd done this for years. The bonds they'd made in the military were serving them well. There was no need to dwell on politeness and manners when you'd seen each other at your worst.

"About this hunt . . ." Mariah began.

"What about it?" Quinn asked as he scooped another spoonful of cereal into his mouth, then proceeded to chew.

"So you're hunting this bear . . . but if you see one, how will you know it's the right one? I mean, there have to be lots of them in the reserve, right?"

"Yeah, sure, the possibility of seeing black bear in the less populated areas of the mountains of Kentucky isn't that unusual. However, from the marks this one's left on trees and the size of its prints, it's unusually large. We also have reason to believe that this bear has either been injured or is sick. Most of the behavior it's exhibited is unusual."

Mariah kept eating, listening without interrupting as Quinn continued to explain. But somewhere between one sentence and the next, she lost touch with the conversation and began watching the play of expressions on his face instead. Some of them she'd never noticed. Some of them she remembered from before.

When he was serious, he appeared to be frowning, yet she knew it wasn't anger. The right corner of his mouth turned up just a little if he was skirting sarcasm, and when he was thinking about making love, his lips always parted just a little, as if he was only capable of quick, shallow breaths.

But it was the laughter in his eyes that stole her heart.

"Do you understand?" Quinn asked.

She blinked. "Understand what?"

He grinned. "Were you listening to a damn thing I said?"

"The bear you're after is probably limping?"

Quinn threw up his hands. "My work here is done."

"It's not my fault I lost concentration. You have an interesting face."

Now he was the one taken aback. "I do, do I? How so?"

Mariah pointed to the clock. "You're going to be late."

He sighed. "If that's the way you want to play this, fine with me. Just remember what I told you. Until we get that bear, no leisurely walks outside."

"Not even on the deck?"

"Not even on the deck."

"I promise."

"That's all I need to hear. Stay safe. Get some exercise and some rest, and I'll see you this evening."

He got up from the table, gathered his things and was on his way out the door when Mariah stopped him.

"Hey, Quinn?"

"Yeah?"

"Be careful."

He could tell she was anxious.

"I'll be fine. I promise. Remember to keep your phone in the pocket of your sweat-pants, so you'll have it handy if you need to call."

"I will."

"See you later," he said, and was out the door.

Jake Doolen and his sons were already on site, along with the local sheriff and a bevy of armed hunters, when Quinn arrived. The Doolens' three bloodhounds were tied to their truck bumper, patiently waiting to be set on the trail.

"We have news that might not be good," Jake said, as Quinn approached.

150

Quinn frowned. "Like what?"

"According to Sheriff Marlow, the Dawes family lost a calf last night in the storm. I'd chalk it up to the storm itself, except Mr. Dawes found part of the innards and some hide caught in the brush."

"It could have been a cougar or a bobcat," Quinn said.

Jake pointed at his son. "Cyrus, show Quinn the chunk of hide Dawes gave the sheriff."

Cyrus pulled it out of the back of the sheriff's truck and tossed it on the ground. When he did, all three hounds were on their feet, barking and straining at their leashes. The claw marks on the hide appeared to match what Quinn had seen on the mossy rock.

Quinn frowned, rubbing the back of his neck in frustration.

"Well, hell. That means the bear was on the move last night instead of holed up somewhere."

Jake nodded. "That was my thinking, too."

"How far to the Dawes's place from here?"

"Less than two miles," Sheriff Marlow said, as he walked up behind them.

Quinn frowned, no longer confident the bear was still above them.

"Jake, what's your thinking on this?"

151

Quinn asked.

Doolen didn't hesitate. "I say we split up. I send Cyrus and Avery with Blue and Red to go upstream with half the hunters, and I'll take Zeus and the others with me and check the area around here to see if we can pick up sign."

Quinn eyed the sheriff. "Are you in on this?"

"No. I've got another problem brewing down the mountain. I just came to bring the news and the skin Dawes gave me."

Quinn eyed the skin and then turned to Jake.

"We're already outside the reserve, so technically I have no authority here. However, I'm going with you. Split the rest of them up the way you want, but this is where I grew up. I know this country like the back of my hand."

Jake nodded and quickly divided the men, sending half of them upstream with his sons and their dogs, while the rest of them stayed behind.

As soon as the others had moved out of sight, Jake untied Zeus.

"The creek runs into the river about a hundred yards downhill, as do a couple of other small creeks. I've a mind to take Zeus down there and see if we can pick up sign on any of those branches."

"We're with you," Quinn said, referring to the eight other men who'd stayed behind.

"Then let's get moving," Jake said. "Hunt, Zeus!"

The hound leaped forward, straining at the leash, but Jake wasn't turning him loose. They'd already seen what the bear had done to a pack of eight dogs. No way was he going to let Zeus go at him alone.

They reached the mouth of the river without finding any tracks. Last night's storm had devastated any scat or sign they might have found.

"Spread out," Jake said, directing a half dozen of the men to backtrack up one of the small creek branches, while he and the others started to track up the other. Between the three search parties, they were now covering every direction the bear could take.

Quinn was looking toward the east and the small spring-fed creek. If they followed this creek, they would be going back uphill. He took out the map and spread it on the top of a nearby bush.

"What's up?" Jake said.

"We're here," Quinn said, tapping the map with his finger. "And this creek right here is the one that that feeds in from the east."

He traced the path of the creek and then

suddenly paused. The skin crawled on the back of his neck as he realized this creek originated at the small waterfall coming out of the mountain just above his place.

"Let's move," he said, and started walking without waiting for Jake and Zeus and the others.

The men fanned out, some of them on one side of the creek, some on the other. Quinn waded into the creek and began walking through the water, looking for signs like he'd found before.

About fifteen minutes later one of the men on the north side of the bank suddenly yelled.

Everyone converged to see what he'd found. When Quinn climbed out of the creek and saw the faint indentation of a large, oversize paw print partially sheltered by an overhang of bushes, he caught his breath. This print had been fresh right before the rain.

Son of a bitch, it was still ahead of them, and if it followed the creek all the way up to the waterfall, it would be the end of the ride. There was no more waterway to follow unless it backtracked, which he doubted it would do. The bear had to have heard Zeus and know it was being hunted.

"I got to let the others know," Jake said,

and pulled out a cell phone.

Quinn walked away as Jake began calling in the other searchers to their location. Anxiety grew as he thought of how isolated the cabin was. He didn't have any livestock. All he had was Mariah. She'd promised to stay inside, and he had to trust that she would stick to her word. It was a good four miles up the mountain as the crow flies to get back to his place.

He took out his phone and tried to call her, but he couldn't get a signal. Frowning, he put the phone back in his pocket with a mental reminder to try calling again soon.

EIGHT

Mariah was in workout mode and putting the stairs leading up to the loft to good use. After a brief test run, she'd opted to use the bottom three steps as her goal and was walking up and then down them, up three, down three, while holding on to the railing until her side was hurting and her muscles shaking.

Back at Fort Campbell, her physical therapist had worked her hard every day while impressing upon her the need to continue her exercises after she was released. She'd skipped yesterday, but that was her last lazy day. If she was going to get back to one hundred percent, she had to put in the effort to get there.

She'd found a radio and tuned it to a country music station, and after a steady hour of reps with fifteen minutes working and five minutes resting, she was sweating and in serious pain.

Finally she groaned and collapsed on the stairs.

"Oh, my sweet Lord," she moaned, and dropped her head on her knees, too exhausted to move.

Her heart was pounding so hard its beat drowned out the song. The bottoms of her feet burned, and her muscles felt like they'd never hold her up again. In spite of all that, she was more than satisfied with the workout.

Finally she straightened and then stretched out on the steps while her breathing slowed and the sweat slowly dried on her skin. It was the need for water that finally made her move.

She eased up to a sitting position, then stood, slowly testing herself until she was certain her leg would hold her weight, before she turned off the radio and made her way to the kitchen. Two glasses of water later she was hunting around for something to eat when she heard a car approaching. After a quick peek she recognized Beth driving the SUV they'd come home from Fort Campbell in, but she wasn't alone.

When Mariah saw the young pup get out of the seat behind Beth, she grinned. Rufus had come for a visit, too.

It was the second day in a row that she'd

had unexpected company, and she was beginning to think there was nothing spontaneous about it. Instead of being irked that Quinn must think she wasn't capable of taking care of herself, she was touched that he didn't want her to spend all day alone.

She answered the door smiling.

"Hello!" she said, as Beth and Rufus came up the steps onto the deck.

Rufus saw the open door and bolted inside without waiting for an invitation, which made both women laugh.

"Just like a man," Beth said. "Can't take 'em anywhere. Do you mind? Quinn always lets him in."

"Of course I don't mind," Mariah said. "This is Quinn's house. I'm a visitor, just like Rufus. Where's the baby?"

Beth grinned. "Oh, I don't think you're *just* a visitor, but that's only my opinion. Sarah is with Ryal. They're visiting Grandma Dolly. I hope you haven't eaten lunch yet. I brought chili for your supper tonight, and chicken salad sandwiches for us."

"I was just poking around for something to eat, and that beats anything I would have come up with."

Rufus bumped up against her leg until she acknowledged him with a pat on the head and a few words of hello, and then he was off, sniffing through the house, then up the stairs.

Beth rolled her eyes. "He's looking for Quinn. They're buddies. Can you make us something to drink?"

Mariah nodded, and proceeded to get ice cubes out of the old trays and put them in the glasses.

"Don't forget to refill the trays," Beth said. "It took me forever to get used to that. Ice makers are a thing of beauty, but they aren't all that easy to come by up here. It has something to do with the mineral content in the water. They corrode and break so fast, it's not worth the trouble to have one."

Mariah absorbed that information. It helped to know stuff like this.

Rufus came running down the stairs and paused in the kitchen long enough to beg for food.

Beth frowned. "Not a chance, you big mooch." She opened the back door. "Go play."

Rufus happily obliged with his tongue hanging out the side of his mouth and what looked like a smile on his face.

Mariah frowned. "Quinn didn't want me going outside until they caught the bear. Do you think it's okay that Rufus goes out?"

Beth rolled her eyes. "Oh, I'm sure it's fine. Now let's eat. I hope you're hungry, because I'm starving."

They sat down and began to eat the sandwiches that she'd brought.

"Save room for brownies," Beth said.

"I always save room for dessert," Mariah replied.

Outside, Rufus chased around the deck several times before spotting a rabbit out in the meadow. He yipped, then leaped off the deck in wild abandon and gave chase.

The other hunters caught up with Jake's team within thirty minutes of his call. It didn't take long for all three hounds to pick up a trail, and they began moving double-time, anxious to put this killing spree to an end.

When it became obvious to Quinn that they had a bona fide trail that was still leading in the direction of his home, he had tried another call to Mariah. He placed it on the move, all the while keeping a watchful eye on the woods through which they were moving. The image of the young hiker he'd found flashed through his mind, and he said a silent prayer that they all came out of this in one piece.

Mariah answered on the second ring with

a smile in her voice. "Hello, Quinn."

"Hi. What are you doing?"

"As if you didn't know. I'm having lunch with Beth. How many more of your relatives do you have lined up to drop in on me?"

"I didn't tell them all."

She laughed. "At least you're honest." When Beth waved and pointed at the phone, she nodded. "Beth says hi."

"Tell her I say hi back."

"She brought chili for our supper tonight."

"Tell her I said thank you very much."

"I will. How's the hunt going?"

"We have a new kink."

"Oh, no, did you lose it again?"

"No, it's actually the reverse. We have the first real trail in days."

"Then what's the kink?"

"It's moving along another creek. We're tracking it, but we have no idea if it's holed up somewhere or still on the move."

"And?"

"The creek ends about a half mile above the cabin."

She gasped. "This cabin?"

"Yes. You and Beth just stay inside. I'll give you a call if we find it, and if you see anything suspicious, *you* call *me*."

"Oh, Lord," Mariah said.

Beth frowned. "What's wrong?"

"The bear is moving in this direction along the creek."

Beth's eyes widened, then all of a sudden she gasped. "Rufus!"

She bolted for the door to call the pup back.

Quinn heard the uproar. "What's happening?"

"Beth brought Rufus. He's outside somewhere."

"Shit. You tell her if the dog doesn't come in, under no circumstance is she to go looking for him. I'm serious, Mariah. Do what I say."

"Yes, yes, I get it," she said. "I've gotta go before she gets away from me."

She dropped the phone in her pocket and had started out the back door when something made her stop. She went back to the hall closet for Quinn's rifle, checked to make sure it was loaded and the safety was off, then headed out onto the deck.

Beth was already running across the meadow, calling the puppy, who was nowhere in sight.

Mariah's heart skipped. "Beth! Beth! Come back. Quinn said to stay inside. Hurry!"

The cave where the bear had taken shelter was in unfamiliar territory, but there was no indication that any other animals were living in it. The poison from the infected hip was spreading and it was weakening. For the bear, weakness always meant a need for food and rest, but time and recent feeding had not improved its situation. It had been sleeping fitfully and had been awakened only moments ago by the distant sounds of baying hounds.

Instinct surfaced, pushing past the pain as it got up and moved to the mouth of the cave, sniffing the air. The dogs bayed again, indicating a hit on the scent they were tracking. The bear rocked from side to side, swinging its head and huffing angrily. The scent of water came from only a short distance away, but to get to it, the bear would have to move toward the dogs.

All of a sudden Rufus burst onto the scene, startling them both. The pup barked in a wild, challenging attack, and the bear charged. The pup fell backward, regaining his footing only seconds before the bear would have disemboweled him. Instead the swipe of the paw just barely caught the pup on the side, eliciting a sharp, frantic yelp before Rufus made a beeline for the cabin.

If the bear had been healthy, the pup never would have been able to outrun it, but fate was on Rufus's side as he tore off down the mountain.

Beth heard Mariah yelling and stopped.

Mariah could tell Beth was torn about returning without Rufus, but she kept shouting and waving until Beth finally stopped and turned back.

Mariah stood watch on the deck with the rifle in her hands, scanning the woods as closely as she had scanned the desert a world away. There were no hidden explosives here to worry about, but the danger here was as real and just as unseen.

All of a sudden they heard Rufus's frantic barking.

The hair on Mariah's arms stood on end. She knew in her gut what was happening, and when Beth stopped and turned toward the woods, Mariah screamed.

"Beth! Beth! Run, damn it, run!"

The panic in Mariah's voice transferred itself to Beth in swift fashion. She turned on her heel, heading toward the cabin in an all-out sprint.

Within seconds the puppy flew out of the

woods, his tail tucked between his legs and his ears plastered to his head. The minute he saw Beth, he headed straight for her and, in his panic, proceeded to knock her down.

Mariah groaned. The dog was frantic. The bear couldn't be far behind.

"Get up, Beth! Hurry!" she screamed.

Beth was back on her feet and running again, with Rufus keeping pace at her side.

And then all of a sudden the bear shot out of the woods, bellowing and running toward them far faster than Mariah would have believed possible. At that point, instinct took over.

She swung the gun to her shoulder and took aim, only to realize Beth was in her line of fire. Dragging her weak leg, she stumbled to the far end of the deck as fast as she could go and once again took aim, this time at the side of the oncoming animal. Nerves almost took over when she realized that not only had she never fired this weapon, it was unlikely she would get a chance at more than two shots before it was too late.

"God help me," she said, and squeezed the trigger.

The first shot went a little to the right, hitting the bear in the backside. It let out a roar as it spun toward the pain, but the shot had been a through and through without hitting an organ or a bone. It tried to charge forward again, stumbling as it went.

Mariah took a deep breath, adjusted for the pull and fired a second shot, hitting the bear squarely in the head. It dropped like a stone, and this time it didn't get up.

Beth was screaming as she leaped up the steps and didn't turn around to look until she realized everything was quiet. The bear was silent. Mariah wasn't moving. Beth looked toward the meadow and saw the bear's body partially hidden in the tall grass, unmoving. She dropped to her knees. Rufus leaped into her arms, shaking.

The smell of gunpowder sent a wave of nausea rushing through Mariah. The sound of gunshots was still echoing in her ears as she laid the rifle on the porch railing and pulled the phone out of her pocket.

Before she could make the call, it began to ring. Her hands were shaking as she answered.

"Quinn?"

"What the hell? We heard gunshots and —"

"The bear . . . Beth's puppy . . ." She shuddered and tried again to explain, but the deck was beginning to roll and she felt herself losing control. "It's dead," she said, then set the phone down beside the rifle, sank to the floor, curled up into a ball against the railing and buried her face in her hands.

The moment Beth saw Mariah go down, she knew something was wrong. She crawled over to where Mariah was sitting and pulled her into her arms, holding her close.

"I've got you, honey. You're okay. You're okay," she kept saying.

It took her a few moments to realize Quinn was still on the line and shouting into the phone. She reached up and grabbed it.

"This is Beth. The bear is dead. Mariah shot it. Wherever you are, come home."

Quinn's heart skipped a beat. Despite the good news, there was panic in Beth's voice, and he was afraid he knew why. He dropped his phone in his jacket pocket as he yelled at the other hunters and ran to catch up.

"The bear's down!" he shouted.

Jake was shocked. "You're kidding."

"No. I'm not sure what happened, but it wound up at my place. Ryal's wife is there. I've gotta get home." He singled out the other rangers from the hunters. "Can I ask a couple of you to bring my Jeep back to my place?"

"Absolutely," one said.

Jake wasn't ready to quit the chase. "Me and my boys have tracked this damn bear all over Rebel Ridge. I want to see it *and* the man who took it down."

"It wasn't a man. It was a woman . . . a friend I served with in Afghanistan. She's going through a lot of what I went through when I came home, and this could seriously set her back. I've got to go. Any of you are welcome to follow, but I can't wait for you to catch up, understand?"

"Understood," Jake said. "Me and the boys will be along."

Quinn nodded, then swerved away from the creek and struck out in a lope, heading in a southerly direction. He had a good mile to go cross-country, but given the anxiety in Beth's voice, he couldn't get there fast enough.

Beth was in a panic. She didn't know what to do for Mariah, and she had no idea where Quinn was or how long it would take him to get there. She tried twice to get Mariah up and into the cabin, but she seemed unable to stand, wouldn't talk and hadn't quit shaking.

Rufus had a deep bleeding cut on his hip and was sticking so close to her side that she couldn't take a step for fear of stepping on him. She needed help, and her first thought was Ryal.

She punched in his number with shaking fingers and then took a deep breath to calm her shaky voice. The phone rang three times and then he answered.

"Hello?"

"Ryal, it's me. I'm at Quinn's. I need you."

"What's wrong, honey? Are you okay? Are you hurt?"

"Thanks to Mariah, I'm fine, but she's not, and I don't know what to do."

The panic in his voice was evident. "What the hell happened?"

"You know that bear, the one they've all been looking for? It was up in the woods behind the cabin. Just hurry. I'll tell you about it when you get here."

"Oh, my God . . . you said something was wrong with Mariah. Was she hurt?"

"No. She killed it, but after she shot it, she sort of spaced out on me. Something's wrong, and I can't get her up."

Ryal knew exactly what was happening. He'd seen Quinn flip out plenty of times since his return.

"Where's Quinn?"

"On his way, but I don't know how long it will take him to get here."

"I'm at Mom's. It won't take me long. Don't worry about Mariah. Just don't leave her alone."

"I won't." And then her voice broke. "Hurry, okay?"

"I'm on my way."

Memories of Mariah flashed through Quinn's mind as he ran. How she made love with as much passion as she fought. Seeing her share a candy bar with a couple of Afghani children. Shooting at the enemy without blinking an eye, then crying over a dead puppy they'd found in the ruins of a bombed-out building. The dichotomy of being a woman and a soldier was hard to explain, but she was a perfect example of how it worked. He'd brought her home to help her heal, not traumatize her further, and he was sick at heart about what had happened. But like life, there was no going back. It was all about moving forward, and whatever she was going through, they would go through it together.

He could hear the thrashing of brush and leaves in the distance behind him, and knew the Doolens were still on his trail. There was a stitch in his side and his muscles were beginning to burn, but he pushed through it. Once he got to Mariah, none of it would matter.

Ryal was flying, driving faster on the rough mountain road than he'd ever driven in his life. His mother was white-lipped and silent in the seat beside him, with Sarah safely in her car seat in the back. When Dolly had heard what happened, she wouldn't be left behind.

There was a knot in his stomach getting tighter by the minute, and when he finally took the turn off the road onto the driveway that led to Quinn's cabin, all he could think about was Beth. He'd come so close to losing her before. He couldn't bear to go through that terror again.

Then the cabin came in sight.

Dolly pointed. "I see both of them. They're on the deck."

Ryal pushed the accelerator all the way to the floor, and when he finally reached the cabin, he came to a skidding stop and was out and running before Dolly even opened her door.

It wasn't until Beth saw his face that she started to cry, which only increased his panic. He leaped the steps in one bound, and moments later she was in his arms.

"Bethie . . . honey, what happened? Are you hurt?"

Dolly came up the steps with the baby on her hip and quickly realized Mariah was in trouble. She handed Sarah to Beth and then knelt beside Mariah.

"Honey, we're here. You're okay now."

Mariah was rocking back and forth, her face expressionless except for her eyes. She appeared to be staring into hell.

"What should we do?" Dolly asked.

"Wait for Quinn," Ryal said, and then noticed the bloody pup cowering at Beth's feet. "What happened to Rufus?"

"The bear did it. You know Rufus, he ran off into the woods right after we got here. Then Quinn called later and said they thought the bear had come in this direction. I went outside to bring him inside, but he was gone. I was out in the meadow, calling for him, when Mariah began screaming at me to come back. I was already running back to the house when Rufus came out of the woods with the bear right behind him."

Ryal's stomach roiled. He glanced out into the meadow, gauging the distance between the trees and the cabin — more than the length of a football field — and shuddered. She would never have been able to outrun a bear.

He pulled her into his arms. "You could have died."

172

Sensing the turmoil of the moment, the baby began to cry.

"It's okay, sweetie," Beth said, as she cradled Sarah close against her. "Mama's right here." Then she looked down at Mariah. "If it hadn't been for her, Rufus and I . . . Oh, Ryal, she was amazing. She never even flinched when she fired, but once it was over, she sort of came undone. I don't think she even hears us."

Dolly came out of the cabin with a quilt and wrapped it around Mariah's shoulders, then sat down beside her.

"This is like watching Quinn all over again," she said, and started to cry.

"It'll be all right, Mama. It has to be," Ryal said.

All of a sudden Rufus jumped to his feet and barked.

They all looked toward the meadow just as Quinn came out of the trees, running in an all-out sprint.

"It's Quinn. Thank God," Beth said, and then knelt at Mariah's feet. "Quinn's coming, honey. Quinn's coming."

NINE

Quinn's heart was pounding in frantic rhythm with his footsteps as he burst out of the trees into the high meadow above the cabin. The first thing he saw was the people gathered at one end of the back deck. When he realized no one was standing, it increased his panic and he ran faster.

A few yards farther on he caught sight of the dark mound lying motionless in the grass. It was about halfway to the house. He couldn't believe they'd chased the damn bear all over the mountain without finding it, only to have it show up at his back door. He kept telling himself that he was almost there. He just had to keep moving, had to keep putting one foot in front of the other.

Even though his muscles were burning.

Even though it hurt to breathe.

With nothing between him and Mariah now but a little distance, he could do this.

As the dog began to bark, someone stood.

174

When he recognized Ryal, his relief at knowing his brother was already on the scene was huge. Whatever had happened, if it was bad, Ryal would have initiated a medical rescue already. The realization gave new life to his step.

He ran past the bear without stopping — only a few more yards to go. Then he saw his mother. She was crying.

No, dear God, no. Where was Beth? Where was Mariah? Why weren't they visible? There was a knot in his belly, and he wanted to cry. He'd brought her here to get better, not to get her killed.

When he finally reached the deck he cleared the steps, dropped his rifle on the deck and began shedding his jacket and his backpack as he followed the trail of blood toward the people at the end of the deck.

At that point everything seemed to shift into slow motion.

He could feel the sweat running down the middle of his back, but Rufus's constant barking sounded like it was coming from down a well. The puppy was covered in blood and Ryal's lips were moving, but he couldn't hear a word. His mother was still crying, and Sarah had begun to cry, too, which scared him all over again.

Everything before him was a blur, and

then he saw Mariah. She was sitting on the deck with her injured leg stretched out in front of her and the other bent in an awkward position. Someone had tried to put a quilt around her shoulders, but it had fallen down around her waist as she rocked back and forth in a steady, repetitive motion. The blank look on her face was deceptive, not an indication of what he knew was going on in her head.

Beth jumped up and ran toward him. "The bear didn't touch her, Quinn. It was after me. She saved my life. She was amazing. I think it was the sound of gunshots that caused this."

Quinn went weak with relief. At least the blood wasn't Mariah's or Beth's. He didn't need to know anything more.

"I'm glad you're okay," he said, and then knelt at Mariah's side, trying to decide what to do. "Damn it. I brought her here to get better, not traumatize her all over again."

Beth knelt beside him. "Now you know how I felt about you after Ryal brought me here to hide. We put you in the middle of a similar situation, and you survived. She will, too."

Quinn was heartsick, but he knew it would serve no purpose. There was nothing about her demeanor to indicate she even knew they were there. He wanted to touch her, but it might trigger an even bigger episode.

"Mariah?"

Her hands were fisted, ready to fight. Her expression was blank, except for her eyes. She was looking at something besides the view before her. He knew where she was. He just didn't know how to get her back.

And she kept rocking.

"Mariah, it's me, honey. It's Quinn. I need you to hear my voice. Wherever you are, I'm right beside you. Remember? We were always side by side." He raised his voice. "Mariah! Look at me."

Still rocking, she had no reaction.

He said it louder. "Move it, Conrad! It's over now! The enemy is dead."

She blinked.

Quinn reached for her hands. "I've got your back, soldier. Look at me. Hear me. *It's over.*"

She tried to pull away, but when he wouldn't let her, she moaned.

Dolly walked away sobbing, unable to watch. Rufus was at her heels.

Beth buried her face against Ryal's chest, feeling guilt for coming and causing this to happen.

Quinn moved a little closer to Mariah, raising his voice even further. "It's time to get up. It's over, and we're going back to base. Stand up, Corporal. Stand up!"

She blinked several times in rapid succession, suddenly gasping as if she'd been holding her breath. By the time she realized Quinn was on his knees beside her, the rocking had stopped.

Quinn sat back on his heels. She was coming out of it.

"Mariah?"

She focused on his voice and then his face. There was something she needed to tell him. Something about the gun. Then she remembered.

"Your rifle pulls to the right."

Oh, my God. He sighed. "Yeah, I know. You did good, honey. You did real good."

She was sick to her stomach and kept trying to wipe the sand out of her eyes, push her windblown hair away from her face, but there was no sand, no wind. It was so odd to feel one thing and yet be completely aware it was absent. As she became more aware of her surroundings, she was shocked to see Beth with the baby. Sarah had been with Ryal, only now Ryal and Dolly were here, too. When had they come? What in hell had she been doing while the world went on around her? This was maddening and shocking and more than a little scary.

She wrapped her arms around her waist, anchoring herself to the present.

"Quinn, I don't know what happened."

"I know, honey. It's going to be okay."

When the pup started barking again she jerked and then looked through the railing. Strangers were coming across the meadow.

Ryal grabbed Rufus to keep him from running off the deck.

"That's Jake Doolen and his boys," Quinn said.

Mariah began trying to unwind herself from the quilt so she could get up.

Quinn pulled her to her feet.

"I'm so sorry this happened to you."

She leaned against the railing, embarrassed and frustrated, wiping shaky hands across her face.

"Don't feel sorry for me. It's the bear who's dead."

Quinn wanted to hold her, but she'd taken a step back instead of toward him. He got the message.

"Okay, tough stuff. I hear you."

Beth ignored Mariah's body language and hugged her fiercely. "You are one amazing woman, Mariah Conrad. You saved my life. You know what that means, right? I am forever in your debt, so any time you want me to give Quinn a good ass-whipping, just say the word."

Humor was just what the situation needed.

Jake and his sons stopped where the bear had fallen and struggled to keep the hounds off it.

"What's that smell?" Avery asked.

Jake pointed to the bear's side. "Gangrene. Quinn was right all along. Looks like the shaft of an arrow broke off in its hip. No wonder it went rogue. Poor critter. Must have been in terrible pain."

"Look, Daddy," Cyrus said. "She got it with a head shot."

Jake turned toward the cabin, gauging the distance from the deck to where the bear had fallen. At least seventy-five yards, with the animal on the run. Damn good shooting.

All of a sudden his eyes narrowed. Dolly Walker was there. He felt a momentary twinge of regret, then let out a breath. Old loves belonged in the past, even though this was a full-circle moment. They'd first met as kids when they were both unattached, and in the twilight of their years they were unattached again. It was the neighborly thing to say hello.

"Come on, boys. It's time we paid our respects," he said, and they started toward the cabin, dragging the dogs away from the carcass as they went.

Mariah felt like she was in pieces. A part of her was still standing on the deck with the rifle in her hands. Another part of her had crawled up into Quinn Walker's lap and didn't want to let go. The bit of her she showed to the world had a calmness belying what roiled beneath the skin. But it was the piece still lost on the other side of the world that she wanted back most. As long as it was there, she would never be all here.

"You ready to go inside?" Quinn asked.

She nodded.

"Good girl," he said, and this time she let him steady her as he walked her toward the door.

Jake's hounds were baying, which set Rufus off again. He was becoming too difficult to hold, and his cut needed attention. Ryal could envision problems arising from the four dogs meeting and decided to carry his pup inside. His mother was already in there putting the baby down to finish her interrupted nap.

Mariah paused as Quinn led her slowly toward the door. "They're coming to the cabin."

"They want to meet you. Are you okay

with that?" he asked.

"I guess, but why would they want to meet me?"

"They've been tracking that bear all over Rebel Ridge for the better part of a week without finding it, then you take it down. They're curious and, I'd say, a little jealous."

"Do you know them?"

"Yes. I grew up with them. The Doolens are trackers, and their bloodhounds are the best mountain foot soldiers you could ever want to meet. You get lost . . . if there's a piece of you still on this earth, they'll find you."

Mariah paused to watch as they strode across the high meadow with their shoulders back, their heads up and their long strides in near-perfect unison.

Quinn was still nervous as he glanced at Mariah, trying to gauge her emotional status. He knew from experience how easy it was to hide what you were thinking, only to have it erupt later, and then, moments later, the Doolens were at the cabin.

Jake lifted a hand as he and his sons paused to tie up the dogs, acknowledging Quinn and curiously eyeing the woman beside him. They took off their hats as they came up the steps.

"Quinn. Ma'am."

"Mariah, these are the Doolens. That's Jake, and these are his sons, Cyrus and Avery. Boys, this is my friend Mariah Conrad."

"Nice to meet you," Mariah said, and shook their hands in turn, feeling the calluses on their palms and, at the same time, the deference in their touch.

"Truly our pleasure, Miss Conrad," Jake said. "You are one damn fine shot."

"I'm not really all that great. It took me two shots to bring it down."

"The rifle pulls to the right," Quinn said. "My fault because I didn't warn her ahead of time."

Beth walked up on the conversation. "Hey, I heard that, Mariah. You *were* all that great and then some. The bear had already gotten a piece of Rufus when it took off after me. If it hadn't been for Mariah, *I'd* be the one lying out there in the meadow."

At that point the back door opened and Dolly Walker came out.

"Beth, I put the baby down on a quilt on the living room floor. She's already falling back asleep."

"Thank you, Dolly," Beth said

Jake couldn't stop the smile spreading across his face.

"Dolly, it's been a while. I have to say, you're looking fine."

Dolly was still dabbing her eyes and blowing her nose from her bout of weeping. She would rather have been in a better state, but such was life.

"Jake . . . boys . . . it's good to see you again."

Ryal came out next, Rufus limping at his side.

The puppy saw Beth and went to her, whining with every step.

"Poor baby," she said. "The bear got a piece of his hip."

An injured dog instantly claimed Jake's attention. "Mind if I take a look?"

"Of course not," Beth said. She sat down in a chair and pulled the gangly pup up into her lap, where he whined, then licked her hand.

Jake ran a hand along the hip, checking for broken bones and then gauging the depth of the claw marks. The bear had cut through skin but not into the muscle, which was good.

"Cyrus! Hand me your pack."

Cyrus dropped the pack at Jake's feet. "What do you need, Daddy?"

"Hand me some of that ointment Aunt Tildy made up for the dogs. The stuff that's

184

in that blue tin box."

Cyrus rolled his eyes. "That stuff stinks."

"Yeah, but it'll heal this cut right up."

Beth glanced up at Ryal and smiled. They'd had their own run-in with some of the old herb woman's concoctions.

Jake quickly doctored the pup, then handed Beth the tin.

"You keep it. Use it on him at least three times a day."

"What if he licks it off?" she asked.

Jake grinned. "He won't do it twice."

Beth sniffed the contents. "So, it tastes as bad as it smells?"

"I haven't tasted it, but the dogs won't lick it, so I'd say you were right."

Mariah's leg was about to give out, and the deck was starting to sway. She'd reached the limit of her endurance.

"Quinn, help me inside."

"Your leg?"

She nodded.

He picked her up and carried her into the house.

"So much for not making a scene," she said.

"You scared the hell out of me today, so just shut up and humor me."

The baby was asleep on her makeshift pallet on the living room floor. Mariah couldn't remember ever being secure enough in her world to have fallen asleep so quickly and soundly. She stretched out with a weary sigh as Quinn laid her on her bed, then pushed a couple of pillows under her leg to elevate it.

Wearily she closed her eyes. "Thank you."

He wanted to stay with her, but when she rolled over, turning her back to him, he took it as a dismissal.

"Back in a few," he said, and rejoined the crowd outside only to find his mother and Jake head to head in conversation, and Ryal and the Doolen brothers on their way out to look at the bear. He ran down the steps to join them.

Ryal pointed at the animal's hip. "Look at that. I think it's the broken shaft of an arrow. And that smell . . . Damn, that's gangrene, isn't it?"

Quinn nodded. "Every bit of this happened because someone was hunting out of season, and in the national reserve at that. That jackass got a man killed and another one mauled, not to mention the misery the animal was in or the number of animals it killed along the way."

"Daddy said the rangers were bringing a wagon to haul the carcass away," Avery said. "Why would they want it?"

"For starters, it killed someone on federal land, and there always have to be answers when the government is involved. I imagine they'll be interested to dig out this arrow, for sure," Quinn said.

Ryal glanced toward the road. "Speaking of rangers, here they come with a truck and a trailer, along with your Jeep."

A short while later the rangers had loaded the bear's carcass onto the trailer with a winch, returned Quinn's car keys and driven away, one bear to the good.

Jake and his sons had gone with them, needing a ride back to where they'd left their trucks. Quinn wasn't sorry to see everyone go. He'd had more visitors at this place today than he'd had in the past year and a half, and his patience for all of them was gone. He wanted to check on Mariah. He needed peace and quiet and his family, and nothing more.

"Is there any more of that apricot cobbler you said Mom brought?" Ryal asked, as he poked through the refrigerator.

Beth frowned. "For goodness' sakes, Ryal, this is Quinn's house. You can't come here and eat everything like you do at Dolly's."

"Why?"

Dolly pushed her son out of the way and

closed the refrigerator door.

"For starters, because Mariah's here and she isn't up to cooking, so you have to leave the leftovers alone."

Ryal had the grace to be embarrassed. "Oh. Yeah. Right. I'm sorry."

"Sorry for what?" Quinn asked, as he walked in the back door, patting the very subdued puppy lying on a mat against the wall with his tail tucked between his legs.

Ryal grinned. "You don't want to know." He quickly changed the subject. "Are they gone?"

Quinn nodded as he washed his hands at the sink. "Are you guys hungry? Except for an energy bar, I haven't eaten since morning, and I'm starved. I think there's some apricot cobbler left."

Ryal turned to the women. "If it's offered, *then* can I eat it?"

Beth rolled her eyes.

Dolly sighed. "I'll get bowls."

"I'm gonna check on Mariah," Quinn said, and pointed at Ryal. "Save some for us, too."

"I will, I will. I'm not a complete pig," he muttered.

"That title falls to James, right?" Quinn said.

Ryal grinned. "For sure. James is the true

garbage disposal of the family."

Quinn was still smiling as he walked past the baby on the pallet to the darkened end of the living room, where Mariah lay sleeping with a pillow clutched against her chest. Just as he started to walk away, he realized her shoulders were shaking.

Oh, shit. She's crying.

He sat down on the side of the mattress and laid a hand on her hip.

"Hey, you," he said softly.

"Go away," she whispered.

"Why?"

"I don't want them to know I'm awake."

"Why?"

"Because I'm crying, that's why. I've made an ass of myself enough for one day, don't you think?"

"Really? You save Beth's life, and you call that making an ass of yourself?"

She rolled over. With her eyes red and swollen, her vulnerability was showing.

"Yes, I did that — and then proceeded to freak out and scare them all to death."

"They weren't afraid *of* you. They were afraid *for* you. They didn't know what to do, Mariah. Truth be told, when it happens to me, I don't know what to do, either, because so far nothing has actually worked."

"Oh, my God," she muttered. "How do

you live with it?"

He shrugged. "This is how I look at it, honey. We came home breathing. The others came home in flag-draped coffins. Do you want to die?"

"No, I don't want to die. What a stupid question."

Her anger was encouraging. He wasn't going to admit that he'd had a few moments when he'd had a different opinion, but fortunately the thought had passed before he could act on it.

"Then are you going to just lie there and let Ryal eat all the leftover cobbler?"

She sat up with a sigh, smoothed down her hair and wiped her eyes with the palms of her hands.

"I guess not."

"Then go wash your face and come to the table with us. I'll even let you sit in my lap."

Her eyes narrowed. "You're kidding, right?"

"Only if you want me to be kidding."

Her eyes narrowed even more, irked that he was still able to get under her skin.

"I want you to be kidding."

"Then your wish is my command."

"Whatever, Prince Charming. You need to move so I can get up."

He stood, then offered his hand.

She took it without hesitation, thankful for the lift.

Her leg was stiff, but she held on to his arm until it loosened before hobbling through the kitchen to the bathroom.

"We saved you some cobbler," Beth said.

Mariah managed a smile. "Thanks, I'll be right back."

As soon as Mariah was out of sight, Beth turned on Quinn, her voice low and anxious.

"She's been crying. Did we do something wrong?"

He shook his head. "She's just overwhelmed and embarrassed, I think."

Dolly sighed. "Poor girl. She's had her share of hard knocks."

Ryal was quiet, leaning against the counter with his arms folded across his chest. When Mariah came back, he handed her a spoon and a bowl of cobbler.

"Does that look good to you?" he asked.

Not sure what he meant, Mariah looked at the cobbler, then nodded.

"It does to me, too, but not for the reasons you might think." He took a deep breath, trying to control his emotions, but he wasn't entirely successful, because when he spoke his voice was shaking. "Thanks to you, I'm here mooching my brother's food and not at Mount Sterling looking for an under-taker."

Mariah's eyes widened, but Ryal wasn't through.

"I can't change what you went through in Afghanistan, and I am as sorry as I can be that you're still suffering. But as far as I'm concerned, you are one hundred percent, A-one perfect on every level that matters, and I'll take out the first person who says otherwise." Then he pointed at the cobbler she was holding. "Want ice cream with that?"

Her eyes welled again, but this time not from shame. She nodded.

He plopped a scoop of ice cream into her bowl and then proceeded to put two scoops on his own before putting the carton back in the freezer.

"Sit by me," Dolly said, patting the empty chair beside her.

Mariah sat, then took a big bite. The crust was flaky, the fruit filling perfectly sweet, and the ice cream put it over the top.

"This is so good," she said.

Dolly beamed. "I can teach you, if you're interested."

Mariah rolled her eyes. "You don't know what you're offering."

Quinn sighed. God bless his family for

always being there. He took a big bite, resisting the urge to roll his eyes. This was his favorite dessert.

He was quietly cleaning the bowl when his phone began to ring. He took another bite before answering, hoping to God it wasn't another emergency. He wanted to be done with lost hikers and crazy animals for at least the rest of the day. Then he saw the Caller ID and knew he was in for another inquisition.

"Hey, James, what took you so long?" he asked.

James was pissed and scared all at the same time. "What the hell has been going on? I just got a call from one of my neighbors — who, by the way, should not know more about my family than I do — saying that killer bear everyone's been tracking showed up at your place and went after Beth. Is that true?"

"Yes."

"Damn it, Quinn! Why didn't someone call me? They said you shot it. Is it really dead?"

"It's dead, but I didn't kill it. Mariah did."

James inhaled sharply. "The friend you brought home from the hospital?"

"Yes."

"Damn." There was a long silence, and

then he added, "Is she okay?"

For the second time in five minutes, Quinn realized how much he loved his family. They honest-to-God got what was happening to him and Mariah, and understood what gunfire could do to a soldier with PTSD.

"She will be."

"When do I get to meet this wonder woman?"

"I guess when you next head this way."

"Is tomorrow too soon?"

Quinn eyed Mariah's pallor. "Yes. What about Sunday, after church? I'll grill hamburgers for you guys if you'll bring some stuff to go with them."

"It's a deal. Can she handle being around the kids?"

"I think we can manage. See you then," he said, and hung up. Then he glanced at Mariah. "That was my other brother, James. He just invited himself and his family to Sunday dinner. Do you think you're up to a little chaos? They won't stay long. They have a couple of kids, one of them still young enough to need an afternoon nap."

"As long as I don't have to feed them," Mariah muttered, and then shrugged as everyone laughed at her. "I open cans. I microwave. I eat takeout."

"I'll grill the burgers," Quinn promised. "They'll bring whatever they want. Don't sweat it, okay?"

She nodded and took another bite of cobbler.

Ryal dropped his spoon in his bowl, well aware that it clattered. When everyone looked up, he was frowning.

"So we're not invited to the party?"

Mariah stopped chewing, thinking he was seriously upset. She looked to Quinn, wondering what he would say.

He shrugged. "I didn't want to overwhelm Mariah with a crowd."

Ryal turned to her. "We're not a crowd, are we, girl? You wouldn't care if we came, too, would you? Look how good *our* baby is. She's quiet as a little mouse."

Mariah blanched. She had no idea what to say.

Dolly frowned. "Oh, for the love of God, stop it right now, Ryal. She thinks you're serious."

Beth laughed. "He *is* serious, Dolly. Can't you see that he's drooling?"

Once Mariah knew it was a joke, she relaxed. "You guys are nuts," she said, scraping her bowl for the last bite.

Beth nodded. "Yes, they are, but they're lovable nuts. On a serious note, honey, if this all sounds overwhelming, it can happen another time."

Mariah shook her head. "No, it isn't overwhelming at all. I'm not breakable. Just a little frayed."

Dolly smiled. "I'll bring potato salad, and fresh-baked cookies for dessert."

"We'll bring paper plates and cups, extra ice and the buns," Beth offered.

"I guess I'll sit around and look pretty," Mariah said.

Quinn grinned. That was the last thing Mariah Conrad would be thinking of doing, which made it even funnier. She was the least prissy woman he'd ever met, and that was one of the reasons she was so intriguing.

After cleaning up the kitchen, his family left, which gave Quinn a chance to focus on what was next. After that race through the woods, he wanted a shower and clean clothes.

As soon as he went up to the loft, Mariah went back out to the deck. If she was going to be able to stay here, she needed to come to terms with what had happened. She couldn't let a fear of the unknown take root and grow into something she couldn't handle.

Ryal had hosed the blood off the deck,

but the planks were still damp. Unsure whether it was slippery, she eased herself carefully toward the railing to look across the meadow to the trees beyond. Before they'd seemed appealing, but now they felt threatening — a harbor for creatures she didn't understand. She'd grown up on the streets and could handle herself in almost any urban situation. She'd fought alongside the toughest soldiers without feeling incompetent, but here on this mountain she was no better than a baby — unaware of where danger might lie.

She wasn't going to admit her fears to Quinn. In his eyes she was already a basket case. Telling him how intimidated she was by the solitude of this place would only increase his worries. If she was going to stay — and God knew she wanted to — it was up to her to get past it.

As she stood there, she heard an odd whistling sound and looked up. Moments ago the leaves on the trees had been motionless, as if the mountain had been holding its breath. Farther up she could see them beginning to dip and sway, as if in deference to the power of the oncoming wind. She frowned. The sky was clear. It couldn't be a storm.

Her heart skipped a beat as she tracked

the wind coming closer, shifting limbs, rattling leaves, then moving down across the meadow, parting the knee-high grass in its wake. It looked like an imminent attack. The urge to run was strong. But she refused to budge, and when the blast of wind finally reached the cabin, she was braced and holding on to the railing.

She expected a slap in the face. Instead it was a cleansing breath. She inhaled the pine-scented air and then lifted her chin as the wind tore through her hair, blowing away the feeling of sand in her eyes and cooling the desert from her blood.

It had to be a sign.

Coming here hadn't been a mistake. Here she would heal. She knew it.

Late that night, long after Mariah and Quinn and all the other denizens of Rebel Ridge had gone to bed, a new predator was on the way to the mountain. A predator who walked on two feet, carrying a weapon on his hip rather than a broken one in his body, but with the same powerful urge to take what he wanted with no apology or regret.

TEN

When Lonnie Farrell turned off the highway and started along the blacktop road up Rebel Ridge, the hair rose on the back of his neck. Up to now the drive from the airport in Frankfort had been relaxing, but the turn changed everything. The last time he'd been on this road he'd been fourteen years old, in handcuffs in the back of the sheriff's car and on his way to jail.

He was years older and wiser now, and a hell of a lot richer, but that gut-wrenching memory had yet to abate. It had given him a hate for the law that drove everything he did, and every time he outwitted them it was another boost to his ego.

The plan he had for the old Foley mine was a good one, but it wouldn't work unless he could pull in enough locals. He could have brought in any number of qualified people who'd worked with drugs before, but bringing in strangers to the mountain would

199

be like hanging out a Come and Get Me sign. The loyalty and silence needed to make this endeavor work would come with the money he paid out. Jobs were few and far between up here. He was hoping that, except for a few self-righteous families who saved their allegiance for religion, having access to local work would be too inviting for most people to turn down. This was where his brother-in-law came in. Buell was a son of a bitch, but he knew the people up here better than Lonnie did, so he was counting on Buell to round up the right kind of crew.

As he drove, he began noticing mailboxes grouped at different turnoffs where narrow one-lane roads disappeared up into the trees. Sometimes there were only two or three boxes, but sometimes as many as eight or ten — an indication of how many homes and families were hidden up in the woods as well as the mountain people's love for solitude and privacy. The houses that were visible along the road varied in appearance. There were simple houses, some in need of a paint job, but neat and well kept, but others looked uninhabitable even though they were still sheltering families. He'd lived in one of those. A muscle in his jaw jerked as he looked away. This trip was a stark reminder of how far he'd come.

He thought about his mother. She'd done the best she could for him and Portia, but growing up without an old man had been tough. She'd turned him into the man of the family, whether he'd wanted it or not, and he'd spent four years in juvie because of it. But when you were the man of the family, you did what you had to, whether it was legal or not. He'd funneled plenty of money back to her over the years and was curious to see if she'd done anything with it, or if she'd let the double-wide he'd bought her fall into disrepair like the house they'd once lived in. Considering their past, he wasn't looking forward to spending the night there, but it was too far to drive back and forth to a hotel in Mount Sterling, and if Buell had done his job, it would only be for one night.

As he continued to drive, he noticed names on the mailboxes that he remembered, but he couldn't recall the faces that went with them. Then he passed one mailbox that actually made him smile. He distinctly remembered Mrs. Venable. Everyone called her Granny Lou. He couldn't believe she was still living. Even back then he'd thought she was old.

He slowed down for a big curve, reading

the names on these mailboxes as he went: Reneau, Samuels and Walker. There'd been a couple of Walker boys close to him in age. He tried to remember their first names but couldn't. It had been too long, and, truth be told, he didn't much care.

As he came out of the curve he suddenly hit the brakes and swerved to keep from running over a kid playing in the road.

"Son of a bitch." He threw the car into Park and took a moment to breathe.

The kid looked as startled as Lonnie felt and darted off into the brush. There was a roof just visible through the trees, and Lonnie assumed that was where he belonged.

His heart was pounding as he put the rented Hummer back in gear and drove on.

Gertie Farrell had begun cleaning house when her grandkids left for school and continued to clean all day as she sent Portia off to shop for groceries down in Boone's Gap. Her son-in-law, Buell, left right after breakfast, and she didn't expect him back until evening. She hoped he was doing what Lonnie had asked him to. It would be a shame on the family if, after all her son had done for them, they failed in their first opportunity to return the favor.

She was very excited about this new

venture Lonnie was starting. It would mean much-needed jobs on the mountain. As she mopped the floors on her hands and knees, she imagined her friends' looks of envy, knowing it was her son who'd brought prosperity to Rebel Ridge.

Once the cleaning was finished she put some dried apple slices to soak while she made up pie crusts. She'd promised to fry up some pork chops for Lonnie and make him a dried apple pie.

As soon as Portia returned from the grocery store, Gertie sent her outside to mow the yard. It was the one job she managed to get out of Buell, but since he was now employed, Portia could do it just as well. Gertie glanced out the window as she rolled out her pie dough, trying not to judge her daughter, but it was hard. Portia had been wearing that same pair of pants and shirt for three days straight, and her hair was lank and greasy. When Portia turned a corner with the mower, her blouse came up, revealing a roll of white, dimpled fat around her waist.

Gertie sighed. She didn't blame her daughter for the ne'er-do-well she'd married, because there weren't a lot of choices in men to be had around here, but she did blame her for letting herself go. As poor as they'd been, Gertie had still taken pride in staying fit and clean. Portia, on the other hand, was a good sixty pounds overweight, and with the nice washer and dryer that had come with their double-wide, she had no excuse for not wearing clean clothes.

Gertie worried how Lonnie would view her own appearance. She'd grown old and wrinkled since he'd last been home.

And then there were her grandchildren. They were often rude and mouthy, something she had never tolerated in her own offspring. Oh, well, Lonnie would be here before dark. It was too late to worry about all this now.

Once she had her pies in the oven, she took some pork chops out of her freezer and set them on the counter to thaw. The fact that her son had not been home in over fifteen years was a sore she couldn't heal. She'd never known if it was fear of the law who'd once taken him away, or shame that this was where he'd been born. What she did know was that he had never forgotten her. That was all that mattered.

For the first time in Buell Smith's life he had purpose. Knowing he was going to be in charge of something was a huge ego boost. He'd been at this hiring business for a day and a half, and already he had twenty-seven men who'd promised to show up at the gates to the old Foley Brothers Mine.

It would be a lie to say he wasn't nervous. All of this hinged on them actually showing up and Lonnie approving of his choices. There was also a slight concern among the men that, knowing Lonnie, this venture would turn into something illegal, but the promise of steady money was too good to pass up.

This morning, when Buell got up he had actually showered and shaved and put on clean clothes. Portia made a big-ass deal out of it, even teasing him, which pissed him off. But he would show her. He could make good just like Lonnie. And if he was going to be a boss, he needed to look like one. Screw anyone else who laughed at the change in his appearance. Buell Smith had come into his own.

He loaded up his meager assortment of tools, including a couple of shovels and a bolt cutter in case Lonnie planned on going onto the actual property today, and drove away. The gates across the driveway to the mine were chained and locked. They'd long since rusted and sagged from the years, but the chain had held, and no one had been interested enough in a shutdown mine to ever cut it.

He arrived far too early, but his anxiety in doing this right was paramount. He parked in the shade just off the road and settled down to wait

Lonnie was only a half mile from where he'd grown up. He was debating with himself about stopping now and saying hello to his mother. But if he did, he wouldn't be able to stay long. He was due at the mine in just over an hour, which meant Mama was going to have to wait. There were no pangs of regret as he passed the road leading up to the home place. Life had long since weaned him from that tie. He kept going over the speech he planned to make to the men — if, in fact, any showed up. His faith in Buell had yet to be proven.

When the first two men showed up at the entrance to the old mine within seconds of each other, Buell's anxiety started to ease. Maybe, just maybe, he would actually pull this off. By twelve o'clock there were more than a dozen waiting — some sitting on the tailgates of their trucks, some trading tales, some nervously silent, as if this was too good to be true.

It was a quarter to one when the last three

men showed. It was all Buell could do not to strut. He'd done it. Lonnie had better, by God, be appreciative, too. He couldn't afford to lose face in front of these men when he was supposed to be their boss.

Five minutes later they heard the sound of a powerful engine approaching, and all of them turned to see who was coming around the bend.

The hair rose on the backs of Buell's arms. Every instinct he had told him this was a turning point in his life. And when the big black Hummer appeared, his eyes widened. One day he was going to drive something like that. He just knew it.

"Is that him?" one man asked.

"Damn, that's a Hummer," another one commented.

The murmurs of appreciation and envy ran through the crowd as the car approached, and they only increased when the driver stopped and got out.

Lonnie knew first appearances made a difference. He also knew that his past and reputation preceded him. He intended to make sure they saw the benefits he had reaped. When it came time to reveal the second part of his venture, it would be crucial to make sure they were willing to take the risks.

He'd left his fancy suits back in Chicago, but he was wearing designer jeans, a blue silk shirt and a chocolate-brown bomber jacket. The skinny body and acne he'd had at fourteen were long since gone. He wasn't handsome by any stretch of the imagination, but he had a look women called interesting, and he was satisfied when he looked in a mirror. His boots were made from alligator, an exotic hide few here would have seen. Add a Rolex watch and a three-carat diamond pinkie ring, and he was going to be the topic of every man's conversation at the supper table tonight.

Buell stepped forward, smiling. For the first time in his life he felt pride in his connection with this man.

"Lonnie, it's good to see you," he said.

"You, too, Buell," Lonnie said, and shook Buell's hand. They'd never officially met except through pictures and phone calls, but he wasn't going to let on.

He needed them to believe he and Buell were tight, so that if they fucked up in Buell's presence they would be confident he would pass the message along.

As he turned to the men, his smile died. He narrowed his eyes against the sun as he looked through the assembled crowd. Buell had done well. There were at least two dozen men of varying ages here, all with one thing in common: a hungry look in their eyes. That was something he could work with.

"Gentlemen, my name is Lon Farrell. Some of you look familiar, some don't, but I've been gone a long time, so if you're someone I should know, you'll have to forgive me. When I began thinking of where to locate my newest business venture, I thought of Rebel Ridge. It's obvious that jobs are still in short supply here, and I understand you're all available to work as of today. Is that correct?"

His answer came in an accumulation of muttering, head shakes and *yes, sirs*. He would take it.

"Good. You're getting in on the ground floor of a new company I'm starting. There's a huge market for organic anything in the cities, and exotic and specialty mushrooms are in high demand. I don't know how many of you are aware that there are actual mushroom farmers, and that the mushroom spores are planted like seeds in a dark, damp environment, then grown to maturity in a relatively short time before harvesting. When I began considering this latest venture, I asked myself where I could go and have easy access to these basic needs. Then

209

I thought of old mines and their long tunnels, which led me to Rebel Ridge. As of a few days ago, I now own this mine and the surrounding land, and as soon as we clear access and shore up the interior of the initial tunnel, we'll be ready to start. As I said before, the turnaround time for harvesting is surprisingly short, so profits come quickly. But before we begin, I need clear access to the mine itself, which means cutting brush, filling potholes in the old road, whatever it takes. Understand?"

They nodded, but he had a feeling that if he'd told them he was going to grow warts, they would still be on board.

"Stay with me on this and I'll make it worth your while. I'm paying fifty dollars a day, cash money, and once the business gets under way we'll adjust the pay scale up accordingly and fill out papers for taxes and all. Is that satisfactory with everyone?"

They were smiling. One had tears in his eyes. Lonnie knew he had them in the palms of his hands. Once they got their first paychecks he would have them in his pocket. He loved it when a plan came together. At that stage he pointed to the Hummer.

"I have some tools in the back. Unload them and get busy. I'll ask you to start at seven and work until 6:00 p.m. every day, and although we didn't begin until afternoon today, I'm counting this as a full day's work. You'll be paid weekly until we get into the actual farming, then twice a month."

One by one they filed past him, shaking his hand and thanking him over and over. He wondered if they would still be thanking him when he added the drug setup, but it didn't matter. By then they would be so hooked on steady cash that he didn't expect much flack.

Buell was riding a high as he took the bolt cutter and strode toward the gate. The chain was red with rust, as was the ancient padlock, but both gave under the cutter's sharp edge. When the chain fell off, the gates followed, leaving only one still attached by a single hinge.

Lonnie approached him as he pulled them aside.

"Three dump trucks are en route," Lonnie said. "Load one, and while it's dumping, you can load the other two. Keep everything in motion. I don't want anyone sitting around waiting."

"No, sir. That won't be happening," Buell said. "You can count on me."

Lonnie's eyes narrowed as he searched Buell's face. "Don't make me regret this," he said softly.

Buell lifted his chin. "No regrets. I swear."

Lonnie nodded. "You'll be getting seventy-five dollars a day. Don't fucking drink it all up. Take care of your damn family for a change. Understand?"

The insult was clear. Buell should have punched him, but he had neither the guts nor the desire to do so. He would take a lot of crap for that kind of money.

All he said was, "I sure do."

At that point Lonnie smiled and clapped him on the shoulder. "I'm counting on you." Then he looked up the overgrown road, anxious for that first glimpse of the mine itself. "What say we go check out that mine?"

Buell glanced at his truck.

"Not in yours. We're taking mine," Lonnie said. "It's four-wheel drive with plenty of clearance. It'll get us in and out with no trouble."

Buell turned to the men. "There are more tools in the back of my truck if you need them. We'll be back shortly."

Then he strode to the Hummer as if he rode in one every day and tried not to smirk. Damn, but this might just be the best day of his life.

Gertie was changing into clean clothes

when she heard the sound of approaching cars. She recognized Buell's truck from the hole in the muffler and the clatter of stuff rattling around in the bed, but the other one was unfamiliar. It had to be Lonnie. Her belly rolled. The anxiety at seeing him again was killing her. The last time they'd seen each other he was being put in the back of the sheriff's car in handcuffs. He'd looked back at her as they drove away like he was trying to memorize what he was leaving behind. It had bothered her then, and it bothered her still, that he'd never cried. Even at fourteen, he'd been a man before his time.

She ran a brush through her hair and checked to see if her makeup had smeared. Her reflection wasn't pretty anymore, but it was as good as she could look. She dropped the hairbrush and hurried to the door.

Lonnie was pleasantly surprised when what had once been the old home place came into view. The house he'd grown up in was gone, and the long, double-wide trailer he'd bought Mama was sitting in the same location. The general disrepair and malaise the place had always worn like an old coat were gone. The old barn had been shored up and reroofed. The pen where they fed out hogs to butcher was actually in good shape, and she'd even added one of those portable carports at the end of the trailer to keep her car out of the weather. He had to give it to his mama. When she had options, she maximized them to the best of her abilities.

It did occur to him that she couldn't live here alone and keep all this up, and with that understanding, a part of the resentment he'd felt at keeping Portia and her family sheltered and fed was gone.

In a way she was looking after their mother in a more personal way than he ever could or would. There wasn't a chance in hell that he would ever come back to this mountain to live. The status quo was the best answer for the situation at hand.

Buell parked and got out, then waited by his truck for Lonnie.

The front door was opening as he parked. When he looked again, Gertie Farrell was standing on the porch with her hands clasped beneath her breasts and tears running down her face. He got out of the Hummer, surprised to be feeling emotion of any kind — but it was there. This was the woman who'd helped teach him to read, who'd doctored his cuts and who'd kept them alive on little more than a refusal to quit. She was also the woman who'd turned him into a man. And the day they'd come to arrest him, it was Mama who'd tried to take the blame for being the brains behind the meth he was cooking and selling.

Buell wisely kept his mouth shut, leaving the mother-and-son reunion to them, and hurried on inside, anxious to tell Portia about the day.

Walking toward the house, Lonnie felt as if he was moving in slow motion. A thought passed through his mind that the day would eventually arrive when she would no longer be on this earth. He was glad he'd come home.

"Hey, Mama, still as pretty as ever."

Gertie smiled through tears as she threw her arms around Lonnie and hugged him fiercely.

"You're still a good liar, but you're definitely a man fully grown now. Look at you, Lonnie! Just look at you! I am so proud that you're my son."

Lonnie grinned. "Thanks, Mama. You can take the credit for making me tough, 'cause that's what it took to get here. Now, where's that pie you promised me? I swear I can smell it from here."

Gertie led him into the house, then to her bedroom.

"This is where you'll stay. There's a

private bathroom through that door."

"This looks like your room," he said.

A look passed between them, and then it was gone. Gertie smoothed her hands down the front of her dress and smiled.

"It *is* my room, but I'm sleeping with my granddaughter tonight. I've done it before, so it's no big deal. Lucy likes it when Granny shares her bed."

"So how old is Lucy?" he asked.

"She's seven and the baby. Marvin is thirteen, and Billy is nine. Portia is really excited to see you again, too."

"I'm looking forward to playing catch-up, Mama."

Gertie hesitated, then lowered her voice. "About Portia . . . She's different now. Living with Buell dragged her down. Maybe with this new job and all she'll take some pride in herself again, but don't say anything to her, all right?"

He frowned.

"He's not mistreating her, is he?"

"Oh, no, no, nothing like that. But you know how it is here. No hope to change where you grew up. That kind of thing. I just didn't want her appearance to surprise you."

When he thought of his older sister, it was as a tall, skinny girl with long hair and a big laugh. Curious as to what he would see, he took off his jacket and laid it at the foot of the bed.

"Okay, so this is my room for tonight. How long until supper? I'm starved."

She grinned. "It won't take me long to finish up. Come to the kitchen so we can talk. I swear I need to fill myself up with looking at you so that when you're gone again, I'll have this face in my head instead of the other one. You remember him, that skinny boy always in need of a haircut."

He smiled, but his conscience pricked. He'd been so ready to put this place behind him that never once had he thought of how his absence had impacted her life.

ELEVEN

To say Lonnie was shocked at his sister's appearance would have been putting it mildly. Even though he'd been warned, he wasn't prepared to see a woman he didn't even recognize. Then she spoke and he saw her — lost inside the oversize body and dirty clothes.

Portia lifted her chin, as if preparing for his disapproval.

"Hey, Lonnie, it's about time you came for a visit."

He heard the accusation and acknowledged it without reminding her that it was his money putting a roof over her head. Instead he made himself smile.

"It's good to see you, sister, and good to be home. Something sure smells good."

And just like that she smiled and the tension was gone. "Mama made pork chops. I'm just finishing up the taters to go with them."

"Sit, son, sit," Gertie interjected. "I'll bring you a cup of coffee. You do still like coffee, don't you?"

"Yes, Mama, I still like coffee. That would be great." He sat, eyeing the ease with which the women worked together, and realized it felt more comfortable to be here than he'd expected.

At that point Buell, who'd changed into his old clothes and gone out to feed the hogs and chickens, came in from outside. Three kids followed on his heels, pushing and shoving, loud and shrieking.

Lonnie stood up.

The kids stopped in their tracks, eyeing the stranger in their kitchen. They knew who he was, but before he'd been a faceless stranger who paid the bills. This tall, well-dressed man was so far removed from their experience that they were momentarily taken aback.

Buell pushed them forward. "Kids, this here is your uncle Lonnie. Lonnie, this is Marvin, Billy and Lucy."

Lonnie eyed them with a quiet gaze. "It's nice to put faces to names," he said.

Buell nudged Marvin. "Remember your manners and say hi."

Marvin mumbled a hello. Billy said hi, and Lucy waved.

Lonnie pointed at Lucy. "You look like your mama."

"No, she don't! Mama's *fat*!" Billy shrieked.

Portia's expression fell.

Gertie sighed. This was exactly what she'd feared would happen. The kids acted like little animals most of the time. Seemed company wasn't going to change them.

Lonnie was appalled that Buell hadn't taken up for Portia or reprimanded their son.

"That shit won't fly with me," he said, and all of a sudden the room seemed to shrink. "Since no one else is going to take up for my sister, then I guess the task falls to me." He pointed at Billy, who was starting to back away, raising his voice until the room echoed with his anger. "It says in the Bible that you honor your father and your mother, so that leads me to believe that you haven't been paying attention, boy. I'm not going to be here long, but while I am, if I hear one more rude word come out of anybody's mouth that has to do with my mother or my sister, I'll take you out back and whip your ass myself. Do I make myself clear?"

Marvin glared. "You're not our dad. You can't tell us what to do."

At that point Portia spoke. "Shut your

trap, Marvin. If it wasn't for your uncle Lonnie, we'd be living with your grandpa Smith, and you wouldn't have nice clothes or none of them computer games you like to play."

Buell's cheeks reddened, but he wasn't sure how to direct his anger. Bottom line, he knew he should be mad at himself, but technically this was his territory, not Lonnie's, so he figured he had a right to be mad at Lonnie, too. Still, all things considered, he opted for the side of safety and kept his mouth shut.

Marvin ducked his head and looked away.

Gertie had had enough. "Everybody go wash up. Supper's ready."

They quickly left the room, once again leaving Lonnie alone with his mother and sister.

"I'm sorry about that," Portia said.

Lonnie shrugged. "I learned a long time ago that you teach people how to treat you. The last person who talked shit to me isn't talking to anyone anymore."

Gertie gasped.

Portia flinched, looking at him as if she was seeing him for the first time. She didn't know whether to be grateful he'd taken up for her — or scared of the man he'd become.

It occurred to both women that looks could definitely be deceiving. It was a reminder that the reality of how he lived his life and made his money was an unknown they didn't want to visit.

Gertie began putting food on the table and talking fast to cover up her confusion. She loved her son, but she realized she didn't actually know him.

The ensuing meal was uncomfortable for all concerned. Lonnie wished he was anywhere but there.

Buell was afraid Lonnie would fire him for not taking up for Portia.

The kids sensed their parents' uneasiness and had the good sense to lay low.

Gertie tried her hardest to make everything right, but it was a case of too little, too late.

When Lonnie finally went to bed, all he could think about was leaving. Around three in the morning he got a frantic phone call from one of Sol's madams back in Chicago. Some high roller had paid big bucks for a woman, then beat her half to death. Retribution was Lonnie's business. He found himself relieved by the call and looking forward to dealing with it when he got back.

By sunrise he was up and already packed. After reassuring Gertie that he would see her more often and telling Buell that he would be back by the weekend to check on the men's progress, he drove away.

Gertie stood on the porch, waving until he was out of sight, then went back inside and, in one of her rare fits of temper, turned a cold shoulder on the rest of the family and shut herself inside her room, leaving them to make their own breakfast and get themselves off to school.

It was an eye-opening moment for all of them. Lonnie's arrival back in Rebel Ridge was causing more commotion than anyone could have predicted. They'd made themselves look bad in his eyes and shamed Gertie. It wouldn't be beyond her to put all of them out, and they knew it.

The Sunday cookout Quinn had promised James was on the horizon. Mariah had been here almost a week now and was settling into a routine that bordered on normal. Quinn was an easy man to share space with, and she was curious to see if James Walker was as congenial as his two brothers.

She continued to work on her therapy, even when it hurt — *especially* when it hurt. And she was figuring out that physical exhaustion was at times a fairly decent deterrent to PTSD. She wanted to be well

— to be normal again — but she was coming to an understanding that war had forever changed who she was. She couldn't get back the girl she'd been, but, given time, she was hoping to accept who she was now.

Quinn was on the back deck scrubbing down his grill, getting ready for tomorrow. He had a list of groceries he needed to buy and was hurrying to get through it. This was going to be Mariah's first visit to Boone's Gap, the little town at the foot of Rebel Ridge. It was a long trip down and back, and he hoped she was up to it.

Just as he was finishing up, she came outside. She was wearing jeans and a long-sleeved white T-shirt. Her dark curls were still a little damp from her shower, and the lipstick she was wearing matched the color in her cheeks. He couldn't remember if he'd ever seen her in makeup and anything but sweatpants, but she looked good. He wanted to strip her naked and make love to her until they were both too weak to move. Instead he whistled low and long.

Mariah blushed. She felt the heat coming up her neck and across her face. It was good to feel attractive, even if it was a fleeting thing.

"If you think this looks good, you've been

alone too long. When are we leaving? I'm ready to go, and you're still dirty."

He grinned. "It won't take me long. I don't have to look pretty like you, remember?"

He put the lid down on the grill and turned off the water.

"Give me five minutes and I'll be ready."

"Take ten and dry off before you try to get dressed. Trust me, it's easier, remember?"

The smile froze on his face. He was remembering, just as she was, the time when they'd nearly gotten caught making love in a makeshift shower at base camp, and the crazy race to get dressed while their bodies were still wet. They'd slipped out through a window in the back just ahead of three female soldiers coming in the front door.

Quinn eyed her slowly from head to toe. "I remember everything about you, pretty girl."

Her breath caught, leaving Mariah tongue-tied. He'd always called her "pretty girl," but this was the first time he'd said it since she'd been here. It felt good and, at the same time, a little nerve-racking. She wanted him back, but not until she had a grip on this life.

Quinn winked as he jogged past, then ran up the stairs double-time, stripping as he went.

Mariah watched until he disappeared, admiring his lean, toned body, and then closed her eyes and took a deep breath.

She started inside, then stopped and looked toward the meadow — into the trees — to the unknown she had yet to conquer. One day, when she was stronger, she would face that down, too, but not today.

The day was sunny, the road on which Quinn and Mariah were traveling shaded by tall trees bordering both sides. The yellow slices of sunlight coming through the gaps in the limbs and leaves gave the blacktop a patchwork appearance. If she had been the fanciful kind, she might have believed they were on the yellow brick road. But she didn't believe in wizards, and the only thing she could have wished for was sunglasses.

As they came to a fork in the road, Quinn pointed.

"That road leads to the ranger station up in the reserve."

"Do you check in there every day?"

"Usually. Sometimes I just call in and they have me go directly to a location."

"At the risk of sounding stupid, what do

rangers do?"

"Technically, I'm a backcountry ranger. I don't normally deal with the day-to-day stuff that a regular park ranger would, like campers and organized treks, but when there's an emergency we're all on board. I'm usually up in the high country, checking for poachers, reports of sick animals, once even a downed plane."

"Do you work with a partner?"

"Rangers aren't like cops. We don't usually work in pairs unless the situation demands it. Why all the questions? You interested in hanging out with me?"

"What? Me? No, I was just —" She sighed. He was messing with her again. "Funny. Real funny."

Quinn shrugged. "I wasn't really teasing you. It occurs to me that you have just as many qualifications as I did when I applied."

Her eyes widened. "I grew up in a city. I barely know the difference between a possum and a raccoon. Besides, I'm not even close to being able to handle a job."

Quinn slowed down for the curve ahead. "You will be one day. How do you feel about the great outdoors?"

She couldn't tell him that it scared her. "I can't be sure. This is my first time around.

Can I get back to you on that?"

He laughed. "You have all the time in the world."

"You'll get tired of me before that," she said.

The smile slid off his face. Before she knew it, he was holding her hand, and his expression was no longer teasing.

"No, pretty girl, that's not true. This might not be the time for it, and it might not be something you're ready to hear, but just so you know, I won't ever get tired of you."

His grip was firm. She got the message.

"Thank you, Quinn, more than you know, but . . ."

His gut knotted when he heard the "but." He didn't want her to say it had been fun sneaking sex back in the day, but she didn't want a permanent relationship with him.

"Don't say it. You have a hell of a lot on your plate, and the last thing you need is more pressure. Your job is just to focus on getting well."

She nodded.

He needed to lighten the conversation. "On another note, see that little road off to your right?"

"Yes?"

"There's a house about a half mile back. It's where Meg and Mama live."

"So now I know where most of your family lives."

He laughed. "Not even close."

"What do you mean?"

"There are at least a hundred or so of us, counting the extended family, maybe more, depending on who's recently given birth."

"You're kidding!"

"Nope."

Her eyes suddenly welled with unshed tears, which shocked her. She hadn't felt sorry for herself in years, but this had taken her aback. Why were some babies born into big loving families while others got thrown away?

"I can't imagine that," she said, and then leaned over, pretending her shoe needed tying so he wouldn't see the tears.

Quinn frowned. The tone of her voice had changed. He knew she was upset but didn't understand why.

"Are you comfortable? Is your leg hurting? If you need to stop and stretch, just say the word."

She straightened up and leaned back in the seat. "It's okay."

He nodded, then wisely kept quiet. The silence between them lengthened. Finally it was Mariah who broke it.

"Can I ask you something?"

"Sure," he said.

"I need you to be honest."

The stipulation surprised him. "I'm always honest. Ask away."

"Why did you come get me?"

He glanced at the look on her face and then back to the road. His fingers tightened on the steering wheel. *Damn.*

"I could answer that a dozen different ways, and they would all be truthful. For me, being with you was never just about sex. I really liked and admired you. And you saved my life. After I was back stateside, I was so messed up, both physically and emotionally, I shut down to almost everyone because I was afraid to admit, even to myself, how bad I was. But my family didn't quit on me, and I've gotten to this point mainly because of their support. I wondered plenty of times where you were and if you were all right. Then I found out you'd been wounded and were close to being released. I didn't want you going through all this shit alone."

This time Mariah didn't bother to hide her tears. "You are a very special man, Quinn Walker, and just for the record, it wasn't just about the sex for me, either."

He glanced at her briefly. "But it *was* damn good, right?"

She sighed. "Yes, it was good, and so were you."

He grinned. "Anytime you want to stroll down memory lane, all you have to do is ask."

She pointed toward the windshield. "I am not talking about sex with you any more today. Just drive!"

He wiggled his eyebrows. "Made you hot just thinking about it, right?"

She laughed, and when she did, her whole body felt lighter — like she'd just shed a year's worth of pain in two seconds.

Once the tension between them eased, the rest of the drive down to Boone's Gap passed quickly, but when they turned onto what Quinn called Main Street, Mariah could only stare.

It was all of four or five blocks in length, and that was it. There were a few houses within the "city" limits, even fewer than she'd expected. The population sign read 300. At a guess, she would say even that was a stretch.

"So this is what you guys call town?"

Quinn grinned. "It tides us over. If we need to do serious shopping, we have to drive into Mount Sterling, which is another thirty or forty-five minutes farther."

"Wow."

"Not much compared to Lexington, I guess."

She shrugged. "Looks better than the parts of Lexington I knew."

Quinn glanced at his watch. It was after 11:00. "I thought we could eat at Frankie's before we pick up the groceries. Is that okay with you?"

"Definitely okay. I'm getting hungry."

He pulled up to the curb in front of Frankie's Eats and then helped her out. He quietly waited until she took the first step, knowing she needed to stretch her muscles and regain her balance.

"I'm good," she said, but held on to his arm as they stepped up the curb, then headed across the sidewalk to the café.

Inside, it was like a thousand other eateries across the country: a few booths in need of new upholstery around the sides of the room and an assortment of tables in the middle.

But it was surprisingly bright and clean, and the aromas of French fries and burgers were familiar enough to make her mouth water.

There were at least a dozen customers already seated, and two waitresses flying about the room in perfect rhythm, laughing and talking as they went. A television had been mounted above the counter, but the sound of the program was drowned out by the camaraderie of the patrons. It was obvious that she was the only stranger, and when they saw her with Quinn, the silence that ensued was almost funny.

He leaned over and whispered in her ear, "I forgot to warn you about the curiosity quotient around here."

She grinned.

"Hey, y'all," he said more loudly. "I suppose I'd better introduce you so you can get back to your food. This is my friend Mariah Conrad. We served in the same unit overseas. As you can see, she came back a little bunged up, but I promised her that this good mountain air would cure what ailed her."

"Hey! Is she the one who shot and killed that bear Jake Doolen was trackin'?"

Quinn smiled. "She's the one. Brought it down with a head shot from seventy-five yards away when it was on the run."

Someone piped up from across the room, "Dang, lady, that's some fine shootin'. If you're still hangin' around here come deer season, you can go huntin' with us. Might save me some cold mornings in a deer stand if you do."

Laughter erupted as the others began teasing the man, claiming he didn't even like venison and just went hunting to get out of the house.

The joking put them all at ease. They shifted from teasing the lazy hunter to praising her service to the country, along with a half dozen promises to pray for her healing. She was both surprised and touched by their sincerity.

"Thanks," she said. "So, what's good on the menu?"

"Burgers and fries," they all said in unison.

One of the waitresses sped by with a pitcher of iced tea.

"Pick yourselves a seat. I'll be right with you."

They sat down at an empty table just ahead of their waitress, who came by with glasses of water.

"Hey, Quinn. Hey, Mariah, nice to meet you. I'm Sue Ellen. Me and Quinn are kin."

Mariah smiled. "It's nice to meet you, too. I believe I'll have a burger and fries. Everything on it."

"Same for me," Quinn said.

"Sweet tea or pop?" Sue Ellen asked.

"Tea for both of us," Quinn said.

Sue Ellen wiggled a finger in goodbye and ran off to put in the order. Conversation resumed around them, which prompted one of the customers to fill Quinn in on the latest gossip.

"Hey, Quinn, you hear about the new business goin' in up on the mountain?"

"Can't say I have. Fill me in."

"Remember Lonnie Farrell?"

Quinn flashed on a skinny, pimple-faced kid who was always in trouble with the law. "Yeah, I remember Lonnie."

"Well, he's back in a big way. Went and bought the old Foley Brothers Mine, and now he's starting up a mushroom farm in it. He hired his brother-in-law, Buell Smith, as manager, and already has more than two dozen men on the payroll. There's big talk about what a good deal this is. Hasn't been work on that mountain since the mine closed."

Quinn nodded. "Mushrooms, huh?"

"That's what I heard." Then he grinned. "It'll be a surprise if it's the kind you eat 'stead of the kind you smoke."

The room erupted in shared laughter.

Mariah leaned closer to Quinn. "What am I missing?"

"Lonnie's a little older than me, but he hasn't been back to Rebel Ridge since he was a teenager. He got busted for making and selling meth, and hauled off to jail. He never came back, but he funnels enough money back to his mama to keep her in a style better than most."

"Oh, that ain't all," the man added. "He came back dressed fit to kill and driving a big black Hummer. He's made it big, that's for sure."

At that point Sue Ellen came back with their burgers and fries, and Quinn filed the info away for future reference. It paid to stay current with what was happening with the neighbors, especially those with iffy pasts.

TWELVE

By the time they finished their food Mariah was no longer the stranger in town. She was Quinn Walker's girl. Even if it wasn't technically true, she liked how it made her feel. She made a trip to the bathroom while he was paying, then they stopped at the small grocery store to pick up what they needed for tomorrow's cookout.

She used the shopping cart for a walker as Quinn filled it up, and though she was in pain as they drove out of town, she wouldn't have changed a thing. The trip off the mountain had been worth it.

When Quinn turned on the radio, she stretched her leg out in front of her, leaned back and closed her eyes. The next thing she knew, they were driving up the road toward the cabin. She sat up with a jerk.

"Did I snore?"

"Something awful," he said. His expression was blank, but his eyes were dancing.

"You lie!"

He grinned.

"I don't even care if I did," she said.

He wasn't going to tell her that she'd cried out, because wherever she'd been in her sleep, it appeared she'd left it behind when she woke.

"We're here," he said, as he pulled up and killed the engine. "Hold on a sec and I'll help you up the steps."

"No. I've got it. I've been practicing, and it's easier going up than coming down. You'll see."

Quinn watched from the corner of his eye until she reached the steps. She paused, as if steadying her balance, grabbed the railing and took the first step up, then the next and the next, until she was on the deck. The moment she reached the top she turned and threw her hands in the air.

"Ta-da!"

He began to clap. "Way to go, pretty girl," he said, then grabbed a couple of grocery sacks, hurried up the steps and unlocked the door, winking at her as he passed.

Mariah sighed. If she could have, she would have done a little dance. She promised herself that one day she *would* dance again, hopefully with him.

Still stiff from the ride, she stayed out on

the deck to walk it off while Quinn carried in the rest of the groceries. She walked the U-shaped deck from one end to the other until the muscle spasms had eased.

Quinn was sitting on the end of her mattress watching TV when she went back inside. The minute she saw his face, her stomach roiled. This had been such a good day, and something told her it was going to hell.

"What's wrong?"

He looked up. "Remember Dewey Pomeroy?"

"The blond-haired guy from motor pool?"

"Yeah. He was killed two days ago in a firefight in Kabul. I liked Dewey. He was a real nice guy."

Mariah felt sick, thinking about the big broad-shouldered guy with the goofy sideways grin being dead.

"Shit."

Quinn blinked. She'd pretty much summed up his feelings, too. He headed for the kitchen and came back with two cans of beer, popped the top on one and handed it to her, then opened the other for himself.

"To Dewey," he said.

Tears burned the backs of Mariah's eyes, but she wouldn't cry.

"To Dewey," she echoed.

They took a drink, then a second, and without speaking went out to the back deck. She sat down in one of the deck chairs, but Quinn moved to the top step and sat down alone, his back to her as he stared out across the meadow. Every now and then he would take a drink, but he didn't talk.

She kept thinking there was something she should be saying, but she knew if she tried to talk she would cry. Time passed as they continued to sip their beer, and as she sat, the peacefulness of the place began to settle the turmoil within.

A thin, high-pitched screech caught her attention. She looked up and saw a hawk slowly circling in the sky above them — a sad reminder that life went on, no matter who was around to live it.

She finished her beer, then crushed the can and went inside. After a quick trip to the bathroom, she crawled into her bed, curled up on her side and closed her eyes. It was a mistake. One image after another of Dewey Pomeroy flashed through her mind: of him sliding out from under a Humvee with grease all over his face; his fingers bleeding in half a dozen places when a shattered fan blade broke in his hand; the way he laughed when he told a joke — and the sweet expression he got on his face when he talked about his wife.

Somewhere his family was in mourning.

She took a breath, then choked on a sob.

The back door opened. She lay without moving, listening to the sound of Quinn's footsteps, then the clink of the empty beer can that he dropped in the trash.

Quinn felt numb. He knew he should be used to this kind of news. It was what happened in a war, but it made him feel empty — like he was all used up. He stopped at the end of the living room. Mariah was in bed. She must have sensed he was there, because she suddenly rolled over to face him.

There were tears on her face. She'd been crying. He wished he could. Maybe the knot in his belly would ease enough that it wouldn't hurt to breathe.

She patted the edge of the mattress, as if offering him a place to sit — a case of grief seeking solace.

He wanted to make love to her.

"Talk to me," she said.

Quinn moved closer, stopping short of sitting down. "I don't want to talk."

Mariah shivered. She knew what he wanted. It had been so long, and she was as vulnerable now as she'd ever been. If they started this up again, would she be strong enough to lose him if it didn't work out?

Then her instinct for self-preservation kicked in. What the hell. She'd been hopping on one foot most of her life without backup. If this didn't work out, she still had the other foot to fall back on. She sat up and pulled off her shirt.

Quinn's heart thudded hard in his chest as a little wave of shock swept through him, but that was the last of his hesitation. He kicked off his shoes and started toward her.

She unzipped her jeans and wiggled out of the rest of her clothes as he stripped and crawled onto the bed, then took her in his arms. There was nothing between them now but the dog tags he still wore around his neck. Three years had come and gone, and she still curled against him as perfectly as if she'd been made to fit. When she wrapped her arms around him, the emptiness vanished.

"I'm afraid I'll hurt you," he whispered.

She leaned back.

"We've already been hurt. I'm tired of hurting. We know how to make each other feel good, remember?"

His nostrils flared. "Hell yes, I remember. You set fire to my blood, pretty girl."

"Then make love to me, Quinn . . . make

love because we still can."

He cupped the back of her head and pulled her close.

Her lips were as soft as he remembered. They opened at his touch like a flower to the sun, yielding to his need. Her hands felt small on his back, but he knew her strength. He cupped her breasts, brushing his thumbs across her nipples. She moaned as they hardened to his touch. When he slid a hand between her legs, she arched upward, pushing against the pressure of his palm.

He knew how she liked it.

She knew what turned him on.

All of a sudden her hands were on his chest, then sliding down his belly and encircling his erection. Now he was the one struggling to draw breath. The heat between them ignited as he rolled her over onto her back, settling easily between her legs.

"Now or never," he whispered.

"Now," she begged, and shuddered when he slid inside.

For Quinn, it was a homecoming.

For Mariah, it was a reunion with the man who made her whole.

Then he began to move — thrusting deep, in and out, over and over — rocking in that slow, steady rhythm she knew so well. In her heart, she was finally dancing — follow-

ing his lead, because she knew all the steps
— and the miracle they were seeking began
to happen. When they were in each other's
arms, the rest of the world ceased to matter.

One moment Mariah was riding a building heat wave, then all of a sudden was hit
with an orgasm that made her think she was
falling. She screamed, first in shock, then in
ecstasy, as the waves rolled through her.

Quinn felt her coming, from the first
tremors inside her, to the orgasm's peak.
But then she screamed and he lost control,
coming so hard he forgot to breathe, spilling his seed in hard, urgent bursts until he
collapsed in utter bliss.

They clung to each other in silence,
remembering why they'd made love, knowing this had happened out of a sense of
shared grief and at the same time acknowledging that there was far more between
them than good sex.

It was Quinn who finally broke the silence.

"That was the best that I've felt since the
last time we did this."

Mariah pushed out of his arms and sat
up.

He sat up, as well, waiting for her response. The scars on her body were as
blatant as a slap in the face, and yet she

wore them like a badge, with no excuses. Her body was damp with sweat, her lips swollen from his kisses. If there had been a way to measure the energy between them, it would have lit up the room.

Unashamed of her nudity, she touched his face, then his mouth, then laid her hand in the middle of his chest. To her surprise, his heartbeat matched the steady rhythm of her own. Her voice was quiet when she spoke.

"I have never denied that you turn me on, but I also have never told you how much you mean to me, and that's stupid. We know, better than most, how short life can be. I grieved for you after you were gone. I didn't know how to find you."

Quinn threaded his fingers through hers, then gave them a gentle squeeze.

"That's because I was lost. It took forever before I trusted myself around anyone, even family. I moved off to an old trailer after my body healed, because I was afraid of what I might do when I forgot where I was. I didn't quit on you, but I almost quit on myself. Can you understand?"

Her shoulders slumped. "Completely."

"I still have moments when I lose it. Hell, for all I know, that may never go away. But I'd given up on believing I would ever have any kind of a life or anyone to share it. Then

I found out what happened to you, and that you were about to be released on your own, and all I could remember was your face and your smile and the way we made love."

"I don't know where you want this to go," she said.

"As far as you'll let it. I don't want to lose you again."

Her voice was as shaky as the hand she cupped against the side of his cheek.

"I don't want to lose you, either, but I won't promise you anything until I'm convinced I'm gaining ground, not losing it."

"But you're —"

"No, Quinn, no buts. I feel crazy in my head, and physically, I can't even run without falling. I feel like a cripple in every way that matters, and until that goes away, or until I learn how to handle it, there'll be no commitment between us. Is that a deal?"

It wasn't what he wanted to hear, but he understood.

"Deal — if you don't shut me out of your bed."

"Deal."

She offered her hand.

He shook on it, and the deal was sealed.

"I'm still sad about Dewey," she said.

And just like that, the reason they'd made love was back between them.

"Hell, honey, so am I. As sad as a man can be and still keep breathing. I'm tired of losing friends. I quit going to funerals. The only thing I can do is keep living the best life I can, because they don't have that chance."

Mariah nodded, then glanced toward the window and frowned. "It's getting dark."

"Night comes fast on the mountain. I'm going to take a quick shower before I make us some supper."

"I need a shower, too," she said.

He grinned. "Race you?"

She rolled her eyes. "We've been here before, and I wound up with a cold ass. The least you could do is be a gentleman and —"

He rolled off the bed and grabbed his clothes. "Whining will get you nowhere, woman. I'll wait until you're standing up, then the race is on."

"Oh, for the love of Pete," Mariah said, as she scooted clumsily off the bed and picked up her clothes. "I demand a handicap. I should get at least a five-step start before —"

He bolted for the stairs, still as naked as the day he was born, except for his dog tags.

Mariah squealed, then laughed and stumbled toward the downstairs bathroom,

247

cursing him as she went.

The grill was hot, and the burgers were shaped into patties and sitting in the refrigerator waiting to be cooked. The cabin felt homey with all the hustle and bustle of preparing for company, and Mariah was actually getting excited. She had taken the sheets off her bed and turned it back into a sofa so that there would be more seating. On her own, she dusted the house and cleaned the hardwood floors until they glistened.

Quinn watched as she worked, gauging her mood by the expression on her face before he finally relaxed. Yesterday had been a turning point for both of them. Making love had been inevitable, but accepting that they both wanted more was even better. It was the first time since he'd come back from Afghanistan that he let himself believe he could be happy again.

By the time she'd finished the floor she was limping. That was when he took the dust mop out of her hand.

"You've done enough. I don't want you worn-out and hurting before they even get here, okay?"

She frowned. "I want to do my part. It's bad enough that I'm letting you and everyone else take care of me. I can't help in any other way but this. Lord knows we don't want to be eating anything I'd try to make."

He laughed, then slid his arms around her waist and cupped her hips.

"I'm not doing a damn thing I don't want to do and don't you forget it."

Mariah locked her hands around his neck and kissed him, feeling the strength in his touch and the gentle demand of his lips as he deepened the kiss. He made her feel safe. He made her feel loved.

Quinn groaned as he finally pulled away.

"If company wasn't coming, you and I would so be taking our clothes off right now."

She smiled. It was a heady thing to know she had "that kind of power" over a man she so adored.

"What time are they due?"

"After church. They'll probably get here just before one o'clock."

Growing up like she had, church had never been part of Mariah's daily routine.

"Do you go to church?"

"I used to."

"So what changed?"

"Me," he said, and looked away.

She knew what he meant and didn't push the issue. It was hard to see the death and destruction they'd seen and not be changed in some way. Faith of any kind was definitely a struggle.

She glanced at the clock. It was just after noon.

"I don't know about you, but I'm sort of hungry. What do you say we open a bag of chips a little early?"

Quinn sighed. And just like that, she'd changed the darkness of the moment without even knowing it.

"I say yes, and let's pop the top on that ranch dip, too."

"Good call. It's our duty to make sure what we serve is edible, right?"

He grinned. "Exactly."

At his bidding, Mariah sat down, easing the weight on her leg, while Quinn brought the chips and dip to the table, along with a couple of cans of Pepsi, and by the time they'd finished their snack the mood had shifted back to a happy one.

As per his prediction, the first of the family began arriving just before one o'clock.

Quinn was on the deck, turning burgers on the grill, when Mariah suddenly pointed.

"Ryal and Beth are coming."

"Good timing," he said. "These will be done soon, which is good, because when it comes to food James's kids are just like him.

When they're hungry, they're impatient as hell."

The more Mariah heard about the brother she had yet to meet, the more she liked him. What could be wrong with a fun-loving family man who liked to eat?

Ryal and Beth came in through the front door on their own, put their food on the table and came out smiling. Sarah was riding Beth's hip, and waving and pointing. Her baby babble made Mariah smile.

"Man, those burgers smell good," Ryal said. "I hope you made enough."

"If we don't let James fix his plate first, there'll be plenty for everyone."

It was obvious to Mariah that there was more truth than humor to the statement, because none of them laughed.

Meg and Dolly arrived less than five minutes later, bringing their share of food and noise to the party. Dolly quickly took Sarah into her lap and began a conversation with the baby that only a grandmother could have.

Quinn was taking the first batch of the burgers off the grill when the final brother and his family drove up.

"There they are!" Dolly cried, and jumped up with Sarah in her arms, then hurried along the deck to greet them.

251

Meg rolled her eyes. "In case you're wondering, Mariah, that excited exit she just made is because they're bringing her other grandchildren."

Mariah smiled. "I take it the pressure is on for the rest of you to reciprocate?"

"You could say that," Meg drawled.

"The only reason Quinn and I have escaped her less-than-subtle hints is because we were partner-free." She wiggled her finger at Mariah. "Consider yourself forewarned."

The look on Mariah's face made everyone laugh. She wasn't sure she would ever trust herself with children. She had yet to prove she could take care of herself. She was still blushing when Dolly came back with two more children at her heels.

"Mariah . . . this little guy is my three-year-old grandson, James Junior, also known as Short Stuff, and the little girl is my six-year-old granddaughter, Meggie, and no she's not named for Meg. Meg is Margaret, and this Meggie is Megan."

The little boy hid his face against Dolly's skirt, but the little girl turned loose of Dolly's hand and walked up to Mariah as if they'd known each other for years.

Mariah had just scooted to the edge of her chair to say hello when Meggie surprised her with a small tissue-wrapped package.

"This is for you."

"For me?"

"Uh-huh, for saving my aunt Bethie's life."

The gesture stunned her. She was struggling with what to say when she felt Quinn's hand on her shoulder.

"Better open that right up," he said, and pointed to the little boy. "Short Stuff is already heading for the food."

Mariah tore into the tissue, then softly gasped as a small wooden badge with the word *Hero* written in red crayon fell out into her lap. A lump formed in her throat.

"Oh, Meggie, thank you! This is the best present anyone has ever given me."

Meggie nodded. Now that she'd delivered her message, she was all about the food.

"Uncle Quinn, did you remember to make my booger flat?"

Quinn grinned. "Yeah, I made your booger flat, just like the ones you get at Mickey D's."

"Hey! We produced those adorable creatures. Surely that counts for something!"

Mariah heard that big, booming voice and was already smiling when she turned around to see the speaker turning the corner.

James. The last brother and his wife had arrived. She liked him on sight and got up to meet them.

James wasn't standing on ceremony. "Oh, wow, Quinn, you must have told a whole lot of lies to get a girl this pretty." Then he grabbed Mariah's hand and promptly shook it. "I'm James, and this gorgeous woman on my right is my wife, Julie."

Julie was half the size of James but obviously able to hold her own in the family. She elbowed her way past James and promptly hugged Mariah.

"It's so nice to finally meet you. We echo Meggie's sentiments. Beth is a treasured member of our family, and what you did in saving her life is nothing short of amazing."

"Nice to meet you," Mariah said. "This is what's amazing," she said, holding up the little badge.

Julie beamed. "It was Meggie's idea. She wanted to make you a medal because, she said, brave soldiers get medals."

Mariah's voice was starting to shake. "Enough already. I'm trying not to make a scene."

"Come on, you guys, don't make my lady cry," Quinn said.

Ryal caught the "my lady" reference and elbowed Beth, who was already grinning at Meg and Dolly.

"I hungry!" Short Stuff yelled, which put

the event into perspective.

Julie rolled her eyes and took her son by the hand, while the others filed into the house behind her.

Mariah had a feeling the day would come when she would look back on this meal as the day she finally learned what family was all about.

The teasing, the laughter, sharing food and memories — and all she could think about was how blessed she was to still be alive to see it.

Once, when she got up to refill her glass, she paused, looked out at the people scattered about the room eating and talking with such ease, and it suddenly hit her. Somewhere, in another part of the country, Dewey Pomeroy's family was probably together, as well. And they might be sharing food and memories, but she seriously doubted there was laughter. It was the only sobering moment in a day full of joy.

Even though they were now sharing a bed, Quinn had moved down to the living room with her, rather than make her climb all the way up the steep stairs to his loft.

Mariah had fallen asleep waiting for him to come back from his shower, and he didn't have the heart to wake her. He checked the locks, turned on a night-light, then turned off the lights and crawled into bed.

Even after he'd scooted up close, spooning himself against her back, the whole scene felt surreal. A few days ago she'd been part of his past, and now here she was, lying in his arms — a part of his future.

As he pulled her close, he realized her breathing was short and panicked. The moment their bodies touched, she began to mutter.

". . . gonna die . . . get a medic."

The fear in her voice brought tears to his eyes. He rose up on one elbow, then whispered in her ear, "You're safe, Conrad. I'm here."

She mumbled something indecipherable, but her breathing began to slow down until it fell into a normal rhythm.

He lay back down and closed his eyes, but what she was going through hurt his heart. Then he thought of Dewey Pomeroy, reminded himself to be grateful that she was still alive, and let go of the pain.

THIRTEEN

According to the Bible, it took the Lord six days to create the heavens and the earth, and on the seventh day He rested.

Lonnie Farrell never got the message.

Three days after he put the crew to work clearing brush and fixing the road, he had two teams of carpenters inside the tunnels, shoring up old timbers, with Buell as site overseer.

The front part of the mine was a natural cavern that was over sixty feet high and more than a hundred yards long. The first actual tunnels branched off in two different directions from there. One had ended quickly when the owners broke through into a natural passage without the veins of ore they were seeking.

They'd abandoned that route and gone in the opposite direction, which had proved to be a good move. For the next forty years the Foley brothers dug, blasted and ripped the ore out of Rebel Ridge, until there was nothing left but a rat's maze of underground tunnels.

The genius of Lonnie's planning came into play with the way he decided to use that cavern.

He'd had a small portable building hauled in and set up just inside the entrance as an office.

The first part of the carpenters' job was to encase a hundred yards of what had been the second tunnel with walls, ceilings and floors, which they did, transforming it into a long, narrow warehouse set up to grow mushrooms in tiers of floor-to-ceiling shelves.

Grow lights and misting systems were in place, along with bins that would hold the nutrients in which the spores would be seeded, and a special ventilation system had been added to ensure safe oxygen and temperature levels that were necessary. It was impressive cover for the rest of the plan.

At the same time, a second set of carpenters were finishing out a section of the abandoned tunnel, but these renovations were entirely different in makeup. Besides the floors, walls and ceiling, he'd left the far end of the tunnel open for ventilation, and had the entrance walled off and fitted with a heavy metal door and lock. Neither tunnel was visible from the cavern entrance, and if anyone came on-site to tour the mushroom facility, he would pass the locked area off as storage.

He planned to set up both a day crew and a night crew in the drug room, with only a small number working in the mushroom nursery. The workers in the lab would be cutting and adulterating the pure cocaine that was coming up from Mexico, then bagging it for street sale before it was flown out by chopper to the distributors he'd lined up.

All the equipment needed to make both ventures happen was in place, his chemists were on notice and the first shipment of cocaine was coming up from Mexico in two days. All he needed was on-site living quarters for the chemists and he was in business.

Buell had been out most of the night and was just sitting down to breakfast. He popped a couple of NoDoz in his mouth and washed them down with coffee just as the phone rang.

Gertie glanced at the Caller ID, then yelled over at him, "It's Lonnie. Probably for you."

Even though Lonnie Farrell couldn't see him, Buell smoothed down his hair and retucked his shirt into his pants, making sure it covered his beer belly, as he went to answer.

"Hello?"

"Buell, it's Lonnie. Glad I caught you at home. Got a new task for you today."

"Yeah, sure. What's up?"

"A trailer house will be delivered up at the mine today. Look for it around noon. I want it set on that concrete slab where the old mine office building used to be."

"Yeah, I can do that. I'll make sure they get it in the right place."

"Some electricians and a couple of plumbers will come out tomorrow and hook everything up. That's going to be where my organic experts will stay. They'll be training the men and working with them to make sure they comply with organic methods. Bigger profit in organic, you know."

"Oh, yeah, sure, sure," Buell said.

"I've leased a small delivery truck and had it painted with the Mountain Mushrooms logo, and that will b e delivered today, too. You'll need to sign for it and make sure I have three sets of keys. I asked for them on purpose, so make sure they're there. I'll check in with you tonight to make sure everything went as planned. If there's a big problem, you have my number."

"I'll take care of it. Don't you worry none," Buell said.

He was stepping high when he sat back down t o breakfast, and, unlike other mornings, he didn't dawdle over his food. He was out the door and on his way to work before the grease had cooled in the frying pan where Gertie had cooked his eggs.

Lonnie had everything lined up in Kentucky. The only thing left was to firm up the deal with Bert Warwick in Chicago, who, for the time being, would be in charge of distribution for all Lonnie's products. Bert already had an established route and runners on both coasts, as well as a large clientele of pushers. Lonnie wasn't demanding that he buy exclusively from him. He just wanted into the pipeline. What was pissing Lonnie off was that Bert was hedging now, wanting a bigger cut of the profits than he'd originally agreed to. He needed an attitude adjustment, and Lonnie was the man to do it, but he would deal with that later in the day. Right now he had other things on his mind.

He tossed his cell phone onto the table beside his bed, and then dropped his bathrobe and turned to look at himself in the full-length mirror.

He'd come a long way from the skinny kid he'd been when he was arrested at fourteen. He'd filled out and grown up. He stood six foot two in his bare feet, and while he wasn't handsome in any sense of the word, money turned heads faster than any pretty face. He was proud of his flat belly and even prouder of the way he was hung. He had a big dick that rose to majestic proportions when he got an erection. Between that and his dough, he could have any woman he wanted, and right now, he wanted the one still asleep in his bed. He couldn't remember her name, but it didn't matter. She was a number in his little black book and as transient in his life as the tissue he wiped his ass with.

As soon as he came again, she would be gone.

He strode to the bed and yanked back the covers. She rolled over, stretching slowly like a big cat waking up in the sun. When she saw him naked, she sat up and looked at him through her sleep-tousled hair, then cupped her breasts and flicked the ends of her nipples just enough to give them their own little erections.

"Tell Mama what you want," she whispered.

Lonnie's eyes narrowed sharply as his head came up, his nostrils flaring. She'd already said the magic word.

"I want to fuck you senseless."

"Who do you want to fuck, little boy?"

His dick was instantly engorged. "You. I wanna fuck you."

She leaned back, pulling her knees up and then spreading them wide, giving him full view of everything she had.

"Who am I, little boy?"

"Mama."

"Come here, little boy. Mama's gonna show you how to be a man."

Lonnie fell on her like a rutting stallion, ramming into her so hard he slammed her head against the headboard time and time again. She was moaning and clawing, begging him to stop, but it was all part of the game.

"Say it," he growled, as the blood hammered in his ears.

"Mama wants it hard," she gasped, and dug her fingers into the flesh around his neck.

He hammered harder, until the bed seemed to be spinning — almost as fast as his head.

His eyes were closed, his entire being focused on the job at hand. Sweat was dripping down his forehead, across the bridge of his nose and onto her chin. All of a sudden he pulled out and turned her over.

She got up on all fours and arched her back as he shoved his erection into the wet depths of her sex, letting him ride her like a bitch dog in heat.

"Say it!" he screamed.

"Mama loves you, little boy. Show Mama how much you love her."

He pulled out just as the orgasm hit. He shot semen all over her back, in her hair and on the bed in a series of hard, convulsive thrusts. When he was spent, he shoved her off the mattress.

"Money's on the dresser. Get your clothes and get out."

A shower would have been nice, but she knew not to linger, and the money was too good to piss him off. She knew what he wanted. He would call her again.

As soon as she was gone, Lonnie showered and dressed without looking at himself in the mirror. He never liked himself after he fucked, but he wouldn't go there in his head as to why that might be. His introduction to sex had been twisted. He'd known early on that none of it was right, but he'd been too young to figure out how to stop it, especially when it felt so good while it was happening. He *had* been the man of the house, and Mama had always told him that meant he got a man's share of everything else, as well.

It wasn't until he'd been arrested and jailed that he'd come to terms with the perversion of what she'd done to him. A subconscious shame had kept him from going home when he'd gotten out of juvie, and it had also kept him from ever going back in all the years since.

Until now.

However, one look at Gertie's wrinkled face and sagging tits had killed his last nagging doubt about not being the one in control. He was the one with the power now, not to mention the money. He told *them* what to do, not the reverse. The fact that he couldn't get it up without the "game" was of no consequence to him anymore. They were just words — the means to an orgasm.

And now that fucking was off his mind, he had more important things to do — like bringing Warwick into line. A deal was a deal, and Lonnie wasn't about to begin this new venture by letting some asshole jerk his chain. He picked up the phone and direct-dialed his muscle, Freddie Joseph.

Freddie answered promptly.

"Hey, boss. What you need?"

"I'm at my townhouse. Come pick me up. We have places to go this morning."

"Be there in fifteen minutes, boss."

"Ring me when you get here."

"Will do," Freddie said, and disconnected.

Lonnie dawdled through a cup of coffee as he logged onto his computer, checked the stock market, then scanned his email. Nothing pressing. He was finishing his coffee when the maid let herself in the door.

As usual, she called out as soon as she was inside, her accent as thick as the day she'd arrived.

"Morning, Meester Farrell."

He strolled out of the office with the empty cup in his hand.

"Good morning, Bonita." He handed her the cup. "There are five suits hanging on the front of my closet door. Send those to the cleaners when they deliver my clean shirts today."

Bonita was from Paraguay. She understood English better than she spoke it, and understood even better that whatever she saw and heard in this place stayed behind when she left.

She nodded, her dark eyes missing nothing. Her boss was in a good mood, which meant he'd probably had sex, which meant she would be changing the sheets, although it didn't really matter. It was all the same job to her, no matter the tasks that went with it.

"Ju gonna eet lunch today?"

He frowned, thinking of what he had to do. "No, don't fix anything. Just leave me some dinner in the refrigerator. I'll heat it up if I want something tonight."

"Okee dokee," she said, and carried the dirty cup to the kitchen as she went.

A few minutes later, Lonnie's cell rang. It was Freddie. He went back to his office, opened the small wall safe and took out a gun, then slipped it inside the pocket of his topcoat and headed out the door to meet Warwick.

The day was clear and sunny, but once out of the shelter of the car, the cold wind cut right through Lonnie's overcoat. He hunched his shoulders as he and Freddie walked between the rusting train cars. The old rail yard was a favorite place of his to do business. Out of the way of prying eyes, but still close enough to keep the drive from his townhouse to a minimum.

Bert Warwick was already there, leaning against the hood of a Silver Lexus and smoking a cigar. His driver was at the other end of the car, standing watch. Lonnie could smell the tobacco on the wind. His eyes narrowed as Bert took a big puff, then exhaled, sending another wave of smoke right at him. He knew exactly what Bert was doing, and it pissed him off. Blowing smoke in his face — in a show of understated intimidation.

Lonnie gauged the distance between Bert and his driver. At least six feet. That was Bert's second mistake — the first being trying to pull a double cross.

Lonnie stopped within a few feet of the car, then jammed his hands in his pockets, as if to protect them from the cold.

"How's it going?" he asked.

Bert shook the ash off his cigar and started to take another puff when Lonnie suddenly pulled a hand from his pocket and slapped the offending smoke out of Bert's hands.

"What the fuck?" Bert yelled.

"That's what *I* thought when I heard you wanted a bigger cut."

A wave of red swept up Bert's neck. It occurred to him that he just might have underestimated the man.

"I didn't —"

Lonnie slapped Bert, then pulled his gun

on the driver when the man started to make a move.

"You! Stay out of this."

Freddie had his weapon trained on the driver now, so all Lonnie had to do was focus on Bert.

"Walk with me," Lonnie said, using his gun to urge Bert away from the car.

Bert knew the ropes. Leaving the scene without backup was suicide.

"Come on, Lonnie. We don't have to do this. You know how it goes. I was testing the waters, so to speak. You're a new kid on the block in this business and —"

Lonnie grinned. "But that's where you're wrong, Bert. Before you tried to pull a fast one, you should have done your homework on me."

"What do you mean?"

Lonnie shoved his gun up under Bert's chin so hard it made the man bite his own tongue. Bert tasted blood but had the good sense not to move. Lonnie's breath was warm on his face as he leaned closer.

"If you'd been a smart man, you would have found out that I had been cooking and dealing meth on my own since the age of twelve. I killed my first man at thirteen for welshing on a debt, and I got busted at the age of fourteen. When I came out of juvie I was eighteen and deadly. I don't like liars. I don't tolerate them. Did you lie when we made our first deal? Did you intend to pull this shit after you knew I'd already invested heavily in my setup?"

It was then that Bert knew how close he was to dying. "No, no, I swear. I didn't lie. You know what I said. It's just my way of testing you, man."

"You suck," Lonnie whispered. "And you don't know how bad I want to pull this trigger just to see how high the top of your head would fly."

Despite the chill wind, sweat was running out of Bert's hair and down the back of his neck. He shuddered.

"I'll do right by you. I swear."

Lonnie took a step back, then lowered the gun.

"We will never have this conversation again," he said, then added, "Just so you know, this is your last chance. Don't fuck it up, and don't ever fuck with me again. The next time we talk it will be when I deliver the first shipment of coke."

Bert nodded.

"Good. So get your ass back in the car," Lonnie ordered, and pointed at Bert's driver. "Lay your gun on the ground, and then the both of you get the fuck out of my sight."

Bert scrambled around the front of the car and jumped in just as his driver opened the door.

"Hurry up," Bert said. "Get us out of here."

Lonnie watched until the car was completely out of sight, then pocketed his gun.

"Let's go, Freddie. I have an appointment."

They walked back to the car and drove away.

All in all, the day was moving along quite nicely, Lonnie thought as they went. Next up was the little matter of taking care of the man who'd beaten one of Sol's girls. The son of a bitch didn't know it, but Lonnie was about to give him a good beating and a solid case of indigestion. He knew stuff about the man that could ruin him. Leverage was a good thing to have.

Mariah poked around the cabin, wishing she had something to do besides sleep and eat. She'd never been much of a television watcher, and having that for her only source of entertainment fell short of satisfactory.

But if someone had asked her what she wanted to do, she wouldn't have been able

271

to answer. She had no marketable skills beyond those she'd learned as a soldier. Growing up, no one had ever encouraged her to pursue a trade, and she'd been too busy trying to survive the foster system to think about anything except getting out of it.

Now here she was, nearly twenty-four years old, with a gimpy leg and a scrambled brain — definitely less than a prime choice for employment. But it was a case of first things first, which meant getting well. Then she could worry about working. Maybe recovery would give her time to figure out what she could do.

Even though it was almost lunchtime, she wasn't hungry. Quinn had been gone since before daylight, and she'd slept in and eaten late. Bored, she walked out onto the back deck and thought about taking a walk in the woods. The fact that they were so close to the cabin and she had yet to even set foot beneath the shade of the trees was eating at her. The mere presence of the forest was a taunt — reminding her of yet one more fear she couldn't conquer. She hated feeling like a failure. It was just another reminder of the tenor of her life.

The longer she stood there, the more determined she became. Before she could talk herself out of it, she went back into the cabin, got the rifle, made sure it was loaded, dropped the cell phone in her pocket and headed out.

The grass in the meadow was knee-high, and the sun was warm on her face. She placed each step carefully, aware that a tumble this far from the cabin could be an issue. She was so busy looking down at where she was walking that she didn't realize how close she was to the woods until the grass began to thin out.

She looked up.

Trees loomed.

There was a moment when she almost turned around and went back. Then she took a deep breath, shifted the rifle from her shoulder to her hand and walked out of the grass into the trees.

The underbrush was thicker in some places than in others, but it didn't her take long to find a well-worn trail. Curious as to where it would lead and knowing she couldn't get lost as long as she stayed on it, she began to walk.

The shade was a welcome contrast to the hot sun in the meadow, and the birds she'd previously heard only from the deck were much louder, their songs more distinct. She paused, trying to identify where the sounds were coming from, but only caught the occasional glimpse of color as they flitted from tree to tree.

She looked down periodically to make sure she was still on the path, as well as to keep an eye out for snakes.

As she passed beneath a tall pine, a sudden outburst of animal disapproval caught her attention right before a pinecone landed at her feet. She looked up through the branches and finally located a small squirrel peering down at her through the needles, still scolding her for trespassing.

She laughed. "Sorry about that," she said, and kept walking, listening, taking mental notes as she went.

The farther she walked, the slower her steps became. Muscles were beginning to protest. It was time to go back, even though the trail stretching in front of her piqued her curiosity.

"Another day," she said, and reluctantly turned around. As she did, something rustled in the underbrush just ahead, and when it didn't emerge, her imagination went into overdrive. She swung the rifle up, ready to take aim should an attack be imminent.

The limbs on the bushes began to flail, and there was a distinct sound of something moving about in the dry leaves on the forest floor. Her heart was pounding. Should she try to get away, or wait and possibly be attacked?

All of a sudden the branches parted and a fat rabbit hopped out. There was a moment of hesitation when it saw her and seemed as shocked as she was, then it leaped off into the underbrush on the other side of the trail.

"Oh, my Lord," she muttered. "A rabbit. I was almost attacked by a rabbit."

Still rattled, she took off, going back down the path as fast as she could move. It was a mistake. Within a few steps she lost her balance and down she went, falling hard on her hands and knees. The rifle went flying, and she bit her lip.

It was the taste of blood in her mouth that made her lose it. Just like that she was back in the desert, crawling on her hands and knees — and without a rifle. The trees were gone. The sound of the wind in the pines, the bird calls, the squirrel's chatter . . . all gone. The only things she could hear were the screams of incoming shells and the ensuing explosions.

Still crawling for cover, she sobbed with relief when the feel of cold steel hit her palm. Grabbing her rifle, she dragged it with her as she crawled behind the wall of a bombed-out house. Blood was running from the corner of her mouth. She spat, then listened, waiting for orders that never came.

It was the cell phone ringing in her pocket that yanked her back into the present. When she came to, her back was against the trunk of a tree, her rifle aimed at the underbrush. Her tongue hurt as much as her lip, and there was blood on her shirt. She had no memory of biting her tongue hard enough to make that happen. The phone rang again. She closed her eyes, answering the call with shaking hands, knowing if she didn't, Quinn would worry. "Hello?"

"Hey, I was beginning to think you weren't going to answer. Are you okay?"

She looked at the trees and the lengthening shadows beneath them. It was getting dark, and she was still in the forest.

"I'm fine. Are you on the way home?"

"Soon. I'm down in Boone's Gap getting gas. Is there anything you need from town?"

She closed her eyes, trying to think of anything that would delay his trip so she would have time to get back to the cabin.

"I'm getting low on shampoo, and I'm going to be needing some Tampax. Will you freak if you have to buy that?"

He laughed. "I have a sister, remember? From the time we learned to drive, Mom made all three of us boys buy stuff like that. It was part of the price of getting to go to town when we were in our teens."

She made herself laugh when she really wanted to cry.

"Okay, so get a couple of boxes, then you won't have to buy it so often. Just regular . . . nothing supersize."

"Will do, pretty girl. Can I assume you'd be okay if I brought home a side of smoked baby back ribs?"

She rolled her eyes. Eating those with a sore tongue was going to be a trick.

"Yes, you can, and if they have sides to go with them, I like anything you like."

"That sounds like a deal," Quinn said. "See you soon. I've got a bunch of stuff to tell you about what's been going on today."

"Drive safe," she said, then disconnected.

As she put the phone back in her pocket, she realized the palms of her hands were scratched and her knees were hurting. She pulled up the legs of her jeans and sighed. Both knees were scratched, as well. No way to hide it. She didn't remember falling, but it was obvious that she had. She didn't know what had triggered the PTSD, but she knew damn well it had happened.

Anxious to get out of the forest before dark caught her, she pushed herself up, wincing sharply as she bent back down for the rifle, and then panicked when she realized she was no longer on the trail. Moments later she found signs of where she'd been crawling and backtracked until she found the path. At that point it was easy to figure out which way to go. The land sloped slightly downward, which would take her back down the mountain toward the cabin.

Ignoring her pain, she started walking. The sounds in the trees were different now. The birds had gone to roost. The squirrels had taken to their nests. Mariah had no idea what kinds of animals came out at night, but she had no desire to run into them.

Her knees throbbed, her hands stung, but she was so angry at what had happened that her fear was gone. By the time she walked out of the trees it was dusk and the moon was becoming visible in the night sky. She knew Quinn wasn't home yet because the cabin was still in darkness. Anxious to get cleaned up before he arrived, she set her jaw and strode through the meadow. When she finally reached the back steps, she was shaking.

She entered the cabin, turning on lights as she went, and then stripped in the utility room, threw her bloody clothes in the washer and headed for the shower.

By the time Quinn drove up her clothes were in the dryer, she had doctored her hands and knees, taken a pain pill, and dressed in a clean pair of sweats and a T-shirt. It would be simple to explain away the injuries without lying. All he needed to know was that she'd fallen. Given her condition, he would never think to question the fact.

FOURTEEN

Quinn came in the door smiling and holding up the to-go sack with the baby back ribs. The scent made Mariah's mouth water, but the thought of what the salt and tangy sauce was going to do to her sore tongue made her wince where she sat on the couch.

"Hey, honey! I'm home." Then he saw her swollen lip and frowned.

She held up her hand. "I'm fine."

He put the sack down on the coffee table and sat down beside her.

"So?"

She shrugged. "So, I fell, okay? It happens every now and then, and I can promise you this won't be the last time."

"Are you okay other than the fat lip?"

She yanked up her sweats and held out her hands.

"I also bit my tongue. Wanna see that, too?"

Quinn heard the anger in her voice but

knew it came from frustration.

"No, but if you'd told me sooner, I would have brought mashed potatoes instead of potato salad, and something easier to eat than ribs."

She slumped. "I feel stupid enough without asking for baby food."

"Now you're feeling sorry for yourself. Suck it up, Conrad, and come eat with me."

She grinned. "Gee, thanks for all the sympathy."

He wanted to hold her. Instead he shrugged. "Just means more ribs for me. Do you want water or a beer? I brought a six-pack."

"Water. I took a pain pill."

That got to him. "Well, damn it. I'm sorry, honey."

She sighed. "So am I, but it's not the end of the world. It was just a fall, okay?"

He tilted her chin, but instead of kissing her lips, he kissed one cheek and then the other.

"My poor baby."

Mariah shivered with sudden longing. It was almost worth the pain just to hear the love in his voice.

"Let's eat, okay?"

He nodded, then helped her up. "Are you too sore to walk?"

"Let's just say I'm too sore to take another fall, so I'll lean on you just in case."

"Just hang on," he said, then picked her up and carried her to the kitchen. As soon as he set her at the table he went back for the food. "You take out the containers. I'll get plates."

She felt guilty for not telling him where she'd been when she fell, but it didn't change the facts of her injuries and would only make him worry, so she let it slide. She was already a burden. The last thing she wanted was to become a bigger one.

Quinn hid his concerns as he doled out the food. It did no good to dwell on what had already happened, and she was sitting in front of him, proof the damage was minimal.

As soon as they began to eat, he started telling her about his day.

"Remember I told you I had some news to share? Well, it looks like we might actually be on to who put an arrow into that bear and turned it into a mankiller."

That was news Mariah had a connection with. "Really?"

"Yes. The ranger station has been getting calls about someone poaching up in the high country. Another ranger and I did some recon today, checking out reported kill sites."

"Kill sites?"

"We found carcasses . . . or what was left of them after he removed the trophies."

"Trophies? Oh, my God, does that mean he's cutting off the heads?"

"And anything else he thinks there's a market for."

"How do you know it's the same person who shot the bear?"

"Remember how the park service hauled off the bear you shot?"

"Yes."

"They removed the arrow and the broken shaft as evidence. The brand and style are the same as the arrows we found in the carcasses today."

"That's awful. Do you think you can find him?"

"I know we're going to try. Want some baked beans? They're probably easier to chew than the ribs."

"Sure, I'll give them a try," she said, and pushed her plate across the table.

He served her up a couple of spoonfuls and winked. She took a bite.

"They're good, and you're right, a lot easier to eat than the meat."

He picked up another rib and took a bite.

"Did you doctor your knees and hands?"

"Yes, boss."

"Just checking," he said.

She pointed to the corner of his mouth. "Sauce."

He grinned. "I was saving that for later, but since it bothers you . . ." He wiped his lips.

Mariah laid down her fork and leaned back in her chair, watching him eat.

When he realized she was staring, he stopped. "What? More sauce somewhere?"

She shook her head. "No. I was just thinking about us, being here together like this. All those months overseas we made love like rabbits without really knowing each other. It's only now that I'm finding out what you're all about."

He didn't know where she was going with this and wondered if he should be worried.

"So what am I about?"

"I'm thinking you are as good a person as you are good in bed. That's not a bad combination."

He knew he had a silly grin on his face, but he couldn't help it.

Mariah picked up her fork and took another bite, chewing slowly, but now Quinn was watching *her*.

"What?"

"You want to know what I'm thinking?"

he asked.

"I don't know, do I?"

"You should, because I'm thinking how hard I'm falling for you . . . that and whether or not to tell you that I brought dessert."

Mariah felt hot all over. "If I wasn't so damn sore, I would be stripping as we speak."

A muscle jerked at his jaw. "*Now* you tell me."

"What kind of dessert?" she asked.

"Pie."

"I want some," she said softly.

He leaned forward. "*I* want some, too."

She smiled. "I'm talking about the pie."

"I'm not."

She put down her fork. "If you help get my clothes off, we can both have some."

"Pie?"

She laughed. "No, you fool. Just get me in bed and we'll let nature take its course."

He grabbed a handful of napkins and wiped the sauce off his face and hands, then carried her to the bed. He stopped to pull the T-shirt over her head and her pants down around her ankles. Her bruises were revealed as he laid her down, which made him frown.

"This is crazy. I'm going to hurt you."

"I already hurt myself. I consider what's about to happen good medicine."

He turned off the lights, leaving a single light burning in the utility room, then stripped and crawled in beside her.

"I don't know where to start. If I kiss you, it will hurt your lips. Your hands are a mess, and so are your knees."

She took his hand and laid it between her legs. "Start here and see what happens."

He laughed.

Mariah closed her eyes and spread her legs. When his fingers slid between the folds of her sex and found the hard little nub, she sighed. This had been the day from hell, but it was going to end on one hell of a high.

Quinn was rubbing her clit in a small circular motion, increasing pressure ever so slightly until there was a steady throb between her legs that matched the thunder of her heartbeat. Over and over, minute after minute, he kept up the motion, and then she felt his mouth on her breast. His tongue flicked across her nipple, increasing the ache growing in her belly. As always, he lit her fire so fast she was ready to burn. She reached for his shoulders, digging her fingers into the muscles.

"Inside me, Quinn. I won't do this without you."

He didn't need a second invitation. He pushed her legs apart and slid in so fast Mariah lost her breath. When he began to move she wanted to move with him, but she was already coming and all she could do was hold on.

Quinn felt the tremors of her oncoming climax surrounding him, squeezing him, blurring consciousness between the past and the present.

The climax hit with a blow that splintered and washed throughout her. She gasped, then she moaned, and when Quinn let go of his seed, she cried.

Weak, spent and utterly at peace, he eased off her, then rolled away. He was motionless, waiting to see if the weakness would pass, or if this would be the day he died. At that point, it was impossible to predict.

"Are you okay?" he asked.

Her voice was shaking as she blinked away tears. "Oh, my God, Quinn. If having sex with you could heal, I'd be the healthiest, sanest woman on the planet. I don't know how you do it, but you do it so well."

"It isn't what *I* do, it's what *we* do that makes the magic. It's us together, baby. It's how God meant us to be. Just so you know, I'm waiting for the day when you believe in yourself enough to let go and trust what's good between us."

Mariah sat up. Her dark eyes were brimming with tears, her swollen lip trembling.

"I trust that my feelings for you are growing, Quinn Walker. But I need to be well to make plans that go beyond good sex, not the burden I still am."

He rolled over, then sat up to face her. "I hear you. I don't agree, but I understand. I won't keep pressuring you, but just so you know, I won't let you go."

Mariah reached for his hand. "For now, that's all the promise I need."

He eyed her closely, loving her even more at that moment for the honesty and bravery with which she chose to live.

"So, are you telling me you don't need any pie?" he asked to lighten the moment.

She grinned. "Uh, no, I didn't say a word about turning down pie. Hand me my clothes, crazy man."

He gathered them up and tossed them toward her. As soon as she scooted into her panties, he helped her with the sweats.

"The T-shirt, too, please," she said.

He hesitated, eyeing her with admiration.

"Are you sure? I always wanted to eat pie with a half-naked woman."

"Damn it, Quinn, my shirt."

He tossed it to her. "Such a pity."

She was laughing as she pulled it over her head, then held up her arms.

"You brought me here, so if you don't mind, would you take me back where you found me?"

"You don't mean Fort Campbell?"

She punched his arm. "You don't get rid of me that easy. To the kitchen, pie man. I'm suddenly very hungry."

Quinn lifted her up into his arms, then paused. For a moment they were so close they could see their own reflections in each other's eyes.

Mariah leaned forward and very carefully kissed the smile on his lips.

"Pie?"

He nodded. "Pie."

It was payday at the mine. Lonnie arrived in a chopper and got out carrying a briefcase.

Buell hadn't known he was coming, which made him uneasy. He didn't like surprises. He watched his brother-in-law swagger as he came toward the office and just for a moment thought about what it would be like to be that rich and powerful.

He had been working his own little racket before this came along but had slacked off since he'd started working for Lonnie. He'd quit taking new orders. He had only a couple of old ones to fill and then he would be done. This gig raising mushrooms was easier and, in the end, more lucrative. But he did like being his own boss. He would miss that part of it for sure.

Then Lonnie reached the entrance. "Buell. I trust all is well?"

"Of course. Your guy has been teaching the men how to propagate portobello spores. Do you really get eight to ten dollars a pound for them big caps?"

Lonnie nodded. "Even more in some areas of the country. People are willing to pay big for organic produce."

"Damn. Who would'a thought a fungus would bring that kind of dough?"

Lonnie eyed Buell, wondering what he would think if he knew how much a pound he was going to get for the coke. He was still on the fence about how the men would react, but he couldn't hesitate much longer. According to his chemists, they were ready. The first load of coke was due in tonight. Now all he needed was to choose a crew.

"I brought the payroll," Lonnie said, and strode into the little office he'd had built just inside the entrance. "Do you have their hours figured up?"

"Yeah. Portia did it for me last night. I

ain't real good with figures, but here it is."

Lonnie frowned as he read the list, but he let it go. Portia was smart enough. Figuring payroll was simply a matter of hours. There would be nothing on paper to indicate what work the men were getting paid for, and he didn't want her getting nosey and asking questions.

"Is everyone here?" Lonnie asked.

"Yeah, they're inside the nursery. That's what your expert calls it."

"Go get them."

Buell hurried away, returning quickly with the men.

Seeing Lonnie made them antsy. He was a hard taskmaster, but they wanted to keep their jobs. When he opened the briefcase, the sight of all that cash put a smile on their faces. When he began to dole it out, their smiles got even wider.

As soon as he was finished, he eyed them carefully. This was make or break time.

"So, we've been in operation a bit over a week now. I have a proposition to offer you, but it involves being willing and able to keep your mouth shut. You'll get double the money you're getting now and work in two shifts. Some of you at night, the rest of you during the day."

The men shifted nervously. They knew

Lonnie Farrell's reputation, and they'd all talked among themselves more than once about him being on the up-and-up. But double the money was hard to turn down.

They looked at each other, then back at Lonnie, waiting to see what he said, but he wasn't talking — just watching them.

Finally one of them spoke up.

"Doing what?"

"If you're interested, tell me now. If you want no part of this, you're welcome to stay on the day shift in the mushroom nursery for the same money and no hard feelings. But know this. If you repeat one word of what I'm telling you, remember . . . I know where you live. Do you understand me?"

Buell's heart was hammering so hard he could barely breathe. He felt guilty for getting these men into this and, at the same time, excited about the prospect of more money.

Then the same man spoke again.

"Double pay you said? That would make us drawin' a hundred dollars a day."

Lonnie smiled. "A hundred dollars a day cash money."

He could see them calculating . . . five hundred dollars a week, which was good money up here. Lonnie needed loyalty, and money bought silence better than anything else he'd ever tried.

"I need a decision now. The men who want in on the big money, stand by Buell. The rest of you stay where you are."

A few seconds passed, and then, one by one, every one of them walked toward Buell.

"Perfect," Lonnie said, and then smiled. "Follow me."

Although they were surprised when he headed across the cavern in the opposite direction, they followed. And when they turned a corner and saw Lonnie unlocking a heavy metal door, they knew in the pits of their stomachs there was no turning back.

One of the chemists was standing beside a long metal folding table, but there were a dozen more scattered around the room, with folding chairs and small scales at every one. Expensive lab equipment only added to the overall incongruity of a room like this existing inside a mountain. The white jumpsuits draped across the back of every chair and stacks of disposable face masks hinted at drugs, but he had yet to say the magic word.

What sealed the deal was the large plastic-wrapped package the chemist was holding. He pierced it with a knife and poured a small mound of white powder into his hand.

"Gentlemen, what that man is holding is

a brick of pure Mexican cocaine. The purpose of this lab is to cut it and bag it for distribution. The chemists will be doing the cutting to insure that the product we put out is high quality. No crap. I want repeat customers. The surest way to get that is a reliable product. Your job will be on the weighing and bagging side."

Their eyes widened and their mouths dropped.

Lonnie took in their reactions, which ranged from shock to fear. Now was the time to make sure they still wanted in.

"If this isn't what you want, the other deal still holds. You can go straight back to the nursery and no hard feelings. I'll still need help in there anyway, so at one time or another, you'll all rotate in and out. But your silence is not an option. It is what will keep you and your family alive. Do we understand each other?"

They nodded without speaking.

"Anyone want out?"

Four men held up their hands.

Lonnie was disappointed he didn't have a clean sweep, but he still had a good crew.

"Come on up. No hard feelings," he said, and smiled as he shook their hands. "You four head back to the nursery. You'll come to work every morning like you've been doing, and go home the same time every evening at the same pay."

They ducked their heads and scurried out, looking back every few seconds just to make sure there was no gun at their backs.

Lonnie turned to the others. "Pay attention to the man," he said, pointing to the chemist. "He's going to show you what to do. Buell, divide up the men into two shifts. Take names of who'll be on days and who'll be on nights. After a month, if need be, we'll rotate. But if those hours suit you men and you want to stay on that schedule, you're welcome to keep it."

Buell nodded, still unable to meet the men's gazes. "I'll go get a pad and a pen. Be right back," he said, and scurried out.

He was so pissed he didn't know what to do. He wasn't above breaking a law now and then, but this was serious business. People got killed doing this. He had Portia and the kids to think of. They could never suspect what was going on. He thought of the big speech he'd given Marvin when he'd turned thirteen about staying away from drugs. Hell. What a hypocrite he was turning out to be.

Goddamn Gertie and Goddamn Lonnie. It was her fault for birthing Lonnie, and

Lonnie's fault for turning into such a bastard.

He grabbed the pad of paper and a pen, and headed back into the lab. The sooner he got this over with, the better.

Lonnie stayed until the men had been divided into two crews, then added one more warning.

"Just so you know, don't try to steal from me. If you think you can sneak any of this out for your own personal use, you have another think coming. You will notice that those jumpsuits have no pockets. What you don't know, but what I'm telling you now, is that every one of you will strip at the main door when you come on shift and put on the uniform. You will take it off when you leave and put your own clothes back on. At no time will you be allowed near these tables unless you're properly dressed for work. Do you understand why?"

"So no one can sneak drugs out in a pocket," Buell muttered.

Lonnie frowned. He sensed attitude in Buell, which he would deal with later.

"That's correct. Basically I'm just removing temptation. You will all thank me later." He looked around the room, meeting each man's eyes.

"Gentlemen, I leave you to your lessons.

If we work together, all of us will get wealthy. If you renege on our deal, someone will die. Do we understand each other?"

They nodded.

He wasn't satisfied. "I'm sorry. I didn't hear you," he said.

They all answered quickly and loudly. He smiled. "Perfect. Thank you for your understanding."

Then he pointed at Buell. "Walk with me to the chopper."

Buell followed Lonnie out and then all the way back to the office before Lonnie stopped.

"Spit it out. Say what's on your mind, and say it now."

"I don't like being made a fool," Buell said.

Lonnie frowned. "How have I done that?"

"You lied to me just as much as you lied to them. We was all tricked, and now we're caught up in something maybe we wished hadn't happened."

Lonnie was startled. He never would have imagined that Buell, fat-ass slob that he was, had an ounce of morality in him.

"You want out?"

Buell shrugged. "There's no way I can quit now without Portia or Gertie being suspicious, which is exactly what can't happen, but I got kids, and I don't want any one of them hooked on no damn drugs."

"Then you have an even bigger reason to make sure this stays a secret, don't you?"

Buell turned red in the face.

"Look, Buell, you're not thinking this through," Lonnie said. "None of this is being distributed for sale around here. It's all going out of state to the big cities. There are pipelines for this stuff running from the East Coast to the West Coast — from Mexico to Canada. I just want my share of the billions of dollars being made in the industry, that's all."

Buell frowned. He hadn't thought of it that way. He still didn't like being tricked, but this made him feel better.

"I guess."

Lonnie clapped him on the back. "And I apologize, brother. I should have explained. Feel free to reassure the men if any of them say anything to you. Otherwise, rest assured that I will slit their damn throats if they talk."

Gorge rose in the back of Buell's throat. Lonnie was still smiling, even as he made the threat. Buell couldn't manage anything but a nod.

"Make sure the crews stay on task. The first load of coke is coming in tonight, so I want the men to start cutting it right away. Another chopper's coming in less than forty-eight hours to take it north for distribution."

Buell was startled. "How much do we have to get done?"

"All of it. So make sure it's finished. We're not talking about six-dollars-a-pound mushrooms anymore. We're talking about millions of dollars in just a few months. Understand?"

Buell was sick to his stomach. His little side business had been shady, but this was over the top — deadly, and there was no going back.

"Yeah. I understand plenty."

Lonnie frowned. "Just because you're married to my sister, you don't get a free pass. I can just as easily make her a widow if the need arises."

Buell's gut knotted. "The need ain't gonna arise."

"Good. Then we understand each other. Now you better hurry back. Make sure you find out what they're supposed to be doing. Part of your job will be to keep them from slacking. I'll be in touch. Tell Mama and Portia I said hello."

He walked back to the waiting chopper.

Even after they'd lifted off, he never looked back.

Buell watched him leave, thinking to himself that if the chopper happened to crash, all his troubles would be over.

FIFTEEN

A storm was brewing.

Quinn looked up into the building clouds overhead and knew the rain was going to wash out the trail of the poacher he'd been tracking, not to mention that he would be soaked before he got out of the high country.

After a solid week of following up on leads that went nowhere, his boss had pulled the extra rangers off the trail to attend to other duties, leaving Quinn to do the best he could on his own. He was worn-out and frustrated that he had yet to set eyes on the man. Except for a fleeting glimpse of someone on the opposite ridge four days ago, he might as well have been trailing a ghost.

After a solid week of hide-and-seek, the only means of identification he had on the poacher was a nick in the heel of the man's left boot. He'd found the same print at a number of the kill sites. It wasn't much, and even that was about to turn into mud.

Thunder rumbled above him. He started downhill toward where he'd parked, moving at an easy jog, wanting to get off the mountain before he got caught by the storm.

A big buck suddenly leaped out of the trees and across his line of vision before disappearing into the bushes below.

"He knows it's time to get to shelter," Quinn said, then pulled his rain gear out of his backpack and dropped the bright yellow poncho over his head just as the first drops of rain began to fall. The rain was cold, and when the wind began to rise, it felt even colder.

He thought of Mariah, thankful that at least she was safe and warm inside the cabin, and wished he could call her. But there wasn't any cell reception on this side of the mountain, and certainly not in this storm. He knew she would be all right. He just wished he could assure her that he was, too.

Then the rain began to fall in earnest, hammering at the poncho like bullets. He ducked his head against the wind and kept moving.

Nearly an hour later he was driving around the curve by the old Foley mine when a Mountain Mushrooms delivery truck came out of the driveway and headed down the road in front of him. It was the color of new grass, with mushrooms painted all over it.

Quinn couldn't help it. He found it hard to believe that Lonnie Farrell would be involved in any honest business venture.

Mariah was on her daily trek up through the forest. It was something she did now on a regular basis, though she had yet to go past the banks of the small creek, even while the path she took led farther up the mountain. The exercise was good for her leg, and hiking helped pass the time. She hadn't told Quinn or anyone else what she was doing and didn't plan to, not until she was confident that she wouldn't screw up again.

She was on her way home, about four hundred yards above the cabin, when she realized the wind had changed. Without a clear view of the sky, she'd had no idea that a storm was blowing in. The last time one had come through here she'd freaked out. But at least that time she'd been safe inside the cabin. If she flipped again up here, there was no telling where she would wind up. She hadn't tried to run since the day she was wounded, but if she was ever going to give it a try, now would be a good time.

She shifted the rifle from her shoulder, checked to make sure the safety was on, then increased her stride. The muscles in her right thigh were stiff, but there wasn't much pain. The wind was whipping the branches now, and the sound coming through the trees was like a high-pitched whine. It was scary, but at the same time it made her feel alive in a way she hadn't felt for a very long time.

She shifted her stride to a jog just to see if the leg would hold her, and it did. Thunder rumbled. The storm wasn't far off. She gripped the rifle a little tighter and tried to move faster, but her leg refused to cooperate, forcing her to run at a lopsided pace.

By the time she came out of the trees into the meadow, the storm was nearly on top of her. With less than a hundred yards between her and safety, she forced her leg to behave as she broke into an all-out run, desperate to get out of the open meadow and away from the oncoming lightning.

Rain was pelting her body, stinging, blurring her vision. When her foot hit the first step, she went up on her hands and feet, then grabbed the back door and leaped inside just as a bolt of lightning streaked across the sky.

She switched on lights as she went, shaking from the adrenaline and the chill of the rain, but she was smiling, too. She'd done it. She'd actually run without falling, and without a huge amount of pain.

She stripped off her clothes, dropped them in the washer, then grabbed a big towel from the bathroom and began drying off.

Thunder rumbled, rattling the windows. Lightning flashed, shattering the air with its electrical force. The skin on her body began to tingle, then tighten, like she was trying to crawl out.

Boom!

It sounded too much like bombs exploding. She reached for the edge of the counter, gripping it tight with both hands.

"That was thunder. That was thunder," she repeated, struggling to stay anchored to sanity.

She ran for the remote and turned on the television. Because of the storm, the reception kept flickering in and out, which was too much like what was happening in her head, so she turned it off.

The elation she'd felt only moments earlier had turned into a heart-pounding fear that she would lose her sense of self.

She was pacing from the kitchen through the living room and back again, talking just to hear her voice, giving herself orders, because following orders was what she knew how to do.

"Do something. Focus, focus, focus on something. On what? What to do? What to do?"

She had skipped eating at noon to head into the forest.

"Food. Make food. Peanut butter. I like peanut butter. And jelly. Get the bread."

Boom! Crack!

Thunder and lightning — repetitive noise, bright flashes of light — turned the interior of the cabin into a dance floor beneath a disco ball.

She got out the bread with shaking hands, and smeared peanut butter across one slice and jelly on another before slapping them together. She ate standing up, moving from window to window, watching for Quinn while night came to Rebel Ridge.

The heater was on in his truck, but Quinn couldn't feel it. He couldn't remember ever being this cold. Despite the poncho he'd been wearing, everything he had on was soaked and sticking to his skin. The headlights bounced as he drove across a pothole in the road, reminding him to tap the brakes. The last thing he needed was to drive off into a ditch.

He was worried sick about Mariah. He'd tried twice without success to get a call through, even though he knew it was futile. When he finally reached the turnoff leading to the cabin, he was miserable in body and spirit. He was driving too fast now, anxious to get within seeing distance of home. The last curve was just ahead. All he had to do was get past it.

When he saw the cabin ablaze with lights, relief washed through him so swiftly he wanted to cry. This had to be a good sign. He parked within a foot of the steps and jumped out on the run, dashing through the rain for the door.

It suddenly swung inward, leaving Mariah silhouetted in the doorway. He could see the worry on her face, but she was smiling.

"You're home!" she cried, and fell into his arms the minute he was inside.

Quinn caught her to him. "I'm filthy and cold, and I'm getting you all wet."

She cupped his face and began kissing him, on his cheeks, on his lips, laughing through tears.

"Just a minute, honey," he said, and began shedding his clothes.

She gasped when she saw what condition he was in and hurried away to go get some dry towels. It never occurred to Quinn that she was running until she ran back.

"Mariah! Baby! You're running!"

"I know," she said, thrusting a handful of towels at him, then gathering up what he'd taken off.

She dumped his clothes into the washer with her own sodden things, and then started it up. When she turned around, he was behind her.

"You can't take a shower while there's lightning. If it hits the house, you could be electrocuted. Water conducts electricity."

He nodded. "It's okay. I know. Getting dry is good enough for now."

"You need something hot. We have soup."

Thankful that there was something she could do, she opened a couple of cans and poured them into a pan to heat.

Quinn felt like an old man as he went up the stairs to the loft for dry clothes. Every muscle in his body ached, along with most of his joints. But the clean socks and dry sweats began warming him up. When he came back down, she thrust a cup of soup in his hands and handed him a spoon to scoop out the bits of vegetables.

He took it eagerly. "This is good."

"There's more if you want it."

"Did you eat yet?"

"A peanut butter sandwich. I'm fine."

"Make me one of those and I'll share the soup."

Happy to be able to help him for a change, she began to put the sandwich together.

"What happened to you?" she asked.

"I was too high up on the mountain when I saw the storm coming in. I couldn't get down in time to beat it."

"Still no sign of the poacher?"

"Actually, I did find new sign, but thanks to this damned weather, it'll all be gone."

"Do you have to keep hunting him?"

Quinn nodded. "What he did led to a man's death. What if it had been me? Wouldn't you want him found?"

Her shoulders slumped. "Yes. I was just thinking about you, and for a moment I forgot about why you're doing this."

"Sometimes I'd like to forget about it myself. It feels like trying to find a ghost."

She shoved the sandwich across the counter toward him. Still sipping his soup, he sat down on the bar stool.

Mariah poured a cup of soup for herself and then sat down beside him.

They ate in comfortable silence, and once again she was struck by how easy it was to be with him.

Gertie Farrell cursed as she ran a wet mop

across her kitchen floor. By the time Buell had come in from work and the kids had come in from their chores, they'd tracked mud all over the place. Portia was finishing their supper, but Gertie couldn't abide filth and was determined to clean all this up before a bite of food crossed her lips.

"Just look at this mess," she said, dipping her sponge mop into the bucket for a rinse.

Portia resisted the urge to roll her eyes. "That's what happens when it rains, Mama. Ain't nothin' you can do about it."

"They could wipe their feet," Gertie insisted. "You oughta be teaching them to wipe their damn feet!"

Portia turned away. It did no good to talk to her mama when she was in one of her moods. Still, the least she could do was carry Buell's muddy boots out to the utility room. Maybe a little "out of sight, out of mind" would calm her mama's ire.

She picked up the boots, then stopped and stared at the odd print left on the floor. Frowning, she turned the left boot over and saw where a wedge-shaped notch had been cut out of the heel. She sighed. Buell didn't take care of his things any better than he took care of himself. These boots weren't much more than two months old and he'd already messed up one of them.

Gertie came right behind her, mopping and muttering.

Portia knew her mama was upset because Lonnie hadn't come back since that first visit. She had blamed all of them for their bad behavior and had been cleaning like a madwoman ever since. She seemed bent on changing something, and since she couldn't make her family into the mannerly people that she wanted, she seemed determined to make the house perfect instead.

Portia sighed. It was going to be a long night.

The next day dawned with a clear sky and a promise of afternoon heat. Quinn was loading up the Jeep for a trek back to the high country, making sure he had sufficient water and energy bars along with his gear.

Mariah was poking through a cabinet in the utility room and came out carrying a container full of packets of seeds.

"Hey, what are you going to do with these?"

He stopped to see what she was carrying, then scratched his head in surprise as he poked through the packets.

"Honestly, I have no idea where they came from."

She flipped through them, separating food

from flower, then spread them out on the counter.

"You could make a garden," she said. "You have green beans and radishes, and these are beet seeds. I like beets. Do you like beets?"

Quinn heard the excitement in her voice. "Yeah, I like just about all kinds of vegetables. Are you interested?"

Her eyes widened. "You mean do I want to do it? Yes, I would like to. I actually know how. One of my foster families grew everything we ate. I lived there almost three years, and learned how to do planting, hoeing and harvesting. The only thing she wouldn't let us kids do was cook what we grew — yet another reason why I never learned to cook."

"James has a little tractor and plow he uses to turn Julie's garden spot. How about I have him come over and break some ground for you to plant?"

"But all the animals around here would be in it nonstop from the time the first shoots popped up. Not such a good idea after all."

He slid an arm around her shoulders and pulled her close.

"For a kiss, I'll have him fence it, too."

The smile on her face was a welcome

sight, and when she wrapped her arms around his neck and kissed him soundly, it was all he could do not to take her back to bed.

"I'll call him on the way to work. Do me a favor and stay out of trouble today," he said, and gave her a quick swat on the backside.

"Same goes for you, Mr. I-Can-Do-It-By-Myself Walker."

He was still laughing when he drove away.

Quinn backtracked to where he'd found the last sign of the poacher, then began to search the area in ever-widening circles, but it was just as he'd feared. The rain had washed away the man's tracks, and what was left of the deer's carcass from the last kill had been dragged away by scavengers.

Back to square one.

He radioed in the update, only to learn another carcass had been found by a pair of workers from the EPA checking water samples. By the time he got the GPS coordinates and made it to the site, it was nearly noon.

Unfortunately, the kill was an old one. Animals had been feeding on the carcass for at least three days, maybe more. It was sickening to see the carnage and waste of such a magnificent animal.

He wanted to catch this man in the worst way, but he needed a break for that to happen. Disappointed that this kill site was too old for him to track from, he started hiking back. Although clear weather was predicted for the entire day, he didn't trust spring weather.

He'd gone about three miles when he decided to stop beside a stream to rest and eat a snack. He shed his backpack, stepped into the ankle-deep stream to wash his hands, then climbed back up the bank and sat down on an outcropping of rock. He got a bottle of water and an energy bar from his pack, and kicked back to rest as he ate. He'd barely taken the first bite when he heard something moving in the brush. Instinctively he dropped his food onto the rock and grabbed his rifle.

As he waited, he heard a whimper, then a whine. Frowning, he scooted down from the rock, remembering the wounded bear and the poacher roaming the area, and wondered if something else had been injured the same way.

The whining grew louder, and the bushes continued to move, but now that the creature was closer, he could tell it wasn't very big. Only the lowest branches were moving.

He squatted down and peered closer, trying to see what he was hearing, when all of a sudden a small, skinny puppy came crawling out on his belly. It was a little redbone hound and obviously starving. Quinn could count every rib on the pup's body as he continued to crawl toward him.

"Lord have mercy," he said softly, slowly offering his hand, uncertain whether the dog would bite.

The pup seemed so grateful for the kind tone of Quinn's voice that he frantically licked every finger instead.

Quinn got another energy bar from his pack and broke off a small piece.

"I know you're hungry, little guy. I wish it was steak."

The pup wolfed it down so fast he didn't even chew.

Quinn fed him the whole bar, then got the one he'd started to eat and fed that one to him, too. By then the puppy was all over Quinn, licking him and trying to climb in his lap.

"What the hell happened to you?" he said, as he picked the dog up and carried him to the rock to check him out.

The pup was a male, and he had cuts and scratches on the pads of his feet. Except for the fact that he hadn't eaten enough in a very long time, he seemed healthy enough.

Quinn poured water into a natural indentation in the rock. The puppy lapped eagerly, licking Quinn between drinks just to remind him of his gratitude.

Quinn looked into the pup's dark, mournful eyes, then at the thin, wasted body, and sighed.

"I know someone you're going to like even better than me," he said softly. "Her name is Mariah, and just so you know, my name is Quinn. But you, my little fellow, are nameless. Do you have a name? Did you just get lost and couldn't find your way home?"

The pup sat while Quinn talked, tilting his head sideways as he listened.

"I don't know where you were going, but I was going downhill when we met. Wanna come?"

The puppy stood, quivering from head to foot, as if afraid to be left behind.

"Oh, damn it, don't look at me like that," Quinn said, as he put on his pack and slung the rifle strap over his shoulder. "I'm not gonna leave you. This is your lucky day, buddy, because you're coming home with me."

He picked up the puppy, waiting until he settled in his arms.

"You okay now?"

The pup looked up and licked him on the chin.

Quinn grinned. By the time he got this dog home, they were both going to need a bath and flea powder.

He started walking, feeling good that the day hadn't been wasted after all. Rocked by the sway of Quinn's steps and his own weakened state, the puppy fell asleep in his arms.

It was nearly an hour later when Quinn reached the Jeep.

The puppy looked nervous when Quinn laid him in the seat but settled after Quinn got in beside him.

"I figured out what we're gonna call you," Quinn said, as he started the engine. "We're gonna call you Moses, because I found you wandering in the wilderness. I think it's a good fit. How about you?"

The puppy crawled across the seat, then laid his chin on Quinn's leg, looking up at him with big mournful eyes.

Quinn grinned, put the Jeep in gear and drove away with one hand on the steering wheel and the other on little Moses's head.

Mariah had been drawing diagrams all morning of how she might lay out the garden plot, scooting the packets of seeds around on the table and trying to remember how much different vegetables bushed out as they matured.

Dolly had heard through the Walker grapevine that Mariah wanted to plant a garden, which got her just as excited as Mariah had been. She gathered up some seed packets left over from the garden she'd just planted, packed up some leftover casserole and drove over unannounced.

She honked the horn as she pulled up to the house, then grinned and waved when Mariah came out.

"Hi, honey! I brought food. I hope you haven't had your lunch."

"Just in time," Mariah said, and held the door open for Dolly, who came in with her arms full.

"I brought leftovers. They just need a little reheating. I'll put this in the oven," Dolly said.

"What is it?" Mariah asked.

"Just a casserole. A little bit of this, a little of that. Truth be told, it's what we always did with leftovers. This one has chicken and vegetables with a biscuit topping. You'll like it."

Mariah grinned. "I'm sure I will."

Dolly put it in the oven, then waved at the

sack she'd put on the end of the counter.

"That's for you," she said.

"For me?"

"Yes, look inside. James told me he's going to make a garden spot for you and fence it in. I'm so excited. I used to help Mama plant a garden up here every year. I know right where the soil is the best. I want to show you, so you'll know where to tell James to plow, okay?"

Mariah nodded, then almost squealed when she saw the seeds Dolly had brought. Okra, two kinds of lettuce and some field peas.

"Quinn can get you some seed potatoes down in Boone's Gap. Do you know how to cut them up to plant?" Dolly asked.

Mariah nodded. "Make sure each chunk of potato has at least one eye, but two is better?"

Dolly beamed. This girl was going to fit in just fine.

"Come with me, honey. I'll show you where Papa had the garden when we lived here. The land is rich and loose, no clay, no rocks, and on just enough of a slope that it has good drainage."

"That would be great. I'm not sure when James is coming, but I hope it's soon."

"I think he's coming tomorrow, after he

finishes his route."

"What route?"

"The mail route. He's the mail carrier for Rebel Ridge."

"Oh, I think I heard Quinn mention that before." Mariah thumped her head. "I'm having a difficult time retaining new information. The doctor said it would pass."

"Eventually everything does," Dolly said, and led the way outside.

Later, after they'd eaten and Dolly had left, Mariah couldn't quit smiling. She was beginning to feel like she could actually fit into this family and this world.

It was just before sundown when Quinn pulled up to the cabin and parked. The pup immediately stood up in the seat, then jumped onto Quinn's lap, once more making sure he wasn't going to be left behind.

"It's like this, Moses, after we cross this still-new-to-us bridge that you're on, you're gonna have to learn some manners."

He gently rubbed the puppy's frail, bony head and then opened the door. Moses jumped out behind him, then stumbled from weakness.

"Come on, little guy, I'll give you a lift up the steps."

He picked up Moses and had started

toward the cabin when Mariah opened the door. She took one look at the puppy and met them at the top of the steps.

"Oh, Quinn! Oh, my Lord . . . what happened to him? He's so thin. Who does he belong to? Where did you find him?" She turned her attention to the dog. "You poor little baby. Will you let me hold you?"

Then she held out her arms, and Moses went from Quinn to Mariah like a baby reaching for his mother. Feeling somewhat abandoned, Quinn managed a grin.

"Well, I thought I found myself a pup up in the high country, but it appears that what I found was *your* pup. He's half-starved and as friendly as can be. He also has fleas and bad breath. Can you handle it? Oh, I named him Moses, because he was wandering in the wilderness."

Mariah headed back into the cabin baby-talking the pup, leaving Quinn on the porch still talking to himself.

He watched her walk off with the puppy, loving her more at that moment than he'd ever loved her before, and then followed them both inside.

A couple of hours later Moses had been fed, bathed and doctored. Quinn cleaned up first, and then sat with the pup while Mariah showered.

The little dog had curled up at his feet, but with his eye on the door where Mariah had gone. Quinn continued petting and stroking him, telling him what a fine dog he would make when he got some weight on him, all the while knowing that when it came to the pup's loyalties, he was going to be second best.

It was the peak of irony that Quinn had brought home the only competition he would ever have with Mariah, but a fact was a fact. Both the males in this house were in love with the same woman.

That night, when they went to bed in the loft, Mariah slept with one hand on Quinn's arm and the other hanging off the bed touching the puppy's back. As she slept, she started to dream, and as usual, the dream quickly turned dark. At first she suffered in silence, but as the dream evolved, so did her fear.

The first time she moaned, Quinn sat straight up in bed. Moses was already on his feet.

Mariah flinched, then kicked, like she was trying to run.

The puppy looked up at Quinn, as if expecting him to fix her. Just as Quinn rolled over to turn on the light, Mariah screamed.

Moses leaped onto the bed and began to bark.

Mariah woke abruptly to find the puppy straddling her legs and Quinn's hand on her shoulder.

"Oh, my God! What did I miss?"

"I think we just found the alarm clock you need to yank you out of an episode."

"What happened?"

"Moses barked. You woke up."

Mariah sat up and put her arms around the little pup's neck.

"Good boy, Moses, good boy."

Quinn added to the praise with a soft pat on the head. "You're my hero, little guy. Way to go."

Moses didn't know what he'd done. All he knew was that the bad stuff he'd sensed was gone and no one was mad. He dropped down onto the bed between their feet.

Quinn turned off the light, and then slid his arm beneath Mariah's neck and pulled her close. She rolled over onto her side and threw her arm across his chest, taking comfort in the steady heartbeat beneath her ear, then closed her eyes.

Outside, the owl that claimed the roof above them for a perch suddenly hooted.

The pup's head came up.

"It's okay, buddy, he lives here, too,"

Quinn said.

After that, peace came in increments.

A quiet sigh without an accompanying sob.

The soft flutter of the owl's wings as it took off into the night.

The clock ticking on the wall downstairs.

And the little snort from a half-grown pup with a gallant heart.

Sixteen

It was what mountain women called the witching hour. The sky was black with clouds, without a star to behold, and the moon was on the wane. The cloud cover was perfect for what Lonnie had come to do.

He arrived at the mine just after midnight. The chopper pilot killed the lights but kept the rotors turning. Lonnie jumped out, ducking beneath the backwash as he ran.

Buell was standing inside the mine with a rifle slung over his shoulder. After a month on a job and more money in his pocket than he'd ever had at one time in his life, he should have been happy, but it was just the opposite.

Guilt lay on his heart like a stone. He was at least twenty pounds lighter than he'd been when they started, and he'd lost that subservient manner he'd once had with his brother-in-law. He hated Lonnie's guts for being trapped in this mess but lacked the balls to walk out.

"Is it ready to go?" Lonnie asked.

"Yes," Buell said. "I told them you were here. They're on their way out with the first load."

Lonnie looked into the darkness at the far end of the cavern.

"I don't see a fucking thing," he snapped. "I can't wait all night."

Buell just stood there, letting Lonnie rant. Within seconds a faint glow appeared in the darkness, and as it grew brighter, it became apparent there were men behind it. When they got closer, Lonnie could see they were driving forklifts hauling pallets loaded with the bales of street-ready cocaine.

He smiled. This was the second batch to go out this month, and the money just kept rolling in.

"Load it up," he ordered, waving toward the chopper and the pilot standing beside the open bay. Then he turned to Buell. "There'll be a new load coming in from Mexico in two nights. I'll be back to make the buy. I'll need you and two of the others here for backup. Make sure you bring your rifles."

Buell glared. "I got tricked into stirrin' up your cocaine, but I ain't turnin' into your bodyguard and windin' up in some gunfight. You want muscle when you do business, bring it with you. And this is your official notice that I am no longer on twenty-four-hour call. You want a night watchman, hire one."

Lonnie flinched. Where was the fear he would have expected? This anger surprised him. He wanted to argue, but not in front of the men.

"On second thought, a bunch of hillbillies used to shooting squirrels aren't who I need backing me up on a drug deal. Forget I mentioned it."

Buell lifted his head in anger. "Just because you're wearin' fancy clothes and a big diamond ring don't change the fact that you're just as big a hillbilly as the rest of us. Gertie's still your mama and Portia's still your full-blood sister, and all the diamonds and money and fancy cars in the world ain't gonna change that."

Lonnie pushed a finger against Buell's chest. "You work for me. You do what I say or else."

"Or else what?" Buell snapped. "You wanna shoot me? Go ahead. Right now I'd rather be dead than keep doin' what I'm doin' for you. But you won't have a single employee to do your dirty work when it's over. And for what it's worth, they wouldn't let you walk off this mountain alive."

Lonnie blinked. He hadn't seen this coming.

"Fuck you. Get a little money in your pocket and you get a conscience," he said.

"I kill animals. Unlike you, I don't kill people. But don't ever threaten me again or I might have to change my mind," Buell snapped.

Lonnie took a deep breath, making himself calm down. He didn't know when it would happen, or how he would do it, but he was going to make his sister a widow. No one threatened his life and lived to tell. It pained him to make her sad, but she would thank him in the long run.

He pointed at Buell, aiming his finger at him like a gun, then mimed pulling a trigger.

Buell flipped him off.

And that was how they parted.

The night crew loaded the cocaine and went back inside.

Buell went home, crawled into bed with Portia, then woke her up and fucked her. Something told him he'd better get it while the getting was good, because if he turned his back on Lonnie Farrell again, he would be dead.

Mariah began hearing the chopper before she was really awake. In her mind she and the other soldiers were watching it come into camp with the wounded. Medics were running toward it carrying stretchers, and the rotors were turning the sand into a maelstrom. In the distance, she could hear shelling from the firefight close by.

She felt something cold against her hand and then sat up with a jerk. Moses was standing beside the bed, waiting to be acknowledged, and Quinn was nowhere in sight. It was then she remembered that he'd been called out just before dark to help search for a child who'd gone missing from a campground.

"Sweet puppy, how do you always know when to bring me back?" she asked, and ruffled the hair between the growing pup's ears.

She started to lie back down when she realized she was still hearing a chopper, and it scared her. Always before, the sounds of war had disappeared when she came to.

She jumped out of bed, her legs shaking and a knot in her belly as she started down the stairs. The sound kept getting louder and louder, like it was right over the cabin. Her heart was pounding, her hands damp with sweat. This must still be a dream. She only thought she was awake. All she had to do was look out the door and there would be sand as far as the eye could see. That was how she would know it was still a dream. That was when she would wake up.

She stumbled to the door as the sound began to recede and ran out onto the deck. There was no desert, no sand. Just trees looming in the dark. She looked up. The sky was black. No stars, no moon — and no lights anywhere in the sky from flying aircraft. But she could still hear it. Frightened, she ran around to the other side of the deck, searching the skies for a sign, but there was nothing. She looked out across the meadow, but without a moon it was impossible to see anything specific. The only thing she could make out was the chicken wire fence around the garden to the south of the cabin.

By now Moses was at her heels, whining with every step she took. He sensed her panic but couldn't understand it.

Mariah ran back into the house with the pup beside her, then shut and locked the door.

"What the hell? What the hell? What's

happening to me?" she moaned, and began to pace.

Moses barked. She turned and touched the top of his head as he thrust his cold nose against her palm. The pup felt her discord. She wished she would heal as quickly as he had. Where he'd been skin and bones, there was now muscle and thick red fur.

All these weeks she'd been getting better, getting stronger, learning to deal with the episodes without feeling like such a failure. But this was new. She'd never had a hallucination like this and been awake.

She ran her hand through her hair, fingering the edges of the scar along her scalp. Was some long-hidden damage just now coming to the fore? Was an aneurysm ballooning, pushing on sensory nerves and waiting to explode, or was she just finally losing her mind?

Shaking from panic, she crawled up into Quinn's chair, pulled her knees up against her chest and hid her face. She should have known the devil wasn't done with her yet. She'd wanted Quinn and this life too much, and this was what she got for wanting. Maybe it wasn't her fate to be happy.

Quinn was tired and itchy. They'd traipsed all over a good portion of the park before

331

the little boy had been found, but it was all part of the job. Except for a few bug bites and being scared of the dark, the child was safe and unharmed.

The sun was just coming up when Quinn drove up to the cabin and parked. He got out, stretching wearily, and couldn't wait to get a shower and crawl into bed. When he unlocked the front door, Moses met him at the threshold.

"Hey, buddy," Quinn said softly, and squatted down to pet the gangly pup.

Then he saw Mariah curled up in the chair. His first thought was that she must have had a bad episode to be down here instead of up in their bed. He stepped inside and shut the door, then hurried to her side.

She seemed okay. No skinned places, nothing bloody or swollen, so he didn't think she'd taken a fall.

He put a hand on her arm.

"Mariah? Honey?"

She jumped. "Huh? What? Oh, Quinn, it's you. Sorry, you startled me."

"I'm sorry, baby, but since you were asleep in the chair, I thought you might have had a bad night. Are you okay?"

Immediately the dread came back into her heart, but when she saw the fear on his face, she knew she wasn't going to tell.

"I had a bad dream, and then Moses and I were awake, so I took him out to pee. When we came back inside I sat down for a bit. I don't remember falling asleep."

"It's just after six. Why don't you get back in bed? I'm gonna shower and then crawl into bed myself. I'm beat."

"Did you find the little boy?"

"Yeah. He got out of their tent to go to the bathroom, and then got turned around and couldn't find his way back. Poor little guy. He was scared, but he's fine."

Mariah got up and started to hug him when he stopped her.

"Honey, I stink and I itch. Let me go shower, then I promise you a big hug and a kiss."

"I'm going to let Moses out. I'll be up in a minute," she said.

Quinn blew her a kiss and then headed for the utility room, stripping as he went, but instead of going back upstairs to clean up, he showered downstairs. When he came out, Mariah was already in bed. Moses was on the floor next to her, curled up on his rug. They were both asleep.

Quinn crawled into bed beside her, kissed the back of her ear and then pulled her up against him and closed his eyes.

■ ■ ■ ■

When they woke, it was almost noon and Moses was running down the stairs, barking.

Someone was coming up the driveway.

They flew out of bed, frantically grabbing clothes.

Quinn managed to get a pair of jeans on and ran downstairs in his bare feet, putting on a T-shirt as he went. Mariah was still struggling with fastening her bra when he yelled up at her, "Don't worry. It's only James."

"That's easy for you to say," she called back. "He's seen *you* naked, but not me, and I have no wish for that to change."

Quinn was laughing when he went out onto the deck.

James waved as he got out, carrying a box.

Moses bailed off the deck and immediately went to James's truck, where he began sniffing the tires.

"Hello, brother! That pup you found is filling out real good."

"Yeah, regular meals will do that," Quinn drawled.

"That they will. As you can see, I am here in my official capacity as the mailman to deliver a package that was too large for your mailbox."

Quinn's interest shifted. "Oh, good . . . that's the stuff I ordered for Mariah. It's a surprise."

James eyed the mailing label, recognized the name of a familiar department store and grinned.

"I'm thinking you're gonna get lucky tonight."

Quinn frowned. "Seriously, James, maybe you could say that a little louder. I don't think she heard you."

James had the grace to look embarrassed. "Oh. Yeah, right, I wasn't thinking. Sorry."

Quinn thumped him on the side of his head and then took the box out of his hands.

"You're such a goof," he said.

Happy to be off the shit list, James grinned again. When he saw Mariah coming out the front door he waved and started toward her.

The pup immediately put himself between Mariah and James, and then growled.

"Whoa," James said. "Good watchdog you got there, Mariah."

"Moses. Sit," Mariah said. The pup sat, tongue lolling out the side of his mouth as if he was laughing.

"What did you bring us?" Mariah asked, as James gave her a hug.

He grinned and winked. "I'm just delivering the mail. I guess the rest is for Quinn to tell. And speaking of mail, I'd better get back at it. You all have a good day."

"Tell Julie and the kids we said hi," Quinn said.

"Will do."

James backed up and drove away as they went inside. Moses nosed at all four sides of the box as Quinn set it on the floor.

"What's that?" Mariah asked.

He cut the packing tape and opened the top. "It's for you."

A big smile spread across her face. "For me? What is it?"

"Look and see, and make sure to save all the tags. If you don't like them or they don't fit, we can send them back."

Mariah dug into the box, pulling out one shirt after another, then three pairs of nice slacks and two pairs of dressy jeans, while her face turned pink and her eyes lit up like it was Christmas.

"Oh, Quinn! Oh, honey! These are beautiful. I can't believe you did all this. It must have cost a fortune."

She stood up, holding a shirt against her for size, then saw there was more in the box and went back in.

"Oh, my gosh, look! A pair of shoes that

aren't army boots or sneakers. What are you trying to do, turn me into a girl?"

He laughed out loud as she threw herself into his arms.

"This is the best surprise, the nicest gift, and from the sweetest man I've ever known," she said, and kissed him long and hard until it made them both hurt with longing.

Quinn groaned as the kiss deepened. He cupped his hands around her hips and pulled her to him, letting her feel his growing erection before reluctantly turning her loose.

"If I wasn't so damn hungry, I'd do something about this," he said softly.

Mariah leaned back in his arms, so full of love for this man.

"If you keep doing stuff this thoughtful, I'm going to have to break down and learn to cook to feed you."

He grinned again. "We'll learn it together," he said. "Why don't you try stuff on while I make us something to eat?"

"Are you sure you don't want me to help?"

"I'm sure. You have your fun. Try on the clothes, so we'll know what to keep and what to send back."

She frowned. "I don't want to send anything back."

"Well, then, pretty girl, better see if everything fits."

She began taking off clothes as he went into the kitchen, and every time she put on something new, she darted into the kitchen to model it for him. He was seeing a side of her that he'd never seen before — a softer, more feminine side — and he liked it.

"They fit. They *all* fit!" she announced as she tried on the last pair of jeans.

"What about the shoes?" Quinn asked.

"Yes, see?"

She pointed a toe, letting him see the tip of the shoe where it poked out from under the leg of the pants.

He whistled. "You look hot, woman."

She paused as the smile froze on her face, then her eyes welled. "I can count on my fingers the number of times I've ever heard a man say that to me. Thank you, Quinn. You are the only man who's ever made me glad to be a woman."

"I'm pretty damn glad myself," he drawled.

She laughed, and the tears were gone. "I just love you," she said.

Quinn's heart did a somersault.

"I just love you, too," he said softly.

There was a moment of silence as they looked at each other from across the room.

"Uh, our eggs are done," he said.

"Be right there," Mariah said, then went to put her old clothes back on before gathering up the new things and carrying them upstairs to be put away later.

By the time she came down her food was on the table. She stopped at Quinn's chair, wrapped her arms around his neck and kissed him again.

"Thank you for saving me from the streets."

"It was pure selfishness."

"Then thank you for being such a selfish ass."

He grinned. "You better sit down and eat your food before Moses gets it."

She eyed the pup, who was already set to beg.

"Just so you know, he's already been fed," Quinn said.

Mariah frowned at the dog. "You little faker."

The pup flopped down on his belly and proceeded to watch every bite she put in her mouth.

After they'd cleaned up the dishes, and Quinn had finished checking email and filing his report on the lost child, he was ready for what was left of his day off.

Mariah was out in her garden pulling weeds, and Moses was lying just outside the gate waiting patiently for her to finish, when Quinn came out onto the deck.

When Moses saw Quinn, he immediately galloped up on the deck for a pat, which he quickly received.

"Hey, buddy, I see you're taking good care of our girl." Quinn scratched the puppy behind both ears and then gave him a quick pat on the back. "You are such a good boy, yes, you are."

Moses licked Quinn's hand and then dashed back to where Mariah was.

Quinn watched as she worked, diligently focused on getting at the weeds without uprooting the new plants that were sprouting. She'd finally found something to do that made her happy. And he'd been waiting for this day ever since she'd come here, waiting until she was physically strong enough to share another part of his world with her: the secret places on the mountain where all the Walkers had played when they were kids.

"Hey, pretty girl, are you about through?" he finally called down to her.

She looked up, her face red from exertion and the sun. "I can be if you need me."

"I will always need you, but the question

is, do you feel good enough to take a hike?"

She pushed herself up, wincing as the muscles momentarily knotted in her calf, and brushed the dirt off her hands.

"I feel fine. Give me a couple of minutes and I'll be right with you, okay?"

"Wear your hiking boots and get a bottle of water."

She hurried inside, excited to get away from the cabin. She loved it there, but it would be good to do something different.

After a quick change of shoes and a trip to the bathroom, she grabbed a water bottle from the fridge and headed outside to find Quinn and Moses both waiting for her.

She saw the rifle strapped on his shoulder but didn't comment. All she said was, "I'm ready. Where are we going?"

He pointed up the mountain.

Finally she was getting a tour of her nemesis from an expert. She took Quinn's hand, and they went down the steps together, then across the meadow and into the trees with Moses bounding along just a few feet ahead.

SEVENTEEN

As soon as they entered the woods, Moses left to investigate.

Mariah looked anxious. "Will he get lost?"

"Honey, he won't ever go very far away from you. He'll catch up. You'll see."

She gave the disappearing pup a dubious look but didn't argue.

As they proceeded up the path, Quinn's promise proved true. Moses came running up behind them and barked once, as if to say, "Wait for me," then fell in line, trotting happily at Mariah's heels.

"I know you've been coming out here for a while. How do you like it?" Quinn asked.

She hesitated. "I haven't thought about liking it so much as I have about conquering a fear."

He frowned. "You were afraid of it . . . ? Of the woods?"

She shrugged. "A little. Remember, the only thing I had seen coming out of these trees was a wounded bear bent on killing."

Quinn stopped abruptly and wrapped his arms around her. His voice was shaking.

"I'm sorry. I'm so sorry. I was so busy worrying about what happened to you in Afghanistan that I completely forgot about what kind of vibes you were getting from here. It's all so familiar to me that I didn't even think. Even after you shot the bear, all I focused on was that the gunshots set off the PTSD, not what you must have thought seeing that bear trying to run Beth down. Damn, honey, damn. I'm so, so sorry."

It was affirming to have her fears recognized.

"Don't apologize, Quinn. I'm getting better, lots better, and in a way, it was good for me to tackle the woods on my own. It gave me back a certain confidence in myself that I thought I'd lost."

He stepped back so he could see her face. He needed to know that she forgave him.

"I want you to know that, no matter what you're feeling, I'm here for you. You can tell me anything. I won't judge, and I won't laugh. Okay?"

"Okay," she said, but now she felt guilty. She was still keeping secrets from him. Something was wrong with her head; something that was causing her to hear things that weren't there.

He hugged her again, then lightly tweaked her ear. "I have something really special to show you, and it's not the least bit scary. In fact, I can promise you're going to love it."

Now she was excited. All the time she'd been walking alone, she'd been stopping at a certain point on the path and coming back without seeing anything remarkable. Now she wondered what she'd been missing.

Quinn talked constantly as they went, pointing out trees and bushes for which she'd had no name, showing her nests in the trees and the birds that made them. A raccoon started out across the path, then made eye contact with Moses and turned tail into the bush.

They laughed, especially when Moses gave chase.

"You don't usually see raccoons out during the day," Quinn said, and whistled the pup back before he got hurt. A grown boar raccoon could do serious damage to a dog, especially if the dog didn't know what he was doing.

Moses caught up, then once again scampered ahead.

Mariah was amazed that this forest had been the Walker children's playground.

"I can't believe your parents let you kids

run wild up in here."

He shrugged. "It's not scary to us. The few animals that could actually hurt humans don't, by nature, attack without provocation. And believe me, we made so much noise they would all have heard us coming and left on their own. They don't want anything to do with us any more than we want anything to do with them."

"That's good to know."

He glanced down at her leg. "How are you holding up?"

"I'm fine. Is it much farther?"

"Nope. In fact, it's just beyond that deadfall, and if you'd been listening to the forest instead of to me, you would already have heard it."

"Heard what?"

He stopped and put a finger to his mouth.

She immediately heard running water. "It's a creek?"

"It's more than that. Wait until you see," he said.

They could hear Moses barking. "He's already found it. We better hurry."

He didn't have to ask twice.

When they came around the deadfall and saw the small waterfall spilling out of a hole in the side of the mountain into the creek below, she gasped.

A big heron, already startled by the dog's sudden appearance, was taking flight through an ethereal mist. Sunlight winked here and there on the surface of the swiftly moving water, while a turtle that had been sunning on a rock slipped into the creek as Moses came too close.

When the pup started to investigate the turtle further, Quinn called him back again.

"That was a snapping turtle. Moses doesn't know it, but he'll want no part of that, either."

"What'll it do?" Mariah asked.

"They aren't called snapping turtles for nothing. When they bite down, they don't let go. You have to kill them and cut the head off to get free."

"Good Lord," Mariah said. "Moses . . . come here, baby, come here."

The pup gladly splashed up out of the creek, then proceeded to shake, sending water all over both of them before he came to heel.

"I saw that coming." Quinn was grinning as he wiped his face with the tail of his shirt.

Mariah seemed oblivious to the water droplets on her face and skin. "This is so beautiful. So you kids played here when you were little?"

"Yeah, and fished here. You have to look

close, but there are actually some small fish here. But this isn't all. There's more. Follow me."

Now she was really curious. This place was like something out of a storybook. What else could there possibly be?

She quickly found out.

"Here it is," Quinn said, pointing to a dark yawning hole in the side of the mountain.

Mariah took a step back. She was not impressed.

"That's a cave."

"It sure is. At least three generations of Walkers have grown up playing in there."

She gasped. "You're kidding. What about wild animals and snakes and creepy stuff?"

"Nope. At least, nothing scary."

She shuddered. "Everything is scary to me."

Quinn handed her a flashlight. "Wanna see?"

She took a deep breath. "Yeah, sure, why not? I've gone into shelled-out houses to look for Taliban, I'm sure I can handle one little old cave."

"I'm here, and so is the rifle. We'll both protect you from the toads and bats."

Shock spread across her face. "Bats? Are you serious?"

"Yes, Mariah, bats. Think what you're saying, woman. You faced the Taliban without hesitation. What the hell's so scary about a little bitty bat? See? Moses isn't scared, which means there aren't any four-legged critters about."

She glared. "Fine, I'm being shown up by a puppy. Bats are my new favorite thing."

She turned on the flashlight and strode into the cave as if she was about to overthrow a government. Quinn swung the rifle from his shoulder into his hand and quickly caught up.

Her defiance faded as she stepped inside, sweeping the flashlight from floor to ceiling and checking out everything in between. Moses was nose to the dirt, following scents he most likely remembered from when he'd been alone in the woods.

"What do you think?" Quinn asked.

When she realized his voice bounced off the walls and ceiling, she grinned. "You echo." Then she laughed when she heard her own words come back at her. "That's so cool."

"Go stand over in the far end against the wall. I'll show you something even better."

She made her way across the dirt floor in short, cautious steps, sweeping the flashlight before her as she went to make sure nothing creepy-crawly awaited her in the dark.

As soon as she got to the place where Quinn had sent her, she turned around.

"Okay, I'm here. What now?"

He had moved to the opposite side of the cave. "Wait for it," he said, then turned his back.

All of a sudden she could hear his voice in her ear like he was standing right behind her. She jumped back in fright.

"What the hell?"

He turned around, grinning widely as he pointed up at the ceiling above. "The ceiling is concave, see? It carries sound just like a microphone, so when I was whispering over here, you could hear me over there."

"Do it again," she said.

He laughed, then turned his back and whispered again.

This time Mariah gasped. "Quinn Walker, I can't believe you said that, and furthermore, I don't believe you can do that."

He grinned. "I said it. I meant it. And I can so do it. In fact, I'll prove it to you tonight."

Before she could comment, Moses barked and then began digging furiously, sending dirt flying in all directions.

Quinn went to see what the pup was digging up, while Mariah wandered around the back wall and soon stumbled onto what appeared to be a passage leading deeper into the mountain. All of a sudden she began hearing voices and turned to see if Quinn was tricking her again, but he was standing at the entrance to the cave, silhouetted by the sunlight, looking at whatever Moses had unearthed. She could see he wasn't talking.

Her heart began to pound. She was hearing things again, just like she'd heard that chopper. It was plain there was no one here, yet the voices were in her head, murmuring, whispering.

Oh, my God.

Her legs were shaking as she stumbled toward the cave opening. She wanted to throw herself into Quinn's arms and tell him what was happening, but she could see the future. Long, expensive trips back to Fort Campbell to see a shrink. Being readmitted to Blanchfield and watching Quinn drive away. Wondering if he would bother to come back for someone who was going crazy.

She choked back her fear and, even though her lips felt numb and her words sounded fake, pretended everything was all right.

"What did he find?"

"Buried treasure," Quinn said.

"You're kidding."

"In a way, but at the time, it really *was*

buried treasure to us."

He handed her a large slotted serving spoon. "It was Grandma Foster's silver spoon, which was actually the only really nice thing the family owned. Supposedly it came from England with her ancestors, who'd pioneered here in the early eighteen hundreds. I have a vague memory of us boys 'borrowing' it to play pirates. I have no memory of putting it back. Lord. I wonder what Grandma must have thought when this went missing. She used it for every-thing."

"Oh, wow, Quinn. It really *is* treasure. I mean, I know your grandmother is gone. Her old house and everything in it are also gone, right?"

He thought of the killers who'd trailed Beth to Rebel Ridge, remembered watching the old house blow up, believing Ryal and Beth were still in it. Mariah was right. This *was* a treasure.

"You know what, honey? You're right. We *did* find a treasure today. If you're ready to leave, let's head back to the cabin. I can't wait to get this cleaned up. Mom is going to be so surprised — and hopefully so thrilled enough we found it that she won't whack me on the head with it for taking it all those years ago without asking."

"I'm ready whenever you are," she said, then slid her arms around his neck and kissed him. "Thank you for this. It's the best time I've had in forever." And then she kissed him again.

"Don't forget tonight. We'll have a better time. I promise."

She grinned. "I still don't think that's physically possible. Have you ever done it before?"

"No."

"Then where on earth did you get such a notion?"

"From a book called the *Kama Sutra*."

Her eyes widened, and then she punched him on the arm.

"Oh, my God, no wonder. And just for the record, both my legs won't go over my head anymore, so you're shit out of luck on that one. Come on, Moses. It's time to go home."

He was still laughing when they passed the waterfall, and the smile stayed on his face all the way home.

Gertie knew something was wrong with Buell. For the past few weeks he'd been off his food, short with the kids and Portia, and half the time he wouldn't even talk to her. It had to be because of Lonnie, but she wouldn't ask for fear of what he might tell her.

Buell used to hunt a lot at night, but he'd even quit doing that. When he was home he stared off into space, and when he was outside doing chores, she could tell his mind was somewhere else by the way he dropped things and slammed around.

She stirred a can of peas into the stew she was making for supper. It was already dark outside, and only half the family was even home. She tossed the can in the trash just as her phone rang and answered absently, still thinking about her wayward son.

"Hello?"

"Gertie, it's me, Mae. Have you heard about the Colvins?"

Gertie sat down, expecting gossip, which was what Mae Looney was known for.

"No, what about them?"

"Oh, it's awful! Just awful. They say Willis went crazy. Killed his daddy with a hunting knife and then headed for his mama when he suddenly dropped into convulsions and died at Sue's feet. They say there's blood all over the place and that Sue near went crazy."

Gertie shuddered. She'd known the family her whole life. Sue was just a little older than Portia, Willis a couple of years older than Marvin.

"That's awful, just awful. Does anyone know what happened or why?"

"Well, they say his symptoms all point to a drug overdose, but that's just gossip. Don't quote me on that, hear?"

"I hear. Do you know when the funeral's gonna be?"

"No. The sheriff took the bodies. Don't know when they'll be released for buryin'. If I hear more, I'll let you know."

"Yeah, okay, thanks for calling," Gertie said.

Her hands were shaking when she hung up the phone. The stew was beginning to bubble. She could hear it from where she was sitting, but she couldn't bring herself to get up, because she was afraid her legs wouldn't hold her. Lonnie hadn't been back to the house since his first and only visit, although she knew for a fact he came and went at the mine. Buell was acting all weird and pissy, and now this. Maybe it wasn't connected, but then again, maybe it was. Only time would tell.

Lonnie's chopper landed just before one in the morning with a new load of baking soda, dextrose and lidocaine, the stuff they were using to cut the pure coke for street sale. The night crew was on the job, waiting to unload.

As soon as the chopper landed the men came running and began to off-load the fifty-pound bags of soda and dextrose, as well as the anesthetics. Lidocaine was used during the cut to mimic the numbing sensation of pure coke, which led the buyers to believe they were getting the "good stuff."

And, per Buell's challenge, Lonnie had brought muscle: his Chicago driver, Freddie Joseph, and three other very large men, all armed with equally large automatic weapons. Both their presence and their weapons were seriously intimidating to all assembled, and Lonnie knew it. It was what he called good PR. It never hurt for employees as well as clientele to know he meant business. Too bad Buell wasn't here. It might have helped *him*, as well. However, when the time came, nothing was going to help Buell, so it didn't really matter.

He got out of the chopper, transferred the suitcase of money he was carrying to his other hand and glanced at his watch. This trip had served double duty, because he was expecting a new shipment of Mexican coke in tonight. It should be here any time within the next half hour. He'd already spoken to the driver while they were inbound and knew the drugs were close.

"Uh, is there anything we can do for you, Mr. Farrell?"

It was a man from the night crew, but Lonnie didn't remember his name.

"Yes, actually there is. You can go down to the road and unlock the gate. There'll be a van coming shortly. Wait there and let them in, and when they leave, lock the gate behind them."

"Yes, sir," the man said, and started off at a jog.

Lonnie turned abruptly and called after him. "Hey, you!"

The man stopped. "Yes, Mr. Farrell?"

"What's your name?"

"Sydney Colvin, but everyone calls me Syd."

"Thanks for helping out, Syd."

Syd jogged off into the dark.

Lonnie made a mental note. He was going to need another foreman after Buell's demise. This was a man with initiative. He might be a good replacement.

Lonnie went back to the office to wait, and less than thirty minutes later he saw headlights at the gate. He smiled, watching as the van came up the road and pulled to a stop at the entrance to the mine.

He stepped out onto the threshold and

waited for them to get out. The door at the back of the van opened, and two armed men got out, quickly taking up guard positions on either side of the opening. Three more armed men got out and stood at the front of the van. The driver, a short, stocky Latino wearing blue jeans and a denim vest over a bloodred T-shirt, walked toward him as Lonnie's hired muscle stepped up beside him.

"We meet again, Señor Farrell."

"Hello, Miguel. It's good to see you again, but we can skip the chitchat. I'm ready to do business."

The man smiled. "We do not chit the chat, either, *señor*. As you say here in the States, show me the money."

Lonnie swung the suitcase he was carrying into the light. "It's all here, just like last time." He flipped it open for Miguel to see, then locked it and handed it to one of his guards. "I assume it's all right that I check what I'm paying for?"

Miguel stepped aside.

"Of course, *señor*. A smart man always tests the product before he pays. Luis! The lights, *por favor*."

One of the gunmen swung a searchlight into the van's interior.

Lonnie got hard just thinking about all

the money he was going to make, then waved at his guards.

"Tell the men to start unloading."

The night crew came running, anxious to get the coke into the lab and out of sight. About halfway through the process Lonnie stopped them and chose a tightly wrapped brick out of the stack. He stabbed a switch-blade into it, then pulled out a powdery substance on the knife blade to sample.

The night was still. No wind was blowing. He licked the tip of his finger, stuck it in the coke, then put it into his mouth, rubbing it into his gums.

The kick was instant, as was the numbing sensation.

"Good stuff," he said, and waved the men on.

As soon as the last load was gone, he opened the suitcase and set it in the back of the van for Miguel's approval.

Miguel checked the bills' denominations and then counted the stacks. When he shut the suitcase and turned to Lonnie, he was smiling.

"It is a pleasure doing business with you, *señor*."

"And you," Lonnie said. "See you in two weeks. Same amount, same money?"

"*Sí*, we can do that. But if I lose any more

to the *federales*, the price might have to go up."

Lonnie shifted his stance. His chin went up, his shoulders went back. There was no mistaking the threat in his voice or that his hand was now hovering on the pocket of his jacket.

"That loss is yours to absorb. You don't pass it on to your buyers. Same amount, same price, or no deal."

Miguel smiled. "So, for you, we make the exception."

Lonnie nodded. "I'll be in touch."

"Safe flight," Miguel said.

"And a safe trip back home to you, as well," Lonnie said.

And just like that, two men who'd been toying with the thought of murder calmly parted ways.

As soon as the van drove off the property, Syd Colvin locked the gate and ran back to the mine.

"Good job," Lonnie said. "You can join the others."

The man hustled off into the shadows and disappeared into the mine.

Lonnie went back in, turned off the lights inside the office and gave orders to the guards to board the chopper. Production was moving smoothly. New product was in the house. It was now up to his men to turn it into salable blow.

"Are you ready, Mr. Farrell?" the pilot asked.

"Yes. Start it up," he said, and climbed into the chopper moments before it lifted up, flying blind into the night. Until they'd cleared the airspace over Rebel Ridge, it was lights out and radio silence.

After that it was back into Louisville, where Lonnie would switch from the chopper to the charter jet and fly back to Chicago. He would sleep on the plane, pop a couple of uppers to get himself going in the morning and be good for the day.

But the time was coming, and he knew it would have to be soon, when he would have to make the break with Uncle Sol. The old man had been good *to* him and *for* him, but he was branching out on his own. He already had Sol's blessing, but it was still going to be a big change. He hadn't decided where he would make his new home, although he had to be closer to the mine than Chicago. What he did know was that he would never live on this mountain again.

Mariah had been unable to sleep after she and Quinn made love, although he'd quickly passed out, sated in body and soul from their passion. Knowing that her tossing and turning would only disturb his sleep, she got up and slipped downstairs with Moses at her heels.

She prowled through the pantry until she found some cookies, then got a can of pop from the refrigerator and curled up in the living room with the pup at her feet, watching every bite that went into her mouth.

She grinned and finally broke off a small piece, which he promptly inhaled.

"Silly puppy," she whispered. "You didn't chew it. You didn't even smell it. You don't know what that was you swallowed. All that mattered was that we shared it, right?"

The pup's tail swept back and forth across the hardwood floor in agreement.

"That's all," she said, brushing away the crumbs, then popped the top on the can and took a slow sip.

The burn of the cola made her eyes water, and she hiccupped as the first swallow went down. But after that she was good to go. She sat surrounded by the silence of the house, thinking to herself how blessed she was, after a lifetime of being alone, to finally belong.

The man she loved with all her heart was asleep up in the loft. The puppy at her feet worshipped the ground she walked on. It was the first time in her life she felt safe and loved.

She finished off the pop, set the can on the table, then curled her feet up under her and closed her eyes, letting the peace envelope her.

She was somewhere in between sleep and semiconsciousness when she realized she was hearing a chopper. Still groggy and confused as to whether it was in her head or part of a dream, it took her a few moments to wake up. By then the sound was beginning to fade. She ran to the window and, just like before, saw no sign of lights, not from a chopper or a plane — no lights anywhere in the sky but the flickering lights of a billion stars.

Moses eyed her from his spot on the floor.

Once again her heart was pounding as she looked up at the loft. Quinn hadn't moved, and neither had the pup. Obviously it wasn't real or they would have heard it. She was the only one hearing things that weren't there.

She thrust her hands into her hair, tugging at the short strands in growing panic as she began to pace. This was the perfect hell. On the outside, she appeared to be healing. On the inside, she was coming undone.

Scared in every fiber of her being, she went up the steps, then got into bed, snuggling as close to Quinn as she could. If she was going crazy, she wanted to get all she could out of her life before she lost it.

Quinn must have felt her presence. He muttered something she didn't understand, then laid his hand over hers and softly sighed.

She closed her eyes, willing herself not to cry, and finally fell asleep.

When Mariah woke, Quinn was already dressed and getting ready to leave for work. The time to confess was once again gone.

He leaned down to meet her eyes.

"You don't know how much I'd like to join you in there," he said, and kissed her on both cheeks before he settled a long kiss on her lips. "Call me if you need me. I'll be home at the regular time, and if I'm delayed, I'll let you know, okay?"

"Okay," she said. "I love you," she added.

He grinned. "I love you, too, pretty girl. Take care."

She nodded, then fell back against the pillow and listened to him going down the stairs, talking to Moses as he went.

"I already let Moses out, so you don't have to get up until you're ready," he shouted up at her.

"Okay, thank you," she called back.

Then he was out the door, and a minute later she heard the Jeep start up. She listened until the sound faded completely, then grabbed his pillow and rolled over, hugging it to her and wondering if this was the day she would finish going insane.

EIGHTEEN

The little green Mountain Mushrooms truck was becoming a familiar sight around the area. It delivered organically grown portabellas as well as criminis, which were just portabellas in an immature stage, to several businesses in Mount Sterling, including one organic grocery store, and there were new orders coming in from a couple of restaurants in Lexington. The carefully packed boxes of the brown-capped fungi were selling at high prices, and the men working the nursery had caught on quickly to the process of growing them at optimum rates. Once the delivery truck had unloaded the mushrooms, it went back up the mountain with a fresh load of the bags of compost and bales of straw used to nourish the spores.

The main workers in the nursery were the four men who had opted out of Lonnie's dirty business. They had become used to the long, narrow work space. They kept their mouths shut and their heads down when the other men were around. It was dicey being the only ones who had openly disapproved of what the others were doing. None of them wanted to wind up dead at the bottom of a mine shaft, but the situation had definitely driven a wedge between them and their friends who'd accepted Lonnie's offer.

Bad news had a habit of spreading fast, and by the next morning, when the day shift started up the mountain, everyone coming on duty had heard about the tragedy at the Colvins and that Willis had died from an apparent drug overdose. Syd Colvin, who worked the night shift, was Willis Colvin's uncle and Faris Colvin's brother, but he'd already gone home and had yet to find out.

The whole thing had left the men stunned. It wasn't like drugs were a rarity here. It was just that no one had ever gone off the deep end like that before, not from smoking meth or popping prescription pills. They'd died in plenty of accidental ways, but not foaming at the mouth in violent convulsions after killing a member of their own family.

What was worse and completely inexplicable, Willis Colvin hadn't been a druggie. He'd been an honor student at the high school in Boone's Gap and had never been a bad kid. So what kind of crazy drug could he have gotten hold of that would have caused such violent behavior?

They didn't believe it had come from here. There was no way any of them could sneak coke out, but even so, the guilt was on all their shoulders. All they could feel was the sadness and the shock of knowing they were a part of the business that had caused two deaths.

To a man, not one of them spoke of it.

Buell's eyes were red and swollen as he stood in the doorway, watching them strip and put on the white suits to tackle the new load of fresh coke that had come in overnight. He knew without asking that they were all thinking the same thing. This had happened because of something they were doing. They didn't know how, and none of them had any way to prove it, but the guilt was taking seed. What had happened in that house wasn't just a murder. It was a mortal, send-your-soul-to-hell, sin. If Lonnie had walked up at that moment, Buell would have shot him where he stood.

As soon as the men had changed and taken their places at the tables, Buell stepped out of the room, then strode through the passageway to the office. He couldn't decide whether to call Lonnie with the news about the deaths or wait for more details before he got in touch.

Syd came home feeling tired to the bone. He didn't want anything but a shower and the comfort of his own bed. He'd been a single man ever since his wife left him for another man, so he dealt with his own cooking and cleaning as it suited him.

After a quick shower, he sat down on the side of the bed to check his messages. There was only one, and it was from his sister-in-law, Sue. He pressed Play, and then all of a sudden he heard her screaming, "They're dead! They're dead!"

His blood ran cold as he sat through the rest of the message, a jumble of words about Willis stabbing his daddy with a hunting knife and then coming after her before dropping at her feet in convulsions and dying from what the cops said looked like a drug overdose.

Syd looked over at his dresser. He was already shaking when he got up and walked toward it. The drawer was slightly ajar. The little box where he kept his extra money had been moved. He took it out and counted. There was a ten-dollar bill missing.

Then it hit him. That was how much he

paid Willis to keep the grass mowed around his place. He ran to the window and looked out at the freshly mowed grass.

"Lord, oh, sweet Lord," Syd moaned, and then ran back to the drawer and dug deeper, beneath the box and his socks, for the small baggie he'd hidden there.

It was gone.

Shock swept through him so fast that he threw up before he knew it was coming, right into his sock drawer and onto his stash of cash.

He staggered backward until he hit the side of the bed and sat down with a thump, staring down at his hands. He knew what had happened, and he knew that he had killed his nephew and brother just as surely as if he'd shot them himself.

He always left money on the table for Willis when he mowed, but yesterday he'd forgotten. Willis, knowing that Uncle Syd wouldn't mind, had gone into his drawer and paid himself, then — being the curious teen that he was — poked around and found something that shouldn't ever have been there.

Syd kept wondering what Willis must have thought, how he had felt, knowing the uncle he idolized had something like that — and wondering why, if it was okay for his uncle, it wouldn't be okay for him, too? And then Willis Colvin had treated himself to pure, unadulterated coke, and the rest, as they said, was now history.

Syd wiped a hand across his face, too stunned to cry. He sat for a few minutes in the silence of his house, smelling the souring stench of his own vomit in the drawer on the other side of the room, hearing a drip in the bathroom where he hadn't turned off the shower all the way, and knew his time on earth had to be over. There was no living with what he'd done.

Without a second thought, he went to the closet, dug into a shoe box where he kept his daddy's old revolver, loaded it with one bullet, put it to his head and pulled the trigger where he stood.

When Syd never called back, Sue went to check on him. She found him on the floor of his bedroom, lying naked in a pool of his own blood, the revolver at his side. She called Sheriff Marlow and then went outside, too stunned to cry.

Syd's hunting dogs were whining in the pen. She guessed he hadn't bothered to tend them before he went to be with Jesus, so she fed them and watered them, and then sat down to wait. A few minutes passed as she sat praying, waiting for God to give her a sign that would explain how all this had come to pass. It wasn't until she saw Syd's blood on her dress that she lost it.

She looked down at the red splotches on her breast and started to shake. At that point horror came welling up in her, growing and growing until she threw back her head and let out a shriek so hideous it set the dogs to howling. Once she started she was unable to stop. She threw herself on the ground, wailing with such power and despair that she gave up her sanity, too empty from the grief to give this world another chance.

When Sheriff Marlow and his deputies drove up, they found her lying near a rick of wood, curled up in a fetal position with her eyes wide and fixed, and her mouth frozen open as if she was still screaming.

No amount of talking got through to her. Not only did they have to call the coroner about Syd, but they had to call another ambulance from Mount Sterling to come get poor Sue.

Mae Looney heard bits and pieces of it on her police scanner, then filled in the blanks on her own and promptly called Gertie, because that was how the mountain smoke signals worked.

Gertie took the call in near silence, grunting when necessary, muttering when a grunt didn't pass for an answer, and hung up on Mae without saying goodbye. She knew Syd Colvin worked at the old mine, because she'd seen his name on the payroll Portia figured for Buell.

Gertie knew people would probably have read Syd's suicide as stemming straight from grief, but she guessed different. It felt to her like Syd had a load of guilt too heavy to carry in this life and had given it up to the Lord. That was what she believed, and nothing was going to change her mind.

She called Buell the moment she got off the phone with Mae, but he didn't answer, so she went in search of Portia to tell her the news. Portia's face turned white, and then she started to cry. Gertie felt like crying with her, but that wouldn't solve a thing.

As they sat out by the barn a sudden wind came through the trees, wailing like a banshee comin' for the dead.

"It's a sign," Portia wailed. "It ain't over, is it, Mama? It's just gonna get worse."

Gertie jumped to her feet and turned into the wind as it ripped through her hair, yanking and tugging the long gray strands out of their pins, and flattened the fabric of her dress so tight against her that it perfectly outlined the wear and tear on her body from her sixty-some years. Then, just like that, the wind was gone, taking all signs of life with it. The animals weren't moving. The birds weren't singing.

Gertie headed for the house. She knew in the very bottom of her soul that it was old sins — *her sins* — that had created the devil come into their midst.

Portia blew her nose on the hem of her shirt, then called out when she realized Gertie was leaving.

"Where you goin', Mama?"

"To get my Bible," Gertie said. "You go on and finish weedin' them green beans. I need to pray."

Mariah was pulling weeds with a vengeance while Moses watched from just outside the garden fence. She worked until she had the entire space weeded, then stopped to stretch her aching back, and as she did, she noticed that Moses had disappeared from sight.

Dusting off her hands, she came out, shutting the gate behind her as she began calling and whistling for the dog. But no long-legged, gangly pup appeared — not from around the cabin or from the forest at the edge of the meadow.

She frowned. Silly puppy. Where on earth

could he have gone? She thought of her daily walks. He went with her every time, but this morning she had skipped their walk and gone to the garden instead. What if he had decided to go without her? What if he'd taken off after an animal that could hurt him? What if he went back to that cave where she'd heard the voices?

Now she was really worried. She ran into the house, grabbed the rifle and a flashlight, then remembered her cell phone and dropped it into her pocket before heading back out.

Her strides were long as she hurried through the meadow, too concerned to dawdle. She had no idea how long Moses had been gone or what kind of trouble he might be in. Within seconds of entering the forest she began to call his name. When there was no answering bark she kept walking, and the higher up she went, the faster she moved. By the time she got to the waterfall, nearly thirty minutes had passed. She had a stitch in her side and tears in her eyes.

"Moses! Moses! Come here, puppy!" Then she whistled, but there was still no answering yip.

She moved to the edge of the creek, making sure his little body wasn't floating somewhere along the banks after falling victim to the snapping turtle, but the only things she saw were small fish darting into the shadows.

Just as she started to turn back, she saw a muddy paw print in the dirt along the bank. She knelt, running her finger lightly along the edge. It was barely dry. The print was fresh.

She stood up. The little shit. He had come this far. Where the hell would he have gone next? God, please not that cave.

She turned and headed farther up the path toward the mouth of the cave. When she walked inside and turned on her flashlight, she saw more paw prints. Granted, he'd left plenty there the last time, but not this many, and a lot of them were new prints over the old shoe prints she and Quinn had made. As she feared, he had been here. Whether he was still here or not was another matter.

"Moses! Moses! Come here, puppy!"

She whistled again and walked farther into the cave. She was so scared she'd lost him that she forgot to be afraid. She walked all the way to the back wall with her flashlight pointed down, and when she finally found puppy prints going into that unexplored passageway, she groaned.

She was about to call out, but before she had a chance she began hearing voices again. Like the last time, they sounded more like murmurs rather than distinct words.

Her heart started to hammer at the onset of panic. She was spinning out of control, with no way to stop herself. She staggered toward the wall, grabbing hold of an outcropping, desperately trying to steady her legs and slow the rapid thunder of her heart, and then sank to the ground, her shoulders slumping as she waited to disappear.

All of a sudden she heard barking and swung her flashlight into the passage just as Moses came running out of the darkness. He leaped against her and began licking her face.

Mariah threw her arms around him. "Bad dog, bad puppy. Don't you ever run away from me again."

She pushed herself up, grabbed the rifle and the flashlight, and headed for the mouth of the cave with the puppy at her heels. And for all the good it did, she scolded him all the way back.

But there was another, far bigger issue on her mind. It was sobering to realize that she might be getting worse. This was the second time she'd heard voices in that cave. She wondered if they were ghosts, or if it was all in her head. By the time she reached the cabin, she'd made up her mind to call Dolly. If there were stories of people having heard or seen ghosts there, she was going to go with that theory. She'd heard of people turning psychic after head trauma, and she was far more willing to go there than to accept the fact that she was genuinely crazy and going crazier by the day.

Dolly was bringing in a load of laundry from the clothesline when her phone began to ring. Meg had gone to Mount Sterling a couple of hours earlier to run some errands, so she hurried to answer, dumping the clothes on the kitchen table before picking up the phone. She was a little breathless as she answered.

"Hello?"

"Hi, Dolly, it's me, Mariah."

A smile spread over Dolly's face. "Hi, honey. How's the garden growing?"

"Good, really good. I think I've finally found my calling. Now all I need is for you to teach me how to cook what I'm growing."

"I'll be happy to do just that," Dolly said. "All you have to do is say the word."

"Okay, thanks. Uh, actually, I called about something else, though. Do you have a minute?"

Dolly pulled up a chair and sat. "I even have two or three. What do you need, sugar?"

Mariah hesitated. She didn't want to give herself away, but she had to find a way to get her questions answered.

"The other day Quinn took me up to see that waterfall and the cave where the kids used to play. It's really something."

Dolly beamed. "It is, isn't it? All us kids did our fair share of leaving tracks up there when we were young. I haven't been up that way in years."

"I was wondering what you knew about the cave. You know, like did early settlers ever live in it, or was it ever a hideout for some outlaw? I know there's a place in a park in Oklahoma called Robbers Cave, where some famous outlaws like Jesse James and Belle Starr used to hide. I heard they even scratched their names into the rocks."

Dolly laughed. "I don't know about outlaws, but I know my great-granddaddy had a still in there once."

Mariah grinned. "Really? How funny."

"Not to them it wasn't. Whiskey was serious business."

"I'll be honest, it freaked me out a little when I first went in," Mariah said.

"Oh, we scared ourselves in there on a regular basis," Dolly said. "It was part of the fun."

Mariah's pulse kicked. Now they were getting to the conversation she needed to have.

"Scared yourself how?"

"We were always imagining bad guys were going to come out of the dark and we'd never see home again. As scared as we were, we still went back for more. Kids are crazy like that," Dolly said.

"I'll bet you saw everything from wild animals sneaking up to ghosts about to grab you, too," Mariah said.

Dolly laughed. "Probably, but us kids never talked about ghosts — or haints, as our grannies called them."

"Haints? What's a haint?"

"It's the mountain way of saying 'haunt.' "

"Oh. Did you all believe in them, too?"

"Everyone believes in ghosts up here, honey. There's too much history not to, you know."

"Did you ever hear or see any in the cave?"

"Lord no," Dolly said. "If we had, we'd all still be running."

Mariah's hopes fell. "Oh."

"I'll tell you one thing I remember about that cave. It was something Granddaddy Foster once told us. He said the passage at the back goes all the way through the mountain and comes out on the other side. Course we never went in to test the theory, but Granddaddy wasn't one to stretch the truth, so I guess we all believed him."

Mariah frowned. That still didn't help her cause. She wanted ghosts, not a hole in the mountain that went in one side and out the other, kind of like the growing hole in her sanity.

"That would be something, wouldn't it?" she said.

"For sure. If Granddaddy was right, it would be over near the park side of the mountain where Quinn works. And speaking of Quinn, when are you two going to come to supper? I'm a real good cook, and it'll be a treat for Meg and me to see you again."

Mariah smiled. "I don't need to be asked twice. As soon as I can get an answer out of Quinn, I'll let you know. How's that?"

"Perfect."

"Well, it was good talking to you, Dolly. Thanks for letting me rattle on."

"Good talking to you, too, honey. Take care."

"You, too," Mariah said, and disconnected, leaving her alone with the knowledge that she was hearing things nobody else seemed to be hearing. And she didn't like the way that made her feel.

It was midafternoon when Quinn started back to the ranger station. As the days moved into summer, it was always good to keep an eye on the amount of deadfall in the forest. That played into how fast a wildfire might spread, which was a constant source of concern for park rangers.

He was coming around the curve in the dirt road where he usually met the mushroom truck and slowed down out of habit, but today it was nowhere in sight. He glanced toward the gates up ahead, marveling at what time and money could do.

The big green-and-white Mountain Mushrooms sign at the gates was hard to miss. It was common knowledge now that the men who worked for Lonnie Farrell took home good money. It was also common knowledge that he was no longer hiring. Quinn surmised it didn't take all that many men to sit and watch fungus grow.

As he neared the entrance he heard something thump hard against the bottom of his Jeep. He hit the brakes and then put the car in Park, hoping he hadn't run over anything living.

He dropped to his hands and knees as he

got out and looked underneath, praying he wasn't going to see some kid's cat or dog squashed beneath his tires. To his relief all he saw was a chunk of a dead tree branch. He pulled it out and tossed it in the ditch, then began checking the underside of the vehicle, making sure the branch hadn't punched a hole in the oil pan. Reassured that everything looked secure, he circled the Jeep, kicking the tires as he went to make sure none of them were going flat. It wasn't until he got to the front tire on the passenger side that he saw a sight that stopped him cold.

It was a shoe print — the kind of print left by a lace-up work boot — and there was a distinct wedge missing in the left heel of that boot, just like the print he'd found at all the poacher's kill sites.

"Son of a bitch," he muttered, and began following the tracks — straight to the gates of Mountain Mushrooms.

The gates were locked, which was odd, considering it was nothing but a mushroom business. He could see nearly a dozen cars parked around the new trailer house. He needed to find out who was in charge and get a list of employees, but he didn't see anyone outside.

He went back to his Jeep, got out his

binoculars and then returned to the gate and began scanning the site, but nothing was moving. He jiggled the gate, thinking about climbing over and walking onto the property, but the clearly posted No Trespassing sign left him without that option, as well, at least if he wanted to stay within the law.

And he couldn't be breaking any laws, especially while he was on duty, which left him with only one option. He headed for the ranger station. This was something the boss needed to know.

Buell Smith had been sitting in the office staring out a window when he saw a man walk up to the gates and then shake them, as if trying to come in.

He could tell that the man was in uniform, and when he came back with binoculars, Buell panicked. His first thought was that the law was on to them and they were all going to be arrested. They would go to jail and wind up getting ass-fucked by their cell mates for the rest of their lives.

He didn't know what to do. Should he tell Lonnie or take care of it himself? It wasn't until he saw the man get into a Jeep and drive away that he realized it was Quinn Walker. He didn't think rangers had any authority outside the park, but even so, the incident was enough to send him into a mood that set the tone for the rest of the day.

He left work that night and headed home with new worries on his mind. What if Walker had seen something that made him suspicious? Made him think there was more going on inside the mountain than a mushroom-growing business? He was convinced his own guilt was written on his face, obvious to anyone who looked at him.

By the time Buell got home that evening he was exhausted. He hadn't slept well in weeks and now, knowing one branch of the law was nosing around the mine, he knew things were only going to get worse.

When he went into the house it was easy to see that Portia had been crying. He sighed, wondering what the hell had happened now.

"What's wrong with you?" he asked, as he took off his boots and hung up his jacket.

"The Colvins."

He frowned. "Oh. Yeah, that's a tough one. Makes you wonder what the hell kids are coming to these days. Poor Sue, losing her boy and her man all on the same day."

Portia shivered. "You ain't heard about Syd?"

Buell's gut knotted. "What about Syd?"

"When he got home this morning and found out about his brother and Willis, he shot and killed himself, too. Sue found him. Mae called to tell us. She said Sue Colvin has went and lost her mind."

Buell reeled as if he'd just been punched. Every scenario he could think of was running through his head, but the ending was always the same. What if Syd had smuggled out some coke and Willis had found it? Why else would he feel bad enough about what had happened to his brother and his nephew that he would kill himself? This was something Lonnie probably needed to know, which meant he would have to call the bastard before he went to bed. He was sick to his stomach but couldn't quite put his finger on the reason for it. All he could think was that this felt like the beginning of the end.

"Where's Gertie? Where's the kids?" he muttered, suddenly aware of how quiet the house was.

"Mama took to her room. Said she needed to pray. Since tomorrow was Saturday, I let the kids go to the lock-in at church. They're gonna watch movies and play games and stuff. One of us will have to go pick them up before ten o'clock tomorrow."

He nodded. Surely church would be a safe place for them to be.

"What's for supper?" he asked.

"Stew and cornbread."

"How long before it's done?"

"About twenty minutes on the cornbread. I just put it in the oven."

"Reckon I'll go feed the critters. I'll be back in a bit."

He quickly changed into his old work clothes and was headed out the door when something stopped him. He turned and looked back.

Portia was standing at the stove with her back to the door, slumped over in her usual self-defeated posture with her hair all slick and greasy. But just for a moment he saw her the way she'd looked when they got married — all young and slim, with a smile always on her face.

It occurred to him then that the only thing that had changed from that time to now, besides the passing of the years, was that he'd come into her life. He started to say something to her about being sorry that he hadn't done better by his family than he had, then changed his mind. It was too late to change what was done, and the less she knew about the way things were now, the better.

NINETEEN

Quinn left the ranger station feeling frustrated but not surprised. A park ranger had authority only in the reserve and nowhere else, but that didn't change the fact that he was beyond pissed, knowing the poacher he'd been tracking all this time probably worked at Mountain Mushrooms and he couldn't touch him. But he knew someone who could.

Sheriff Marlow had already been involved in investigating the case of the hiker killed by the wounded bear. Quinn guessed he would be interested in talking to the man who'd been hunting game animals out of season on federal land and wounded that bear. If they could nail him for involuntary manslaughter, then so much the better.

Quinn knew it was too late to drive down to the sheriff's office in Boone's Gap this evening, but he would call Marlow at home tonight. He wasn't going to let this slide.

As he started for home, he wondered what Mariah and Moses had been doing in his absence. Between the two of them these days, there was no telling. The odd thing about the pup's presence was that Quinn no longer worried so much about Mariah sliding into a PTSD episode alone and getting hurt. So far the puppy's presence had been a remarkable tool for stopping them at the onset. His one wish in this world was to spend a long and happy life with her at his side. But she needed to believe in herself again before that could happen.

As he took the turnoff leading to the cabin, he thought again how blessed he was to be able to call this place home. The cabin was small, but they didn't need that much space. Acquiring things like gas and groceries was an inconvenience because the place was so far off the beaten path, but the solitude suited them and their . . . situation.

The cabin came into view as he drove around the curve. When he saw Mariah and Moses on the deck, his delight was immediate. There was his family — something he'd almost given up on ever having.

When she saw him coming, Mariah waved, then came down the steps to meet him as he parked and got out.

"Welcome home, Quinn." She slid her

arms around his neck for a kiss, and he quickly obliged.

"Mmm, you smell good. Are you wearing perfume?"

She laughed. "No, I don't even own perfume. It's vanilla. I tried to make cookies. They're not completely successful, but they're edible."

"Honey! Way to go!" he said, lifting her off her feet and swinging her up into his arms, which set Moses to barking. "Hush up, boy, I saw her first."

Mariah grinned. She wasn't used to being the center of attention, but she could learn to like it.

"Moses is in trouble anyway," she said, as they started up the steps.

Quinn frowned. "What did he do?"

"Ran away while I was gardening. I trailed him all the way up to the waterfall, then into the cave. I could tell he'd been in there, but he was nowhere to be seen. Just when I was about to give up, he came running out of that passageway and jumped into my lap."

Quinn eyed the pup who trailed them inside.

"Boy, you don't know how lucky you are that she went to find you." He glanced at Mariah. She was still upset. "You may have to start tying him up when you're busy with other activities outside, at least until he gets a little older."

"I hate to, but I know you're right."

"So where are those cookies you made?"

She pointed at the cooling rack on the counter.

"They're pretty lopsided, and we didn't have any raisins to put in them, but we had oatmeal and cinnamon. Like I said, they're edible."

Quinn popped one in his mouth. "Mmm! These are good, really good. And I'll make sure to put raisins on the list next time we go shopping."

She couldn't wipe the smile off her face.

"Your mom has promised to teach me how to cook. Hang in there with me long enough and I just might catch on to more of this girl stuff."

Quinn swallowed the cookie and grabbed two more to take upstairs.

"You do whatever makes you happy, but just so you know, you're all the woman any man could want just the way you are."

"So you say," Mariah said. "But as you can see, we don't have any food cooked for supper."

"These will tide me over until we get something made," he said, and popped another cookie in his mouth. "Be right back." Then he headed for the utility room to strip off his work clothes.

To his surprise, he saw she'd hung a clean pair of old sweats and a T-shirt for him to put on without having to go upstairs.

"Hey, you," he called.

Mariah turned. "What?"

"Thank you for thinking of me."

Her eyes darkened. "I think of you all the time, but you're welcome."

"It's funny. All this time I lived here alone I never once thought of doing that. Instead I stripped down here, then went all the way upstairs to shower and change, even though there's a shower right beside the washer."

The praise filled her up, but in the back of her mind she couldn't help but wonder how long the good times would last. If she was losing it, then surely one day she would lose *him*, as well.

She turned away before he saw her tears.

But Moses knew something was wrong and nosed at her heel.

Mariah sighed, then knelt and pulled the puppy into her arms and whispered in his ear. "You know my secrets, don't you, boy?"

Moses licked her ear, then her cheek, whining softly as he sensed her unsettled state.

By the time Quinn got out of the shower

she had prepped as much as she could for their supper and was making a fresh pot of coffee.

Quinn kissed the back of her neck, then patted her rump before turning on the stove to heat up the skillet. Soon the house was filled with an array of enticing aromas.

Moses was eating his puppy kibble and Mariah was setting the table when Quinn remembered what he'd discovered.

"Oh, hey, you won't believe what I ran into today. Footprints that match the poacher's prints I found at the kill sites."

"You're kidding! Do you know who it is? Did you arrest him yet?"

"No arrests. Not sure who they belong to yet, but I think I know where he works. At Mountain Mushrooms, that business that went in at the old mine site."

"What are you going to do?"

"It's more about what *can* I do. I'm going to have to tell Sheriff Marlow. This is all out of my jurisdiction, but I sure want to be around when they ID and arrest him."

"Good job!" she said.

"It's been a good day all around." Then he stopped and looked at the pup crunching away at his dinner. "Except for one very naughty puppy."

"I'll second that," Mariah said.

Moses stopped chewing and looked up toward the ceiling, then woofed softly.

"He does that every evening," she said. "What's the deal?"

"It's probably the owl. It perches up on this roof just about every night."

"Oh, wow! Those are some pretty good ears he's got."

"And his sense of smell is even better," Quinn said. "Nothing beats a hound for following a trail, and our little redbone has the makings of a real fine dog."

Mariah glanced up at the ceiling, imagining the owl perched just overhead, and then finished setting the table.

After supper was over and the dishes were cleaned up, Mariah took Moses outside for a last trip before bedtime.

Quinn took the opportunity to call Sheriff Marlow and tell him what he'd found. Marlow answered on the third ring.

"Marlow residence."

"Hey, Sheriff, this is Quinn Walker. Sorry to be bothering you at home, but I have some information about the poacher that I think will interest you."

"I'm all ears, son. What do you know?"

"I don't know if you were aware of it, but I found a distinctive boot print up at the kill sites that has a notch out of one heel."

"No, I didn't know."

"Yeah, so today I happened to stop up near the gate to Mountain Mushrooms, and I saw that same boot print in the dirt. I trailed it all the way to the gates, but the gates are locked and I didn't see anyone around to let me in. I wanted a list of the employees, however my boss reminded me that my authority ends once I'm outside the reserve, but I damn well don't want this man to get away. He's indirectly responsible for one man's death and another man being crippled, never mind the loss of an entire pack of hunting dogs, as well as who knows how much livestock."

"I'll get that list," Marlow said, "and I'll find out myself who's wearing them boots."

"Excellent. I would consider it a favor if you'd let me know if and when you're ready to make an arrest. I'd like to be there."

"I can do that," Marlow said. "However, I'm a little tied up at the moment with this mess with the Colvin family. Got lab tests back from the coroner's office just now, and it appears we've got a new drug dealer in the area, so you might keep an eye out for anything suspicious on your rounds."

Quinn frowned. "What makes you think there's a new player?"

"Willis Colvin had cocaine in his system. Nearly pure, which is probably why he flipped plumb out."

"We've had drug issues around here for years," Quinn said.

"Yeah, meth, pot, prescription drugs, but this is high-dollar shit. And this is not a place where high-dollar drugs would be in demand, mostly because no one on Rebel Ridge has that kind of money. However, that doesn't exclude the possibility of a new drug setup around here. This would be a real good place to hide something like that. Ship it in and cut it. Ship it out and sell it. That's how some of them work."

"The only new business I know of is Mountain Mushrooms, where my poacher probably works."

"Yeah, I know all about . . . Well, shit. I didn't put it together until just now," Marlow suddenly said.

"What?"

"Syd Colvin works — worked . . . up there on the night shift. It was Syd's nephew, his brother's son, who had the coke in his system when he killed his dad. The kid was going after his own mother when he dropped dead at her feet. This morning, when Syd got home and found out what happened, he offed *him*self, too. That's about one too many coincidences for me."

The news gave Quinn the creeps. No one had said the name Lonnie Farrell yet, but he knew they were both thinking it.

"But you can't get search warrants based on coincidence, can you, Sheriff?"

"No, son, you can't. But that won't stop me from digging around until I find me a good reason to get one."

"I know you'll do all you can," Quinn said. "So I'll let you get back to your evening, but if there's anything I can do to help you, don't hesitate to ask."

"Will do, and thanks again."

Confident he'd done all he could from his side of the badge, Quinn disconnected. Now it was up to Marlow to tie up all the loose ends.

As soon as Buell finished supper, he went outside to make a call to Lonnie. He didn't want what he had to say to be overheard.

While he waited for the call to go through, he began thinking about how to begin such a deadly conversation. He knew someone was going to pay for what had happened and was damn glad he didn't cover the night shift. Considering the fact that Syd Colvin's brother and nephew were dead because of drugs, and Syd worked the night shift and killed himself after finding out what happened, it all felt like too many clues pointing at their operation. Shit was gonna hit the fan for sure, and Buell planned to be upwind when it happened.

Then Lonnie answered, and Buell shifted focus.

"I'm in the middle of something," Lonnie said. "What do you want?"

"I thought you'd be interested in knowing that Syd Colvin, a guy who worked the night shift, went home this morning and killed himself."

Lonnie blinked. Syd was the guy who'd opened the gate for Miguel and his men during the delivery.

"What the fuck for?" he asked.

"It's just a guess, but I'm thinking it's because when Syd got off work, he found out his brother and nephew were dead. It seems the nephew was all freaked out on some drug. He went and killed his daddy, then was going after his mother when he dropped at her feet, had a fit and died. Granted, Syd could have killed hisself out of grief . . . or he could have done it because he felt guilty. And if I think that, you can damn well bet the cops are gonna be thinking it, too."

Lonnie felt all the blood draining from his

head. "Does anyone know what kind of drug he was on?" Lonnie asked.

"I ain't heard, but you can be sure if the cops don't know yet, they will soon."

Lonnie felt sick. "If it came from us, then how the fuck did you let this happen? There were all kinds of safeguards set in place. Were you in on it, too? Were you getting a cut of the money?"

The skin crawled on the back of Buell's neck. This was exactly where he'd known Lonnie would go.

"You forget. I only work the day shift. One of your hotshot chemists is doing oversight on the night shift, not me, so don't you fuckin' try to pin this shit on me, you hear? All I did was call to give you a heads-up. What you do with your night crew is your decision."

"Have the cops been out?"

"No cops — not yet anyway — but there was a ranger out at the gates today, and he was looking at the mine with binoculars."

"Fuck, fuck, fuck. Who was it?"

"Quinn Walker."

Lonnie's eyes narrowed as he shuffled through the past for a face, but all he could remember were a bunch of really tall dark-haired boys.

"And where does this Walker live?"

"I don't know. He's an army vet. Came back from Afghanistan all fucked up. I heard he's living way up on the mountain, away from the rest of polite society."

"If you see him around the gates again, get him."

Buell frowned. "What the fuck do you mean, 'get him'? I'm not doing any of your dirty work. If you want him hurt, do it yourself."

"I didn't ask you to off him," Lonnie snapped. "I'll take care of that. If you see him again, I'm telling you to wrap him up for me. I'll tend to the rest, and if you screw that up, don't forget, I know where you live."

Buell's bowels roiled. "You telling me you'd actually come to this house and do me in right in front of your own mother and sister? If you think you can do that, then you better be prepared to kill them, too, because Portia would shoot you dead where you stood before she'd let you walk out."

This was spinning out of control, and Lonnie knew it. He had to rein it in before he said too much.

"Look, Buell, we're family. I'm just pissed, and I blew up at you. I didn't mean it. Thanks for letting me know about Syd. I'll check into what drugs the kid was on when he died. If it's something else, then we're in the clear. You forget, no one knows what's going on up there. We're growing mush-rooms, remember? The little truck goes out loaded with 'shrooms,' money goes in the bank under the company name, the truck comes back with supplies to grow more. If at any time the cops want to take a tour of the facility, they'll need a warrant, and there's nothing to tie us to those deaths. It's just a family tragedy. It's all cool. I'll be there before daylight, and I won't leave until this is all cleared up. This is on me, and thanks for calling."

Buell shifted the phone to his other ear.

"So, we're cool?"

"Definitely. We're cool. Just keep an eye out for Walker. If you see him hanging around the entrance again, I want him detained in any way you see fit until I can talk to him on my own."

Buell sighed. He should have known he wouldn't get all the way off the hook.

"Yeah, if I see him again," he said, and sincerely hoped that didn't happen.

It took one phone call to a computer hacker Lonnie knew to find out the results of the drug tests the M.E. had run on Willis Colvin's body. He read the email in silence, but when he got to the words "pure cocaine" his gut knotted.

He knew good and well he had the only pure cocaine on Rebel Ridge, which meant what killed the kid came from his lab. And if Syd Colvin worked the night shift and had already offed himself, then he had to assume that was how the kid had gotten the coke. What he didn't know was how Syd had managed to get it off the property, but he was going to find out and put a stop to it before all hell came down on his head.

Despite the hour, he called his pilot out to arrange a flight south, and in what felt like no time he was back in a chopper and on his way to the mine. The only plus side of this mess was that he'd been in Virginia looking at rental property, so it was going to be a quick trip back to the mine.

TWENTY

The silence inside the cabin was the result of a serious night of lovemaking. Quinn was flat on his back, so deeply asleep that he was lightly snoring. Mariah's head was on his shoulder, her arm across his chest and her leg across his knees, wearily lost in a dreamless sleep.

Moses was the first to wake up. He took off down the stairs and then ran to the window, looking up into a dark cloudless sky.

Mariah woke up next, in an immediate panic that it was happening again. The *whup-whup-whup* of spinning rotors was an unmistakable sound. She sat straight up in bed as her heart began to race.

Dear God, please make this stop.

Instead the sound got louder, and that was when she realized Moses was gone.

She rolled out of bed and looked over the railing. The pup was staring out the window, looking up. That was when it hit her. If this was just her imagination, he couldn't be hearing it, too.

She ran back to the bed and began shaking Quinn.

"Quinn! Quinn! Wake up! Do you hear that? Wake up. Listen. *Listen*. Do you hear that?"

Quinn woke abruptly, and when he saw her panic, he grabbed her arm.

"What's wrong, baby? Are you okay?"

"Listen! Do you hear that? Please tell me you hear that?"

He frowned. "Are you talking about the chopper?"

She felt like weeping. "You hear it? You really hear it?"

"Hell yes, I hear it. You'd have to be deaf not to. Why?"

She headed down the stairs, desperate to get outside before the chopper disappeared.

Quinn followed, confused by what was going on. The moment she opened the door, Moses was out on the deck and barking.

But just like before, the sky was dark.

"Where is it?" Quinn asked.

She grabbed his arms. "You hear it, right?"

He frowned. "Yes, baby, I hear it, but I don't see it, and we should. As loud as it is, it has to be low."

His frown deepened. He thought about what Marlow had told him about the possibility of a new drug operation in the area. If someone was making a pickup or a delivery, there was every possibility that he would fly blind until he'd cleared the area.

"Oh, my God, oh, my God," Mariah whispered, and started to sob.

Quinn misunderstood what was happening and thought she was spinning back into PTSD.

"Look at me, Mariah. Talk to me. Don't give in to the feeling. You're not there anymore. You're here on the mountain with me. With Moses. Can't you feel him? He's licking your bare feet."

Mariah threw herself into his arms.

"You don't understand. I don't feel like I'm about to lose it. I thought I was already gone."

Now he was really scared. "I don't know what you mean, honey, but let's go back inside out of the chill. Whatever you have to say, you know you can tell me. Okay?"

Still sobbing, she let him lead her inside and then collapsed on the sofa.

He took an afghan from the back of a rocker and put it over her bare legs, then called Moses inside and locked the door.

The pup curled up at Mariah's feet as

Quinn sat down beside her.

"I thought I was going crazy," she said.

"Why, honey? Why would you think that?"

"I've been hearing that chopper for days now, but every time I looked, nothing was there. I thought I was having hallucinations. I thought something bad was happening inside my head and that I would keep getting worse until I died."

"Oh, my God," Quinn muttered, and pulled her into his lap. "Why didn't you tell me?"

"I was scared. I didn't want you to know I wasn't getting better. I didn't want to lose you."

He held her closer, his chin on the crown of her head as his own tears welled.

"You can't lose me, no matter what," he whispered.

"But it wasn't just the chopper. I was hearing voices, too."

He frowned. "Here? You were hearing voices *here*?"

"No, in the cave. I heard them the first day you took me there, and then again the day Moses ran away."

"Why didn't you say something?"

The tears rolled unheeded down her face.

"For the same reason I didn't mention the chopper. I thought I was getting worse. I even convinced myself I might be hearing ghosts. I called your mother and asked her if she'd ever heard anyone say the cave was haunted. She said no to the ghosts, but that she'd been told when she was little that the passage inside the cave goes all the way through the mountain and comes out in the park."

Chills rolled through Quinn's body. If that was true, the only open passage he knew of that was up that high and on that side of the mountain was where the old mine had been — the mine that Lonnie Farrell now owned. If there was a new drug operation, that would be a good place to hide it. And if Mariah was hearing voices in the cave and that passage went all the way through to the old mine, then — given the way sound traveled in the cave — she could have been hearing Lonnie's employees. As to what they were doing, that remained to be seen.

"I'll tell you what, honey. Tomorrow we're going back to that cave, and I don't care how long it takes, we're gonna stand there until we both hear the voices. Okay?"

"What if we don't? What if it really is just me?"

"Then I'll assume I have hearing loss, that's what. That's how much I believe in you. And there's something you don't know.

Sheriff Marlow thinks there might be a new drug operation on the mountain. If there is, there's a possibility that it could be hidden in that old mine where they're growing those mushrooms. If Mama was right and the passage goes all the way through, the old mine is in the right spot for where it would come out. Those workers might be what you're hearing."

She tucked her head beneath his chin. Just the thought of a rational explanation gave her peace.

He pulled the afghan around her shoulders and closed his eyes, but he couldn't stop his tears. It was the terror he'd heard in her voice that broke his heart. All this time and she'd carried the burden alone. Would the day ever come when she finally trusted him enough to share her heart as fully as she shared her body?

Lonnie landed at the mine just after 1:00 a.m. Because of the hour, it was only him and his pilot, who he'd left outside on standby. No armed muscle, just his flashlight and a semiautomatic.

The cavern was dark, and there was only a small outside light burning at the office door, while the office itself was in darkness. He punched a number in his speed dial and waited while the phone rang several times before he heard a man answer.

"This is Davis."

"It's me," Lonnie said. "I'm at the office. Unlock the door. I'm coming in alone."

"Uh . . . yeah, sure, Mr. Farrell. Do you need someone to walk you down? Do you have a light?"

"I have a flashlight. Just open the fucking door."

"Yes, sir. Right away."

Both Lonnie's long stride and the set of his body would have been warning enough to those who knew him that he was angry enough to kill.

The chemist was standing in the doorway when he arrived, and from the expression on his face, Lonnie knew the men had been expecting the visit. He strode through the doorway without talking and slammed the door shut, then dropped the metal bar.

Eleven men in white jumpsuits wearing disposable masks sat at their work spaces, all frozen in the act of measuring or bagging the adulterated coke. Their street clothes were hanging on hooks on the wall where he was standing, and their work shoes were on the floor beneath the hooks. Except for disposable booties, their feet were bare. It was a cool sixty-one degrees year-round in here. He figured they were all uncomfortable, but he wasn't paying them for comfort. He couldn't see an obvious way for anyone to walk out with the coke without an accomplice, and in this case that had to be the man in charge.

Lonnie turned on Davis, his voice just above a whisper when he spoke.

"How the fuck did Syd Colvin get out of here with pure blow?"

Davis gasped. "He didn't. He *couldn't*."

Lonnie strode toward the first table. "But he did. His nephew died of a drug overdose. It's on record. But it's not this shit," he said, flinging what was sitting on the scale into Davis's face. "He had pure coke in his system when he died. Pure coke . . . like this." He grabbed Davis by the arm and shoved his face into a stack of unopened kilos.

Blood spurted from the man's nose and lip.

Davis moaned but didn't fight. He knew how close he was to dying.

"Where did Colvin sit?" Lonnie asked.

Davis pointed at the empty chair in the middle of the room.

The men sitting on either side knew they would be next on the hot seat.

"Walk me through your exit process. Now!"

Davis grabbed a handful of paper towels, wadded them up and stuffed them under his nose.

"They get up one at a time and bring me their work tray with the baggies. There's nothing but the scale and their mask left on their station when they go to change. They stop over there —" he pointed "— and strip. Their jumpsuits go into that bin. Their booties go into that basket. They have absolutely nothing on them when they go over by the door to get dressed."

"Then what?" Lonnie asked.

"Carter, the other chemist, is always at the door waiting to come on shift. He lets them out one by one. They're never together. No way can they pass anything between them unseen."

"And Colvin did the very same thing as everyone else?"

Davis nodded. "Yeah. Exactly the same. He was a hell of a worker, too. He was always going above and beyond, ready to pick up the slack if someone needed to take a shit — that kind of thing."

Lonnie's eyes narrowed thoughtfully. Colvin had been real helpful to him, too. Maybe he'd been playing them all.

"What kind of extra work are we talking about?"

Davis mopped at his bloody nose. It was beginning to throb.

"Well, after everyone leaves, we always clean up between shifts so nobody's walking out of here with blow in their hair or whatever. Syd helped with that a time or two. Said since he didn't have a woman to go home to, he didn't mind."

"Clean up how? Show me," Lonnie said.

Davis pointed to a small upright vacuum. "We use that on the floor. If you sweep, it just stirs it up into the air, and then we all go out of here with it in our eyes and hair, which isn't good."

Lonnie stared at the vacuum for a few seconds, looking at the way it was made.

"Show me how it works," he said.

Davis plugged it right in and ran it back and forth, then turned it off.

"Now what?" Lonnie asked.

Davis shrugged. "Now nothing. The floor's clean and ready for the next shift."

"What about what's inside?"

Davis turned and stared, then his cheeks turned red as he popped the container off the shaft. It was empty.

"I guess Carter dumps it."

"Where's Carter?" Lonnie snapped.

"He's in the trailer — asleep."

"Call him. Tell him to get his ass here now and not to waste time getting dressed."

Davis nodded and made the call without looking at the crew. Less than three minutes later Carter was knocking on the door.

"Let him in," Lonnie snapped.

Davis unbarred the door.

Lonnie caught the look that passed between the two chemists. He didn't know what it meant, but he was about to find out.

"You! Get in here," he said.

Carter stumbled in his haste to obey.

"You see that vacuum?"

Carter nodded.

"Did you let Syd Colvin use it?"

"Uh, no, sir, I didn't give him permission. He's not on my shift."

"But you saw him using it, right?"

He glanced at Davis and then nodded.

"So what happened when Syd was finished 'helping' you two?"

"He changed clothes like everybody else and went home."

"Did you empty the vacuum when Syd was finished?"

"Nobody emptied the vacuum," Carter said.

Lonnie picked up the empty canister and flung it at him.

"Then one of you better tell me how the fuck it got emptied and where it was dumped."

Both men looked nervous, but they were old pros in the business. They knew bosses blew up and spouted off, but they also knew that their expertise was invaluable. They hated to get an ass-chewing, but they didn't fear for their lives.

Davis shrugged. "I didn't see Syd anywhere near it when he finished."

"Neither did I," Carter added.

"Then one or both of you were in on this with him. He didn't get out of this place with my blow on his own."

"Hell no! I've been in the business for years. I'm not that stupid," Davis insisted.

"Me, either," Carter said. "You can check everything. All the totals balance out. We're not missing a fucking ounce."

"Except for what got vacuumed up," Lonnie snapped. "You two hotshots come in from the city, think you're smarter than one of these hillbillies because they talk and walk slower than you, and now you know different, don't you? Somehow Colvin slipped enough unadulterated coke out of here to get his family killed. We may never know exactly how, but we all know it happened, don't we?"

The hush that hung over the lab was like the calm before the storm. All of a sudden someone farted.

Davis grinned.

Lonnie pulled his gun and shot Davis in the foot.

The echo ricocheted off the walls and out into the open passage that led deeper into the mountain.

Davis dropped to the floor, screaming as blood ran in every direction.

Lonnie jammed the gun against the man's forehead.

"You wanna laugh at that?"

"No, no," Davis sobbed. "I'm not laughing."

Lonnie waved at Carter. "Clean him up and get this blood off the floor." He turned toward the other men, who sat frozen in their seats. "Get back to work. All of you. And if anyone tries to pull shit like this again, I'll kill the whole damn lot of you. I'll be long gone and in another country before anyone ever knows you're dead. Do you understand?"

Everyone nodded.

"Work, and do it fast!" Lonnie screamed. "Because Colvin was a greedy bastard, we may have the cops breathing down our necks. I want all of this cut and packaged within the next thirty-six hours."

The men's hands were shaking as they went back to what they'd been doing. Davis was in the corner, moaning with every breath as Lonnie walked past him.

"Shut the fuck up," he said.

Davis shuddered, then bit his lip without uttering another sound.

Lonnie threw the bar aside. "Lock this fucker up behind me. Don't make me come back here like this again."

He strode out of the mine, jumped into the waiting chopper and flew off into the night.

Quinn was dressed and gone before Mariah woke up. There was a note on his pillow.

Love you. Duty calls, but you can call me, too, if you want to hear the sound of my sexy voice. We'll check out that cave this evening, after I find out a little more about Lonnie Farrell and his "new venture."

She laughed, then rolled over and got out of bed. Her heart was lighter than it had been in weeks. Just knowing she wasn't losing her mind was the best medicine she could have hoped for. Moses was lying at the foot of the stairs. He looked like he was laughing with her.

"So, little guy, what trouble are we going to get into today?"

Since he didn't answer, she went to get dressed.

Quinn couldn't stand it, knowing in his gut that his poacher was likely inside the old mine, growing mushrooms or bagging coke or whatever the hell else Lonnie Farrell was up to in there.

Even though his boss had warned him about following up on the lead, when he came to the entrance to the mine again he slowed down. To his delight, the gates were open and the little green delivery truck was on the way out. He pulled over onto the shoulder and jumped out to wave down the driver.

"Hey! How's it going?" he asked.

The driver paused as the man with him refastened the gate. Everyone on-site had heard about the boss's late-night visit and what Syd Colvin had done. They were all antsy. Even though he knew a ranger wasn't a real cop, the uniform and the gun in Quinn's holster made him nervous.

"Fine."

"Wonder if I could ask you a couple of

questions?" Quinn asked.

The driver frowned. "We got a delivery to make."

"It won't take long. I just want to talk to the manager."

"That would be Buell Smith. He's in the office."

"Got a number?" Quinn asked, pulling out his cell.

The driver shrugged, then rattled it off as Quinn punched in the call.

"Thanks a lot," Quinn said.

The guy drove off, leaving Quinn standing in the middle of the road with his cell phone to his ear.

Buell was coming out of the nursery when his phone began to ring. He answered without checking Caller ID.

"This is Buell."

"Buell, this is Quinn Walker. I'm out here at the gate. I wonder if you'd have time to come talk to me for a sec."

Buell's heart stopped. How the hell had this man gotten his number, and why was he here? This shit just kept getting worse, and he had Lonnie's orders ringing in his head. Detain Quinn Walker.

"Uh . . . I'm real busy. What did you want to talk about?"

"I wanted to get a list of the employees working at Mountain Mushrooms."

Buell frowned. "Why do you want that?"

"Let's just say it's park business and leave it at that."

Buell sighed. Walker was askin' for it. All he had to do was go on about his business and Lonnie would never know the difference. No, it was bound to get back to Lonnie that they'd spoken, so he had to snatch the man and bring him in for Lonnie to question. On the other hand, if shit went wrong when Lonnie showed up, they couldn't have Quinn's vehicle on-site. He had to figure something out and do it quick.

"It's not my place to give out information like that, but if you want to come up to the office, I can call the boss and see if it's okay with him."

"That would be great," Quinn said.

"Just leave your car on the side of the road. I'll come get you. We're kind of limited for parking space up here."

Quinn frowned. The place didn't look all that crowded, but he would take what he could get.

"Yeah, okay."

"I'll be right there," Buell said, then hailed one of the men, a guy named Goslin, working in the nursery. "Ride down to the gate with me and unlock it while I pick up a visitor."

Goslin nodded and jumped into Buell's truck. They took off down the road. When they got to the gate, Buell handed the keys to Goslin, who got out, unlocked the gate and then held it open for Quinn to walk through.

"Thanks," Quinn said, and couldn't help checking the tracks the man left in the dirt. They were clean. No notch in the heel. He got into the truck and nodded a hello. "Buell, I'm thinking you married Lonnie Farrell's sister, Portia, am I right?"

Buell nodded.

"So what's it like working for your brother-in-law?" Quinn asked.

"Interesting," Buell said, watching in the rearview mirror as Goslin jumped into the truck bed, then putting the truck in gear and turning around.

"How's the mushroom business?" Quinn asked.

"Growing daily," Buell said. "Picked up another buyer down in Mount Sterling this week, and a couple in Lexington. That makes almost a dozen regular customers now, and they're buying everything we can give them." He pulled to a stop.

"We're here. Come on into the office. I'll

give Lonnie a call."

Quinn got out, waved to Goslin, who jumped out and headed back deeper into the cavern, and then waited for Buell to lead the way.

Instead Buell stopped.

"Go right on in and take a seat. I'm gonna make the call to Lonnie out here. Better signal and all. If he says it's okay, then I'll dig out the list for you."

"I appreciate it," Quinn said, and went inside.

Buell watched him head into the office and waited until the door was closed behind him, then quickly called Lonnie's number.

He answered promptly.

"This better be good news," he snapped.

"I have Quinn Walker sitting in the office. He says he wants a list of the employees."

Lonnie's pulse kicked. "Don't let him get away. Knock him out. Tie him up and put him in the passage at the back of the lab where he can't make any trouble. I want to talk to him myself."

"If I do that, then we both know you aren't gonna let him go. It means I'll be aiding and abetting in a man's death."

"You've already done that, damn it. Three men. Their names were Colvin. Now do what I tell you or we'll all go down."

"We could just give him the list and let him go about his business."

Lonnie snapped. "Listen, you dumb fuck. His business is obviously to nose around in our business or he wouldn't be there. Now do what I told you. I'll be there after dark."

The line went dead in Buell's ear. He sighed, wondering how everything had gone wrong so fast. He went back to his truck, got a couple of things out of the truck bed and headed for the office.

Quinn was looking at a chart that had been tacked to the wall and showed different varieties of mushrooms when Buell walked in behind him.

"What kind of mushrooms are you guys growing here?" he asked.

Buell hit him in the back of the head with a crowbar. Quinn dropped.

Within moments Buell had him tied up and blindfolded. He searched Quinn's pocket for the keys to his Jeep, then threw Quinn's body over his shoulder and headed for the tunnel where the lab was housed, phoning Carter as he went.

"It's me, Buell," he said when Carter answered. "Open the door. I have a package."

"Okay," Carter said, and after a quick glance at the crew, he went to the door and lifted the bar. He opened the door just as Buell arrived.

When Carter saw the body over Buell's shoulder, his eyes bugged.

"Who the fuck is that?"

"The law," Buell said. "Lonnie said to hold him." He walked past Carter and through the cutting room.

The men sitting at the tables stared.

"Who is that?" someone asked.

"Quinn Walker," Buell said.

"Is he dead?" another asked.

"Not yet," Buell said, and walked out the open end of the lab and into the natural passage at the end.

He kicked a couple of rocks aside, dropped Quinn against the wall then untied the ropes and rearranged them so Quinn was hog-tied, his hands and feet bound together behind him, with a loop around his neck connected to the ropes at his hands and feet. There was no way he could move without strangling himself.

He looked down, eyeing the dark patch of blood in Walker's hair, and then out of curiosity felt for a pulse in his neck. It was still there. He went back into the drug room, peeled a strip of duct tape from a roll on Carter's desk, then went back into the shaft and slapped it across Walker's mouth.

Confident he'd done what he'd been ordered to do, he walked out and grabbed
another worker from the nursery.

"I need you to come with me," he said.

"I don't want no part of what's going on
over on the other side," the man complained.

Buell frowned. "Yeah, neither do I, but
we're here, and in the eyes of the law, we're
all guilty as sin. I gotta go move a vehicle. I
need you to drive behind me in my truck
and bring me back."

The man frowned but had no recourse.

A short while later, Buell was in Walker's
Jeep and heading into the park. The man
was a ranger. It stood to reason he would
be doing ranger business all day. Wouldn't
be the first time someone went missing in
the Daniel Boone Reserve, and it probably
wouldn't be the last. About four miles in he
pulled over and killed the engine. He got
out of the Jeep, left the door open and the
keys in the ignition, then told the other man
to shove over, got into his truck and drove
away. Neither man spoke a word on the way
back to the mine, where they went their
separate ways in silence.

TWENTY-ONE

Quinn came to in darkness and pain. He could hear voices, but there was such a roaring in his ears that he couldn't make out the words. He couldn't remember what had happened or how the hell he'd got here — wherever here was.

When he tried to move his arms, it felt as if they were being ripped from their sockets. The coppery scent of blood was in his nose, and there was duct tape over his mouth. He quickly realized that if his nose started to bleed he wouldn't be able to draw air and he would suffocate. Even worse, every time he tried to roll, a rope tightened around his throat. His only effort at a scream emerged as nothing more than a muffled groan. Mariah's face slipped through his mind. It hit him that he might never see her again. The sadness that came with that thought overwhelmed him.

Mariah was trying not to panic.

It was after dark, and Quinn hadn't called her all day. Even more concerning, he hadn't answered her calls. According to his note he'd planned to be home before dark. Surely if there'd been an emergency at the park he would have called. She didn't know what to do, but her gut feeling was that something was wrong.

After another hour of pacing she finally sat down and called Ryal. She needed a shoulder to lean on, and his was the first that came to mind. His voice was full of laughter when he answered, and she knew she was about to ruin the mood.

"Ryal, it's me, Mariah."

"Well, hello, sister. How goes it?"

"Quinn hasn't come home."

The humor in Ryal's voice disappeared. "When did you talk to him last?"

"I wasn't even awake when he left this morning. There was just a note saying he'd be back before dark. But he never called all day, and he hasn't answered any of my calls. I didn't know who to contact at the ranger station to see if there'd been any emergencies, so I'm dumping my fear at your feet."

"Give me a couple of minutes. I'll call you right back," he said.

The line went dead, but Mariah already

felt better.

She paced, waiting for Ryal's call. The time stretched from a couple of minutes to five and then ten, and she was ready to panic when the phone finally rang.

"Ryal?"

"Yeah. Sorry it took me so long. I couldn't get any answer at the station and had to run down one of the other rangers at home."

"Has there been an emergency? Has Quinn been sent someplace where he just can't get a phone signal?"

"There's no emergency. He never checked in at the station this morning. No one knows where he is."

Mariah's legs went out from under her. She sank to the floor, her heart pounding in her ears.

"Mariah? Are you there?"

Her voice was shaking. "Yes. What do we do?"

"They're already initiating a search. They'll look for his vehicle first, and if he's not with it, they'll go from there."

"Oh, my God, I can't believe this is happening."

Ryal was worried, but he wasn't going to let on.

"It's probably nothing. He's probably stranded somewhere and pissed off because he's stuck on foot."

"Yes, maybe that's it," Mariah said, unconvinced. "Did you call Dolly?"

"Yes. She's on her way over to you."

Tears welled so fast that Mariah never felt them coming. "She is?"

"Yeah, and Meg's with her."

"They didn't have to do that," she whispered.

"Yes, they did, honey. It's what family does. You don't go through shit alone, okay?"

"Okay, and thank you, Ryal. I didn't know what to do."

"We'll find him, and he'll probably be upset at the uproar we've caused."

"I won't care how upset he is. I just want him to be okay. If you hear anything at all, call me."

"I will. Beth sends her love. If you need us, you know where we are."

"Okay."

She hung up, then took a deep breath and prayed to God that this wasn't as bad as she feared. About fifteen minutes later she saw lights coming up the driveway. For a few fleeting moments she let herself hope it was Quinn, but when Moses began barking she knew it had to be a strange car.

She turned on the porch light just as Dolly

and Meg came up the steps.

"Oh, honey," Dolly said, and held out her arms as Mariah walked into her embrace.

"I got scared," Mariah said, and then started to cry. "This isn't like him. I was afraid he was somewhere hurt and expecting me to help."

"You did exactly the right thing," Meg said, and shut the door behind them.

Moses licked Meg's knee and Dolly's leg, and then followed Mariah back to the sofa and sat on her feet.

"Look at that pup," Meg said. "He's right on your feet."

"That's what he does when he knows I'm upset," Mariah said, and laid her hand on the puppy's head.

"Talk to me, honey," Dolly said. "Did Quinn mention anything about what was going on at work last night?"

"Yes. He was all excited because he'd finally gotten a big break in locating the poacher he's been tracking. You know, the one who wounded the bear."

Dolly leaned forward. "What did he say?"

"He said his boss wouldn't let him follow up because he had no authority outside the park."

"Yes, that's true, but do you know what he found or where he found it?"

"Apparently the poacher has a wedge cut into the heel of one boot that makes his footprint unique. Then yesterday evening on the way home he saw it again, just outside the entrance to Mountain Mushrooms. He tried to get in, but the gate was locked. He said he wanted to get a list of the employees' names but his boss told him to drop it. But you know Quinn — he wasn't ready to let it go. He called the sheriff from home last night and told him what was going on."

Dolly felt sick. She knew her son well enough to know that he wasn't the kind of man who would quit on anything.

"What did Marlow say?" Dolly asked.

"That he'd take care of it. That's all I know."

Dolly kissed Mariah's cheek. "You've done everything right. Have you eaten supper?"

"No. I was waiting for Quinn."

Meg caught her mother's look. "I'll rustle something up for all of us. Sit tight."

"I'm going to call Ryal and let him know what you just told me," Dolly said, and gave Mariah's leg a quick pat. "You sit tight, sugar. When the Walkers get behind a project, stuff starts happening."

She got up to make her call, then couldn't

get a signal.

"Darn mountains. I'm going to go out on the deck and see if I can get through," Dolly said, and went out the front door.

Moses was still sitting on Mariah's feet with his chin resting on her knee. The look in his eyes was so loving and so trusting that she wanted to weep. She was among people who cared about her, and yet she'd never felt more alone.

Quinn had been in and out of consciousness for what seemed like hours. He still had no memory of what had happened or where he could possibly be. Even though men were talking nearby, none of what they were saying clued him in as to where he was.

The pain in his arms and legs had moved to a level he'd never lived through before, and he wondered how long he could stay like this without dying. Someone kept moaning nearby. He didn't know he was hearing himself. He prayed to pass out and stay that way, but even that was denied him. He was losing hope fast when he began to hear a commotion nearby. There was a flurry of footsteps, and then a sharp, angry-sounding question.

"Where is he, Buell?"

"Out in the shaft, Lonnie. Right where

you said to put him."

And just like that Quinn remembered getting in the truck with Buell Smith and coming to the mine. So that was where he was and who had put him here.

But why?

"What the fuck?" Lonnie yelled when he saw how Walker had been tied. "I said restrain him, not strangle him before I even got to talk to him. Untie him now, and get that rope off his neck."

Buell sighed. There was no way to make this man happy, but he did as he was told.

Even when the ropes loosened and Quinn's arms were momentarily free, he couldn't feel them. All that mattered was that the rope around his neck was gone and he could take a deep breath without fear of strangling.

There was a sudden scent of mint beneath his nose, and then someone yanked the duct tape off his mouth. He moaned.

"Sit him up," Lonnie snapped.

Hands yanked at Quinn's body, dragging him backward and pulling him upright until he was leaning against a wall. He felt like a rag doll. His mind was working, but there were no bones in his body to hold him up.

"Open your mouth," Lonnie said.

Like hell.

"I said open your mouth, damn it," Lonnie snapped, and splashed water in his face. "It's just water. I want to talk. Your mouth has to be dry."

Quinn licked his lips, tasted the water and opened his mouth.

Lonnie poured a good half a bottle into Quinn's mouth, then laughed when he choked.

"Sorry. Didn't know you needed to be told to swallow. I thought you knew enough to do that on your own."

Rage came swiftly, blinding Quinn to everything but the urge to silence that laugh.

"So, Quinn Walker, you've gotten yourself into a mess of trouble, haven't you? I understand you wanted a list of my employees. Exactly why is that?" Lonnie kicked the bottom of Quinn's boot. "I'm here. You wanted to talk, so talk. Why did you want the list?"

"Take off my blindfold," Quinn said.

Lonnie frowned. "That's not a question. It wasn't even a request. In fact, it sounded like an order to me, and I'm the only one who gives orders around here."

Quinn didn't move. He wasn't giving the bastard an inch.

Lonnie leaned over and slapped the side of Quinn's face so hard that his head bounced back against the wall.

Quinn grunted from the impact, tasted blood in his mouth and spat.

"You bastard. You spit on my shoe," Lonnie snarled, and slapped him again.

"If you hadn't made my damn mouth bleed I wouldn't have had to spit, and if you'd taken off my blindfold I could have seen where I was aiming."

Lonnie thought about being pissed but surprised himself by grinning.

"You're absolutely right. I take full responsibility for that error. My bad."

He yanked the blindfold off Quinn's face and then leaned in so close Quinn could smell that same scent of mint on his breath and realized it must be mouthwash.

Lonnie smiled. "Now that we're looking at each other in such a congenial fashion, what the fuck did you want with a list of my employees?"

"Because somewhere on that list is the name of a man who's been poaching up in the backcountry. He thinks he's real smart, killing the animals using a bow and arrow instead of a gun, because an arrow is silent. But he made a real big mistake a while back. He shot a bear — a real big black bear — but he didn't kill it. That arrow festered, and it got sick and couldn't hunt, and then it came across a pair of hikers. The bear killed one man and crippled the other. The federal government wants the man for poaching, and the law wants him for involuntary manslaughter, because it's his fault that bear went rogue and killed a man."

Lonnie blinked. He couldn't believe what he was hearing. This didn't have a single damned thing to do with his operation. All this fuss, and it could have been avoided. He turned and looked at Buell like he'd never seen him before.

"You couldn't just ask him why he wanted the list? He could have had it. This has nothing to do with us, and yet you had to make it into a big deal."

Buell glared. "I did exactly what you told me to do. That and nothing more."

Still pissed, Lonnie looked back at Quinn.

"So tell me, how do you know it's one of my employees? It could be anybody, even an outsider who doesn't even live around here."

"No, it's someone who works here. I know because of the prints I found at the kill sites. There's a notch in the heel of one boot, and yesterday, when I stopped along the road to check my vehicle, I saw that same print in the dirt. I trailed it to the gate before it disappeared. For starters, I want the man who is wearing those shoes to explain how his boot print wound up at those kill sites."

Lonnie frowned. "But you don't have any authority here, do you, ranger man?"

"No, but Sheriff Marlow does, and I've already told him what I found. He'll be here on his own soon enough."

Lonnie leaped to his feet. "You already told the sheriff?" He turned on Buell. "Damn you. All you had to do was ask a couple of questions and this could all have been avoided."

Buell glared.

Lonnie frowned, then squatted down beside Quinn and looked him in the eyes.

"What am I going to do with you? You're useless to me. I have no reason to keep you alive."

It was no more than Quinn had feared, but hearing it said aloud was shocking. He had to find a way to make Farrell think he had a secret they needed to know. Then he realized Farrell wouldn't know about the lab results on Willis Colvin. He wouldn't know the authorities already suspected him. He grinned.

Lonnie frowned. "What's so funny?"

"You'll find out soon enough," Quinn said.

Lonnie hit him several times in rapid succession with no more emotion than if he

436

was brushing crumbs off his shirt.

"I don't hear you laughing anymore. Are you still laughing?" Lonnie asked.

Quinn groaned. His vision was blurry, and the area he could see was growing smaller. But instead of begging for mercy, he looked up, locked gazes with Lonnie and, even though he knew what was coming, smiled again.

After that he lost count of the blows, until finally he passed out in the middle of a curse raining down on his head.

As Quinn slid sideways onto the floor of the old mine, his dog tags slid out from beneath his shirt onto the dirt. Lonnie eyed them curiously, then rocked back on his heels and stood up. His knuckles were burning. The rage-sparked adrenaline was beginning to ebb, leaving him shaking and spent.

"Stupid, hardheaded fucker." He pointed at Carter, who was standing by in silent horror. "You, throw some water on his face, and when he comes to, come and get me. I'll find out what he's smiling about, and then I'll drop his ass down one of these shafts. No one laughs at me."

Long after midnight had come and gone, and at Mariah's urging, they'd sent Dolly to sleep in the loft. Meg and Mariah pulled the sofa out into a bed for themselves. Meg drifted off to sleep with her hand on Mariah's arm.

Mariah couldn't sleep for worry, and she didn't even want to try, because she knew the turmoil of the evening had set her up for combat. She didn't want Meg and Dolly to see her flip out again.

She lay quietly in the bed with a knot in her gut, staring up at the ceiling, wondering if the owl was up there tonight, wondering if it knew about Quinn. Had he seen him on his night flight? Was Quinn lying at the bottom of some cliff? Had he been attacked by an animal? Every scary scenario she could think of came and went until exhaustion claimed her, and then so did the war.

Mariah had never known there was a taste to fear until Afghanistan, and then it was with her daily — sharp, metallic, with just a pinch of blood. Tonight the taste was strong as they took cover from a sniper who had them pinned down in the bones of a shelled-out house. Her training kicked in as their unit returned fire. Mortar fire was exploding all around them. The night sky was lit up like the Fourth of July, and someone was screaming in pain. Seconds later the house they were in went up in a ball of fire.

Mariah sat up with a gasp, her body

bathed in sweat, her heart pounding against her chest. She rolled out of bed and ran to the window, but the night sky was clear. When she turned and saw Meg, not Quinn, in the bed, she remembered and wanted to weep. If she could only wake up from this nightmare as easily as she had awakened from those of the past. She'd come here to heal and find peace, only to learn that some wounds never heal, and there was no escaping evil, no matter how far you ran or how high you went.

Her fear was so strong that she felt as if she were choking. She looked toward the kitchen, half expecting to see Quinn standing at the stove teasing her about something she'd done, but he wasn't there. She'd lost her anchor. Tears would have been a relief, but she was too numb for emotion.

Moses padded across the floor to where she was standing and put a cold nose on the back of her leg. She knelt and put her arms around his neck.

He whined once, soft and low.

"I know. I'm scared, too," she whispered. Then she got up and went to the door. "Do you need to go out?"

Moses trotted outside onto the deck, paused at the steps and looked back.

"Go on," she said. "I'll be right here."

The pup bounded down and into the grass, made a few quick circles out in the starlit meadow, did his business then ran back. She locked the door, and then, after sharing a cookie with Moses, she went back into the living room, curled up in Quinn's chair with the pup in her lap and finally drifted off to sleep.

It was just after daybreak, and Mariah had already showered and dressed, and coffee was freshly made. Moses was noisily crunching his kibble. Dolly was still asleep, but the scent of fresh-brewed coffee had gotten Meg out of bed. She was sitting at the kitchen table sipping her first cup when Moses looked up and barked.

"Someone's coming," Mariah said, and ran to the door. "It's Ryal."

Upstairs, Dolly began stirring as the others ran out to meet him.

Mariah knew the moment she saw him that he'd been up all night, and from the look on his face she could tell there was news.

He didn't waste time. "We found his Jeep four miles into the park. The door was open. The keys were in the ignition, but he was nowhere in sight."

Mariah moaned as Ryal put his arms

around her and gave her a hug.

"Come inside, both of you," Meg said. "Ryal, there's fresh coffee. Mariah, come sit with me. We can hear what he has to say sitting down as easily as not."

"What's happening?" Dolly called down from upstairs.

"Come down, Mama. There's news."

As soon as the women had gathered, Ryal began to talk.

"Here's what I know. It took a little while to notify Sheriff Marlow, then get the search team organized and decide on starting points. Considering the size of the park, our immediate resources were small, and without knowing which direction to look, any decision we made was automatically going to leave most of the park unexplored. One of the other rangers found the Jeep, and he also found an interesting clue beside it."

"What?" Mariah asked.

"A boot print with a wedge-shaped notch in the heel."

Mariah felt sick. "The poacher. Quinn went after that poacher on his own, even after his boss and the sheriff told him not to, and now he's . . ." She couldn't make herself go on.

Dolly slid into a chair at the table.

"So what's happening now?" she asked.

"They're setting up a new search site where they found the truck."

"No, that's wrong," Mariah insisted. "They need to be looking at the old mine where Quinn found the footprints. We won't find Quinn until we find out who the poacher is."

"She's right," Dolly agreed. "Has anyone called Jake Doolen? He and his dogs could find Quinn. I just know it."

Ryal frowned. "I've told you everything I know, which isn't much."

Mariah felt helpless. "This is ridiculous. Everything bad that's happening is coming from that mine. Quinn said the sheriff thinks there's a new drug operation on the mountain. There was pure cocaine in that dead boy's body. I grew up on the streets. I know that unadulterated drugs are just as deadly as drugs cut with bad stuff. If there's a drug operation at the mine and Quinn was nosing around there looking for his poacher, some very bad people could have gotten the wrong idea about his interest. People who run drugs are as lethal as the shit they sell. If Quinn's in there and still alive, he won't be for much longer."

Ryal was stunned. "I didn't know about the drug report on Willis Colvin."

"It's probably not public information,"

she said.

He stood abruptly. "I'm going home. I need to make some calls, and all the numbers I need are there. If I hear anything new I'll let you know."

Mariah was pale, but oddly calm. "Thank you for coming, Ryal."

He turned and hugged her. "You're family, and you're welcome. I'll be in touch."

At that point Dolly stood up. "Meg, get your stuff. We're going home to tend to the chickens and milk the cow, and then I'm calling the Doolens. There's nothing that says I can't hire them on my own." She looked at Mariah. "Will you be all right here on your own for a bit? We're coming right back."

"I'll be fine," Mariah said. "Besides, I won't be alone. I have Moses."

Moses heard his name, sidled up beside her and put his nose in the palm of her hand. Mariah slid her hand along his muzzle to the top of his head.

Within minutes they were gone, but there was a plan forming in the back of Mariah's mind as she began digging through the closets, and then out in the storage room off the deck, looking to see what was available.

■ ■ ■ ■

Beth met Ryal at the door as he parked. Rufus barked once from where he was lying but didn't bother getting up.

She could see how tired Ryal was, and she saw the worry in his eyes.

"Any news?"

"They found his truck with the keys in it, door wide-open and the poacher's footprint in the dirt beside it."

Beth felt sick. "No, oh, no, what are they doing? Do they think he's —"

"I don't know what they think," Ryal muttered. "But something Mariah said set me to thinking. Do you happen to know where we put Agent Ames's phone number?"

Beth's eyes widened. "As in FBI Agent Ames? The man who helped get me back to testify at Ike Pappas's trial?"

"Yeah, that one."

"I think so. Come with me. You need food and a shower and about eight hours of good sleep."

"I can sleep when Quinn is home, but I'll take some breakfast. And that number."

Beth dug through the desk drawer and finally pulled out a business card.

"Here it is. Do you want your eggs fried

or scrambled?"

"Fried, please, and two pieces of toast. I'll be there as soon as I've gotten hold of Ames."

Ryal sat down in a chair by the window as he made the call. Two years had come and gone since Beth had testified at the trial. He hoped Ames remembered him. The phone rang three times, but just as Ryal feared it was about to go to voice mail it was answered.

"Ames speaking."

"Ames, this is Ryal Walker, from Rebel Ridge, Kentucky. Do you remember me?"

Ames smiled. "I'm not likely to forget you and your people. You did something the FBI failed miserably at. You managed to keep your girl alive and help us put a very bad man behind bars. So what can I do for you?"

"Do you remember my brother Quinn?"

Ames thought. "Isn't that the one who'd been in Afghanistan? The sharpshooter?"

"Yes. Listen, he's gone missing, and it's kind of an involved story, but I'd appreciate it if you'd hear me out, because I'm calling in a favor."

Ames leaned forward, resting his elbows on the kitchen table. "I'm listening."

Ryal began to explain what had happened, all the way from when Quinn found the hikers to the suspicious "new mushroom" business to the Colvin family's drug-related deaths, ending with finding Quinn's abandoned vehicle only a few hours ago.

"The problem is that the sheriff's hands are tied because he doesn't have enough evidence against the owner of the mushroom farm to get a search warrant. And the park service has no authority off the reserve."

"That's quite a mess you have going," Ames said.

"You have no idea. Will you help?"

Ames frowned. "Here's what I can do right away. I have a friend in the DEA. We'll do some digging and see what we can turn up on this mine owner. What was his name again?"

"Lonnie Farrell. He's been living in Chicago for years, but he was born and raised here on the mountain. He got arrested for making and selling meth when he was fourteen, and spent the next four years in a juvenile detention. When he got out he went to Chicago, and he's been working for some shady guy up there ever since."

"You said this Farrell set up his mushroom business in an abandoned coal mine?"

"Yes, sir."

"Do you happen to know the name of the mine?"

"Everybody up here knows it. It was the Foley Brothers Mine but it's been shut down for twenty or thirty years, at least."

"Okay, thanks. That gives me a place to start. Let me see what I can find out."

"One more thing. I realize I'm not telling you anything you don't already know, but if, by some small miracle, my brother is still alive, he won't be for long. If there *is* a new drug operation in the area, once the people running it hear they're under suspicion, they'll just pick up and leave. And they're not going to leave my brother alive when they do."

"I hear you. I'll call you as soon as I know something."

Ryal sighed. He'd done all he could do. "Thank you for hearing me out."

"Hey, like you said, I owe you. Tell your Beth that Agent Ames says hello."

"Yes, sir, I will."

"Ryal. Your breakfast is ready," Beth called.

Ryal said goodbye to Agent Ames and hung up the phone. "Be right there."

When Jake Doolen heard Dolly Walker's voice on the phone, he was so startled that he sloshed coffee out of his cup.

"Well, good morning, Dolly. This is a nice surprise."

"Thank you, Jake, but this isn't a social call. We have trouble. Quinn's gone missing. They found his truck early this morning, but he was nowhere around, and the law is fiddle-footing around wasting time on warrants and judges while my boy's life may be hanging by a thread. Will you help me?"

Jake sat the cup down and turned off the fire under his eggs.

"Me and the boys will be there within the hour."

"Thank you, Jake, and I just want you to know that I'm ready to pay you whatever the going rate is for tracking."

"No, ma'am, you won't," Jake said. "We're friends, Dolly. We go back a long ways. If this was my boy you'd do the same. I don't want to hear any more talk about money passing between us, is that understood?"

Jake's kindness was her undoing. Dolly's chin began to tremble.

"Yes, I understand."

"See you soon."

Ames knew the FBI wasn't going to be pleased about what he was doing, but in his mind the bureau owed the arrest and successful conviction of crime lord Ike Pappas to Beth Venable's willingness to testify against him even after the agency had failed to protect her. After Pappas made three failed attempts on her life, she had given up on the feds and enlisted the help of her relatives in Kentucky to keep her safe, which they had done. He firmly believed she would not be alive today if she hadn't left L.A.

The search he had run through the FBI database on Lonnie Farrell had come up with interesting information, but nothing he could use to get a search warrant for the old mine. He had also done a search on the mine itself, and found the recent sale and the name of the new owner, but that was old news. They already knew Farrell had bought the mine.

Ames was curious to talk to the original owner, a woman named Sylvia Dixon whose current residence was in Louisville, Kentucky. But since he was on the West Coast and the need for haste was strong, there was no time for him to travel down there. What he did have was the name of a DEA agent in Kentucky who could rattle Ms. Dixon's cage for him.

The agent's name was Mike Lancaster. He was a former NFL running back and a bulldog when it came to chasing down the bad guys.

He put in the call and then began thinking how he could best introduce the problem.

"Lancaster."

"Uh, Mike, this is Joe Ames."

"Hey, Joe, arrested any bad guys lately?"

Ames grinned. "More than you, I'm betting."

Mike laughed. "That's a hell of a way to talk if you called for a favor."

"You're so right. I take it all back."

"So, you *do* want a favor. What's going on?"

Ames began to relate Ryal's story as it had been relayed to him. He was surprised that Mike never once interrupted or belittled what he was hearing as unworthy of the DEA's interest.

"And that's all I know for sure," he said after wrapping up. "Does your team have anything on Farrell that would get a search warrant for that mine?"

"Hang on," Mike said, and keyed in some names on his computer, then waited for the info to come up. "Here's something interesting about Chicago's drug trade. There are reports of a dealer bringing in some high-quality shit and ruffling a few feathers, but no one seems to know where it's coming from."

"That's not what I needed to hear," Ames said. "Okay, I knew this wasn't going to be easy. Now comes that favor."

"Talk to me."

"The previous owner of the mine lives in Louisville. I need you to go talk to her face-to-face. Scare the crap out of her if need be, and see what she says about the man who bought her out. Find out what he paid for it. What he told her he was planning to do with it. That kind of stuff. I know we're just fishing here, but we're desperate."

"Yeah, sure, I can do that," Mike said. "Give me her info."

He took down the specifics, then logged off his computer, grabbed his gun and his partner, Louis Townsend, and headed for the door.

They arrived at the condo without incident, rode up in the elevator talking about the upcoming football season, and were still talking odds and players when Sylvia Dixon came to the door.

Sylvia was feeling good. She'd just gotten a manipedi at her favorite hair salon and was getting ready to meet a friend for lunch when the doorbell rang. After a quick peek through the security peephole, she frowned. Strangers.

"Who is it?" she called out.

Mike and Louis flashed their badges. "DEA, ma'am," Mike said. "We just want to ask you some questions."

Sylvia's heart skipped a beat. In the back of her mind she'd been expecting something like this ever since the sale of the old mine had gone through. She was nervous, but she just reminded herself that she'd done nothing wrong as, reluctantly, she opened the door.

Mike took the lead. "Ma'am, my name is Agent Lancaster. This is my partner, Agent Townsend. May we come in?"

"Yes, of course," she said, and led the way back into the living area. "Please take a seat."

Mike and Louis sat beside each other on the sofa, opposite the single chair Sylvia had chosen.

"Now, what's this all about?" she asked.

"We understand you recently sold some property near Rebel Ridge, Kentucky, to a man named Lonnie Farrell. Is this correct?"

She smiled politely, as if rewarding them for the right answer.

"Yes, it is, although to be fair, I never met him."

"Then how *did* this sale take place?" Mike asked.

"I got a call out of the blue from a man who said he represented a company who wanted to buy my granddaddy's old mine. I told him that the mine had played out long ago, but he assured me he wasn't interested in mining."

"What did he give you as his reason?" Mike asked.

"He intended to put in a mushroom farm."

"I see. And what exactly were you asking for it?"

"Oh, I never had it up for sale. In fact, I was surprised to find out he even knew of its existence."

Mike leaned forward. "He just cold-called you?"

"Uh, yes, I think so, if that means what I think it does."

"It means he called you and offered to buy a property you didn't have for sale."

Sylvia smiled again. "Yes, that's what he did."

Mike eyed Louis, then made a few notes before questioning her again.

"So obviously you sold it to him, but do you mind telling me what he paid for it?"

She fidgeted slightly behind the smile she

still wore. "I don't mind at all. It set me up nicely after my recent divorce, so I was glad for the offer. He gave me a half million dollars."

A muscle jerked at the corner of Mike's eye.

Louis Townsend leaned forward and grinned.

"You must have thought you'd just won the lottery," he said.

Sylvia's smile slipped. "Well, I wasn't going to turn it down, that's for sure. After all, it was a played out old mine. If someone wanted to buy it, I was certainly willing to sell."

Mike didn't bother to hide a frown. "You knew damn good and well he wasn't going to pay you that kind of money to grow mushrooms."

Sylvia's chin came up. "It was of no consequence to me what he did with it. I had land that was just lying there. He wanted it. I sold it. There's nothing illegal about that."

"You're right. There's nothing illegal. I'm curious, though. I don't suppose he was giving you a cut on the 'mushroom' profits?"

Sylvia's cheeks turned red. "I never met the man. I got the amount agreed upon after I signed the papers and that was that. Now, if you have nothing further to ask me, I'd like you to leave. I'm late for a lunch date with a friend."

Mike and his partner stood up. "Thank you for your help," he said. "If we have any other questions, we'll know where to find you."

Sylvia didn't comment, and when they stepped out into the hall she slammed the door shut behind them.

Mike looked at Louis and grinned. "I think we hit a nerve."

Louis nodded. "Let's go talk to the boss. I'd seriously like to pay a visit to this mine and talk to the owner myself. Maybe take a little tour of the property. I like mushrooms on my pizza. I'd be interested to see where they're grown."

"I like them sautéed in butter and piled on my steak," Mike said.

"Um, you're making me hungry just talking about it," Louis said.

"Then let's see what we can do about rattling this rat cage. I'm curious who and how many will fall out."

TWENTY-TWO

Mariah was still digging through the storage room off the back deck when her cell phone began to ring. She crossed her fingers that it would be Quinn, and her heart sank when she heard Dolly's voice.

"Hello, honey. I'm just checking on you," Dolly said.

Mariah stepped outside and stared off across the meadow. It was so beautiful today. How could everything be so messed up when the world was so pretty?

"I'm fine. Moses and I are outside. Have you heard anything?"

"No, but I wanted you to know what I'm doing on Quinn's behalf. I called Jake Doolen. You remember him? I told him everything you told us, along with what's going on with the sheriff and the rangers. He and his boys and their dogs are already on the job. He said there's plenty they can do to help find Quinn. Have faith, honey."

Mariah pinched the bridge of her nose to keep from crying.

"I do have faith."

"Then we're doing our part," Dolly said. "Either Meg or I will be over later, so don't worry, okay?"

"I'll be fine on my own," Mariah said.

"You might be, but we wouldn't. The only thing we can do for Quinn at this point is take care of you, and that's what we're doing, so you're gonna have to deal with us."

Mariah managed a chuckle through the tears. "Well, all right, then," she said. A moment later she hung up, then went back into the storage room and continued to dig.

So far she had a good long length of climbing rope laid out on the deck. A can of neon-yellow spray paint. A hunting knife and a large backpack with an internal frame. It had been a while since she'd carried one, but her muscles hadn't gotten that soft. She had two flashlights, a set of extra batteries, two bottles of water, a roll of duct tape and a first-aid kit.

What she was looking for, without success, was extra ammunition for his rifle. All she had found in the house was in a box on the shelf in Quinn's closet. Twenty-two rounds. It wasn't much if she wound up in a firefight.

She glanced at her watch. It was just after noon. Time to get moving, before someone came back and tried to stop her.

She stuffed everything into the backpack, loaded her rifle and put the extra ammo in a side pocket for easy access, then went back inside with Moses still at her heels.

She stood for a few moments, letting the quiet of the house surround her, then closed her eyes and dropped her head.

"God, You know what I need. All the help You can spare would be appreciated."

It was the closest thing she had to a prayer.

After a quick trip to the bathroom, she tied a jacket around her waist, filled up a third water bottle from the tap and grabbed the last two oatmeal cookies from the batch she'd made the other day. It felt like a lifetime since that evening. God willing, they would have another day like that again — and soon.

She went out, carefully closing the door behind her, then shouldered her backpack, grabbed the rifle and headed off the porch. Moses was right beside her, bouncing through the grass and looking up at her as if to say, "Isn't this grand?"

She stopped suddenly, realizing she couldn't take the puppy where she was going.

"Oh, Moses, I'm sorry, buddy, but you can't go with me this time," she said.

She dropped her backpack and rifle in the meadow, then called him and started back toward the cabin at a jog. Moses didn't care which direction they went as long as they were going together. But when she stopped on the deck and tied him up with a length of soft cotton rope, the look on his face broke her heart. It was a combination of shock and betrayal.

She dropped to her knees and gave him a hug. "I'm sorry, Moses, but this isn't just a walk. I'm going to find Quinn, and I need you to stay here. Be a good boy and don't cry, or you're going to make me cry, too."

When she walked off the deck, the pup barked once. She kept walking, refusing to look back. He barked again and then whined. Blinded by tears, she staggered as she picked up her gear and kept on going. By the time she reached the trees, Moses was howling. It was the saddest sound she'd ever heard.

Once inside the tree line, she couldn't walk fast enough. Her search couldn't even start until she'd reached the cave, and that was a good thirty minutes above her. And now that she was officially in search mode, it was only prudent to let someone know what she was doing in case she didn't make it back.

She punched in Ryal's number, pacing her steps so she wouldn't be breathless while she talked, and when he answered, she said what she had to say quickly before he could argue.

"Hey, Ryal, it's me, Mariah. I'm on my way up to the cave as we speak."

"What the hell are you —"

"Just listen, because I'm not going to say this twice and I don't want your opinion. I know in my heart Quinn is in that mine. I believe that the passage in the cave leads into that mine, because I've heard voices twice in that cave, and there's no other explanation for where they're coming from. If Quinn's in there, I *will* find him. If he's alive, I *will* bring him back. If they've killed him, I swear to God I *will* take as many of them as I can with me. Tell everyone how much I love them, and how I appreciated the love with which I was accepted into your family. Moses is tied up on the back deck. Don't let him starve."

Ryal was in shock. He was yelling at her not to hang up when the line went dead.

Beth came running. "What's wrong? Is it Quinn? Have they found him?" she cried.

"No. It's Mariah. She's convinced the passage in the old cave is connected to the mine Lonnie Farrell bought. She thinks Quinn is in there, and she's going after him."

Beth gasped. "No. You can't let her. That'll get her killed."

"She's already aware of the risks."

Beth started to cry. Ryal wanted to cry with her, but there was no time. He needed to tell the sheriff. It might be helpful to know he had a soldier bringing up the rear.

Quinn's eyes were swollen shut, and he didn't know how many ribs were broken, but it was enough to make breathing normally an impossibility.

He'd quit thinking of escape. He wasn't even trying to stay alive anymore. He was in so much pain it would have been a blessing to die. Even Farrell had given up on the beatings, accepting the fact that Quinn wasn't going to tell him a thing. But instead of shooting him on the spot, he seemed to have abandoned him to his fate. Quinn knew that however long it took for his heart to stop beating, that was how long he would lie there before he died.

The only thought in his head now was Mariah, remembering how her eyes crinkled at the corners when she laughed. How upset and angry she was when she woke up from a PTSD episode. She would heal, but she was going to have to do it without him.

His big regret was that once they buried him, he knew she would leave. She wouldn't stay on the mountain without him, and he couldn't bear to think of her out in the world on her own.

Something crashed to the floor a few yards away, and then a long string of curses followed. He'd heard Lonnie ordering the men to get the last stuff cut and packed up. He suspected they would be abandoning the mine after dark. Everyone there felt the urgency, including Quinn. He so desperately wanted to be dead before that happened. Dying alone in the dark was the closest thing to hell he could imagine.

Everything was spinning out of control, and Lonnie could feel it. In hindsight, the worst move he'd made was coming back to this godforsaken mountain. He'd been so sure of his initial plan, and he'd been wrong. But he was a survivor. They'd counted him out at fourteen when they'd hauled his ass to jail, and he'd come out and turned a rap sheet into a résumé. He could do it again. All he needed was to cut his losses and regroup.

A search warrant was undoubtedly imminent, but he knew the law well enough to know how slowly it worked, so he was betting he had at least one more night. He had two choppers inbound, both due to arrive just after dark with armed guards on board. He would have his coke loaded and gone before daylight, leaving the men and the mushrooms to their own devices. He was disappointed, but such was the business of crime. Fair play was never part of the equation.

He glanced out the office window, keeping an eye on the gate at the end of the driveway. Even though he'd seen more traffic than usual — along with some men with their hunting dogs howling up the road — it was a case of so far, so good.

The little green delivery truck was being loaded for a trip down into Mount Sterling. It was ironic that the business meant to be nothing but a cover was beginning to thrive, while his big-money operation had turned into a hot mess. As he watched, Buell came out of the nursery carrying an armload of flats and loaded them into the truck.

"Score one for Mountain Mushrooms. Zero for the coke express," Lonnie muttered, then realized he'd never seen a single flat of mushrooms going out and decided it was now or never.

He left the office and strolled out to the truck.

"How's it going?" he asked, as Buell slid the flats inside.

"Fine," Buell said, and headed back inside for another load.

Last night he'd checked his boots after hearing what Quinn said and realized he was about to catch shit for poaching on top of everything else. He'd thought of every reason he could come up with to go home, change shoes and throw his boots down the old well out beside the garden. But with Lonnie there pushing everybody to the breaking point, there'd been no hope of getting off the property. During the night he'd developed a sort of fatalistic attitude about the whole thing. He might as well quit worrying about something he couldn't change.

Lonnie watched his brother-in-law's molasses-lazy stride and wondered what the fuck Portia had ever seen in him. As he turned, he noticed a mushroom had fallen out of a flat onto the ground. Curious to see what was coming out of here with his name on it, he reached down to pick it up.

When he saw the footprint beside it, he froze. The muscles in his chest began to tighten, then he straightened up and turned toward the nursery, his face expressionless as he waited for Buell's return. At that moment he was a very dangerous man.

Buell saw Lonnie waiting by the truck and wished he would go back into the office. The man got on his last nerve.

He sauntered by Lonnie without meeting his gaze and slid the flats into the truck, then turned right into the blow Lonnie launched and dropped like a felled ox. Before he could get up, Lonnie was kicking him — in the ribs, in the face, in the balls — anywhere he could land a blow.

Buell was screaming like a girl with his hands cupped over his groin, willing to take the kicks anywhere else but in his balls again.

It was Davis who hobbled out and pulled Lonnie off.

"Stop, boss!" Davis yelled. "Stop! You're gonna kill him. Whatever he did, you don't wanna kill him. He's your family."

Spit was glistening from the corner of Lonnie's lips. His eyes were wild, the pupils dilated to the point that they appeared to be black.

"There's no Farrell blood running in that pissant's veins!" He turned back to Buell. "It's your fault." Then he pointed at Buell, his voice barely above a whisper. "You're the fucking poacher they've been looking for. You knew it. You knew it, and yet you still brought the law into my house and pulled it down around us. If you'd been half the man you should be, you would have walked out of here and turned yourself in without ruining my setup."

Davis gawked. Even the others who'd begun gathering on Buell's behalf started backing away.

"Fuck," Buell moaned. "Somebody help me up."

Lonnie's hand slid toward the gun in his pocket, and then he remembered where he was and closed his eyes, shuddering over and over as he struggled to maintain control. Once he could breathe without shaking, he opened his eyes. There was no one left at the truck except him and Buell. He kicked him once more, then walked away and disappeared into the office.

At that point Buell passed out.

Lonnie walked back out of the office and yelled at the top of his voice for someone to get over there. A half dozen men came running. He pointed at Buell.

"Get him out of my sight."

"What do you want us to do with him, boss?" one of the men asked.

"Drag him into the back of the cavern. I

don't want to see him every time I come out."

They dragged Buell Smith's body behind the office while Mountain Mushrooms continued to come undone.

Sometime later Buell regained consciousness. He crawled to the back of the office on his hands and knees, then braced himself against the wall and slowly dragged his battered body into a standing position. Everything hurt, and the world kept tilting on its axis, but he finally managed to take that first step. Once he did, he couldn't get to his truck fast enough, expecting, with every step, to get a bullet in the back.

When he finally got behind the wheel and jammed the key into the ignition, he was shaking. It took all his concentration to start the engine and put the truck in gear. The moment it started to roll, he stomped the accelerator and just hung on. Instead of getting out at the gates to open them, he drove through them, hitting them square in the middle, shattering the chain and the lock. The gates buckled on impact, and then one got caught on the front of Buell's bumper as he sped through the opening. He dragged it down the road until it finally fell off into the ditch.

He cried all the way home.

Mariah had no idea whether the puppy had
quit howling or she had just gotten so far
away that she could no longer hear him, but
it didn't matter. She kept putting one foot
in front of the other until she was standing
at the open mouth of the cave with the
worst part of the journey still ahead of her.
She paused long enough to get a flashlight
out of the pack and shift her rifle to the
other hand, and then she walked inside.
Before it had seemed dark and threatening,
but now it was simply the road that would
get her to Quinn.

Small bats hanging from the ceiling began
to stir as she swept the flashlight ahead of
her. Rats scurried out of her way into the
shadows, but there was no hesitation in her
step. The earth inside the mountain smelled
different, and it took her a while to realize
that the ground she was walking on had
never seen the light of day. Whatever had
managed to exist in the mountain's belly
had done so without benefit of the sun. She
was scared, as scared as she'd ever been in
her life, that when she got to the end of this
tunnel Quinn wouldn't be there, or that the
tunnel would come to an impenetrable end
before she found him. She'd banked every

hope she had on this tunnel connecting to the mine.

Every hundred yards or so she shot a spray of neon-yellow paint from the can onto the wall. Even though she had yet to come to any other passage, she was playing it safe.

When she suddenly walked through a wall of webs, her scream was instinctive. The flashlight went flying as she began swiping at the webs, certain she crawling with spiders. The webs easily brushed away as she scrambled to pick up the flashlight and check her clothing just to make sure.

"Oh, my God, oh, my God," she kept muttering as she swung the flashlight in a high arc, making sure there weren't any giant spiders lurking overhead. Then she gritted her teeth and moved on.

Soon after she began to hear the voices again, and her hopes rose. This was it! This was what she'd been hearing all along. Even though the tunnel was becoming narrower and the ceiling lower, she moved faster, the sounds she'd been hearing muted now by the thunder of her heartbeat.

One second she was on her feet and striding forward, and the next she caught a glimpse of something shiny in the narrow beam of light. Before she could stop, she stepped off into a wall of racing water.

Her scream was swallowed up by the roar of the rapids as she struggled to find solid ground. The weight of the backpack was pulling her down, and the rifle was caught underneath a ledge beneath the surface.

Help me, Lord.

And just like that there was solid rock beneath her feet as she struggled to stand, balancing the heavy backpack against the rush of the water's power. Coughing and spitting, she made her way through the chest-high torrent and then out on the other side. It was with some surprise that she realized the flashlight was still in her hand as she crawled out onto her hands and knees. Within seconds she felt a new spurt of panic. There was no longer headroom to stand upright. The possibility of getting trapped in this tunnel was almost enough to make her turn back, but then Quinn's face slid through her mind, and just like that she was grounded.

Readjusting the pack, she started forward slowly, crouching. Within minutes her leg began to pain her, and then the muscles started to burn. The stress of her crouched position was taxing her weakened muscles.

On top of everything else, her sodden clothes were beginning to chafe, and her hair was matted to her head and face. She could feel the mud beneath her nails drying and hardening like little bits of cement. Her eyes were burning and her skin had begun to itch, but she kept on moving until all of a sudden her low-ceilinged tunnel turned into a crawl space. When the backpack began catching along the top of the tunnel, she pulled out all the extra ammo and put it in the pocket of her pants, then began redistributing the weight.

When she started hearing the voices again, instead of hope, she felt overwhelming despair, because they were no longer ahead of her. They were behind her. And the only way that made sense was to accept that it had never been voices she was hearing. It had been the sound of the water, spilling through the mountain and rolling along the rocks down into the natural spring that fed the waterfall down by the cave.

Swift tears gave way to a flood of disappointment, morphing into a defeat she hadn't felt since the day she'd been turned out onto the streets by the welfare system. If there were no voices, then there was no reason to believe Quinn was anywhere in the mountain, alive or dead.

She cried until her head was throbbing and she was verging on throwing up, and then rage kicked in. She still believed in

Quinn. He thought the drug operation was in the old mine, and this might still be a way to get to it. She'd come this far. She wasn't going back until she knew for sure. She cursed God for ever letting her be born, for sending her back from Afghanistan in such a mess, for taking away the only thing she'd ever loved. Then, somewhere between hiccups and despair, she began to scream.

"Damn it! Where are You, God? If You aren't going to help me out of this mess, then You can kiss my muddy ass!"

With her head throbbing and her throat raw from screaming, she got up on her hands and knees and promptly hit the top of her head on a rock. The warm rush of blood rolling down from her hairline made her madder. She lowered her head, channeled her pain into anger and began scooting the backpack in front of her as she went.

Within another fifty yards the tunnel began to widen again, and the ceiling began to lift until she was actually able to stand upright. Every muscle in her body was screaming. She was so weak she was shaking, but she had to believe she'd made it through the worst. She dropped the coil of climbing rope off the side of the backpack and left it lying against the wall. It kept coming undone and was hindering rather than helping her.

Trying to gauge how far she'd come against how long she'd been in here, she looked down at her watch. It had stopped. So much for shock- and waterproof.

Accepting that she had no idea of time or distance, she found it was also freeing to know that such things no longer mattered. She was going all the way to the end, and wherever it came out was where she would be.

She took a deep breath, and as she did, she suddenly realized that the air smelled different here. The odd odors of the earth's belly were being mixed with something new — something that seemed faintly familiar. A few yards farther and it suddenly dawned on her that she could see shapes and shadows without aiming the flashlight.

Sweet Lord, there was light up ahead! It was time to get serious. She turned off her flashlight and slipped it into the pack, then flipped the safety off on her rifle. She had no idea if it would even fire after being dragged through the water, but it felt good in her hand.

She began walking, staying close to the wall as the natural passage gave way to a tunnel with sagging timbers shoring up the sides and ceiling. Dolly's grandfather had been right! The cave *did* come out on the other side of the mountain, but through a man-made mine shaft, not by nature's hand.

She was hearing voices again, and this time there was no mistaking them for anything else. She heard a sudden burst of laughter, the clink of metal against metal, a sharp word from one man to another.

Wherever she was, she was no longer alone, and she was uncertain how to proceed. If there really was a drug operation in this mine, she was in serious danger.

For a soldier, the first order of business on entering new territory was to reconnoiter. She eased the heavy backpack onto the ground and slowly moved forward. Once she passed the next set of support beams, she would be too near the lights to remain undetected. She dropped down as close to the wall as she could get and began crawling along the floor.

With her eyes drawn by the light, the first thing she saw was a room that had been built inside the tunnel. Her gaze went to the men in masks and white suits, and then to the scales and the bricks of what had to be uncut cocaine, and she knew the sheriff's guess had been right. There was a full-blown drug business in place inside the old mine.

Then she blinked and realized something

was lying between her and the room, shoved up against the wall — in the darkest part of the tunnel. She blinked until her eyes readjusted to the darkness. That was when she realized it was a man's body, and she could see the side of his face.

Her heart slammed against her rib cage. Even though his features were unrecognizable, the dark green ranger jacket was not. It was Quinn! She'd actually found him, but she had the sinking feeling that she was too late. Swept by a fresh wave of despair, the urge to stand up and start shooting was strong. But she hadn't come all this way only to blow her one chance to save him. She had to be sure he was really gone.

Still on her belly, she crawled closer until she could reach out and touch the top of his head. His hair was stiff and matted, and the amount of blood and swelling on his face was beyond horrific. She could only imagine what he'd suffered before he'd died, and the hate that swept through her erased the last vestiges of fear. She moved her fingers along the side of his face and down toward his neck to confirm the absence of his pulse, and as she did, shock was replaced with an unspeakable joy. Instead of the cold, lifeless body she'd expected to feel, his skin was warm. And then she found a pulse! But, oh, God, how to get him out?

His hands and feet were bound, and there was duct tape on his mouth. Wishing the bastards to hell and back for what they'd done, she slipped the hunting knife out of her boot and was about to cut him loose when a large door at the far end of the drug room swung inward and an angry man appeared in the doorway.

Shit!

She flattened herself against the wall, struggling with full-blown panic. Retreat was not in her vocabulary, but she couldn't do Quinn any good if they found her before she had a chance to cut him free. Moving as fast as she dared, she scooted backward until she was out of sight, then ran back to where she'd left the backpack, picked it up and ran all the way out of the tunnel and into the natural passage, where she propped the pack up against the wall. After making sure she was still unobserved, she crept back toward the lab to listen.

Lonnie was feeling the pressure. It was getting dark, and he wanted this last shipment packed and ready to go the moment the helicopters landed.

Buell had surprised him with his daring

little escape, but Lonnie wasn't about to chase the man up and down the mountain.

He wanted to believe Buell was running — running from both the cops and the park service — but he couldn't be sure. The fat-ass had already surprised him once with that unexpected dose of morality. Despite that, he couldn't really imagine Buell going to the cops and turning himself in, but there was too much on the line to ignore the possibility.

He headed inside to check on the progress of the coke and was immediately unhappy with what he was seeing.

"Davis! Work faster! I have two choppers on the way, and you're nowhere near ready."

"Well, we will be if we don't have any more interruptions," Davis said, glaring pointedly at the gun-shaped bulge in Lonnie's pocket, then scooting behind his worktable, anxious to put something between himself and his boss.

That whack job had already shot him once, and he was going to be lucky if he didn't lose some toes. The man was a bona fide psycho.

Lonnie ignored Davis's attitude as he stormed back out of the room.

Mariah heard bits and pieces of the conversation, then waited until the crisis had passed before easing her way back along the shaft to Quinn's body. She had no way of knowing if he was cognizant. Her biggest fear was that if she cut him loose he would lash out in confusion, but she had to chance it. It was why she'd come.

Once more she eased the knife out of her boot, and this time she proceeded to cut the ropes from his wrists and ankles. He rolled slightly, but she caught him before he went facedown, and then held her breath as she slowly eased him onto his back.

The fact that his arms were limp at his sides and he'd made no move to take the duct tape off his mouth was both good news and bad. Good news that he hadn't alerted them by a groan. Bad news that he might have so much brain damage he would never wake up again.

But she'd found him, and if they had a chance in hell of living through this, it was up to her to make it happen. Still on her belly, she slipped her hands beneath his armpits, tightened her grip and pulled.

He didn't budge. Between his deadweight and the fact that she had no room to angle her body for leverage, it seemed an impossible task. Getting a firmer grip, she pulled again, until her arms were trembling and her muscles felt like they were tearing. Using nothing but her upper body strength, she finally felt him move. It was only a couple of inches, but it was a start.

Little by little she continued to inch him backward, away from the light, farther into the passageway, deeper into the dark.

Jake Doolen pulled up in front of the sheriff's office. "Cyrus, you and Avery stay in the truck with the dogs. I won't be long."

He entered the office and went straight to the dispatcher behind the front desk.

"Is Marlow in?"

"Hello, Jake. Marlow's in, but he's pretty busy."

"I won't be long," Jake said, and strode past the desk and down the hall to the sheriff's office. He knocked once and walked in, wasting no time on manners.

"Damn it, Marlow, you and I both know Quinn Walker is likely in Farrell's mine. Whether he's alive or dead is another story, but I don't see how you can sit behind that desk and wait when you know his life is at stake."

Marlow stood. "I don't know anything for sure, only a whole lot of maybes, and in the eyes of the law, maybes don't cut it. What do you know that I don't?"

"I had my dogs at the site where they

found Quinn's Jeep. They didn't pick up his scent anywhere within three miles in any direction, which tells me he never left that Jeep on foot. But when I took them back to the mine entrance where Dolly said he was the evening before, they had themselves a royal fit. My Zeus don't bay like that for old spoor. Quinn Walker was there within the last twenty-four hours, and I'm saying he never left the property."

Marlow knew in his gut Jake was right, but his hands were tied.

"I've been on the phone half the afternoon with three different judges, and not a one of them will sign a search warrant to get me into that mine. Not even with three deaths on my hands. One missing ranger isn't going to up the ante for them."

"That's a crock!" Jake yelled. "If the law won't help us, then I'm saying there's those among us who are ready to go in on our own and take the consequences."

Marlow threw up his hands. "Well, hell yeah, why don't you go right ahead and do that. On the off chance Walker is in there and still alive, that will pretty much seal his death warrant."

And just like that, all the fight went out of Jake. "I can't stand to see Dolly Walker cry."

Marlow sighed. "Yesterday I saw a woman

lose her mind. Sue Colvin is in the mental ward in Mount Sterling General, and I'd bet a year of my life that she don't never come out alive."

Jake shuddered. "This is one fucked-up mess, and all because Lonnie-damn-Farrell decided to come back to Rebel Ridge."

Before Jake could press his case further, the dispatcher poked his head in the door.

"Sheriff, there are two DEA agents up front who want to talk to you."

"Why not?" Marlow muttered. "Everyone else does, too. Send them back."

"We're already here," Lancaster said, flashing his badge. "I'm Agent Mike Lancaster. This is my partner, Agent Louis Townsend." He eyed Jake curiously. "I know you from somewhere."

Jake shrugged. "Jake Doolen. I've been known to work for the law now and then."

Mike Lancaster smiled. "I remember you now. Saw you and your dogs work about two years ago upriver. We had an agent go missing. You found him. Not alive, but you found him just the same."

Jake nodded. "Yeah, sometimes the searches don't always work out the way we want."

Mike shifted focus. "Sheriff Marlow, we're here about a man named Lonnie Farrell.

Would you happen to know him?"

Marlow rolled his eyes. "Yes, although I wish I'd never laid eyes on the man. I've got three family members dead and a park ranger missing. He's at the top of my guilty list, but I don't have enough evidence to nail him."

"That park ranger wouldn't happen to be Quinn Walker, would it?"

Marlow was startled. "Yes, but how did you know?"

Lancaster took a paper out of his jacket pocket and handed it to the sheriff.

"This is a DEA search warrant for the property once known as the Foley Brothers Mine, now known as Mountain Mushrooms. It covers the land around the mine, the mine itself, the mushroom business and any other businesses and buildings on the property."

"How on earth . . . ?"

"Just paying back a favor to a friend," Mike said. "And we're part of the package."

"I can always use a couple more hands," Marlow admitted.

Mike pointed out the window. "There are more than two of us," he said. "Three vans — eleven armed agents. We're just waiting for you to show us the way."

"We're coming, too," Jake said.

Marlow shook his head. "You three stay away from the mess until we've secured the area. If we can't find Walker, we'll set the dogs on the trail again. How's that suit you?"

"Just fine," Jake said, and headed back to his truck on the run to tell his boys what was going on.

TWENTY-THREE

Buell Smith cried all the way home. Today was the end of his life as he'd known it. If he lived through to tomorrow, he would likely be behind bars. But his first duty was to his family. The kids were in school, but he had to warn Portia and Gertie. There was no telling what Lonnie Farrell would do next.

He saw Portia sweeping the front porch as he drove into the yard, then skidded to a halt just outside the fence. She started to wave and then stopped. He watched her expression shift as she saw the crumpled front end of the truck where he'd gone through the gate. She dropped the broom and came running as he practically fell out, leaving the keys hanging in the ignition.

When she saw his face she started screaming for Gertie.

"Mama! Mama! Come quick! Buell's had a wreck!" She slid an arm around his waist.

"Lean on me, honey. I'll help you into the house."

"It wasn't a wreck," Buell said. "It was Lonnie."

Portia's screams got louder. "Mama! Mama!"

Gertie appeared in the doorway as Portia was helping Buell up the steps and into the house.

"Lord'a mercy!" she cried. "What happened?"

Portia spat the bitter words out of her mouth. "Lonnie did it! Like everything else that's ever gone wrong with this family, Lonnie caused it."

Gertie moaned. "He ain't all bad. He gave us this home."

"With blood money," Buell muttered, staggering into the house. "And you don't know the half of it."

"I'll get the first-aid kit," Portia said, and ran off down the hall as Buell dropped into his recliner.

"What happened?" Gertie asked. "Is Lonnie hurt, too?"

Buell sneered, then winced because even that small movement was agony. "Hell no, Lonnie's not hurt. I didn't fight him. He caught me off guard, and when I went down he kicked the holy shit out of me. Most of this is from his boots."

Portia returned and shoved Gertie aside.

"Damn it, Mama, Buell comes in looking like this and all you can ask is if Lonnie is hurt? Get out of my way!" She knelt by the chair to begin cleaning Buell's face, but he needed to get this said.

"There's more, and you need to know it now. I'm the one who shot an arrow into that bear and drove it crazy. It wasn't on purpose. I was just trying to get some extra money for my family by hunting trophy heads for a taxidermist down in Mount Sterling. I never meant for anyone to get hurt, but there's one hiker dead and another crippled because of what I did. I'll probably go to jail for it, but that's okay. Gertie, you need to know that your son is a mean, crazy man. He tricked all of us up at Mountain Mushrooms. We signed on to raise mushrooms, not work in no drug business, but as soon as he had the one going, he started the other one up. He pretty much told us that we either work for him or our families would suffer. He said he knew where we lived. None of us signed on to do that, but there we were."

Portia was horrified and began crying, telling Buell how sorry she was for what Lonnie had done, but Gertie had gone quiet.

"I'll go talk to him," she said at last. "I'll make him let them go."

Buell shook his head. "You don't understand. The Colvins are dead because the drug Willis got high on came from your son. Syd probably smuggled it out. The cops are gonna know it's not meth or pills that killed him. I watch TV. I know how that works. They'll figure it out. And that's not all. Quinn Walker is being held prisoner inside the mine. Lonnie told me to grab him and tie him up, and God help me, I did. I don't even know if he's still alive."

Portia stood up and stepped back, staring at Buell as if she was looking at a stranger. "I can't believe you did that," she gasped.

He shrugged. "I can't believe it, either. Worst part was that Walker wasn't there about the drugs. He was looking for the poacher. He was looking for me. I'm going to jail, Portia. I'm sorry for the shame I've brought on you and our kids, but there's nothing I can do to take it back."

Gertie left the room mumbling to herself, and then came back moments later carrying her purse and walked out the door.

Portia was sobbing so hard she never saw her mother leave, and Buell was on the phone calling the sheriff's office to turn himself in.

Buell had parked behind Gertie's car, so instead of moving it so she could drive hers, she just got in his truck and drove away. It was her fault Lonnie was like this. It was her fault he'd turned out all wrong. She had to tell him she was sorry. He needed to understand how much she'd loved him, even though that love had come out all wrong.

Her mind was set as she drove up the mountain. She knew what she would say and how she would say it. He would be angry. He had a right to be. But he was a man full-grown, and there was a price to pay for sinning.

It was nearing sundown as Lonnie stood outside the office watching the darkening sky. He had just made contact with the first chopper, which would be arriving shortly. All he had to do was stay focused, and he would soon be out of this and on to new and bigger things. Looking back, he realized he'd been too greedy too soon. He should have started off smaller and grown the business rather than starting at the top and watching it crumble beneath him.

As if this day couldn't get any worse, he'd been watching the gate for the men on the night shift to arrive, but they were suspiciously absent. He could only guess what rumors were flying, but it didn't matter anymore. He was done with this place. He and the guards who were coming would load the goods. All he needed was three more hours, and this place and these people would be nothing but a bad memory.

Suddenly he saw headlights as someone paused for a moment at what was left of the gates. When he realized it was coming onto the property his heart skipped a beat, and then he recognized the truck.

It was Buell. The sorry son of a bitch was back. Good. Lonnie had a point to make, and he no longer cared if it made his sister sad. It was her own damn fault for marrying such a loser. The headlights were blinding, but he walked straight toward them anyway. With little more than twenty yards between them he pulled his gun and started firing — sending three shots into the windshield right above where the steering wheel was. Glass shattered. The engine slowed as the driver's foot slipped off the accelerator. When the truck began to veer slowly to the right and then slammed into a stand of trees, he felt a surge of satisfaction.

Fat bastard played me once, but never again.

He jogged toward the truck to make sure

Buell was well and truly dead, ready to deliver the kill shot if he wasn't.

He opened the door and then froze. The body was slumped all the way over onto the passenger side of the seat, but it was plain to see that Buell Smith had not been driving.

Bile rose in his throat like vomit after a binge.

"Mama?"

A wave of panic swept through him. It felt like the same panic he'd felt the night she'd first come to his room. A smothering, weightless kind of feeling that he was leaving his body and watching the debacle play out from across the room.

"I didn't mean to. I thought you were Buell." He pulled the hem of her dress down to cover her exposed leg.

He turned off the key, and closed the door. His gorge was rising as he absorbed the shock of what he'd done. Then he glanced up. He couldn't see it, but he could hear the first chopper approaching. As he went back toward the mine, it occurred to him it might be coming too late. He'd created a hell that was going to take him with it.

Ryal was in a panic. He'd tried to call

Sheriff Marlow and gotten a vague response from the dispatcher about him being out of the office and unreachable. From the moment Mariah had told him where she was going, he'd known he couldn't get there in time to stop her. He'd tried to call James, but the call wouldn't go through. Wherever James was on his route, there was no service.

The update he got from Dolly about Jake Doolen's search wasn't good. In her words, as far as Jake was concerned, Quinn had never made it into the park. He was either dead or being held captive somewhere else, most likely inside the mine. It was the scenario no one but Mariah had wanted to accept. He couldn't sit by any longer. Mariah was the smart one. Right or wrong, she had made her move and he was going to follow. He needed to find James, wherever he was. He would call Uncle John and Uncle Fagan. They would round up as many kin as they could muster and meet him up at the cave. He didn't hold much hope of Mariah finding Quinn, but he owed it to his brother to save Mariah before she got herself killed.

Mariah had to rest. Her arms were shaking from the exertion of pulling Quinn's dead-weight, but they were far enough away from the drug room to feel safe, if only for a moment.

Quinn's pulse was still steady, but the fact that he hadn't come to was a huge concern. She kept thinking brain damage and wondered if she was saving him, or dooming him to life as a vegetable.

She stood, sweeping the flashlight around the tunnel until she located the pack she'd left earlier and brought it back to where she'd left Quinn. She sat the flashlight on end so that the beam of light was pointing upward, and began digging through the pack for water and the first-aid kit.

The first thing she did was remove the duct tape from his mouth. Then she used a wet wipe on the dried blood sealing his right eye. It was slow going, but if they had a chance of getting out, she was going to need every break she could get. If he ever regained consciousness, it would be helpful if he could see.

In the end, it was his groan of pain that gave her the first ray of hope. Already aware of how sound carried through the tunnel, she kept her voice low.

"Quinn, can you hear me? It's Mariah."

He inhaled slowly, his nostrils flaring slightly.

She leaned closer to his ear.

"Quinn. It's Mariah. Follow the sound of my voice. You can do this. I need you to do this. I need you to come back to me."

He moaned again. This time she took his hand and put it to her cheek.

"Feel me, Quinn. It's me, Mariah. Your hands are free. Your feet are free. All you have to do is wake up and come with me."

His lips parted. She poured water on another wet wipe and mopped the blood away from his mouth.

"You want a drink? I have water. Open your mouth, sweetheart, and I'll give you a drink."

Quinn was hearing voices. Someone wanted him to open his mouth. The last time he'd done that they'd nearly drowned him. He wasn't playing that game again. What pissed him off most was that he was still alive. Why couldn't he just give up and die?

Someone was beside him, running their fingers on his face. He waited for the pain to increase, but it didn't happen. A sharp astringent wafted under his nose. He came to with a jerk, his throat burning, his lips too swollen to form words.

"Quinn, it's Mariah. Can you hear me?" she asked as she dropped the smelling salts back into the first-aid kit.

A quick wave of longing swept through him that was so real it was as if he could actually hear her voice.

Mariah poured a thin trickle of water at the corner of his lips.

"It's water, sweetheart. Open your mouth. I won't let you choke."

When the water hit his lips and slid into his mouth, he swallowed instinctively.

"Good job," she whispered. "A little more?" She tilted the bottle again. She was about to put it aside when he suddenly grabbed her wrist.

"It's all right. It's me, Quinn. Mariah."

"Am . . . dead?"

Tears welled and spilled down her cheeks. "No, baby, no. You're not dead. I found you. But we're not safe. We're in the tunnel in the mountain, and I need to get you back to the cave. Remember the cave above your house? We need to get back there. Can you help me?"

Quinn was pretty sure this was another episode of PTSD, but it was an improvement over most of them, and he knew better than to fight it. He squeezed her wrist in answer.

"I'm going to wash the rest of this blood off your left eye. Your right eye is too swollen to open, but this one might if I can get it clean. Don't move. Don't fight me. I need you to be able to see to help me do this. Okay?"

He squeezed her wrist again.

She began wiping dirt and picking bits of crusted blood from his lashes until the lid was free. She had no way of knowing whether he would be able to open it, or if it was too injured to see, but it was the best she could do.

"Okay, that's as much as I can manage," she whispered. "Try to open your eye."

Quinn heard her but couldn't figure out what he had to do to obey.

Mariah groaned. "Honey. Open your eye. All you have to do is blink. You remember how to blink, right?"

It was an involuntary response to a specific command, but the moment he did it, a seed of cognizance came with it. At first all he could see were shadows and the silhouette of someone sitting beside him. Was that her?

Mariah felt like cheering. She watched his eye open and saw him trying to focus. She leaned into his line of vision.

"It's me, honey. Mariah. I love you, Quinn. I love you so much."

His heart skipped a beat. Mariah? This wasn't a dream?

He squeezed her wrist again. She took his

hand and laid it against her cheek. He felt the softness of her skin, the warmth of her flesh, and knew that by some stroke of fate that she had found him.

"Help?"

She smiled through her tears. "Yes. I need you to help me. If I get you to your feet, do you think you can walk?"

He ran a hand over his ribs and winced.

"Oh, God, are they broken?"

He blinked once and quietly passed out.

Mariah shuddered as she laid her head against his shoulder.

"I understand. They hurt you, didn't they? So after I get you home and get you well, if the people who did this aren't already dead, I will find them and kill them myself."

She sorted through the backpack, stuffing the most necessary supplies into her pockets, then took off her jacket and stuffed it inside the pack to make it softer for him.

Now that she could stand up, it would be easier to drag him, but not on his back — not without protection. As she'd looked at the backpack, a thought had occurred to her. It had a sturdy internal frame and wide shoulder straps. What if it was on his back instead of hers? It was long enough to pillow his head, and the internal frame could act as a body brace for his broken bones and keep the entire upper half of his body from being dragged against the tunnel floor. All she had to do was get it over his shoulders and strap him into it.

The first helicopter was loaded and ready to go. The second one was inbound, ETA five minutes. Lonnie waved off the pilot and the two armed guards, then looked at his watch. There were two pallets of street-ready coke yet to load. Thirty minutes tops and they would be gone.

"Come with me," he ordered.

The five remaining guards followed him inside and, at his direction, began stacking a new pallet. He moved quickly through the room, making sure there was nothing left behind with his name on it, and then he looked into the darkness behind him and thought of the ranger. In all the excitement he'd completely forgotten about the man, who had to be on the verge of death by now, if he hadn't already fallen off that cliff. He hurried to the end of the room and looked out into the passage.

A ripple of shock went through him. The body wasn't there. He quickly found the ropes that had bound Walker's hands and feet. They'd been cut. He had no idea how the man had managed that, but he was pissed. All this time and the bastard had been faking. He turned, grabbed a flashlight off a table and waved at the guards.

Mariah moved the rifle out of the way and was about to try maneuvering him into the backpack when she heard a burst of commotion, voices shouting and the sound of people running in the tunnel — running toward them.

She heard someone shout, "Shoot him on sight!" and swung around with the rifle in her hand. She couldn't let the fight come to her with Quinn helpless and in the open. Her only option was to stop them en route. She flipped the safety off, checked her pockets for the ammo and started running toward the voices.

When she saw the first lights, she leveled the rifle and started firing as she ran.

Shouts turned to screams. Beams of lights went up, some went sideways, some fell to the floor. Someone got off a shot that whizzed past her head, but she kept firing methodically, aiming at the sound and the lights until no one else came and the lights were lying motionless.

Mercenaries were men of habit used to following orders. They hired on to the man with the most money, no matter how dirty the job, and when the boss gave the order, they blindly obeyed.

They had followed Lonnie into the tunnel with their little lights and big guns, and when he ordered them to shoot on sight, they took aim on the run, waiting for a target to appear.

They didn't expect the prey to come to them, or that it would come armed and without warning. One moment they were on the attack and the next they were blind-sided. With no defense against an invisible enemy and nothing to hide behind, the ones that weren't hit turned tail and ran. Seconds later the mountain opened up and began to swallow them whole.

Out of nowhere the ground beneath Mariah's feet began to shake, and then she heard a groan and a rumble, as if the mountain was rejecting the foreign objects in its belly. The first support beam came loose less than twenty feet in front of her. That was when she turned and ran, sprinting into the darkness. If she was going to die, she wanted to be in Quinn Walker's arms when it happened.

Lonnie saw the first beam as it came down,

and it was like watching it in slow motion. It fell from the ceiling and split J. R. George's head like an overripe melon. The earth was breaking with it, spilling down in dust and chunks, tons of the ancient mountain caving in, readjusting to the thunder of gunfire that had disturbed centuries of rest.

It was the only time in Lonnie's life that being at the back of the pack was fortuitous, because it meant he was the first one out of the collapsing passage. He leaped toward the lights while the mountain came down behind him, bolting past the tables and the pallets of unsold blow, beyond the metal door and out into the cavern leading to the opening of the mine. A cloud of dust caught up and then passed him, leaving him running blind in the mountain's bad breath.

He didn't know he'd made it out of the cave-in until he felt fresh air on his face. The pilot of the newly arrived second chopper looked at him in shock. Lonnie appeared more ghost than man as he emerged covered in dust.

"What happened?" the pilot yelled.

"Cave-in," Lonnie said, and then choked, gagged and vomited up the dirt he'd swallowed. "Start it up," he said, and then hacked some more. "We need to leave. Now."

The pilot crawled into the cockpit just as a convoy of vehicles appeared at the gates.

Lonnie saw them coming and tried to run toward the chopper, but he stumbled and fell, then rolled over onto his back. The stars on Rebel Ridge had always seemed closer than they did in the city, but in reality, like success, they were always just out of his reach. Suddenly the stars disappeared, blacked out by the silhouette of a person standing over him.

"What did you do?"

He grunted as the cold steel of a rifle barrel jammed into his cheek.

"Portia? What the fuck?"

"What did you do to Mama?"

His gut rolled. "It was an accident. I thought it was Buell."

A high-pitched whine suddenly split the air. He thought the approaching cops had turned on a siren. It took him a second to realize it was her, and she was crying.

"You are the devil incarnate. You are an abomination and a scourge unto this earth. You take and take with no thought about who you hurt, only what you can take next."

"I said it was an accident," he repeated, and realized his voice was shaking.

"Well, this is not," she said, and pulled the trigger. It put a neat hole in his face, and blew brains and shards of bone out the back into the ground beneath.

DEA agents spilled out of vehicles with guns aimed at the pilot in the chopper. The guards inside the chopper dropped their weapons and came out with their hands up. They knew when to cut their losses.

Half an hour later the Doolens watched from the sidelines with sinking hearts. The DEA was having a field day. They'd confiscated a butt-load of drugs, and after interrogating the pilot, had arranged for agents to be waiting in Chicago to meet another chopper that was already in-flight.

Everything in the mine itself was a mess. A bunch of strangers were in custody. Gertie Farrell had been shot dead by her own son, and Portia had taken out her own brother in plain sight of a convoy of lawmen, apparently in revenge.

Buell Smith was already in custody in Mount Sterling, and after what Portia had just done, her three kids would most likely wind up in the Kentucky welfare system while their mama and daddy went to jail.

The mine had caved in, and from first reports there was no easy way to dig out. Whoever had been in there was gone. Jake didn't want to be the one to tell Dolly that

her youngest son was most likely dead, so
he gathered up his boys and the dogs and
went home.

Twenty-Four

Mariah came to flat on her face and spitting dirt, surprised to be alive, and even more surprised that she'd been in a firefight without succumbing to an episode of PTSD. The darkness inside the mountain was so absolute that she couldn't tell if there was a way out somewhere nearby or if surviving what had just happened only made her situation worse.

And what about Quinn? She'd left him alone in that tunnel. There was no way of knowing if he, too, was trapped by the cave-in, but one thing was certain: he would never get out on his own. She wouldn't let herself believe she'd lived through this only to be unable to get both of them out. She felt for the rifle, but it was gone. She clenched her fists in frustration.

"I know this may come as a shock, but I'm praying again today, Lord. Help me find Quinn, and help me get us out of here alive.

I've lived this life you gave me without too many complaints. I'm asking this much back for me."

Then she dropped her head, rolled over onto her hands and knees, and cautiously stood, feeling the air above her as she went. Her immediate area was open and — so far — clear. She started walking in what she thought was the direction she'd been facing when she'd been running, her arms outstretched like a blind woman moving without a cane. She prayed she hadn't gotten turned around when she fell, because she needed to get to Quinn. And long minutes later, when she rounded a bend and discerned a faint glow in the distance, she let out the breath she hadn't known she was holding. It was the glow from the flashlight she'd left with Quinn.

Quinn came to again, this time immediately aware that he could open one eye and was no longer bound. His vision was blurry, but he could see well enough to know he was still in the tunnel. There was a flashlight by his head, pointing at nothing, and after a few moments he made out a backpack next to his leg.

His head was spinning. Vomit was coming up his throat. The pain in his body was so intense that he physically wanted to die. He no longer knew what was real and what had been a dream. Was he still in Afghanistan? Maybe everything with Mariah had been a hallucination and this was reality. There was his pack. Where was his rifle? Had he ever gone home?

Someone was calling his name. He knew who it was. Mariah. She'd pulled him out of a fire. She would find him again.

Then all of a sudden she was at his side, running her fingers across his face, checking his pulse and saying his name in her sweet Southern drawl.

"Quinn! Can you hear me?"

"Hear . . ."

"Oh, thank God," she said. "Sweetheart, we've got troubles, but I promise I'm going to get you home. It's going to hurt like hell and I have no way of stopping the pain. So when it gets too bad, just let go."

" 'Kay."

She rocked back on her heels as she looked at the pack. It really would be a great makeshift stretcher. All she needed to do was get it on his back.

"This is going to hurt like a big dog, and I'm sorry," she said, grabbed him under the arms and, little by little, by pulling up and backward, angling his arms into the straps until he was wearing it like a coat.

He'd passed out again from the pain, which was just as well. After checking his pulse, she duct-taped the flashlight to her arm and was ready to go. The body sled she'd made out of the backpack had been a stroke of genius, and she was the first to admit it.

She'd used the last bottle of water, pouring some down his throat, then drinking the last bit herself. She was exhausted, both emotionally and physically, and despite the cool temperature in the tunnel, every thread of her clothing was stuck to her body with sweat. Satisfied that he was good to go, she bent over, grabbed on to the pack straps and began to pull him along, moving backward through the tunnel.

Long agonizing minutes passed as she pulled and then rested, pulled and then rested, trying to give the blisters forming on her hands a little break. They were coming up on what she called the belly-crawl passage and she was worried that she wouldn't be able to get Quinn through it.

He was bigger than she was, plus she'd elevated his body a couple of inches with the backpack frame, and now she was going to have to find a way to get both him and herself through. She couldn't see how that was going to happen. It had been all she could do to get through on her own the first time. She wasn't strong enough to push him, and if she pulled him, she would have to go through backward, which seemed impossible. That was when she remembered the rope she'd discarded on the way in.

After a few sweeps with the flashlight, she saw the long coil of climbing rope and staggered toward it on shaking legs. She dropped to her knees, her head swaying between her shoulders as she blessed her luck in finding the rope so easily and prayed for strength for what lay ahead.

Quinn moaned behind her and she hurried back with the rope, then touched his forehead. Fever. He was getting worse.

"I'm sorry. I'm going as fast as I can. And I love you."

She began by tying the rope through one shoulder strap and then the other, to equalize the weight. But once she finished, she realized there was a good chance she would simply pull it out from under him.

She thought about the problem for a few moments, then got the duct tape out of the pack and began duct-taping him and the pack together into one mummylike wrap. Then she fastened the rope around her waist, rolled over onto her belly and began snaking her way through the shaft.

The rope played out easily as she crawled, and she was congratulating herself on the success of her makeshift harness when she was yanked to a sudden stop. The constriction around her waist was worse than she'd expected. She was stuck and about to panic.

"Dear Lord."

She couldn't roll over, because the ceiling was too low, and untying herself would solve nothing. He was on one side of the narrows. She was nearly on the other. The only way to do this was to shift the distribution of her load. With the side of her face against rock, she reached down blindly and began pulling at the rope around her waist until it was up around her breasts, and then she paused, her heartbeat roaring in her ears, her body bathed in sweat.

The mountain was squeezing her. She could feel it tightening, trying to push her through the narrows like a baby through the birth canal. She didn't belong here, and it wanted her gone.

Teetering on the verge of a full-blown episode of PTSD, she managed to slip one arm out of the loop, which automatically shifted the pull from her waist to one shoulder, with the rope now angled between her breasts. Pulling anything like this was going to hurt like hell, but it was her only option.

Digging her fingers into the rocks, she flexed her muscles and pulled herself forward. Between the immobilizing frame of the backpack and the slick surface of the duct-tape wrap, she got Quinn into the shaft with a little clearance to spare. When the weight of the load dug into her shoulder, she groaned but kept going, and the farther she moved, the deeper the rope ate into her neck, until it was bleeding and she was screaming. Tears rolled as she cursed and she begged, but she kept on crawling until she had breached the narrows. With one long, heartfelt sob, she slipped out into the relative freedom of the far side and began clawing at the rope to get it off her neck. However, there was still the little matter of getting Quinn out, too.

So tired she was trembling, she rolled over on her butt, braced her feet against either side of the shaft and began pulling the rope hand over fist until Quinn all but slid out into her lap.

Half laughing, half crying, she leaned forward and hugged him.

"You will never believe what we just did," she sobbed, and then straightened the flashlight that was still taped to her arm and got up.

There was still not enough headroom to stand, but she would take a crouch over a belly-crawl anytime.

Quinn moaned, mumbling something she didn't understand, but it didn't — couldn't — matter. Not until they were free. She grabbed the rope, slipped her arms through the loop and started forward, pulling him and the makeshift sled behind her.

When she began to hear "voices" again, she knew they were nearing the inner falls. The water was talking to her now, whispering secrets, warning her of the treachery of its speed. It was strong and fast, and it could sweep even a strong man off his feet and down to glory before he knew it was happening. There was no way she could pull Quinn through it. This was where he had to wake up and help. If he didn't go upright through this, he wasn't going at all.

Every time Quinn came to, he was in motion. He didn't know where he was at, only that it was dark. Once, in a moment of panic, he thought he'd gone blind until a flash of light above his head caught his eye and he relaxed. He kept thinking he could hear Mariah's voice, although he didn't believe that was possible.

He had no anchor to this life other than the heart beating in his chest and refusing to quit.

He kept trying to stay under, but dream-Mariah was always there, pushing him, prodding him, shouting louder and louder, trying to shake him awake.

He tried to open his eyes, but only one lid would work. It was a startling experience when body parts gave out like that. He wondered what would be next to go.

Mariah was crying. Quinn wouldn't wake up, and they were at the water's edge. The flashlight beam was going dim, and somewhere during her repacking in the tunnels she'd lost the batteries and the second flashlight. Whatever she did, she had to do it now. All she needed was to get him across the water and then the rest of the way she would be walking upright. Even if the flashlight failed at that point, there was only one way to go. She couldn't get lost. She would find the way out.

"Wake up!" she screamed. "Don't you quit on me! Don't you do this! You have to hear me, Quinn Walker. That's an order! Open your damn eyes!"

Quinn groaned, his lips parting as he tried

to inhale. Instead the pain in his chest was so sharp that he choked.

"Good. Sorry that hurt, but I need you awake," Mariah said. "You're not going to like this, but we're going upright through this water. It's fast, chest-deep and cold as hell. But you hang on to me and I'll get us across. I won't leave you behind. Do you understand?"

Quinn saw Mariah's face and marveled. She seemed so real. "Love you."

"I love you, too. I hope you remember that," she said, and then spun him around until he was aimed feetfirst at the water.

When she stepped off backward into the icy rush she momentarily lost her breath. Frantic now to get them through as fast as she could, she aimed the flashlight behind her, gauging the distance they had to ford, and then she braced her feet against the rush and pulled him straight toward her, off the ledge and into the water.

His legs went in first and when he screamed and then moaned, she knew it was from the pain of his injuries rather than the cold.

"Steady, steady, I've got you," she said, as she slowly pulled him and the backpack into a fully upright position.

The water was laughing now, yanking at

her feet, teasing her toward slippery rocks, taunting her with its power. The bulk of his weight was against her chest as she slid her arms beneath the pack. Locking her hands around his waist, she took her first step backward.

The beam of the flashlight was centered on the passage through which they'd come, but the pinpoint ray of light quickly melted in the chasm.

Quinn lurched, and when he did his head lolled forward, bumping her nose hard enough that it started to bleed. Eyes watering from the pain, and pissed at God and life in general, Mariah lowered her head beneath his chin and braced herself again while voicing one more complaint.

"Son of a bitch, that hurt! I thought You were the all-seeing, Almighty God. Can't You see me here? You couldn't make this any easier?"

She took another step back, fighting against the drag of the water and pulling him with her.

"Quinn! Move your feet! Move your feet! Listen to my voice, damn it, and walk!"

And all of a sudden he *was* walking. It was a piss-poor example of the act, but she felt the momentary relief when he suddenly bore some of his own body weight, and it was enough to help her get them across. One last step and they were finally at the other side.

Shivering uncontrollably, she quickly turned him around, then closed her eyes, grounded her center and literally lifted him out of the water, angling his body until the backpack cleared the water and she could shove him onto dry ground. Then she crawled out of the water and up onto the ledge beside him before she collapsed, shivering from exertion and cold.

It took her a few moments to get her breath and shift mental gears for the last leg to freedom. They'd come so far. All she needed now was a little luck. She got up, but her feet were so cold that she couldn't feel them, and she stumbled and fell, jamming her arm and head against the wall. Yet another wound that would bleed before it would heal.

She groaned as she pushed herself upright again.

Quinn moaned, which shifted her focus.

She was just so tired.

But he could be dying, and all she had to do was walk.

She reached down and picked up the rope, then started forward again, pulling him behind her.

A few feet farther on, the flashlight died.

The complete absence of light and the waning presence of her strength were a powerful temptation to stop. But she wouldn't give up. Convinced she could do this, she moved forward, until, instead of taking a step, she staggered and fell to her knees.

Quinn was muttering now, and moaning, but her heart was pounding so hard she could hardly hear him above the blood rushing through her veins. Her head was swimming. Not only had she lost her center of gravity, but the last of her strength was gone, as well. With despair in her heart, she followed the rope back to Quinn, then lay down beside him.

The thunder of mortar shells was coming closer, and there was gunfire behind her. She was trapped. So this was where it ended. She put her arm across his chest and closed her eyes. It was a good place to die.

Something was crawling on Mariah's face. Something warm and wet. She thought she was dreaming, then felt it again and opened her eyes. Almost instantly she gasped, then she laughed, and then she started to cry.

It was Moses! The rope was still tied around his neck, but he'd obviously chewed himself loose. She wrapped her arms around his warm, wiggly body and pulled him close.

"Moses! My sweet puppy! You found us, didn't you, boy? Yes, you did, you found us."

Moses was whining and yipping, frantically licking her in a need for reassurance that what he'd done was okay.

Mariah felt along Quinn's body until she was able to check his pulse. It was still there, but so was the fever. She had to get up. She had to get moving. But she'd completely lost her sense of direction. She slung the rope loop over her shoulder and got a good grip, then grabbed the end of the rope tied around Moses's neck and stood up.

"Let's go home, Moses. Home!"

The pup barked but stayed waiting by her feet.

She tried again. "Come on, Moses. We're lost. It's up to you, buddy. Let's go home! You can do it! Let's go! Want a treat? Let's go get a treat!"

Moses whined once and then took off at a trot.

Mariah kept a death grip on Moses's rope, waiting for it to go taut so she would know which way to go. And when it suddenly yanked against her palm, she followed him, pulling Quinn with her.

Just like his namesake, Moses was leading

his family home.

Eight members of the Walker family, along with DEA Agents Lancaster and Townsend, were moving up the mountain above Quinn's cabin in the dark. Lancaster had promised Agent Ames that they would go the distance on this case and not leave until they knew what had happened to Walker.

Sheriff Marlow was bringing up the rear, dragging a stretcher.

The ethereal glow of the fluorescent lanterns they carried cast stark, eerie shadows along the path. Animals that would normally have been out had abandoned the slope for quieter hunting, leaving this trail to the men who had disturbed their night.

When they finally reached the cave, Ryal moved inside, shining his light as he went, which sent the bats into a frenzy as they swarmed from the cave.

Marlow dropped the stretcher and began swinging his hat. "I hate bats."

Ryal didn't comment as James walked up behind him and asked, "What do you want to do, bro?"

"I'm going in as far as I can. That's where she said she was going in, and with the cave-in at the mine, this is the only way she can come back."

Lancaster approached, eyeing the tunnel. "It's risky doing this at night."

Ryal frowned. "It's just as dark in there in the daytime as it is right now. And I can't go to bed tonight without knowing that we tried."

Though none of them had voiced their fears, Ryal knew they were all thinking the same thing: if Quinn and Mariah had actually been inside the mine when the cave-in occurred, they were almost certainly dead.

"I'm ready if you are," James said.

"I'll be waiting out here," Marlow said. "Someone's gonna have to go back and get a rescue crew to get you people out if you get yourselves lost. Might as well be me."

"I'm not getting lost," Ryal muttered, then aimed his flashlight into the black hole and started walking.

James followed behind him, and when Ryal heard more footsteps, he swung the flashlight to see who it was. Two of his cousins and both the DEA agents were grim-faced but marching. He nodded, then swung the light back toward the tunnel and moved deeper into the mountain.

They were ten minutes in when Ryal suddenly stopped.

"Is that a dog barking?"

"Quinn's pup was gone," James said. "You

said he was tied up on the porch, but he wasn't there. Do you suppose he went looking for her?"

"God, I hope so," Ryal said, and started to run.

The dog's barking was louder. Ryal began to shout.

"Mariah!"

The dog yapped again, closer now.

"Mariah!"

Then he heard a faint cry. "Here! We're here!"

The men started running, their flashlights bobbing in the dark like corks on a pond when the fish begin to bite.

That was what she saw first, lights coming through the darkness like fireflies.

And then Ryal saw her, coming out of the guts of Rebel Ridge, pulling his brother behind her on some crazy-ass sled. Her face was streaked with mud, blood and paint — an odd shade of neon-yellow — and her clothes were almost in rags. But her chin was up, her shoulders back, and when she saw him, she collapsed in his arms in weak tears.

"I found him, Ryal. They nearly beat him to death, but I found him. I promised him I'd get him out. No man left behind. No man left behind."

Ryal could feel her shaking, and he wanted to cry. "Here, hon, give me the rope. I'll pull him the rest of the way."

She hesitated. They'd come this far together. It was hard to let go.

"He's broken up really bad. We need an ambulance."

Mike Lancaster was staring at Mariah like he'd never seen a woman before, and then he looked at what was left of Quinn Walker, trussed to a backpack like an Egyptian mummy. He saw the bloody rope burns on her neck and shoulder, and the blood-soaked spot on the rope where her hands had been, and he remembered someone saying she and Walker had served together in Afghanistan. The skin crawled on the back of his neck. That woman was one hell of a warrior. Then he took in the situation, and his cop skills kicked in.

"I'll call for Med-Flight. We'll get him down the mountain, ma'am, don't you worry. And I'm calling an ambulance for you, as well."

He took off running, with his partner behind him, and she was too numb to disagree.

"Hey there, sister, come lean on me," James said, and slid an arm around her waist to steady her steps.

By the time she walked out of the cave into the fresh air and starlight, she was moving on instinct. If it hadn't been for her grip on Moses's rope, she wouldn't have been able to focus.

They got Quinn on a stretcher, then started moving him down the mountain at a swift pace. Until they knew his true status, they had to consider his condition grave.

Mariah paused, then staggered again.

James grabbed her arm.

"Can you make it, girl?"

She took a breath, inhaling the pine-scented air of Rebel Ridge. She was crying as she took a firmer grip on Moses's rope.

"Yes, James, I will make it. Come on, Moses. Take me home."

EPILOGUE

Seven months later

A log popped in the fireplace, sending a shower of sparks flying up the chimney. Moses looked up from his rug by the fire only long enough to make sure nothing was amiss and then dropped his head back down on his paws. Snow had been falling for the past six hours, blanketing the high meadow like a flurry of goose down spilling out of an old feather bed. It fell silently and without wind, muffling all sound.

At the living room window, the flickering lights from Quinn and Mariah's first Christmas tree took center stage. They'd decorated it two weeks earlier and, after adding the star at the top, made love on the rug beneath it.

Now, whenever Quinn looked at it, he thought of the blinking lights as tiny diamonds bathing the ivory of Mariah's bare skin.

The presents beneath it were wrapped, all but the one for Moses, who'd immediately sniffed it out and carried it to Mariah with a "please can I have it now?" look days earlier.

And of course she'd obliged, tearing the packaging off the rawhide bone and laughing as he trotted back to the fire with it in his jaws.

Quinn was at the kitchen table, finishing a report he'd been working on for the past two days. He hit Send, waited for the email to go through, then logged off and closed his laptop.

Curious as to why it had gotten so quiet, he glanced up and caught Mariah looking at him from across the kitchen. He smiled.

"What?" he asked.

"I was just counting my blessings."

The smile tilted. "Am I one of them?"

"You are *the* blessing of my life."

He sighed. They didn't talk about it much, but he had very few memories of what had happened to him in the mine. It had taken nearly three months for him to heal, and one eyelid still had a tendency to droop when he was tired. He was also officially afraid of the dark. Even now, if he woke abruptly in the night, the walls in the room started shrinking inward until he focused on the light.

"And you, pretty girl, are mine. Is supper ready? Something smells good, and I'm starved."

"It's short-rib stew. As soon as the corn-bread comes out of the oven we'll be ready."

He praised her daily for her attempts at domesticity, but he knew better than most that he owed his life to the skills she'd learned in the army, not the culinary skills she still struggled to perfect.

"The food will be great. I'll go put another log on the fire before we sit down."

She began setting the table as he moved the fire screen, threw another chunk of wood on the fire and put the screen back in place, pausing long enough to pet Moses, who was sleeping with his chin on his bone.

"Good boy," Quinn said softly, then straightened up and moved to the window to look out at the snow.

He heard her footsteps as she came up behind him, and then smiled as she slid her arms around his waist and laid her cheek against his back.

"So, Christmas dinner tomorrow at your mom and Jake's. Who knew all this would result in a wedding? I can't wait. It will be my first Christmas ever as a member of a family," Mariah said.

Quinn ran his thumb back and forth across the surface of her wedding ring, hearing the confidence in her voice. Her exploits were already legend in his family, and they loved her without boundaries.

He smiled. "It will be a constant state of chatter, football and kids underfoot. Do you think you can handle all that?"

"Are you kidding me? I kicked ass in a firefight and lost your rifle in a cave-in. A few dozen kids underfoot should be a breeze."

He shuddered. She didn't often mention what she'd gone through to save him, and when she did, he was always stunned by the bravery it had taken.

"I have something to tell you," she said.

Quinn turned until they were standing face-to-face.

"I know what I want to do with my life," she said.

He smiled. "You mean besides spoil me rotten?"

She laughed. "Yes, besides that."

"So tell me."

"Jake Doolen is going to help me train Moses. I want to do what he does, Quinn. I want to help find people who are lost."

Quinn blinked as the contours of her face blurred through his tears.

"I think that's a grand idea," he said softly, and laid his cheek against the crown of her head.

"I've already talked to Moses, and he agrees," she added.

Moses heard his name and looked up, and the expression on his face made them laugh.

"Supper's ready," she said.

Quinn slid an arm around her shoulders as they walked back into the kitchen and sat down to their meal while, outside, the snow continued to fall.

From the roof, the big owl suddenly took flight.

Moses lifted his head toward the ceiling, then looked into the kitchen and softly woofed, just so they knew who was really in charge.